MYSTIK WARRIOR

DARK WARRIOR ALLIANCE BOOK 2

BRENDA TRIM
TAMI JULKA

Copyright © 2015 by Brenda Trim and Tami Julka

Editor: Amanda Fitzpatrick
Cover Art by Patricia Schmitt (Pickyme)

∽

This book is a work of fiction. The names, characters, places, and incidents are products of the writers' imagination or have been used fictitiously and are not to be construed as real. Any resemblance to persons, living or dead, actual events, locales or organizations is entirely coincidental.

All rights reserved. With the exception of quotes used in reviews, this book may not be reproduced or used in whole or in part by any means existing without written permission from the authors.

Our biggest supporters from day one have been our mothers and they continue to believe in our dream. Their love and devotion is as endless as the energy drinks we consume. We love you!

We want to say a heartfelt thank you to all of our readers who have joined us on this thrilling adventure. You enjoyed Dream Warrior enough to beg for the next book, so here it is. Buckle up, baby!

CHAPTER 1

"Thanks for picking me up tonight, especially this late. I owe you," Cailyn murmured as she embraced her best friend on the curb outside baggage claim at San Francisco International airport.

"Anytime, you know that. And thanks for letting me drive your car, I love it. It's the nicest car I'll ever drive," Jessie joked while holding the trunk open for Cailyn to throw in her bags. "So how was the wedding? And more importantly, did you spend *quality* time with the hot Doctor Jace?" her friend finished as she slammed the trunk closed. Cailyn was still reeling over the fact Zander had placed some of his Dark Warriors in human occupations to keep the supernaturals' existence secret. Jace was one of those undercover supernaturals, a renowned ER physician in Seattle. But he certainly wasn't like any doctor she'd ever been to; he looked more like a model.

Thinking of Jace, a smile crept over Cailyn's mouth. She shook her head and crossed to the driver's door and jumped into the plush leather seat. She thought about the question as she put the car in drive and headed away from the airport. "Surprisingly, the wedding was incredible...magical. Elsie is so happy with her sexy Scot," she finally responded. Jessie would come unglued if she knew Zander was a vampire, let alone the Vampire King. She was dying to tell her, but some things you couldn't even share with your best friend, like how your sister was turned into a vampire to save her life and mated to the Vampire King. "And, you should see the huge house these guys live in. It was a perfect setting, with thousands of twinkling lights...it looked like a scene from a fairytale. How were things here?"

"You didn't miss much. I'm glad your sister is happy, after everything she went through when Dalton was killed. There is no one who deserves it more. But, you, my friend, are avoiding the real issue. You broke off your engagement to John months ago because of your attraction to this doctor. Now, spill it, MacGregor."

Cailyn heaved a breath of exasperation. She loved Jessie, but wished she wasn't so tenacious. She had no desire to talk about Jace. The smallest thoughts about him caused an intense arousal she had never experienced before with anyone else, not even while in the throes of passion. Then, there was this unexplainable pull, drawing her toward him. His strange, stunning amethyst eyes, and his incredible body all drew her in, like a moth to the flame.

From the moment Jace had entered Elsie's apartment, Cailyn had been captivated by him, which surprised her. Typically, the kind of man who had a long braid, and wore a large, silver cuff wasn't her type. The combination made her think of an effeminate man, but there certainly wasn't anything effeminate about Jace. He was all masculine strength, and a fierce warrior to his core. She would never forget the vicious battle that destroyed Club Confetti, where he had wielded his weapons with expert precision.

She had found herself in the middle of a supernatural war, and had been terrified beyond reason, but the way Jace had moved so fluidly, and fought with confidence and vigor caused her heart to pound for different reasons. She recalled how she'd stood there unable to do anything to help or defend herself. She had been way out of her element. On one hand, she was horrified at the blood and violence, and wanted to run and hide, but on the other hand, she was captivated and enthralled by this mystical warrior. Needless to say, the situation had caused her a whole load of turmoil.

Like Jessie had said, that unrelenting attraction and confusion had made her call off her engagement to John months before. Thoughts of John reared an ugly, yet familiar guilt. He was attractive, caring, loyal, and supportive, everything she wanted in a husband. It was ridiculous to be lusting after Jace. After all, there were plenty of good-looking men in the world. Not to mention that Jace didn't see her as anything other than Elsie's big sister.

She glanced in her rear view mirror at the dark, empty highway behind her, contemplating how to answer Jessie. "I didn't spend any time alone with him. It was a short trip and he was at the hospital nearly the entire time. I sort of danced with him at the reception. Well, we were all together in a big group, but we were so close we touched several times and the heat between us...." Cailyn trailed off as her body shivered in remembrance.

"How are you supposed to figure out your feelings for John versus Jace if you didn't spend any time with him? I thought you were going to get him alone." Jessie waggled her eyebrows at Cailyn, making her chuckle.

"You make it sound so easy. What was I supposed to do, walk up to him and drag him to the nearest closet? Look, you know how confused this whole situation has made me. I was committed to John, and I love him, yet I can't stop thinking about Jace. Honestly, I didn't trust myself to be alone with him. My body tends to have a mind of its own where he is concerned."

"I have got to see this guy. He has to be smokin' to make you, the most faithful person I know, question yourself. Did you at least finally tell your sister that you broke your engagement to John?"

"No, I didn't have the heart to tell her. It was her big day and she has been through so much the past two years that she deserved it to be perfect. If I had told her, she would have spent too much time worrying about me. I will tell her if it becomes necessary. Things may still work out you know." She hated how her voice sounded so uncertain. She typically had no problems making decisions, big or small. This was infuriating.

She meant what she said though. It was possible that things with John would work out. She and John had continued talking since she broke things off, and he continued to try and win her back. She refused to go back to him until she extinguished her desire for Jace though. She kept telling herself that the draw to Jace was a phase, and that it would end. The problem was, her attraction was stronger now than it had been before.

"If you don't want Jace, can I have him? Does he make house calls? I'm suddenly feeling under the weather," Jessie moaned and leaned her head back against the seat, placing the back of her hand over her brown eyes.

Normally, Cailyn would have laughed that off, but jealousy hot and vicious stabbed through her veins. She wanted to punch her best friend in the face, repeatedly. What was wrong with her? This was out of control. She needed to escape the confines of the car. She was close to harming her best friend. The drive to her condo in Potrero Hill was going to be a long one tonight.

"No, you can't have him," she bit out before she could stop herself, immediately regretting her words. "I'm sorry, Jess. I get a bit crazy where Jace is concerned. Remember, I nearly clawed some girl's eyes out for kissing him. If you have any advice about how to resolve this, I'm all ears."

"Cai, you need to stop being so hard on yourself. You did the respectable thing and broke up with John despite the fact that you still love him. I know you would never hurt…"

An engine revving drew Cailyn's attention. Peering into her side and rearview mirrors she noticed a big, dark colored SUV quickly closing in on them. Cailyn got the sense that something was wrong. The aggressive manner of the other driver had panic setting in.

The large SUV loomed closer, and she realized her convertible didn't stand a chance against the beast barreling toward her. And, it was obvious they were gunning right for her car. Her heart sped up as adrenaline dumped into her system.

"What the hell? What's their problem?" She blurted and switched lanes getting out of their way.

"What?"

"That car behind us is all over my ass," she replied, tension lacing her voice.

Jessie turned around in her seat. "They changed lanes with you. Are they following us?"

Cailyn had the ability to read the minds of those around her, and despite the fact that she had come to loathe her power, she lifted the barriers she had in place to protect her mind and opened her telepathy toward the inhabitants in the vehicle behind her.

She recoiled as malevolence and anger coated her mind like slime on a bog in the bayou. Cailyn could read human thoughts like an open book, but it was difficult for her to read supernaturals. The jumbled mess she was picking up on told her that she was being followed by supernaturals. The intentions of the SUV's occupants were tinged with dark malice, causing a shiver to run up her spine. She tried to get enough information to know what they were facing, but it became difficult for Cailyn to concentrate through her growing fear.

She had to get ahold of herself if they were going to get out of this alive. Tuning everything else out, she focused on the driver and finally caught a few disconcerting words: mate, vampire king, Triskele Amulet, Kadir, capture. These few words caused a lump to settle in her stomach. This was connected to Elsie and Zander and the archdemons desire for the power of the Triskele Amulet. They must think she had information, or worse, they planned to use her to force Zander to give up the amulet. That meant big trouble for her and Jessie.

Flooring the accelerator, she flew back into her seat as the car sped. She glanced in the mirror again and saw that she had managed to put space between her and the SUV. She clutched the steering wheel so tightly her knuckles were white. Her victory was short-lived as the engine of her pursuer roared and a quick check told her the vehicle was closing the gap. They were in deep shit.

"Hang onto your seat, Jess. They're after us," she advised, glancing around at the closely grouped houses of South San Francisco, searching for an escape route. The last thing she wanted was to take this chase into the suburbs and place innocent people in danger. She contemplated going to the police, but dismissed the idea right away. The individuals chasing them were not human, and the police would be ineffectual against their power. Having seen the violence in Zander's world firsthand, she knew no human was capable of protecting her and Jessie.

"Why would they be after us? Do you recognize the vehicle?" The tremor in Jessie's voice made her want to reassure her friend, and tell her that everything was going to be okay, but she knew that would be a lie. Cailyn had no idea what was going to happen.

A jolt, followed by the sound of metal crunching, cut off her reply as she was sideswiped. The wheel swerved, and she tried to steer away, but they managed to push her car, forcing her to exit the freeway. She realized why when she saw the signs for San Bruno State Park. That was as close to being in the boondocks as they could get her in the middle of the city.

From the corner of her eye she saw that Jessie had turned in the passenger seat and was wide-eyed, gaping at the car behind them. She wondered if Jessie saw the red-ringed eyes or fangs of the young men. She guessed not, since Jessie wasn't screaming bloody murder.

As she opened her mouth to tell Jessie to call Elsie, Cailyn saw two creatures that had haunted her nightmares for months. Shock and horror coursed through her, as she saw Azazel and Aquiel mere yards in front of her car. Azazel was a terrifying archdemon working for Lucifer's right hand demon, Kadir, who wanted Zander's Triskele Amulet to free Lucifer from hell. Aquiel was a gorgeous, but dangerous Fae helping the demons. Both of these supernaturals together meant deep trouble for Cailyn and Jessie. The fact that they had found her, and clearly believed she was a way to obtain the amulet, terrified her.

Dread engulfed her at the malicious intent on their

attractive faces. Azazel's red eyes glowed with rage, and Aquiel's silver eyes glowed bright with anticipation. Her heart sank when she scanned the area for an escape, and found nothing but trees and green shrubbery. They were well outside of the suburbs, which meant her and Jessie were left to face them alone.

The SUV pulled alongside her, threatening to hit her again. "There's nowhere for me to go, Jess," she blurted. Flooring the accelerator didn't give them any headway. The sound of cars colliding echoed before her body was thrown to the right. She struggled to maintain her grip on the steering wheel determined not to be driven off the road. She gritted her teeth as she clutched the steering wheel.

"They are going to kill us! Oh, God. Watch out, Cai!" Jessie screamed.

Ear piercing metal screeched, and she was jolted in her seat when she steered as hard as she could into the other car. She lost control of the steering wheel, and as gravity left her, she could no longer tell which way was up. As the car rolled end over end, glass shattered and air rushed through the broken window, the wind slapping her face. A loud snap was followed by excruciating pain in her right leg. The limb was on fire and engulfed by sharp pain. Without looking, she knew that she had broken a bone.

Jessie shrieked, and despite the fact that the both had on seatbelts, they were tossed around the vehicle. Cailyn's purse smacked her face, and before she knew what was happening, their bodies were thrown forward as the car slammed into a hard object. The front airbags exploded, knocking the breath from her lungs. She felt like one giant bruise from head to toe.

The car slammed down onto its roof, sending debris raining around them. The sound of glass hitting the pavement was the only noise in the aftermath. Cailyn prayed that the hard top roof would not collapse and crush her and Jessie. One look out the spider-webbed windshield told her they had hit a tree. The sound of screeching tires meant they had no time to waist. The SUV full of skirm had reached them. She had no idea if the archdemon and Fae were still in the street or not. Her fear was a bitter tang in her mouth as she prepared to die. She had no way to combat these powerful creatures.

They needed help. Her telepathy had never enabled her to communicate with others, but she had to try. She stretched her mind and screamed out an SOS to anyone who may be close enough. She begged for someone to send the police, fire department, anything to distract her pursuers. She was beyond worrying about who else became involved. She was desperate for her and Jessie to survive this.

Speaking of Jessie, there was only silence from the seat next to her. Was she alive? Terrified of what she would see, she glanced over to see blood dripping from Jessie's temple into her long, bleach blonde hair. Hand shaking, she reached out to feel for a pulse. It was faint but there, thank God.

Leaves rustling and twigs snapping drew her attention. Outside the passenger window she saw the demon in his black combat boots approach her vehicle. "Jessie, wake-up, we need to get out—" She yelped as a knife cut through her seat belt and someone grabbed her hair, dragging her from the car. Craning her neck, she saw that Aquiel had a firm hold of her.

When Azazel snatched Jessie from the car she screamed, "Leave her alone! She has nothing to do with this."

"Unfortunately for her, now she does," Azazel taunted.

Jessie whimpered and cried out. Jessie had come around, and her eyes were wide with fear. Cailyn would have preferred that Jessie remain unconscious and unaware of the danger they were in.

"What do you want?" Cailyn asked, distracting the demon while she focused on the thoughts and snippets of conversations running through her mind. She was typically bombarded and overwhelmed quickly when she lifted her barriers, but she was far enough away from a heavily populated area that it was easy to focus on what was coming through. A spark of hope ignited when she heard Zander's name accompanied by a sense of loyalty and dedication. Whoever was thinking of Zander respected the Vampire King and she prayed they were his Dark Warriors. She knew they were close by, but would they reach her and Jessie in time?

"You'll know soon enough. I must say you're a pretty one, princess. Much more voluptuous than your sister, the Queen," Azazel purred. She shuddered as he ran a claw-tipped finger along Jessie's cheek while maintaining his hold around her neck. She knew that all he had to do was flex his fingers and he would end Jessie's life. She opened her mind again and screamed her plea for help.

"Who is that I hear tearing through the brush? More playthings?" Nausea rose at Azazel's words. She cursed supernatural senses. She was hoping that there were Dark Warriors headed her way, supernaturals who could take them by surprise. She didn't want to die like this, and they could end her and Jessie in the blink of an eye. They must want them for something, she reasoned. Otherwise, they'd be dead. She had to stall him.

"What do you want with me? I have nothing to give you. Let us go or you will regret it. The Dark Warriors are seconds away from us," she brazened. "You won't get away with this," she threatened.

"Ah, but that is where you are wrong. We already have. Cast the spell now, Aquiel. I'll take care of her friend," Azazel ordered. Immediately, the Fae began chanting in a lyrical language and as her body became heavy, she fought the hold he had on her. She met Jessie's frightened eyes and watched the tears flow. When Azazel palmed her friend's breast, Jessie struggled against his hold. Cailyn screamed out her anger.

"No, leave her alone, you sick bastard!" She had to get free from Aquiel's grip and help Jessie. She tried to kick out, but her feet felt like they were encased in concrete. She missed the Fae by a mile and her broken leg burned with pain. She lifted her arm to push at the Fae, but it too became weighed down. She wondered what he was doing to make her movements sluggish and uncoordinated.

When the demon sank his fangs into Jessie's carotid, Jessie stopped struggling and went limp in his arms. "No... Jessie! Don't hurt her!" Cailyn pleaded. Spots winked in her vision and her head lolled as she spent the remains of her energy fighting when she heard Azazel's grating voice. "She will be my most beautiful skirm yet."

～

JACE CLOSED the front door of Zeum and heard the sound of Elsie's frantic voice in the hallway followed by Zander's deep Scottish brogue. The compound the Seattle Dark Warriors called home was silent but for the king and his mate. Jace hurried to the war room and came to a halt in the doorway. Elsie was in tears and clearly upset about something.

"Zander, I am telling you Cailyn is in danger. The

archdemon and the Fae are going to hurt her. This premonition was different. I saw events unfold, unlike before, when I only experienced feelings of doom. They are going to take her. Please, call," Elsie pleaded. Anxiety, anger, and a sense of urgency bombarded Jace at hearing Cailyn might be in danger. The idea didn't sit well with him, and he had no idea why. Sure, he was a doctor and his focus was on healing people, but it went beyond that and he barely knew the female.

"I see it too, *a ghra*. Apparently, we now share your premonitions. Doona worry, I will do everything in my power to make sure she is safe." Zander vowed, grabbing his cell phone and making a call. The magic behind a mating amazed Jace. He understood that Fated Mates would share any special abilities they had with each other once the mating was completed, but he had never actually seen it, because Zander and Elsie were the first mated couple in over seven hundred years.

"What's going on?" Jace asked, recalling the first time he had met Cailyn. He had been immediately captivated. Not one to be aroused by females, Cailyn had inspired arousal so hot and painful, he'd lost his breath. The pull to her had not diminished in the least over the months. If anything, it had become stronger. At Zander and Elsie's mating ceremony, it took all his years of celibacy to keep some distance. Simply recalling her sweet face and voluptuous curves had his body hardening.

Elsie's sharp gasp intruded his reminiscing. "They have her Zander, do something," she said frantically. His heart stuttered before it began racing with his worry for Cailyn.

"Thane," Zander barked into his phone, "where are you?" Zander's Scottish accent deepened with his agitation.

Jace heard Thane's voice echo on the other end of the

phone. "We are right outside San Bruno State Park. Cailyn's flight landed early and we have been rushing to catch up with her."

"Pick up the pace. My mate and I have both seen Aquiel capture Cailyn. Do whatever you must to get to her," Zander ordered the warrior.

"Yes, Liege," Thane responded.

"Call when you have her. And, Thane, failure is no' an option."

"Are they going to make it to her in time?" Jace demanded after Zander ended his call with the San Francisco Dark Warrior. His protective instinct was in overdrive. As a healer, the welfare of others always drove him, but this was altogether different. He didn't understand why, but he had to get to Cailyn and protect her.

"Is she going to die? I thought no one lived once you had a premonition about them," Jace asked Elsie, switching gears as the thought occurred to him. He was shaking and couldn't contemplate Cailyn dying. His body shuddered and it was unnerving, to say the least. His reactions to Cailyn were intense, and continued to baffle him.

"My premonitions have changed," Elsie explained. "Now, I get pictures of the events that are going to occur. Earlier, I had a vision of Cailyn being chased by skirm who ran her off the road. Then Aquiel grabbed her from the wreckage of her car. There is an urgency beating in me that tells me we are in a race against time."

That was enough for Jace. Aquiel had proven to be a wicked creature, and skirm were once humans who had been turned into mindless killing machines by an archdemon. The thought of Cailyn being harmed by either one had his anger turning to rage. "Are Ryker and Gage with Thane?" Jace inquired about the other San Francisco Dark

Warriors. Given what Elsie described, Thane would need the help.

"Aye, they are. Jax is also with them. They have taken to patrolling in larger groups with the increase in skirm activity, and that is paying off for us tonight," Zander replied, pulling Elsie into his arms.

"Why haven't they called yet? This waiting is driving me mad. She can't be hurt," Elsie sobbed. Zander wiped tears from her cheeks and kissed her lovingly. Jace marveled at how patient Zander was with his mate. He held and comforted her rather than pointing out that it had been less than a minute since he hung up with Thane.

Panic made it impossible for Jace to sit down, and he paced restlessly around the room. He had enough adrenaline running through his veins to sprint to San Francisco. He'd do anything to get to Cailyn in time. His protective instincts were stronger then they'd ever been. At that moment, his mate's soul stirred in his chest, making him wonder if it was possible that Cailyn was *his* Fated Mate.

He dismissed the idea without giving it another thought. The Goddess would never curse a female as heavenly as Cailyn with a mate like him. He wasn't fit to be a mate. Lady Angelica had seen to that.

The main line rang and Zander hit the speaker button before Jace made it a step. "Dark Warriors," Zander growled.

"This is Thane. We're at the scene of the accident. The moment we cleared the trees, the demon sneered at us, grabbed the Fae and disappeared. We have the females. The Queen's sister is alive but hurt. Her friend has an obvious demon bite on her neck. How do you want us to proceed? Normally, we let the human medical teams take over at this point. Do you want us to call for an ambulance?"

Jace stopped dead in his tracks as his anxiety over Cailyn

riddled him. He was relieved to hear she was alive, but hearing she was hurt made his heart drop into his feet. "A human hospital would be a bad idea," he blurted before anyone else could answer. "Take it from me, this situation will bring too much attention to the realm. We must handle it ourselves." He turned to Zander, determination riding him. "I need to get to them," he declared. No one was keeping him from going to Cailyn.

"I agree. The fastest way will be to portal to Basketane," Zander pointed out, referring to the San Francisco compound. "Do you think you can afford the energy drain? We doona know the extent of their injuries."

"I will do whatever it takes to get to her as fast as possible and I will heal her...even if it kills me," Jace vowed, ignoring the shocked gasps and questioning looks.

"Text Gerrick and tell him to return," Zander said, saving Jace any further explanations. Jace had a message sent to Gerrick and Killian, fellow sorcerers, before Zander finished talking. Their reply was instant, causing Jace to curse as he fired off another text.

"What?" Zander asked.

"They are fifteen minutes away. I'll have to do this alone." They didn't have that long. He needed to be there, now.

"Take the females back to Basketane," Zander said into the speaker phone, holding Jace's gaze steady.

"We are loading them now and will be waiting for you," Thane responded.

"We will be there shortly. Gerrick is five minutes oot and they will set the portal immediately upon his return. Send another crew to clean-up the accident scene. We doona want the human authorities getting involved," Zander instructed.

Sweat beaded Jace's brow and his heart was racing. He listened to Zander comfort Elsie and the others who had joined them discuss this turn of events. Jace was worse than Elsie had been, cocking his ear for Gerrick or Killian every ten seconds. Sitting around waiting was not something Jace did well. He needed to take action. Another lap around the room didn't help. The moment he thought he would go mad, Gerrick walked in the front door.

Jace raced to the double doors. "Come on, Gerrick. You can get caught up later. We need to cast a portal to Basketane. Now!" he snapped when Gerrick made no move to assist him.

"My sister is hurt and at we need to get to her," Elsie told the surly warrior from the doorway to the war room.

Jace knew Gerrick hated hearing a female was in danger, which was no surprise, given that his mate had been brutally murdered centuries ago by skirm. Thankfully Elsie's words kicked the warrior into gear. With only the two of them casting the portal, it would take all their energy and deplete them both, but he couldn't wait for anyone else.

Needing to bolster his magic, he summoned his sorcerer's staff from the Goddess' realm. A bright, white light flashed and then he was gripping the familiar Alder wood of his staff, the additional hum of power radiating into him. The serpent that adorned the top of the seven-foot, weathered pole gleamed in the overhead light. Jace took a deep breath to center his energy. He could do this.

He glanced over and saw that Gerrick had summoned his own staff. He nodded at the warrior and they began chanting in the ancient tongue. Jace felt the magic build beneath his skin. Green, blue and purple lights similar to the aurora borealis undulated all around them. The power increased until Jace thought his skin would split. With a sideways glance to Gerrick, they threw the magic into the giant foyer. A mystical doorway formed, and an elegant drawing room with antique furnishings and wood paneling was visible on the other side of the portal. A sultry cinnamon scent wafted through the opening.

Jace's heart stopped as Jax walked into the drawing room cradling Cailyn.

CHAPTER 2

"Cailyn, oh my god. Are you okay?" Elsie cried out, making Cailyn turn her aching head. Elsie, Zander, and Jace looked back at her. Her heart sped up when she saw Jace. He was as sexy as she remembered and he was there to save her. The house behind them looked familiar. She realized they must have created a portal to get to them. The magical doorway looked exactly like the one they had created the night of her sister's graduation party, when they had fled the battle with the demons outside of Club Confetti.

Elsie rushed to her side, cooing words of comfort. Cailyn wanted to erase her sister's worry and reassure her. She had always hated seeing Elsie afraid or unhappy. Not that her sister had needed her much of late. Elsie had changed in more ways than just becoming a vampire. She had always been confident and capable, but now there was a power about her that demanded respect.

The Goddess Morrigan had chosen wisely, Cailyn thought, when she picked Elsie to be the queen of the vampires. Cailyn recalled seeing the Goddess at her sister's mating ceremony. Her mythology course in college had taught that Morrigan was the Goddess of War and Death, but Cailyn had come to learn that was a small aspect of her Godhood. She was also the Goddess of Birth, and had created the Tehrex Realm, along with the supernaturals that dwelled there. It was odd to think that this realm of beings co-existed on earth with humans. Elsie was now a vital part of these supernaturals, but old habits die hard, and Cailyn didn't think she would ever stop mothering her baby sister.

"El. I'm going to be fine. These guys got to us in time," Cailyn soothed, trying to mask her agony. A low masculine growl had her turning in Jax's arms. Unable to hide the wince the pain caused, she noted Jace was rapidly approaching her.

"Give her to me," Jace demanded, anger etched into his masculine features. The gentle way he eased her from Jax's arms to his was surprising, given how angry he appeared. Still, she had to grit her teeth against the movement. Her leg felt as if a hot poker was being rammed through the muscles and bones, and her head was killing her.

"*A ghra*, your sister is safe. We must get back through the portal to Zeum so Jace can regain his strength and tend to her. Jace will have her up and running in no time. Stop fretting. Let's get back through," Zander instructed as Bhric, Zander's brother, took Jessie from another warrior. Cailyn breathed easier and watched Elsie and Zander turn back to the portal.

"Has Jessie regained consciousness?" Cailyn asked the Vampire Prince. She was terrified for her best friend. She would never forget watching the demon bite her.

"No' fully. Jace, you need to do something for this puir lass. She's writhing and moaning. Here, I'll take Cailyn and you can take her," Bhric answered.

"Unfortunately, Bhric, there isn't much I can do for Jessie, yet. That bite mark on her neck is not from a skirm feeding. It's an archdemon's bite. She has been envenomated. The portal is ten steps away. Suck it up and stay close behind me. The portal is going to close quickly. Our power is waning and we can't keep it open much longer," Jace replied, not missing a step. That sexy voice jolted and soothed her at the same time. She could only describe his voice as raw. It made her entire body come to life.

Cailyn nestled closer to his warm chest and relished when he responded by clutching her tighter. She was right in not wanting to be alone with him. Being this close to him was fogging her mind, which didn't help with her dilemma.

She loved John, and wanted Jace, but saw no quick and easy fix to her feelings. Instead, she forced her thoughts to an easier topic. "What's wrong with Jessie? What did he do to her?"

"First, tell me what happened?" Jace countered as he continued walking and carrying her. She looked around while thinking how best to condense what she'd just gone through. It was mind boggling to think that with a couple steps they had skipped an entire state and went from San Francisco to Seattle via a magical portal.

Cailyn was still trying to wrap her brain around all that went on in the Tehrex Realm, which she only learned about a few months ago. Given her own special abilities, it hadn't been a stretch for her to believe that there was more out there, but this was something else entirely.

The silence in the room was uncomfortable and she realized that there was a large group of people all waiting for her to respond. It surprised her that some of the San Francisco Dark Warriors had come to Zeum with them, and were looking at her expectantly.

She focused on the events of the evening. "We were driving back from the airport and an SUV full of skirm forced us off the freeway. Once they had us isolated, Azazel and Aquiel appeared in the middle of the road. The skirm in the car hit me from the side and I lost control. We rolled over several times before I hit a tree. It was the scariest thing I've ever been through." The memory of it had her palms sweating. She looked over to her friend to reassure herself that Jessie was alive. Small tremors shook Jessie's body, and Cailyn didn't think she was aware of what was going on around her, despite having her eyes wide open.

"Before we were able to get out of the car, the Fae grabbed me and the demon grabbed Jessie." Cailyn fought back her emotions and blinked back before continuing. "He bit her after he heard you guys coming to save us. He said something about her being one of his skirm, his most beautiful or something like that. I tried to fight back and help her, but the Fae said some foreign words and I couldn't move. Nothing else happened before they disappeared seconds later," Cailyn finished.

"What exactly did the Fae say?" Jace asked, tension lacing his every word. The severity in his tone took her back. She assumed his anger was directed at the Fae and demon, not her. Either way, he looked as if he could rip something apart piece by piece.

"I have no idea. I couldn't understand the language he was speaking. It could have been Chinese for all I know. It doesn't matter what he said right now. I want to know what's going on with Jessie. Tell me she is going to be okay," she pleaded.

"I need to know what the Fae said. Fae are capable of casting spells none of the sorcerers in the realm know how to counteract," Jace retorted, his hold on her tightening. "As for Jessie, I believe she is indeed becoming a skirm. And that means she is going to be under the influence of the archdemon who turned her."

"What a bluidy fucking mess," Zander cursed. "Kadir and Azazel are bold but not verra bright if they think we will give this skirm of his free reign in our compound." Cailyn didn't like the sound of what Zander was saying.

"We should take care of her now before she is a risk," Gerrick added.

A cold dread slid down Cailyn's spine. "No one will be *taking care* of Jessie, not unless it is to heal her and make her better," she said, indignant at what they were implying. How could they be so callous talking about killing her friend? Cailyn was determined to prevent anything else from happening to Jessie. She had been through enough because of Cailyn and her association with these creatures. Cailyn refused to let her go through any more pain because of her. She wiggled, trying to get to Jessie, but Jace refused to let her go.

"Stop it. Cailyn, we have no idea what we will be facing once she is awake. Normally, skirm are consumed with bloodlust and kill when they feed. They feed from humans, and right now you are the only human in this compound," Jace told her, keeping his gaze locked on her. The empathy and sadness he reflected back at her only angered her further. He had already concluded that her friend was a liability, too. It was clear that he agreed with the position of confining her, then killing her.

"I can't believe I ever thought you people were any better than the dregs of humanity. None of this is Jessie's fault. It was *your* enemies who did this, yet not one of you is willing to fight for her life. Her condition is a forgone conclusion to you. Well, I refuse to believe there is no hope, and I will not allow anything to happen to her," she declared, wishing she was standing on her own to make a better stance. It burned even further that in the state she was in, Cailyn wasn't going to be able to stop anyone from harming Jessie.

Zander placed a gentle hand on her shoulder. "Calm down, *puithar*. No one is going to harm her, but I have to tell you that in all the decades of research, our scientists have no' been able to find a way to deal with skirm venom, let alone reverse the effects of an archdemon bite," Zander explained. The pity in his eyes told her that he believed Jessie would eventually need to be killed. Not going to happen.

"But we've never seen a female changed before either," Jace added. "Perhaps the process is different with females. Look at her neck. The bite is tinged blue around the edges rather than black. Her blood is still red, and from the brief scan I did, her brainwaves are active and normal, if not enhanced. Now, I haven't done a thorough exam, but every indication shows that she is not developing in the same pattern as a male skirm, at least not physically." Jace had turned so he was facing Bhric and Jessie. Cailyn reached out and grabbed Jessie's limp hand, hating the way her twitching was becoming more pronounced.

Jace shifted Cailyn gently and ran his hand down her arm. Cailyn shivered from the pain his movement caused her, as well as the intense arousal from his touch. Dazed, she watched as he opened Jessie's mouth and examined her teeth. "Her incisors are loosened so I do believe she will grow fangs. The question is, what we will face when her transition is completed?"

Cailyn refused to believe Jessie was becoming a mindless demon minion. "It can't be too late to reverse this. She's not aware of your realm, or that supernaturals even exist.

And now she's going to have fangs? She's going to have to drink blood for God's sakes!" she said, her fear for Jessie sharp and pointed. Once again, Cailyn blamed herself for her friend's condition. If she hadn't asked Jessie to pick her up from the airport, her friend would be sleeping safe and sound in her bed. Right then, she hated herself for being so materialistic that she had refused to park her Mercedes at the airport. It all seemed so unimportant now.

"Jace is right, they havena turned a female before. I always assumed females died if they were envenomated. I understand your concern for your friend, Cailyn, but I canna allow her to be free in the house until we understand this more. It is my duty to see to Elsie's and your protection, and I willna place either of you in unnecessary risk."

Cailyn noted the way Jace stiffened at Zander's words, and was curious as to why. She wondered if he too bristled at the King's dominance. It took great effort for Cailyn to step back and consider the danger she was in. She had seen what the skirm were capable of, and didn't want to place anyone else in that position. But what were they going to do?

As Cailyn contemplated how to protect Jessie, she watched as her friend's skin suddenly smoothed, and any fat she had disappeared, replaced by muscle. She could become the threat they feared. Could Jessie rip out someone's throat and suck the life from them? The Jessie Cailyn knew was too kind hearted and caring to become that being. But no one understood exactly what Jessie was becoming, they said so themselves. Jace had already seen differences in Jessie. That didn't mean Cailyn was going to accept that she had to be eliminated, and she refused to stand idly by while Zander or Gerrick killed her. No, there had to be another way.

"We can contain her. What we need to be asking right now, is what Kadir gains from this. He canna be planning to use her to harm us directly. He has to know we wouldna allow her to roam freely in the compound, which means no opportunity to search for the amulet. He has upped the ante in his bid for the Triskele Amulet, and taken greater risks than any archdemon before him. I just doona see what he accomplishes with this. Perhaps he hopes to create dissention among us. Look at how we argue aboot it already. I willna allow this to cause a split between us. Now, more than ever, we need to stand together. The stakes are higher than they ever have been. 'Tis clear he is still after my mate. Neither she, nor Cailyn, is to leave the compound without protection. Jace, send Jessie's blood to the scientists for testing, and make sure it's their highest priority. We must learn all we can, as fast as we can. Until then, she will be locked in the dungeon," Zander ordered.

"Jessie is not a danger to be locked up and she is no one's guinea pig. She is a twenty-eight year old accountant and she matters," Cailyn protested. Jace grabbed her chin between his thumb and forefinger, forcing her to meet his gaze, trapping her there for several seconds. Something flared between them, fanning the slow-burning fire in her abdomen, despite the excruciating pain in her body.

Finally, he broke the silence, making her realize the entire room had gone quiet. "Cailyn, we have to contain her. We need to study her in order to help her. She is changing, yes, but I can't say with certainty what will happen next. I promise you that she will not be tortured or harmed with the testing," Jace said to reassure her. Problem was, it did the exact opposite.

The hurt that welled up was potent. Given how protective he had been acting, and how close he was holding her, she thought he felt something for her. The moment he had taken her from Jax's arms, electricity had sparked between them. His statement felt like a betrayal of all that. It was ridiculous to feel that way, especially, since it was impossible to forge such an expectation in a short time. Still, it was there. Cailyn needed to keep her head about her. Jessie and Elsie were everything to her, and she'd never forgive herself if anything happened to either of them.

∽

SHAKING UNCONTROLLABLY, Jace feared he would drop Cailyn if he didn't calm down. He was drowning in the flood of his emotions. He was awed by her beauty, and at the same time, arousal ran a hot race through his body. Saliva pooled in his mouth, and his stomach churned. He silently cursed the revulsion his body had to any arousal. He wanted to beg the Goddess to give him one night where he didn't get sick to his stomach and could indulge in a female. He should have known that after seven centuries of nausea, he wasn't going to experience anything else.

Thankfully, he had lived with the sensation long enough that he functioned perfectly well. However, that didn't stop the shame from running hot through his veins. He wished he were a normal male, rather than the ruined shell he had become.

He wanted more than anything to be able to lose himself in a female's body. But not just any female. He wanted this one, more than he had ever wanted a female. Problem was, he'd never pursue Cailyn, because he refused to taint her. It could never go any further between them. No one needed to live with the hell that he dealt with night and day. Still, he was drawn to her like a moth to the flame, and he'd gladly burn to ash for one night with her.

He wanted those lush full lips pressed against his. Or better yet, wrapped around his aching cock. He could imagine her down on her knees, licking the fleshy head teasingly while she smiled up at him. And that fast, he was hard as steel in his pants, certain his zipper was going to break.

The fantasy playing out in his head brought his gaze down to her beautiful face. He breathed deeply of her spicy cinnamon scent. He knew his eyes had to be glowing, displaying his arousal more evidently than his erection. He was unable to look away, and watched her glare turn wary. She had no idea what his eyes were telling her, but she wasn't frightened. He saw the curiosity and desire she tried to hide.

"Promise me that nothing will happen to her. Even if she becomes a mindless killing machine, no one hurts her. And you find a cure for what happened to her," Cailyn demanded. He was awed by her strength and determination, and in that moment he would promise her anything.

"I will do everything in my power to help your friend, but we need to contain her until we know more. I have worked closely with the scientists for centuries, but this is a first. We need time."

"I, for one, promise that nothing will happen without your involvement, Cai," Elsie vowed, grabbing Cailyn's attention.

"*A ghra*, doona make promises you canna keep," Zander chided.

"Oh, but I can keep this promise, I am your Queen, after all. And, you, my King, will make sure that happens," Elsie told him sweetly. Jace watched the interaction and felt a tightening in his chest. He envied them their connection. He had never wanted someone to belong to him, but sometime in the past few months, he had begun to hope for more. From the moment he had met Cailyn he'd felt something more than an appreciation of a beautiful, intelligent female. He had to continue to remind himself that he'd never have a female of his own.

"Thank you, El. I feel better knowing that," Cailyn whispered, her eyes drooping a bit. This entire night had to have taken its toll on her, and her body was still injured.

Without thinking, he leaned down and brushed his nose against Cailyn's slightly pointed one. His gaze went straight to her mouth. She had a mole on the right side of her delectable mouth. A mouth he desperately wanted to taste. Her startled gasp stopped him before he acted on that particular desire and had his gaze searching her hazel depths. He suddenly realized that her eyes matched the serpent's eyes on his staff. Once again, he wondered about this female that had been brought into his life.

The tension in the room reminded him that they weren't alone. He ignored the concerned stares he felt burning into his back from Elsie and the others and shouldered the door open to what had now become Cailyn's room. "Let's get you healed and taken care of, shall we?" Jace asked as he tried to lay her on the bed. His arms refused to cooperate, pulling her closer to his chest.

With half the compound's residents following him, now was not the time to give into desire. He forced his fingers to uncurl and laid her gently on the bed. She winced in pain and a light sheen of sweat coated her body. Her complexion had gone even paler, and he knew she was in tremendous pain, yet she didn't make a sound. He admired her strength. Even the warriors bitched at him when he had to patch up their wounds. This tiny female continued to amaze him.

"I'm sorry. I will take the pain away and you'll be as good as new," he soothed, tucking her loose hair behind her ears, needing the contact. Touching her soft skin brought a sense of relief and calmed him, while at the same time it wound him tight with arousal. A dark, insidious need had taken root. For the first time in his life, he needed to taste a female, to explore her lush body, and get lost in her heated depths. It scared the hell out of him.

Jace hated how his hands shook nervously when he ran them down her arms, not ready to heal her and lose his excuse to touch her. He held her hands for several silent moments before he moved them to her broken leg. She was so soft and supple beneath his palms. It took great effort to shove his lust aside before calling upon his healing ability. Surprisingly, his power came readily to his fingers without much effort, despite the energy expenditure from the portal. He sent his magic into her body and his blood turned to ice when a blast suddenly knocked everyone in the room off their feet. He flew from her side and landed roughly against the wall.

"What the hell just happened?" Cailyn murmured as Jace scrambled to get back to her side.

"Nothing good. Remember those words the Fae was saying? It was a spell that I just activated," Jace replied grimly as everyone else stood up, looking baffled.

"What kind of spell? Can you undo it?" Cailyn asked, lethargy clearly weighing her down.

"I have no idea. What I wouldn't give to have the Mystik Grimoire appear right now," Jace mused, but knew better. Dread settled in his gut at the thought of what could happen to Cailyn now.

CHAPTER 3

Jace groaned out his discomfort, as the familiar slab bit into his back. He had nothing to cushion his body or protect him from the ice cold marble. He shivered from the cold and nausea. How long before she came to him this time? For that matter, how long had it been since she had left him? Time had come to mean nothing to him. He had no way to know how many days or months or years may have passed since his capture, never mind whether it was day or night, winter or summer.

"Goddess-damned-bitch," he grated. Rusted metal cuffs surrounded his wrists and ankles, and were connected to chains that held him to the marble altar. He had prayed night and day to be free of his prison, but had given up hope of any rescue or escape.

Water dripped from the ceiling into a shallow hole in the ground. Goddess, he was so thirsty, would give anything for a drink. But that was part of her torture. Deny him everything, and offer food, water, or a shower for what she wanted. He refused to give her anything. Not that he was able to give her what she wanted anyways though. He didn't have the book and didn't know where it was.

He opened his eyes and gazed around at the rough stone walls. No windows, no pictures. Nothing but endless stone surrounded him. He could scarcely recall the color of the sky, or the smell of the outdoors. As his body shook, he tried to conjure a fire in his palm. Chanted the spell over and over, like he had thousands of times before, but nothing happened. The dampening collar around his neck made sure of that.

He tugged the chains again, wanting to rip them free and wrench off the collar, but he couldn't manage to budge them one bit. She had rendered him weak as a human. Every rusted, moldy inch of his prison was mystically reinforced by one of her spells.

His body stiffened, and bile rose in his throat as sandalwood incense reached his nostrils. She was coming for him. His cock tried to crawl into his body to escape her clutches. If he could have, he would have chopped the damned thing off. Anger at his predicament rose, and he uselessly struggled once more.

He hated what she did to him, and his body hated it even more. He pushed aside his despair, hatred, and revulsion. Showing her any emotion only fueled her desires and made things worse. The door creaked as the heavy wood was pushed aside by one of her worshipers. He shut down in preparation for what came next.

She glided through the door in her emerald gown. With a wave of her hand and a word, she lit the torches that lined his cell. He could do without having to see her flawless features. Her mocha skin gleamed with health and radiance. She was truly beautiful, with her dark brown locks hanging straight to the middle of her back, but he had never seen anything more disgusting.

"Hello, sweet. Have a nice nap?" Lady Angelica whispered next to his ear. She ran her tongue along the shell of his ear as her fingernails scraped down his stomach, forcing him to inch away from her touch.

He glared defiantly into her black as night eyes, refusing to answer. The white pupil always unnerved him, forewarning of her evil nature.

"No? Well, you know how you can sleep in my bed with me." She paused for an effect that was lost on him. Tell me where I can find the book."

It was the same song and dance they had been doing for Goddess only knew how long. Again, he deployed his only weapons, his defiance and his glare. He relished his fantasy of cutting her into tiny pieces, hoping she saw how he felt.

"I hate hurting you, sweet. Tell me where the Mystik Grimoire is. We will rule together," she murmured as she rubbed his arm. What a crock of shit, she loved hurting him. In fact, he was certain she climaxed as soon as she began torturing him.

"How many times do I have to tell you that I don't know where it is," he uttered before he could stop himself. He had no idea where the book had disappeared to when his father was killed, and even if he did, he would never tell this wretch where it was.

His family had been charged with keeping and protecting the Mystik Grimoire for as long as the Tehrex Realm had existed. The book contained all spells of the sorcery, and the prophesies of the realm, as well as information on the spells of other creatures. It was magically connected to his family's blood-line, but the book decided who could access it, and when.

He wasn't one of the ones who had access to it. He could not count how many times during his incarceration he had needed the book, but it had not answered his call. He was convinced he was cursed. That was the only explanation for why the book refused to help him. He wanted it more than she did, but not for the same reasons. There were spells contained within that he could use to break the enchantments on his bonds.

She slapped him across his face, leaving furrows from her fingernails. The blood dripped into his hair, sticking with the years of grime and dirt.

"Now look what you made me do. Cooperate and you can have a real meal this night. It will help you heal that gorgeous face."

He spat in her face in response.

"You will regret that, slave," she shrieked.

His regret was instantaneous, as the Gaelic words of her spell tumbled from her mouth, and bile turned in his throat. He heaved the moldy bread he had been fed the night before while he felt his shaft fill with blood and stiffen against his wishes. He prayed to the Goddess for an end to his torment.

"No, Angelica, don't do this. I have no idea where the book is. It won't respond to me. I swear," he promised, hating how weak and helpless he was. He hated even more that he was pleading with a heartless bitch.

"Mmmm, that's better," she purred, fueled by the sound of his desperation and the sight of his growing erection. He clamped his lips shut, refusing to give her more.

He went stock-still as she ran her fingers over his testicles. Any movement and she would sink her claws into his flesh.

"Bring me the oil," she ordered a servant.

Shuffling footsteps echoed followed by scorching hot liquid pouring over his chest and abdomen. Angelica's hands played through the oil, spreading it across his taught body. He couldn't stop the flinch when her hand encircled his shaft. He was rewarded with her nails embedding in his erection. Unfortunately, her spell prevented him from deflating. She climbed onto the altar with him, straddling his hips. He once again tried to access his powers and counteract her spells. Nothing.

"You cannot refuse me. Let's make this interesting." She snapped her fingers. A cane was slapped into her waiting palm. She crawled her way to his face, and placed her core on his clenched mouth. Rubbing herself across the slash of his lips she brought the cane down on his erection. He screamed out in pain and she climaxed on his face. She loved causing him pain and humiliation. He gave up praying to the Goddess to save him from this hell. He was never getting out.

Jace jolted upright, confused and drenched in sweat, his heart pounding. It was difficult to push the fear and anxiety back so he was prepared to deal with whatever Angelica forced upon him next. Getting his bearings, he looked around the room and saw Cailyn sleeping fitfully on the bed next to him. Clarity struck, and he realized that it had only been a dream, and he wasn't back in that dungeon. Thank the Goddess. His relief was short-lived as nausea overtook him and he hurried to the bathroom.

He bent over the toilet and in between his stomach's heaves he rubbed his Cuff de Draiocht. He hated these nightmares, and in the past six hundred years they had yet to leave him, and he rarely got a full night's sleep. It wasn't enough that his captivity had robbed him of the ability to be intimate with a female. Lady Angelica had taken everything from him, and continued to do so.

More than anything, he wanted a normal life. The problem was, he had no idea how to take control and make that happen. She had dug her claws in and left her venom behind, and no matter what he did he was unable to purge it from his system. He flushed the toilet and washed his hands before reentering the bedroom to see Cailyn still sleeping.

He locked his nightmare down, and recalled why he was in a room with the female who had been occupying his fantasies for months. He checked his watch and saw that he had slept for a couple hours. Everyone had gone to their rooms to rest for the day shortly after he had failed to heal Cailyn. His failure still burned. She was suffering because he had walked right into the Fae's trap.

Setting his guilt aside, he texted Bhric to make sure Jessie was secured in the dungeons. The warrior's reply was instant - the female was sleeping peacefully in a cell, something that had upset Cailyn, but they had no choice with so many unknowns. At least she was still alive.

He cocked his head listening for the other warriors. The house was quiet this time of the morning with everyone sleeping. Jace had used his position as a physician to be the one to stay at Cailyn's side so Elsie could take her day rest. It had been difficult to pry Elsie from her sister's side, but as a new vampire Elsie was forced to rest during the early morning hours. Checking the time, Jace saw that he had a couple more hours alone with Cailyn.

Jace crossed to the bed and sat next to Cailyn who was far from peaceful in her sleep. He pressed his fingers into her wrist and noted that her pulse was still racing. Lifting the covers he saw that the splint and wrap was snug around her broken leg. The bruising and swelling were rising above the bandage. His healing hadn't done anything except set off that Fae bastard's spell. He watched his thumb run over her wrist when a noise had his head snapping up to her face. She stirred and her eyelids fluttered open.

"Hi, beautiful," he murmured.

～

"Hey," Cailyn croaked out, swallowing to wet her arid throat. She felt far more ancient than her twenty-nine years. "God, I need some water," she groaned, trying to sit up and reach out to the glass on the nightstand. Jace was there helping as soon as she stretched her arm out.

"Let me get that. You don't need to be moving too much. Here, I'll prop you up against the pillows," he said as he piled pillows up and stretched his arm behind her. Cailyn leaned into the warmth of his chest and inhaled his masculine scent. He smelled like a thunderstorm, strong and potent. Rather than lying back against the pillows he had prepared she remained tucked into his side. She felt him stiffen around her before he relaxed and placed the glass to her lips.

"Thank you," she whispered in between sips.

"Not too much. I don't want you getting sick on me. How are you feeling?" he asked as he ran his hand down her head and arm. She liked the feel of his caress a little too much.

"I feel as if I have been hit by a wrecking ball a couple dozen times. Can I get some ibuprofen for this headache?"

"Let me exam you first. I want to make sure it wouldn't cause more damage than good. I'm going to unwrap your leg and that's going to hurt, but I want to make sure its stable," he said as he laid her back into the mattress. She immediately missed his warmth. Being close to him felt natural and right, like she belonged there. Apparently, pain made her mawkish.

He grabbed a penlight from the table and shifted so he was facing her fully. Bright light shone in her eyes, making her wince. "Ugh, that hurts like hell," she complained as her head exploded and stars winked behind her closed lids.

She squinted open her eyes when the light abated and noted that his handsome features were now twisted in concentration as he proceeded to take her blood pressure. Something was wrong. She attempted to send her telepathy out but it hurt too much. "What's wrong?" she asked.

He paused with the cuff around her arm and his stethoscope pressed in the crook but didn't say anything. He finished taking her blood pressure and pushed back her covers. Instinct had her grabbing for the blanket to cover her bare legs. She had to remind herself that he was a doctor and had seen plenty of naked women and that it was no big deal that she was in nothing but a t-shirt and panties. She still blushed to the roots of her hair.

He stopped her with his hand on hers. The moment their skin touched, electricity zapped straight to her abdomen. The heat built and she fought to keep it from spreading lower. She looked into his amethyst eyes and saw they were glowing purple. Knowing he was as affected as she was made it easier to let go and allow him to exam her. He lifted her shirt and probed her stomach. His touch felt more intimate than any doctor's exam she'd ever had.

"Without having scans done I can't say for certain what is going on, but something isn't right. Like I told you this morning, you have a minor concussion along with bruising and your broken leg," he said as he settled his warm palm on her stomach. He stayed with his hand like that for several long minutes. She felt the heat build and thought his hand was trembling. As she opened her mouth to ask if he was ok, he rolled her to the side, exploring the area just below her rib cage. She heard his heavy sigh and glanced back to see him looking furious.

"I don't like that look. Tell me what you are thinking."

"Like I said—"

She cut off what was sure to be more of his platitudes. She didn't need him to protect her right now. She knew something was wrong. "Don't keep anything from me. I have a right to know. Besides, I'm not so fragile that I will break."

He lifted his hand and cupped her cheek. Automatically,

she turned into his palm and kissed it. "You are fragile, so very fragile. Your head injury has worsened when it shouldn't have. I can't say for sure but I think you may be bleeding internally. Your liver is slightly enlarged on palpitation. None of this should be occurring. Aside from the broken leg, your injuries from the accident weren't that bad. I believe it's the spell and I have no idea how to break it, and I don't know anyone who does."

She reached up and smoothed the crease between his eyes, ignoring her own fear. She wanted to reassure him and had no idea why. She was the one under some nefarious spell. "But that doesn't mean there isn't a way. Zander said he was going to see the Fae Queen. Surely she will help, right?"

He closed his eyes and leaned into her touch. Hope furled in her that maybe he did like her. "The queen isn't sentimental or helpful unless it benefits her or her people. Giving away Fae secrets goes against that entirely. Asking her for help is a long shot, but it's our only option."

Her stomach clenched when she detected the bitterness in his tone. It was so at odds with what she had seen of him so far. It made her wonder about his history with the Fae. She tried to reach out and grab his hand but she was so weak her hand fell clumsily onto his arm instead. She was getting worse. "I have to say, I'm not feeling optimistic about my chances here. What about what you mentioned this morning? Some mystical grim something? You said you wished it would appear. Can it help?"

"The Mystik Grimoire," he said and twined his fingers with hers. She didn't think he was aware of what he was doing, but her heart skipped a beat. Touching him eased the pain and settled her heart into a more regular rhythm. It was frightening and confusing how much he affected her.

"Grimoire, that's like a book of magic or something, right? If it has the answers, go get it. Or Zander can get it, just tell him where it is," Cailyn offered.

"That's impossible, Cai." She shivered at hearing him say her name like that. Only Elsie and Jessie had ever called her that. He said it like benediction, making her melt. "It disappeared over seven hundred years ago and hasn't been seen since. There is no way to simply retrieve it."

"How does a book disappear?" The idea that a book simply disappeared was unbelievable enough, but to think they had been unable to find it in *seven hundred years* was outrageous. How any of it was even possible baffled her.

Jace's eyes took on a faraway look as if he was lost in time and he reached out with his free hand, twisting a lock of her hair around his finger. "It's a long story. You need to understand more about the creatures the Goddess Morrigan created that make up some of the Tehrex Realm. Sorcerers are one of those races. We wield magic, as you know. Well, my father, head of the Miakoda family, held the position of Guild Master for millennia, up until the Great War killed both he and my mother. After that, my cousin, Evzen, was appointed to the position of Guild Master over the sorcerers in my absence." He paused, and swallowed thickly. His features contorted in pain and he fisted her hair tightly. The action sent pain shooting through her already aching head, but she stifled her wince, sensing he needed the contact.

He realized how tightly he was holding her hair and loosened his hold, but didn't let her go. "The Grimoire had disappeared many years before the war. The Goddess endowed the leather-bound book with magical powers and it appears and disappears of its own accord. My father always told me that it was the book's way of protecting its contents. It is bound to my bloodline, and will only appear to one of us...either me or Evzen since we are all that's left. Anyway, the book not only holds spells and incantations but prophecies from realm Oracles, as well as ways to counteract various types of magic."

Cailyn tried to scoot closer to his body, needing more of his warmth. She was getting colder. He noticed and brought his body closer. She sighed in contentment and focused on what he'd told her. "All of this is so outside anything I've ever known," she mused. "I can understand why you'd want the book. Call it to you again, and keep calling for it. Until it answers, we need to find a way to convince the Fae Queen to help us." This was not going to be easy, but she refused to give up. And, she wasn't going to let him either.

CHAPTER 4

Zander and Elsie entered Cailyn's room, causing Jace to fall off the bed as he quickly pulled away. The action nearly caused him to rip out a handful of Cailyn's hair and she missed the contact right away. Hell, she wanted to crawl into his lap. She had a feeling Jace didn't show others the vulnerability he had just shown her. She clearly saw the defenseless, lost child he had been when his parents had been killed. The intimacy of the moment had connected them, even if she sensed he was fighting it every step.

Zander looked at them with a raised eyebrow in question. Cailyn turned to her sister and gave a slight shake of her head. Zander caught the exchange and let it go. "I'm ready to visit Elvis and question Zanahia about the spell on Cailyn. I want you to come with me, Jace. Or Gerrick. I need someone who knows aboot magic."

"I'll go," Jace said at the same time Elsie asked "Who's Elvis?" Elsie's question brought images of the famous rock star in his blinged-out polyester suit to Cailyn's mind. Could he be a supernatural and still be alive? She smiled at the image of the famous rock star's curled lip with fangs protruding.

"He is the troll under the Fremont Bridge and he controls one of the portals to the Fae Realm," Zander replied. Ok, not at all what she had expected. She had a picture on her digital frame at home of her with Elsie beside the troll from her first visit to Seattle. It was difficult to think that big concrete sculpture was a living, breathing part of this realm. Things just kept getting weirder.

"You mean to tell me that the huge statue is an actual troll and protects a portal? I've said this before. You really need a handbook explaining your world. You could be cliché and call it Tehrex Realm for Dummies," her sister teased, patting Zander's chest.

"Aye, that's Elvis. And I've placed Gerrick on that assignment, mate. You should have the book in aboot a decade." Zander leaned down and kissed Elsie with an indulgent smile on his face.

"Are you guys at it again? Unlock those lips, we have a crisis to deal with," Orlando blurted as he entered the room followed by about half of the warriors. Cailyn heard the longing in Orlando's tone and knew he hadn't gotten over his feelings for her sister. The warrior was careful with his feelings out of respect for Zander, but the feline shifter couldn't hide it entirely from Cailyn's telepathy.

Cailyn glanced at the men in the room and suddenly felt very naked under the covers. As if reading her mind, Jace leaned down, pulling the blanket to her neck and smoothed them down, his hand lingering on her thigh.

"Later, mate," Zander whispered to Elsie who had a dreamy, love-struck expression before turning to the newcomers. "Orlando is right. We need to figure this oot for your sister. While Jace and I are gone, I want all of you but

Bhric oot on patrol, keeping an ear open for any talk of the accident. If we are lucky one of the skirm will boast aboot Kadir's intentions. Bhric, you keep an eye on Jessie."

"No problem, *brathair*, but Kyran isna here right now," Bhric said, referring to their other brother as he reclined against one wall. It wasn't necessarily a bad thing that that particular Vampire Prince was gone, Cailyn thought. He had always frightened her.

"Where the fuck is he?" It was impossible to miss the anger in Zander's tone.

"Where else? Bite."

"Of course he is. I'm going to castrate him when he gets back. He is never here when I need him," Zander growled. "Go patrol your sectors, now." The room began to empty with Zander's order.

Elsie turned in Zander's arms and Cailyn could see that her smile was forced. "Do you want to call John while the guys are gone? I'm sure he's worried about you. He is your fiancé after all."

Cailyn's heart twisted at the thought of John. She felt guilty that she hadn't told her sister that she had broken off their engagement. She hadn't wanted to ruin her sister's big day, and had kept her news to herself. Now wasn't the time to tell her either. Cailyn had no desire to deal with Elsie's upset over that until she was feeling better.

She looked away from her sister and her gaze went directly to Jace. She noted how he had frozen halfway up from the bed beside her, and those remaining in the room were all looking at him. The tension between them could be cut with a knife, and she had no doubt the others sensed their attraction to each other.

"Um, I'm not sure I'm ready to talk to him yet," Cailyn told Elsie. Aside from not wanting to tell her sister, she didn't want to have to explain in front of everyone, especially Jace, why she had broken off their engagement. She didn't fully understand the reasons herself. What she knew was that from the moment Jace had entered her sister's apartment all those months ago, something inside Cailyn had snapped to attention and locked on him, like a heat seeking missile.

His sexy body had captivated her, and caused her to have fantasies about a man other than her fiancé. It was something she had never before experienced, and it was what ultimately led to her breaking off her engagement.

She met Elsie's gaze and saw her disbelief and confusion. That made Cailyn's guilt all the worse. "You're right. I will call him." Cailyn was not looking forward to the conversation. The last time she had spoken to him, she had once again rejected him, and she didn't want to twist the knife any further.

∽

KYRAN'S GROIN tightened as he placed a metal nipple clamp on the female. The beautiful nymph bit down on the leather strap in her mouth and whimpered. He loved the fear and arousal in her silver-blue eyes. And hated it. The sound of her mewling fueled his deviant desires. Lost to his passions, he clamped the other nipple and stood back to admire the picture she created. Her come-fuck-me-thigh-high boots gleamed as he perused her body from head to foot.

As his gaze made its way back up her body, he noticed blood trickling from one of her breasts. The reason he used metal clamps instead of plastic. Pain and pleasure. The sight of blood hardened his shaft further. He bent over and licked the blood from her moist skin, tasting a note of salt mixed with copper elements. He groaned as pre-cum leaked from his cock.

The blood sent him over the edge of his control. He roughly grabbed her hands and pulled her to a bench. She stumbled and fell onto the wood face down. Perfect. He strapped her wrists into the leather cuffs under the bench. The position kept her upper body immobile with her delectable ass in the air. He ran his hand across the glistening globes and smacked one cheek. She moaned. He needed more force than his hand allowed and he swiveled to take in his options.

Skipping the huge four-poster bed, he contemplated strapping her to the wooden X, or placing her in the swing hanging from the ceiling, but decided he was too far gone. He was on a razor's edge, and needed to make his selection before he lost even more control. Along the opposite wall was an assortment of whips. He stalked quickly across the room, his large steel-toed boots echoing loudly throughout the room. He ran his fingers across the various wooden canes. He skipped those, and decided the knotted cat o'nine tails would fit his current mood.

Weapon in hand, he strode back to the waiting female. As soon as he was within range, his hand arched back and the ropes hit her back, eliciting a deep moan from them both. He hadn't even given his hand the order to strike. He was wound tighter than he realized.

He reached down and ran his hand through the curls between her legs and found wet female flesh. He loosened the tension on the leather straps and flipped her over. He brought the leather down on her breasts, enjoying the red welts that immediately formed. Returning to the chest of drawers, he bypassed the toys and other implements to grab a black candle off the top. The strike of a match widened her eyes; she knew what was coming, and was as eager for it as he was. He reached her side and caressed her red swollen breasts while he dripped black wax onto her clit. She arched back and screamed.

He slid the leather strap from her mouth and lowered to whisper in her ear, "What was that?"

"More, whip me more. Please, sir," she whimpered.

He stood up and smiled. This was why he came to this Goddess forsaken club. The cat bit into her flesh repeatedly, amplifying his arousal. His leathers hit his knees and his cock was in his hand before he blinked. He stroked himself then flipped her back over. Her ass was so soft and plump. The cat hit her plush globes, causing them to redden enticingly. He thrust his cock into her ass and stilled.

Grabbing a fist full of her hair, he pulled her head up to him and growled in her ear, "Tell me, bitch. Tell me now."

"Mmmm," she groaned in pleasure as he felt her orgasm begin. He yanked on her hair again and grasped it tightly, anger burning through him. She blurted, "Please don't kill me..."

Hearing her words was his cue, and he set into a punishing, brutal rhythm, seeking a brief moment to silence the voices from his past.

∼

"That could be the nastiest thing I have ever seen, I think my retinas are fried," Jace remarked as he and Zander drove down North 36th Street toward Elvis' home under the Fremont Bridge. He had no idea trolls had sex, and wished he was still ignorant of that fact. The female troll's body was grotesque, her backside was as big as a house, and Elvis was using a small car as a toy in places nothing should ever be shoved.

"Och, I agree. The Queen is going to be pissed off that her portal is being used as a sex toy. I doona think I'll tell her she is crawling through a device that was shoved up a troll's ass," Zander shuddered.

"I haven't seen the female troll before," Jace observed as he twisted his head upside down to get a look past intimate body parts to her face, "and I would've paid two tolls to avoid this whole fucking scene."

Zander chuckled and glanced over at him. "Aye, me too. I think she is new to the Montlake Bridge. I heard a rumor that there was a new transfer. Elvis looks to be quite the player."

"That's not right, Liege. Should we wait for them to finish or do we interrupt? I'm not sure of troll mating habits and we don't have all night, but I don't want to cock-block him either. He could crush us both with one swing of his fist."

"I doona know aboot troll habits either but from the frantic sounds, I think they are close to being done," Zander observed. "I'll park here and take our time walking over that way we can stop them before they begin another round."

Jace stepped onto the damp sidewalk, grateful the late summer weather hadn't turned too cold yet, and looked back to Zander. "I hate that your Eve of Eternal Union was interrupted. I know you aren't in the dog house with Elsie seeing that you have been busy saving her beloved sister, but you guys should have been in bed for weeks. We had a poll going on how long you two would be holed up in your rooms. I lost a bundle on my bet."

A secret smile inched across Zander's face, telling exactly where his thoughts were at the moment. Locked in that bedroom with his beautiful mate. For the first time, Jace was jealous of what Zander had with Elsie. "I will rip that fucking demon limb from limb and shred his insides for interrupting our night. I should be inside my Queen right now rather than watching these trolls go at it. But, no, that Goddess-damned demon had to go and up the ante."

"Do you feel any different now that you are fully mated?" Jace wanted to eat his words as they escaped his lips. Except that his curiosity about what he would never experience wouldn't be denied. The Goddess knew better than to gift a broken male like him with a Fated Mate.

"Aye, I feel verra different. Like I can take oot the archdemons and their skirm with a flex of my little finger, then take on the demons in hell withoot breaking a sweat. This new strength is invigorating. I never knew what I was missing before...but having both our souls complete and intertwined is beyond words. I havena had an opportunity to explore the new powers I was given through the blood exchange of our mating, but I look forward to it. Any description you have been given on the sexual changes you will go through is woefully inadequate," Zander murmured.

Jace wondered what it would be like to actually ejaculate when he had an orgasm. Not that he knew what it felt like to have an orgasm. At this point, he wondered what it would be like to be aroused by a female and not vomit. Unfortunately, he was doomed to never know any of it.

Tinkling sounded in his ears, and strong pheromones reached his nostrils at the same time. None of which, he realized, were coming from the randy trolls. He glanced over and Jace's eyes bulged at the sight of ice crystals dripping from Zander's fingertips. Those were major new powers for the Vampire King, and Zander needed to control them

ASAP. "Uh, Liege, did you know that you're icing the sidewalk?"

Zander snapped to attention and the ice immediately disappeared. "Och, I was thinking of Elsie. She consumes me completely."

The bellow of a T-Rex interrupted their conversation. "I hope they didn't just topple the bridge."

Zander chuckled, "From the look on his face, I would say that was the grand finale. Och, I'd wager that registered on the human's Richter scale."

The sound of boulders scraping echoed and Jace realized it was Elvis talking. "Now you understand why I have my reputation. I'm sure you're glad that you transferred here." Apparently, that was Elvis' version of pillow talk. Suddenly, that large gray head swiveled their way.

"Vampire King, you're lucky you weren't here any sooner and didn't interrupt us before we were done, or you would be missing a limb or two," Elvis drawled and withdrew from the female troll.

"Bluidy hell. Losing a limb would be preferable to my eye sockets bleeding from the sight. Elvis, you've ruined the bliss of my Eve. I'm surprised the Queen allows you to use her portal in such a fashion," Zander countered.

"The magic's vibration is irresistible, isn't it, Priscilla?" Elvis cooed, ignoring Zander. Jace shuddered at the thought of where that VW had been. There wasn't enough bleach to remove that image from his brain.

"Mmmm, yes it does. Who are these handsome creatures, Elvis?" The female troll purred.

"Your name is Priscilla? As in Elvis and Priscilla?" Jace blurted.

"Yes, but I'm much better looking than that human.

What do you want?" Elvis asked tersely. "We have much to do before dawn turns us to stone."

Zander removed a large ruby pendant from his pocket and held the offering out to the troll. "There has been an incident with my queen's sister and we need an audience with her Highness."

"Oooh, that's beautiful." Jace shivered at the tone of Priscilla's voice. It grated like fingernails on a chalkboard, and the high pitch didn't match her large frame.

Apparently, Elvis was anxious to get back to his extracurricular activities as he wasted no time palming the ruby and calling the Queen. Elvis' eyes gleamed bright silver, growing larger than hubcaps, and a mist shrouded the area around the VW. Jace's heart leapt with hope when Zander leaned in and whispered, "The Queen agreed to meet with us."

Jace shoved down the desperation he felt as the enchanting Fae Queen emerged from the vehicle. Idly, he wondered if the contraption smelled vile, given where it had been.

"Zander Tarakesh, what a surprise. I did not expect to see you on such an important night for you. I do hope your mating ceremony wasn't interrupted," Zanahia murmured, catching his attention. The queen's long blonde hair flowed freely down her back, and her silver crown matched her silver eyes. Jace had never seen her before, and had to admit the Fae Queen was mesmerizing.

"Your Highness," Zander bowed and took Zanahia's hand and kissed her pale knuckles. "The ceremony was completed, but our evening was interrupted when Elsie received a vision regarding her sister, Cailyn. I'll get right to the point. My sorcerers tell me Cailyn is under some type of

Fae spell, and as you know, Aquiel is responsible. I need your help reversing it."

"I am glad to hear the ceremony went well. You must tell me about the experience. Surely there is something new to be learned, given the uniqueness of your mate." The Queen's interest was genuine, yet unease at that interest skittered down Jace's spine.

Jace understood the need for politics and niceties, but wanted to scream. They didn't have time for this. Cailyn did not have time for this. He had not experienced anxiety or fear since his imprisonment several centuries before, but he was buffeted by both regarding Cailyn's condition. The longer Cailyn was under the magic, the worse she became. He feared that the longer they took, the greater chance Cailyn wasn't going to make it. She was human, and time was not their friend.

"With all due respect, Zanahia, I doona have time to share anything aboot my mating right now. Cailyn is in trouble and we need to act quickly to help her," Zander interjected. Jace was relieved that Zander cut to the chase.

"Yes, of course. I apologize, I am as curious as everyone else is about your mating. It was a momentous event, after all. With regards to Cailyn, I am afraid that I will not be of much help. All I can say is that if you were to ask the right people, they would tell you that seeking the Voodoo Queen is a dangerous and impossible trip. I can't say anymore. I must protect myself and my people, you understand." Her smile held more venom than her innocuous words. Jace didn't stop to consider her mood. They had a place to start, and if rumors were true, the trip to Marie Laveau was going to be deadly.

The Voodoo Queen was a myth as far as he knew, so he had no idea how to find her. He wracked his brain for other options, but there were none. "We don't have time to go to New Orleans and seek Marie Laveau. Cailyn is not stable enough to make what is sure to be a treacherous journey. If you don't help us, she is going to die," Jace cursed impetuously. Sweat poured down his back as palpitations slammed his heart against his rib cage with his anxiety.

"Calm doon, Jace. Zanahia, surely there is something more you can offer. I know you doona want to see an innocent suffer," Zander implored, trying to appeal to the Queen's empathy. Zander had lost his mind if he thought this female was going to give them any helpful information.

The Queen paused and clasped her hands in front of her body. "I am truly sorry, Zander."

CHAPTER 5

Elsie sat on the bed next to Cailyn and laid her head in Cailyn's lap just like they had done countless times when they were children. They'd always had a special bond due to their unique abilities. When they were little, it was Cailyn that Elsie went to when she was teased ruthlessly by her peers. It was Cailyn who had taught her sister how to cope, and made it better.

Elsie had had premonitions for as long as Cailyn could remember, and the other kids called her names and ostracized her for them. Cailyn had learned early on to keep the fact that she was able to hear what others were thinking to herself. It only took her parents threatening to take her to a psychiatrist and have her medicated for her to realize that she needed to keep her ability secret and pretend she was normal. She didn't have anyone looking out for her, or helping her, so she made certain that Elsie's sanity was never questioned, and she had the support she needed to cope.

It wasn't easy being different. It had been difficult for Cailyn to make friends as a child when she knew what the other kids were thinking, both good and bad. It only worsened when she became a teenager and could go out on dates. Dates were short-lived most of the time because she wasn't one to sit at dinner with someone while they thought about her breasts or having sex with her. She hated how men lusted after her body and didn't see her as a person.

Her telepathy was one of the reasons she vowed never to get married. She wanted to be accepted by someone who knew about her ability. She wanted to be able to share all of herself with her spouse, without seen as psychotic. The fact that she could hear the thoughts of her parents, thoughts that were never meant to be shared, had also put Cailyn off of getting close to anyone, especially romantically. The truth can be very hurtful. That desire changed when she met John. He was different. Sure, he desired her, but he also saw *her*. He loved how devoted she was to Elsie and Jessie, he appreciated her work ethic, and never griped about her long hours. She had not yet shared her abilities with him, but that was more about old fears than him rejecting her. She was sure that he would love her despite her abnormality.

She came out of her thoughts to realize her sister was watching her. "I want to call John, but I need to tell you something first."

"You know you can tell me anything," Elsie reassured.

"I know," Cailyn paused, thinking about how best to tell Elsie. No pretty words came to mind. Nothing to do but tell her. "I broke off my engagement with John."

Elsie's mouth dropped open and did an imitation of a fish before she responded. "When, Cai? Why, what happened?"

"Several months ago. I don't know how to explain it, but this has to do with Jace. Things got to the point where I felt like I was doing both of us a disservice if I didn't call things off until I got my head on straight."

"Oh my God! I had no idea that you and Jace had a thing going. How have you hidden it? Why in the hell didn't you tell me sooner? I'm your sister, and I know you have Jessie, but I thought we were closer than that," Elsie questioned, the hurt clear in her eyes. Cailyn felt terrible for keeping this from her sister and needed to make it better.

Cailyn took a deep breath that sent pain shooting through her chest. When she tried to lift her hand to run it through Elsie's hair, her arm wouldn't respond. Her body was simply too fatigued to move. She settled for getting her hand to her sister's arm. "It's not like that. Jace and I don't have anything going on at all. Before earlier today he had not said more than a few words to me. I wasn't even sure he remembered my name, or who I was other than your older sister. My problem was my reaction to him. From the moment I met him I was enthralled. I thought about him constantly and still do. I just couldn't continue my engagement to John while I wanted another man as much as I did...and do," she whispered, trying to muster some energy.

"Oh Cai, you should have told me. I would have understood, and may have been able to help. You have always looked out for me, it's time I returned the favor."

"I didn't want to ruin your mating ceremony, and before that you had enough on your plate and didn't need my crap. Besides, what could you do? I need to figure out why I am drawn to him and what to do about it. I still love John, yet am unable to deny wanting Jace. And, now I feel this connection to Jace, making matters more difficult."

"Your life isn't crap, and you are my sister. I will always be here for you no matter what is going on. And you'd be surprised at how much I understand what you are going through. I mean, I loved Dalton and made a vow to him for life, and never thought there would be another for me. Yet after he was killed, I found myself yearning for..." Elsie trailed off, her eyes going saucer-wide as she put her fingers over her gaping mouth.

Cailyn's gut clenched with fear. She wasn't sure she wanted to know what her sister was thinking right then. "I wonder if you could be Jace's Fated Mate. It sure sounds like how I felt with Zander."

Cailyn felt the blood drain from her body. She couldn't be this man's mate. She lived in San Francisco, and loved another man, despite what she was feeling right now. "I can't be. How would I know? How did you find out?"

"Fated Mates find out when they have sex with one another. There isn't another way that I know of. I have no idea who we could ask about this. I wish they were back already, maybe Zander has some answers."

A knock at the door interrupted their conversation. "Please don't say anything to anyone until we talk some more," Cailyn begged Elsie, as Orlando peeked his head into the room, his gaze going straight to her sister. Cailyn held Elsie's gaze, and was relieved when she nodded minutely.

"Hey, O. What's up?" Elsie asked, turning to the Dark Warrior. His white-blond hair was sticking out in every direction. Cailyn had to admit the guy was good looking, but paled in comparison to the sexy sorcerer. From the moment she'd met Jace, he had become the standard against which she judged all others.

"Just wanted to come and check on you guys. How are you feeling, Cai?"

"I've had better days. I wish the pain would go away. I have no energy for anything, and between the two I can barely function, but Jace and Zander will be back soon with the cure." She had to believe that they were going to bring something back with them to help her. She refused to accept that this spell was going to kill her.

"You both need to be prepared that they may not have the answers you want. The Fae are fickle fucks and not likely to help. But we won't give up. We will all search every corner of the realm for a way to lift the spell," he promised, sitting on the bed next to Elsie.

"I'm so sorry, Cai. This is all my fault. You would be safe at home if it wasn't for me," Elsie whispered.

Before Cailyn could respond, Orlando interjected. "You can't blame yourself. As you have learned, no one is safe from the ravages of this war," Orlando replied solemnly. Cailyn knew Elsie better than to think his words placated her.

Another knock echoed throughout the room. "Hey Chiquita, Cai, you both look beat. Is my partner bugging you again?" Santiago asked entering the room with grim purpose. The lines set into his face told her something was up. She said a silent prayer that Jace and Zander were okay. She didn't know if she could take any more bad news right now. He and Orlando were homicide detectives with Seattle Police Department, as well as Dark Warriors, and she hated how she hoped it was a human issue on his mind.

"What's going on? Have you heard from Zander or Jace?" Elsie asked sitting up.

"I haven't heard anything from them. Here, I brought you one of those energy drinks that you love. I figured you could use a pick me up. O, I need to talk to you about a call I got from the Lieutenant." The obvious tension in Santiago's voice had Cailyn chomping at the bit as to what he had to say.

Something was up and she wanted to hear what it was, but she didn't have the relationship that her sister did with these formidable warriors. Cailyn was still intimidated by their presence, especially these two. Orlando was a feline shifter and she had seen him shift into a rather large snow leopard during the battle outside Confetti. Santiago was a canine shifter and she watched him become a huge wolf. Seeing them become wild animals coupled with the archdemon, Kadir, who looked like an incarnation of the devil, made for some of her most frightening moments.

"Be right back—"

Her sister's terse response cut Orlando off. "You cannot waltz in here sounding all serious and keep me in the dark, Santi. You guys can have this conversation right here. I'm the queen and I won't be left out of anything."

"It's not that we want to leave you out, Chiquita. This is official police business and there is no need to worry you over things unnecessarily."

"If this has to do with the Tehrex Realm, then it *is* my business." Cailyn's chest swelled with pride in her baby sister. She had come into her own, standing up to such fierce warriors.

Orlando chuckled, "She schooled you, bro. Is this about more skirm attacks on women?"

"Yes and there's been another one," Santiago relayed somberly looking at Elsie, "and the latest victim was a member of SOVA."

Elsie's gasp echoed loudly in the room. Clearly this was distressing for her sister, even if Cailyn had no idea what they were talking about. "What? Oh my God. What was her name? Was it Mack?" What was Elsie talking about?

"Who is Mack, and what is this SOVA?" Cailyn interjected, she'd never heard of them.

"Mack is the leader of a group called Survivors of Vampire Attacks, or SOVA, for short. They hunt vampires, or what they think are vampires, but are really skirm. Who was this victim, Santi?"

"The victim didn't have any ID on her. All I can tell you is that she had dark hair, was five-foot-six-inches tall and was wearing a leather SOVA jacket," Santiago said.

"Was her hair black? And short? Did she have sleeves of tattoos?" Her sister's frantic questions had Cailyn's adrenaline pumping.

"No her hair was dark brown and she had no ink," Santi responded.

"Thank God, it wasn't Mackendra. Ellen had dark brown hair, but I've been out of touch for a while. O, you mentioned there being more attacks on women. Has there been an increase lately, then? What are the victim profiles?" Cailyn was shocked at how her sister took control and delved right into this issue with confidence. Like a Queen.

"There has been a marked increase of female victims and missing women since your abduction, El. They are from various walks of life and do not fit any one profile. There have been blondes, brunettes, and red heads and they have been anywhere from the poor to the filthy rich. There is no clear pattern to the attacks which is frustrating, because we don't know which areas to target," Orlando explained.

Prickles ran down Cailyn's spine as she realized that she and Jessie had also been victims when they were attacked and nearly killed. The scum who did this to them had plenty of time to snap their necks before they had been rescued, but didn't. Her gut turned when she considered that the demon and Fae had something more planned for her and Jessie. She was thankful that Zander had taken the precaution to have his Dark Warriors following her, and that they made it to them in time.

"The Lieutenant is up in arms about this latest victim, thinking there is a crazy vigilante group trying to reap justice for the victims of the 'Twikills.' You were a part of them, Elsie, and there is no one better to help us tell Mackendra that they need to stop what they are doing. They take too much risk with their lives and now the Lieutenant wants their heads. None of us want anything to happen to your friends," Santiago added. What was he talking about? Her sister hadn't mentioned being part of the vigilante group. What he was suggesting was crazy.

"What is he talking about El? Were you a part of that group?" Cailyn watched her sister squirm and fidget. Apparently, she wasn't the only one who'd kept secrets.

"Yes I joined after Dalton was killed," Elsie said turning back to Santiago. "Mackendra isn't going to like that at all, Santi. I can call her and setup a meeting, but she isn't going to close up shop. She feels as if hunting vampires is her calling. Her pain runs deep..." Elsie's voice trailed off and the room descended into silence.

"What is it, El?" Orlando asked, crossing to her side.

"I'm getting flashes of numerous women, both human and realm. They are locked up and filthy. Some of them are naked and covered in blood. I can't see their faces clearly, but they are being tortured by the demons," Elsie moaned, grabbing her head. Hearing voices was bad enough, but having the images in her head that Elsie had just described would give her nightmares for weeks.

Cailyn inched her fingers across the blanket and tried to squeeze her sister's leg, offering reassurance as Elsie continued. "I don't know where they are, but I can sense that they are important to the realm. Is there anyway the demons would be able to detect if these females were mates? I know the markings don't appear until after sex with your Fated Mate, but is there another way?"

"Goddess. Hearing the demons are kidnapping females and keeping them captive is just about the worst news we could get. To answer your question, I have no idea if there is a way the demons could identify Fated Mates. Zander and Jace need to return. We need to have a meeting," Santiago said, cursing soundly.

At the mention of Jace, Cailyn thought back to the day she first saw him. A wild fire had lit and burned unchecked throughout her body from the moment he had walked into her sister's small apartment. It had burned so hot that she had been unable to douse it. Her attraction to the sorcerer was atomic, and caused her heart ache.

She was torn between reconciling with John and pursuing Jace. She loved her life in San Francisco, her job, and John. Anything with Jace meant giving all of it up. It would be worth it, an insidious part of her whispered.

She pictured his lips and how she wanted to kiss him and explore his body. His lean, muscular frame ignited arousal so intense she longed to be taken by him. Their lovemaking would be so hot she imagined it would burn her to cinders.

With that thought, uncertainty plagued her. Was she pretty or funny enough for him? She had seen that woman he had been with at the club. She had been the opposite of Cailyn, tall and skinny with a perfect body. Cailyn carried an extra ten pounds, which only added to her insecurity. Sometimes she hated being a woman as doubts played through her mind.

∽

The second Jace entered the compound, sultry tendrils of cinnamon danced into his nose. Cailyn was aroused. For some insane reason he hoped she was thinking of him. His cock jerked eagerly at that notion. He placed a hand over his churning stomach and closed his eyes, breathing deeply. Goddess, he wanted that female, had never wanted one more in his entire life. The intensity of his desire had him once again questioning if she could be his Fated Mate. Like before, he dismissed the notion. The Goddess was infinitely smarter than that.

He shook his head and placed one shaky foot in front of the other as he ascended the stairs behind Zander who was taking them two at a time, clearly eager to reach Elsie. In moments, Zander burst through the door to Cailyn's suite of rooms and the King's expression lost the hard bitter edges and softened.

"Lady E, your mate has returned," Zander growled and grabbed her up into his arms.

Jace met Orlando's awkward stare while Zander thoroughly kissed his mate. "Get a room," Orlando said, and Jace didn't miss the bitter undertone. Was the warrior as jealous of what they had as Jace? None of them had ever contemplated having a mate until Elsie. Now Jace wondered how many of them longed for it like he did. His gaze slid to Cailyn and he noticed that the circles under her eyes were darker, and her skin was paler. An invisible magnetic pull had him crossing the room to Cailyn's side.

"Good idea. Let's go," Zander responded with his lips still pressed to Elsie's.

The Queen playfully slapped his arm. "Later. First, tell me what you learned." Elsie responded.

"The Queen didn't tell us anything really. She hinted that the antidote is in New Orleans and we need to travel there immediately," Zander said as he stroked a finger across Elsie's cheek. The love between the newly mated pair was tangible. Jace envied the King his fortune.

"Why can't one of you give her blood to heal her? You guys brought me back from the brink of death with your blood," Elsie pointed out.

Words tumbled past Jace's lips before he could stop them. "No one will be giving Cailyn blood but me and even that isn't going to happen, because blood will not solve our problem. This is magically induced and the spell needs to be reversed." He took a deep breath to regain control of his emotions, not sure what had come over him. He didn't have time to evaluate it at the moment. "We need an appropriate agent to break the binding of the magic to your sister, and blood isn't that agent."

"Okay, so we have no easy solution. You mentioned New Orleans. What is there that can help me?" Cailyn asked weakly. Jace reached down and grabbed Cailyn's hand, hating how cold her skin was. She was definitely getting worse. Panic surged through him, setting off a new urgency.

"Orlando, call everyone back. Patrols can wait. We have to strategize and plan a trip. I want you guys on the road ASAP," Zander ordered, ignoring Cailyn's question.

"Wait just a minute. What do you mean you guys? Aren't you going too?" Elsie asked, leveling the mighty vampire king with a glare.

"Nay, *a ghra*, I will remain here with you and Cailyn. Jace and two others will go," Zander replied, trying to bring his mate back into his arms. She pushed his arms away.

"No. Zander, I need you to go. I won't be able to stand it if I don't have the peace of mind knowing someone who cares as much as I do is on this mission. I know that you won't let me leave this compound, especially, with women being targeted by skirm. I hate the thought of you being in danger, but I can't be selfish. Cailyn needs this," Elsie said, her gaze remaining on Zander.

"You all can stand around and argue all day, but I'm going. I don't care who goes with me, but I'm leaving soon," he declared, keeping his gaze locked on Cailyn's. Her eyes flared with surprise when his fingers stroked her hair. The silky stands wrapped around his fingers, keeping him close. He cradled the back of her head with his palm. "You will get better. No one will fight harder to get the antidote than I," he promised, shocked to realize how deeply he meant every word he said.

"I trust you, but you have to be safe and come back to me," Cailyn whispered.

Her trust melted something in him. No one had ever looked at him the way Cailyn did. Something was happening between them, and the connection he'd felt between them intensified. Before he knew what he was doing, he leaned down and touched his lips to hers. Sparks flew where their flesh met, and his breath was stolen from his chest. He pulled away and saw that Cailyn was just as affected. He wished no one had witnessed the intimacy of the moment, it belonged to them alone. He'd never had a more intimate moment with a female, and it had nothing to do with sex.

CHAPTER 6

Watching the clock until nightfall so they could leave for New Orleans was going to kill Jace. He needed to be retrieving the cure for Cailyn, but instead he was in the war room arguing with Kyran about Jessie turning into something unknown, not skirm but no longer human either. His fists balled at his sides, and fury raced through his veins. Jace was going to punch the shit out of Kyran. The bastard had been out with his whores when they had needed him, and now he wanted to change the decisions that their group had already made without him.

Jessie had fangs and craved blood, but still had her appetite for food. It was unclear if she would eventually subsist solely on blood like all skirm. The biggest relief for Jace was that she wasn't a mindless drone, and didn't appear to be driven by the archdemon who turned her. Her bite wound had turned blue rather than the typical black, and her blood had remained red instead of black. Most astonishingly, her brainwaves were enhanced beyond what anyone expected. Jace and the scientists were excited to learn more about what she was becoming, but Kyran kept arguing the issue of destroying the poor girl.

Jace stalked from the war room as his patience hit its limit. Lost in thought, he paused on the marble floor in the entry. The front doors loomed in front of him, with their intricate Celtic symbols. They were his favorite feature in the entire mansion he had called home for over a century. He identified heavily with his mother's Native American heritage, but the door always brought him closer to his father, and this part of his heritage.

He, along with Zander and the other Dark Warriors, had built the home piece by piece. It had been Zander's sister, Breslin, who had the idea that the entrance to the home they shared be a symbol of the heritage they all shared, uniting them despite their differences. The massive twelve foot doors had taken many weeks to carve, and contained the blood of each warrior. Jace and Gerrick had used that collective blood to cast powerful shielding and glamour spells over the building and surrounding property, ultimately providing the realm's strongest protection.

As he continued his search for Evzen, thoughts of protection had him wondering if there was a way to keep all realm females safe. It had been a blow to hear that the archdemons were targeting females, and the thought that they had a way of detecting whether or not they were Fated Mates was frightening. The very idea was appalling.

Jace entered the library and saw Gerrick and Evzen deep in conversation. Seeing Gerrick made him realize that the rising tensions and tempers in the house made the surliest warrior of the compound seem the least unpleasant at the moment. Gerrick had always worn his bitterness as openly as the scar marring his handsome face, but since the accident the night before, he was the only of them who had managed to shove his negativity aside. He was focused and ready to help. Jace had learned recently that the loss of Gerrick's Fated Mate drove him to ensure no one suffered like he had. He appreciated having the formidable warrior at his back.

Jace clapped Gerrick on the shoulder as he crossed the room to Evzen. "Sir," Jace bowed his head in deference to Evzen, "you wanted to see me before we leave?"

Evzen tipped his head in acknowledgment. "Yes. Have a seat," he said gesturing to the nearby leather sofas. He sat next to Gerrick, and contemplated his cousin and their roles in the realm.

Jace had been in line to become Guild Master until he had been abducted by Angelica. During his captivity, the Great War claimed Jace's parents, and so the position fell to the next person in their family line - Evzen. Initially, after his rescue, he had been angry over all that Lady Angelica had taken from him. Now, he was glad that Evzen held that role, as he had become one of the most powerful sorcerers the realm had ever known.

Jace's churning thoughts turned to the matter at hand as he scanned the shelves, looking for a book that may help. There was everything from the history of the Valkyrie, to books of witchcraft spells and incantations, to ledgers documenting various demons encountered during the course of the war.

"I wanted to provide you with all the information I have about Ms. Laveau," Evzen said as he sat across from him. "Marie is a cunning, dangerous, and enigmatic female. And paranoid, with good reason of course. As the Voodoo Queen, she has many enemies. It is said that she has obtained various tomes containing spells and potions for many different species, and that is how she is able to develop and sell her tinctures. No one, especially the Fae, is happy that she has learned how to counter their enchantments. Needless to say, she uses everything at her disposal to hide and protect herself. The God Kalfu is capricious, and you can guarantee that, as her father, he has added to her arsenal. You must also know that you won't be able to approach her without going through one of her Mambos. They are her gatekeepers, so to speak. Rumor has it that she lives deep in the swamps, but no one knows for sure. Wherever she lives will be glamoured, and protected with various layers of magic and creatures."

Just an average day in the life of a Dark Warrior, Jace thought wryly. He had known Marie was powerful, but not that she was the daughter of a God. "Magic we can deal with, but what kind of creatures are we talking about?"

"Don't be so sure about your abilities against her spells. While she doesn't use black magic, she does combine light and dark forces, and that combination is sure to challenge you. You and Gerrick will need to pool your energy and use every resource at your disposal."

"That won't be a problem. We've linked our energies for centuries, but we will need all our focus to be successful," Gerrick replied. He was right. Jace needed to keep his head in the game. Ever since he had rescued Cailyn, his mind had been preoccupied with her, and he needed to be on his A-game if they were going to succeed.

Instinctively, Jace's finger traced the moon and nighthawk etched in his silver cuff. His father had given him the Cuff de Draiocht when he passed his stripling years, and his words came back to him. His father had told him that the cuff couldn't be removed once it was placed on his wrist, and that it provided Jace with immense power. When Jace encountered new or stressful situations, all he had to do was touch the cuff and access what waited beneath the surface. Unfortunately, when he had been chained in Angelica's dungeon, he was unable to access its power. He hoped it didn't fail him now.

"Let's get Zander and Bhric and head out," Jace told Gerrick. He was ready to be on the road.

∽

"Shit, Nikko," Jace cursed at the council member flying the plane, "can you cruise at a higher altitude for fucks sake?" Jace barked as they hit another pocket of turbulence and his nausea surged again. Recalling the all-too-brief kiss he had shared with Cailyn wasn't helping matters. It struck him that he had never felt ill for so long after an encounter with a female. Then again, he had never been aroused like he was at the merest thought of her. It didn't help that images of her naked and spread on his bed plagued him about every five seconds.

"Working on it Jace. Hey, can someone bring me one of those sandwiches and a drink?" Nikko hollered from the cockpit. Nikko was one of the most even-keeled males Jace knew, which was why he was the best suited to train new Dark Warriors.

"Aye, but all you get is a coke because you did a shite-job of stocking the bar. What's up with that? You knew we were going to be on the plane for several hours," Bhric griped as he reclined in the pale leather seats.

"Fuck you, lush. Do it yourself next time," Nikko teased. Jace would bet his last dollar that Zander had told Nikko to remove all the alcohol from the plane given Bhric's tendency to overindulge. Hoping to settle his stomach, Jace got up and made his way to the fridge and grabbed a soda.

"I will. And, when I do I'll bring some lasses along with the booze. Why do we even have a bed back there if I canna pound a willing nymph into the springs?" Bhric shot back.

Jace also grabbed a sandwich then handed them both to Nikko before he sat back down. Unable to relax, he crossed and uncrossed his shit-kicker over his knee, pulling at a loose string on his faded blue jeans. Sweat dripped down his spine and his heart raced as images of him putting that bed to use with Cailyn filled his overactive imagination. He wanted to punch Bhric in the face for putting that image in his head. He was wrongly blaming the male, but he was okay with that.

Needing a distraction, he ran through preparations in his mind. "Who is meeting us when we land?" he asked Zander.

Zander finished off his food and lobbed the trash into the can in the corner. "Aison and Luke will meet us at Lakefront and take us back to Les Augres Manor." Jace smiled at the mention of the New Orleans Dark Warrior compound. He hadn't been there in at least a century.

"I say we go straight to the voodoo shops Micah researched, not the manor," Gerrick proposed. For once, Jace appreciated how focused Gerrick always was on the mission at hand. The warrior was the epitome of ruthless focus and determination.

Jace wanted to get this done and get back to Cailyn. Oddly enough, he already missed her. Her scent...her body. He wanted more of Cailyn. The kiss he stole was a tease. He wanted to trail his lips and tongue across her mouth to her neck and lower to her breasts and then even lower to her sex.

He imagined her head thrown back with her eyes screwed shut while her back bowed off the bed with her release. Would she scream out her pleasure? She was going to be a sight when he got her beneath him. His cock hardened, bringing on more nausea, reminding him why this little fantasy was destined to remain just that...a fantasy. But he still wanted more than anything to enjoy this erotic fantasy.

He had never been more bitter or angrier about Lady Angelica's torture. For the millionth time he considered hunting Lady Angelica down and ripping her limb from limb. He knew he wouldn't, and hated that he didn't understand what stopped him.

From the time Zander rescued him six centuries before, he had planned to exact his revenge for the torture he suffered at her hands. Countless times he had outlined his strategy, but something stopped him every time he attempted to take action. He questioned if magic was at play, but dismissed the notion, as he was unable to detect anything. He left the past and refocused on the present.

"I agree with Gerrick. We have the names of some voodoo shops. I say we don't delay and start right away. It's going to take some time to find an authentic Mambo, and then convince her to disclose Marie's location," Jace suggested as he restlessly shifted in his seat.

"Sounds good, but I'm going to call Aison and make sure he brings booze and beignets to the airport, and lines up a lass or two for later," Bhric said between bites of his sandwich. "I for one, need to get drunk then laid."

"Dude, why do you always lead with your dick?" Gerrick scoffed.

"Because my dick usually leads me...straight to *Annwyn*," Bhric chuckled as a big smile spread across his face. Jace rolled his eyes at Bhric's brash sense of humor. This was going to be a long trip.

∽

"Hell no! You aren't leaving," Orlando insisted. "You heard what Zander said."

Elsie threw her hands up in exasperation. She wasn't helpless any longer. She was a strong vampire, and she had a friend she needed to talk to. "I am going, Orlando. Zander cannot dictate everything I do. I can protect myself. I killed skirm before you guys came along and now I am a powerful vampire. You know I can kick some serious ass. This is important to me. I have to be the one to tell her about the dangers to SOVA. I care about her and the others, more than you know. Besides, she's more likely to listen to me," Elsie said as she climbed behind the wheel of Rhys' Denali. She yelped when Rhys picked her up and tossed her into the passenger seat.

"Unlike him, I get that you are going, but I'm driving, sweet cheeks. That's how I roll," Rhys purred, insinuation dripping from every word. It was easy for Elsie to ignore the cambion's innuendos, because nearly every comment he made was sexual in nature. It's just how he was.

She rolled her eyes. "You are such a chauvinist, but thank you. I didn't want to go alone."

"You are the most stubborn female I have ever met," Orlando grumbled as he jumped into the backseat. "I just got back into Zander's good graces. He is so going to kill me, or remove vital body parts. I like my body parts where they are and in working order, thank you very much." She glanced back and laughed when she noticed the grimace as Orlando protectively cupped his groin.

"Don't worry, I'll make sure they stay where they are," she promised.

The garage door on the far right opened and Kyran pulled in. Crap, she wanted to be gone before he returned. He, unlike the others, would not hesitate to chain her up to keep her in the house. She chewed her lip when he loped over to them and tapped on her window. "So, where are we off to?"

"I am going to meet with Mackendra from SOVA—"

Orlando cut her off. "She insists on leaving the compound."

She ignored him and continued talking, "so I can inform her about the death of her friend and warn her about the danger and the police involvement—"

Orlando's voice rose above hers, trying to drown out her words as he continued, "She won't listen to reason and let me and Santiago handle this."

Again, she ignored Orlando. "And, *they* are coming along to protect me. Want to join us?" she finished, figuring she wasn't going to win with Kyran, given her brother-in-law's protectiveness of her. Besides, it couldn't hurt to have more warriors with her.

Rhys laughed at Orlando's groan when Kyran nodded and silently climbed into the other back seat. The air became thicker in the quiet of the vehicle as they pulled out of the compound. The three hulking men took all the free space in the vehicle. Elsie felt claustrophobic with them surrounding her and rolled down her window, letting in fresh air.

Kyran finally broke the silence as they drove across town. "So what's the plan?"

"You guys are going with me so I can speak to Mackendra. She is the leader of SOVA and my friend, so you guys need to hide your weapons and don't be so intimidating. This woman is a soldier and won't miss anything. Friend or not, she will be skittish if she suspects something. I haven't told her that I am a vampire, and I don't think it is a good idea that she knows that right now. She has hunted skirm for many years and would likely shove a dagger in my chest if she knew."

"Sounds like my date from Saturday night," Rhys quipped.

"Be careful of your emotions, Elsie. You are new to vampirism, and your control is so-so at best. Your fangs tend to come down and your eyes glow when you get riled up," Orlando warned when they parked close to the busy square.

"Okay," she breathed as she climbed out of the car. Control, she told herself. Remembering that was going to be a challenge. She wasn't going to back down now though, she considered this woman her friend. After all, Mack had helped her through the toughest times of her life.

Mackendra was easily spotted across the crowd with her short, spiky, black hair and sleeve of tattoos. She grinned to herself as she read the pink t-shirt stretched across Mackendra's ample bosom. The woman was an activist to the core, sporting a top that read 'Check Your Boobies Bitches' with a pink ribbon. The message was clear, and cut to the chase, much like the wearer. Elsie wanted a shirt for herself.

"Hey, thanks for meeting me," she called out as they approached. She embraced Mackendra and held her close for a moment. She had missed her friend. "I love your shirt."

Mackendra looked down then met her gaze with a small smile. "I wear it in honor of my aunt. One in eight women are affected by breast cancer, and we've got to get the message out. It's been way too long, El. What happened to you? And who are your new friends?" Mackendra eyed the guys suspiciously, lingering on Kyran for several moments.

Elsie noticed the dichotomy between Kyran and Rhys. Kyran stood rigidly with his arms crossed over his chest while and Rhys was flirting with a couple women to their left. Rhys was no surprise, but something was up with Kyran. His tension was palpable. She didn't have time to ferret that out at the moment though, and focused back on Mack.

"I'm sorry for not calling sooner. My life took an unexpected, but wonderful turn," Elsie said then turned to the guys. "This is Detective Orlando Trovatelli. He is one of the detectives who investigated my first husband's murder."

Mackendra's head snapped back to Elsie, then Orlando, and returned to Kyran, whose eyes had yet to leave the female's face. "You said first husband. Does that mean you remarried?" Elsie wasn't surprised that her friend had honed in on that little fact.

Elsie felt bad for not including her friend in her life of late, but didn't allow the censure to rile her. "Yes, I have and I want to tell you all about it, but that's a story for another time. Orlando and I are here for much less pleasant conversation, I'm afraid."

Orlando stepped forward and held out his hand. "Nice to meet you Ms. Callaghan."

After a few seconds consideration Mackendra shook Orlando's outstretched hand. "I'm not sure if it's nice or not. What can I do for you?" Elsie had missed Mack's direct and brash personality. With her, what you saw was what you got.

"Ms. Callaghan, I wanted to ask you about a member of your organization. Elsie told me that you formed the vigilante group SOVA. I'm sure you are aware there have been a rash of unexplained murders in the city...well, we found one victim wearing a SOVA jacket."

"Oh God, no. Who?" Mackendra's voice cracked.

"That's the problem. We aren't sure. She was a Caucasian with dark brown, shoulder length hair, approximately five feet six inches tall, and around one hundred thirty pounds. That's all we have at this point," Orlando replied gently.

"I was thinking it may be Ellen," Elsie suggested.

Mack turned back to Elsie and then once again turned to Kyran who was staring intently at Mack. "Could be. I haven't heard from her for a few days, but there are a couple women in my organization who could meet that description. Can you tell me more?" Mackendra asked, crossing her arms over her chest, pushing her breasts against the tight t-shirt. Elsie heard Kyran suck in a breath before he darted off. She wasn't sure what was up with him, and didn't have time to decipher it.

"What the fuck is his problem? And, how did he move so fast?" Mackendra demanded. Elsie wanted to curse at Kyran. There was no way Mack was going to miss his movements.

She glanced around and saw Kyran standing in an alley then turned back to Mack. Kyran had taken a huge risk by showing his preternatural speed. "I have no idea. He is difficult to understand on the best days. We are here because my new friends care about the victims of these evil creatures as much as we do. They have fought against them far longer than even you have. I haven't given up the fight, either, and have been working with them. We want to help keep you guys safe. There have been reports that there has been an increase in the number of women who have gone missing. After finding this latest victim, the police are now looking into SOVA and ways to stop your patrols."

"I can't believe you left us for some guy. I never pegged you for one of those women, but I appreciate your help now," Mack said, looking around, likely searching for Kyran. The woman never let anything go. It gave Elsie time to calm her nerves before her vampiric nature slipped. Showing Mack her fangs or glowing eyes would earn her a dagger in the heart.

"That's not fair, Mack. I never left the cause. I have done far more than you know," Elsie protested.

"So, do you have anything else you can tell me?" Mackendra asked Orlando, ignoring her completely.

"She had a bite mark on the left side of her neck and a dove tattooed on her right wrist. You're being too harsh on Elsie. And, you have been misinforming your members. Vampires do exist, but what attacked you and your friends weren't vampires. They are called skirm, minions created by archdemons. Now, what can you tell me about your friend? I'd like to notify her family," Orlando responded.

"I don't even know where to begin with all that. Are you telling me that vampires are real, but they aren't evil? I know evil. Evil did this to me and so many others," Mack spat as she pulled the neck of her shirt away to reveal her scars. "And, you were right, Elsie, it was Ellen. I will tell her family," Mack insisted, and Elsie noticed the weight Mack carried, weighing her down even more.

Elsie hoped that their friendship wasn't ruined as she tuned them out while Orlando clarified the difference between vampires and skirm and they began to talk about the dangers and how the two groups could collaborate. She looked around for Kyran, surely he hadn't left. Where the hell was he? Rhys was still happily flirting with the humans, and finally saw Kyran pacing in front of the fountain.

He was clearly struggling with something. Their eyes

locked across the square and he shook his head then vanished. Elsie wanted to throttle her brother-in-law for sifting in the presence of so many humans. Fifty feet away Elsie saw him reappear in a dark alley. He looked at Mackendra one more time and took off running. She looked over at Rhys who had ditched the bimbos and was gaping in shock. The last thing they needed with Zander out of town was Kyran going off the deep end.

CHAPTER 7

"This whole city is filled with fakes and phonies," Bhric grumbled. He hadn't gotten his booze, babes, or beignets. Normally, Jace would have laughed and made sure to visit a realm club to allow the vampire an outlet, but today he had no patience for anything but the mission. He had to find a cure for Cailyn, and time was of the essence. He didn't allow himself to scrutinize why this was such a driving force. He didn't have the time to go down that path at the moment. He needed to focus entirely on the task at hand. Simple thoughts of Cailyn always led him down a path of lust and desire that wreaked havoc on him, both physically and emotionally.

Zander's voice brought Jace back. "Not all are fake, *brathair*. And from the looks of it, I need to remind a subject of his proper place," Zander quipped, shaking his head as they left the latest bogus curio shop. Jace followed Zander's gaze and noticed a vampire and a human female. They were having sex against a brick wall at the end of the alley while the vampire openly fed from the human. Because he was a sorcerer, Jace saw the aura as Zander sent out a burst of his power and froze the couple's action. The vampire and human were paralyzed, only able to move their eyes, which bulged when they saw the vampire king.

"Let go of the female, now," Zander barked, then turned midnight eyes on the human. Jace saw the deep purple of the magic emanating from Zander as he held the human's gaze. "You left the bar early because you were no' feeling well and took a cab home," Zander told the female as he erased her memory of the encounter, and nudged her towards the cab Bhric had hailed. She teetered off pulling her skirt down.

"Now, Jacque. Pray tell, what were you thinking? I am one step from ripping your head from your shoulders. You know the rules. Never expose our existence to the humans!" thundered Zander, fists balled at his sides as he loomed over the shaking vampire. "Feeding openly in an alley off one of the busiest streets in the country is pretty fucking visible."

"Liege," Jacque's body quaked with his fear. Jace expected him to piss himself any second. "Th-this k-kind of thing happens here all the time. Let me explain," he rushed out when he saw Zander's anger rise further. "In this city, the humans are steeped in the paranormal. They seek it. There are nighttime tours of graveyards, and people pretend to be paranormal creatures, especially vampires. They are on every street corner. I would have erased her memory of the bite, Liege. I swear. We never leave their memories of the bite, but we don't worry about being seen."

Lucky for Jacque, a human male chose that moment to wander down the street and pass the opening of the alley a few feet from where they stood. The human male was heavily tattooed with piercings and wore a cape over black clothing. The guy turned his head and smiled at their group, proudly displaying fangs in his mouth. Jace shook his head.

He would never understand humans and the things they did.

"You disgrace the name of vampire. You fail to consider how others in the realm will view this behavior. You will work with the Dark Warriors here in New Orleans to deliver my message to every bluidy vampire in this city. Engaging openly in feeding of any kind is unacceptable and forbidden. Use discretion in your dalliances. I will have eyes and ears everywhere. Anyone caught will become my personal guest in the dungeons of Zeum. Now, get yourself together, you have work to do," Zander turned on his heel and stalked away. If this guy knew what was good for him, he would follow orders. Zander never made threats he didn't follow through on.

As they turned to leave the alley, Bhric picked up where they had left off. "I say we go to Old Absinthe House like Killian suggested. We are running around this city blind, maybe someone there can help. 'Tis too bad none of the NOLA Dark Warriors have ever had a need for Marie Laveau."

"Despite the fact that the only reason you want to go to Absinthe is to get your booze and babes, I do think it is the wisest course of action," Gerrick added. Jace didn't know if he agreed or not. If they went into this club it wasn't going to be a quick visit with Bhric sating his needs, but they were running out of options.

"Lead the way, *brathair*," Zander replied tersely. The king was still clearly upset by the vampire's behavior.

Undaunted by the irritation in Zander's tone, Bhric took out his cell phone and pulled up directions to the well-known bar. The bar had been established over two hundred years earlier by two cambions, and contained various levels. The ground floor was for humans while the levels below ground were for the supernaturals. Only select humans were aware of the lower levels.

"We aren't far. Follow me, I know the way," Bhric said as he waved his phone in the air.

As they got closer to Bienville and Bourbon, more and more supernatural creatures were milling about. A group of imps, Valkyrie, and nymphs giggled as they passed, waving at Bhric. Jace grabbed hold of Bhric's arm and kept him moving forward. If he stopped with that large group they'd be there all night.

Tendrils of various types of enchantments flooded the night sky. He scanned the area searching for enemies, but with so many supernaturals in one place his senses were bombarded with energy. The rush invigorated him. He needed to concentrate so he could distinguish and separate the various colored lights associated with the different creatures. Magic wielders were the only creatures capable of seeing the festival of colors emitted by magic.

He focused and the first species he noticed was the Valkyrie and the luminescent threads of the spell they used to bind and hide their wings. There was a large group of the females standing outside the club. He continued his search and detected no threat. He took a moment to soak in the power around him. It fed his soul like nothing he had ever known. If it wasn't for his magic, he'd have lost his mind centuries ago.

The red light the vampires gave off flared, drawing his attention. A nearby group of vampires caught sight of their king and bowed to Zander, while a couple light demons nodded their heads in recognition. Zander acknowledged them as they entered the busy establishment, and encountered wall-to-wall humans. Jace looked around for the entrance to the supernatural section.

"Killian said we enter the lower levels through the janitor's closet. The entrance is monitored by a brownie," Bhric shared as if he'd read Jace's mind.

They made their way past the ancient wood bar, which proudly displayed its centuries of use. The antique fixtures winked in the low lighting. They were a contrast to the jerseys and helmets hanging from the exposed cypress beams of the ceiling. Somehow the combination worked for this place.

They reached a short hall, and Jace noticed several doors lined both sides. They stopped at the one labeled "Janitor". Zander opened the door and led the way into the small space.

Jace watched a smile of recognition spread across Zander's face as he addressed the brownie. "Clarence, 'tis been too bluidy long. How have you been?" Zander bent his large frame and held his hand out towards the four-foot male. Zander's hand engulfed the small, delicate-looking hand.

Clarence smiled wide, revealing yellowed, blunt teeth. "It's good to see you too, mate. I'm doing well. Pedro and Francisco are good to me. Rumor has it that you've mated, and now I can see that is true. The colors of your completed soul are truly amazing. You must tell me all about her." The elf-like creatures had the ability to see people's aura, and work earth magic so it was no surprise that he could see the colors of the mating. Jace only hoped Zander didn't indulge the small male or they would never get out of there.

Zander settled his free hand on the small creature's shoulder. "Aye, the rumors are indeed true. I have found my other half and she is beyond anything I ever hoped for, but, that is a story for another time. I'm afraid we are here for an urgent matter involving my mate's sister. She was enchanted by a Fae, and we need assistance. Are either Pedro or Francisco here?"

Large brown eyes became even bigger. "Oh no, that is terrible. Yes, they are both here. I will let them know you wish an audience. Go right on through to one of the back tables." The brownie nodded his bald head to Bhric, then Jace and Gerrick as he crossed to the back wall and began muttering words in his native tongue.

Jace watched the orange and yellow light emanate from his fingertips, and a door appeared where there was once a smooth wood-panel covered wall. Jace had never cared for the smell of nightclubs, he thought, as sex, sweat, cigarette smoke, and alcohol hit him the moment Clarence opened the glowing door.

A steep, stone staircase led the way to the revelry below. Torches hung on the walls and provided the only illumination. As Bhric brushed past and began descending, Jace noted the vampire's fangs were out and his eyes were glowing. They'd be getting no help from him until the vampire had a drink, or two. Sighing, Jace followed the others down.

The bump and grind of bodies enveloped Jace as he reached the bottom step. The supernatural floor of the club was much like upstairs, with the antique wood floors and a large aged bar. The difference was in the clientele. Supernaturals came in all shapes, sizes, and colors, and most couldn't blend in with human society without drawing attention. He looked around and saw Bhric hadn't wasted time grabbing a drink at the bar. Several empty shot glasses were already upside down in front of him and he was grabbing a bottle from the bartender.

The atmosphere of the club was intimate, and Jace found himself missing Cailyn something fierce. He wanted to explore and learn every inch of her, from her breasts to her sex. It was more than a want. He needed to have her as much as he needed his next breath. For the millionth time he wondered at his reaction to this particular female. He didn't ponder that long, as nausea hit him, and bile rose in his throat. He hated the way his mouth watered and turned sour.

He forced a deep breath in and out. Where was the bathroom? He frantically searched over the patron's heads. Goddess, he was pathetic. A little arousal and he couldn't get to the toilet fast enough. Long ago he'd given up the expectation that his suffering would ever end, or that he'd have a normal relationship. But one tiny human entered his life, and breathed new life into his hope. It was a useless emotion in his opinion, and he hated that he had even a smidgen of it. As he started to spiral downward, a large heavy hand landed on his shoulder, bringing him back from the edge. He looked back and held Zander's steadying gaze. He was the only person who knew what Jace had gone through all those centuries ago.

"Put it oot of your head, I need you to focus right now. Cailyn needs you. Are you good now?" Zander asked after a few seconds.

"Yeah. I'm good." It was a struggle, but the reminder of the danger Cailyn faced pulled him back from the edge.

"Okay, follow Gerrick to that back table over there," Zander instructed, as he pointed to an empty table in the corner. Together they crossed the busy dance floor and he slid into the booth before Zander.

A male fire demon approached the table. Fire demons were creatures whose flawless, luminescent skin and earthly beauty masked a deadly interior. It was unwise to piss one off, unless you enjoyed regenerating burned flesh, but they were always good to have on your side seeing as they were loyal to their core. "What can I get you guys?"

"House whiskey, double," Jace ordered, scanning the crowd, once more thinking about Cailyn. He avoided thinking about how much he lusted after her, and wondered how she was currently doing. Was she frightened by the predicament she was in? The thought of her frightened had his gut churning and his teeth clenching. When he got a hold of the Fae who did this, he would relish torturing the bastard. No one would hurt her and get away with it. As a healer, he could slice away limbs, cut out his heart and have him on the brink of death only to bring him back and do it all over again. A feral growl escaped his throat.

"Here, drink this. 'Twill help," Zander's voice brought him out of his violent fantasies. He hadn't even heard the other's order, let alone the drinks being delivered.

"Zander, it's an honor to have you in our establishment. Next time we expect to meet this mate of yours," Francisco boomed as he approached their table.

"My mate hasna been to your fine city, but expressed a desire to visit, so I'm sure I will be bringing her here soon enough. 'Tis good to see you both again." Zander stood and held out his hand to greet the two cambions.

"We will hold you to that. Now, what can we do for you?" asked Pedro, smiling like he had found a long lost friend. Zander shook their hands and retook his seat in the red leather booth.

Jace was anxious to get to business, and nearly jumped out of his shit-kickers. Thankfully, Zander got right to the point. "We need information about Marie Laveau. Killian said you guys have your ears to the ground and little happens in your city without your knowledge. As I'm sure you know, we have searched numerous voodoo shops to no avail. We need to find one of her Mambos."

There was a pause as Francisco ran his long fingers over his blue silk shirt and considered his words. "Dante informed us that you may be stopping by, and why, so we did some digging. We had to call in some huge favors for this, so you owe us. Our source said to visit Tia at Marie Laveau House of Voodoo. We can't guarantee she will give you any information, but she is the one you want."

After Zander had failed to inform the Dark Alliance Council about Elsie breaking the mating curse, his relationship with them had been strained. Jace thanked the Goddess that Zander had made amends because Dante was an invaluable asset to have on their side. Not only did the Cambion Lord keep his subjects on the straight and narrow, which was difficult with sex-demon-human-hybrids, he still managed to keep them happy.

"Are you serious?" Gerrick burst out. "Aison had discounted that particular shop thinking it a sham, given the name. She's clever, I'll give her that. I bet not many go there."

"You have to admire hiding in plain sight," Pedro observed.

Glass shattering, followed by a male's shout, drew their attention. As one, their heads swiveled to the bar where a fight had broken out. Jace was not surprised to see that Bhric was in the middle of it. A large shifter was punching him. Jace cocked his head and heard the shifter yelling about the siren Bhric had half-naked being his date. Jace noticed healing fang marks on her neck. Apparently, Bhric had moved on from alcohol.

Bhric shook shards of glass from his hair while he balled his right fist and introduced it to the male's face. The shifter came back swinging and the two fell to the floor where blows were exchanged. The crowd began cheering. The shifter must be possessive of the siren, given that Bhric was bigger than two linebackers combined, and few took him on. Glasses on the nearby tables shattered from the pitch of the siren's screams. Jace noticed that Bhric's t-shirt was ripped as he rose and grabbed a chair up over his head. This was going to get ugly, real fast.

"Drop that fucking chair!" Francisco yelled. "Zander, stop your damn brother before he tears up my bar and get him out of here. This is no way to thank us for all the trouble we went to for you!"

"Aye, you are correct. I owe you a debt and I will stop this." Zander assured the cambions. Using preternatural speed, he rushed toward Bhric, and caught the chair before it broke over the shifter's back. "You are no' doing this, *brathair*. We're leaving, now," Zander snarled, grabbing Bhric by the collar and dragging him toward the exit.

"Thank you for your help," Jace told Pedro and Francisco before following the king and his wayward brother. Gerrick echoed his sentiments and followed suit.

"Damn, that was fun. Where are we going next? I need another drink." Bhric smiled, showing bloody teeth.

Everyone remained quiet, ignoring Bhric as they left the building. Zander pulled his brother down the nearest alley and slammed him up against a brick wall. With his fists bunched in the torn fabric of Bhric's shirt, Zander got in Bhric's face, "Straighten the fuck up or go home. I need your head in this. My mate is counting on us and her sister needs us. Am I clear?"

"We will get to that, but first I need another drink," Bhric replied, his tone unrepentant.

Before he knew what was happening, Zander punched

his brother in the face and had a *sgian dubh* at his throat. "Get your head oot of your drunk arse. The liquor is controlling your life. This is not the time for your shite. You made a promise, are you going back on that? Are you no' a Dark Warrior and all that stands for? We are all that stands between humans and the darkness. We each made a vow to the Goddess to protect and defend those weaker than us against all evil. If you canna live up to your word then I should slit your throat right here and now." Jace had never seen Zander so angry with one of them, especially not one of his brothers. There was no mistaking how serious the king was, and it was a chilling sight.

Jace saw Bhric sober and pale within seconds. He lowered his head, his chest heaving with his breaths. The tight clench to his fists told Jace that Bhric was as angry as Zander. For a second, Jace worried that they would lose Bhric in this dirty alley. After several tense moments, Jace watched the tension ease from Bhric's shoulders. Finally the warrior murmured, "You are right, *brathair*. Doona worry, I have your back. Let's do this."

Zander met Bhric's gaze when his head lifted and a silent message passed between the brothers. Finally, the king released his hold and they turned to head down Bourbon Street.

Zander pointed his knife at Gerrick and Jace and asked, "I hope one of you knows where we are going?"

"I've got it," Gerrick replied.

"Lead the way," Zander snapped, returning the blade to his boot.

They fell silent and remained on alert as they followed Gerrick to the shop. As a unit, they halted across the street from the establishment. The small, weathered, one-story structure looked out of place surrounded by much larger ones. It was in desperate need of a paint job, and was so rickety a strong wind could blow it to pieces. As they crossed and stood on the corner of St. Ann and Bourbon, Jace read the sign above the door. At first glance it read 'Strange Gods, Strange Altars', but then it magically morphed into 'I bind and confound you.' Couldn't anything go their way tonight? He reminded himself why he was here. He needed to get a cure and get back to Cailyn.

"You see that, Gerrick? Our powers will be bound once we cross over. We will be vulnerable," Jace warned the others. He hated the idea of going into an unknown situation with only the steel in his boot. He was a warrior, but his sorcery was his best weapon. The last time he went into a situation unprotected it didn't turn out so well for him. He rubbed his cuff as he tried to think of a way around the binding.

"No matter, we have weapons and we look like idiots standing oot here. Surely she has seen us by now. Come on, let's go," Bhric said as straightened his ripped and bloodied t-shirt, and brushed off his leathers. Jace shook his head.

"Wait," Zander put out a hand, stopping them all. "I am getting a feeling aboot this Mambo. I doona understand what I received from Elsie in terms of her gift, but I strongly sense this female is tied to shifters." The king fell silent and cocked his head to the side, lost in thought. "I'm getting nothing else and have no idea what it means. Let's go."

Gerrick swept past them and entered with the rest hot on his heels. They stood in the entry taking in the chaos of the shop. Objects were crammed into every inch of space. There were traditional voodoo dolls with pins, masks, charms, creepy skeletal dolls, totems, necklaces, and candles all in one small, antique curio across from the door. Talismans hung from the ceiling, incense burned, and skulls of various creatures littered the space. The stained cement floor was covered with threadbare rugs. It was overwhelming to the senses. Jace caught tendrils of magic from so many objects, that the room glowed. With his magic bound, it took a moment for him to adjust.

"Come in, don't be shy. I don't bite...unlike some of you," the slender female behind an antique counter purred in a thick, Cajun accent. She had skin the color of the chicory coffee she was sipping. Her long black hair framed a beautiful face, and was a shocking contrast to her light-green eyes.

Zander pushed Bhric behind him before he could offer to share his bite with the Mambo. "We need information and we have been told that you, Tia, can help. My Fated Mate's sister has been enchanted by a Fae spell and we must see Marie for an antidote."

Dozens of gold bangles jangled on her slim wrists as she gestured, "Look around you, we have many charms and talismans. I am not sure any of dem will lift a Fae spell." Tia stood from her stool and smoothed out her billowy purple skirt, clearly not willing to share anything more.

"Tia," Zander's Scottish accent was terse, "we appreciate your mandate to protect your Queen, but know that we mean her no harm. As the Vampire King, I give you my word that we seek only an antidote for Cailyn. I vow that on my mate's life." Jace hoped Zander knew what he was doing because what he'd just said to Tia was unbreakable in their realm.

"I appreciate your assurances, but I can offer what is in my shop, no more."

"We doona have time to waste here, and I didna want to interfere with fate, but I know where you may find your mate. I received the gift of premonition from my Fated

Mate," Zander tested. Tia's head snapped around faster than a cobra strike. That got her attention telling Jace the female wanted to know about her mate. Problem was, Jace knew Zander was bluffing. There was no way to know you were mates until the relationship was consummated.

Tia placed her hands on her hips, the picture of feminine pique. "You mean ta blackmail me for da information on my Queen in exchange for da information on my mate. Bastard," she hissed, anger lighting her eyes.

"Like I said, we mean Marie no harm, and I would no' have involved your mate, but I am left with no other choice. Time is of the essence. You know the Goddess has led us here. Surely, you can sense Fate's hand at work," Zander coaxed.

Silence descended over the shop, and Jace thought the tension was going to shatter his bones. Tia closed her beautiful, green eyes and sighed in resignation. "She is in da swamps off 45 in da depths of Jean Lafitte territory. Now, about my mate?"

"Thank you for helping. I hope you like the rain. You will find your mate among the Seattle shifters," Zander told Tia. Jace cursed and sent a prayer to the Goddess that Zander wasn't wrong. Otherwise, this mambo would have her revenge.

Jace expelled the breath he was unaware he had been holding. *Hang on Cailyn, I am close, Shijéí.*

Wait, *Shijéí?* Sweat broke out over Jace's skin at the automatic endearment.

CHAPTER 8

"Get out of my way, sex fiend," Jessie shouted. What in all that was holy was going on now? And who was Jessie screaming at? Sex fiend? Realization dawned on Cailyn...fucking Rhys.

For the millionth time in the past hour, Cailyn wished she had the energy to get out of the bed. She felt herself weakening by the moment, and knew she wasn't doing so well. To say her nerves were fried was a vast understatement. She was propelled from annoyance to rage over the situation in the blink of an eye.

"Now you're just turning me on. Come and feel," Rhys teased.

"You are a sick son-of-a-bitch if me pushing you is a turn-on." The sound of flesh hitting flesh echoed and Cailyn knew Jessie was beating the crap out of Rhys.

"Ooomph. You pack a mean punch. Now I'm even harder," the warrior taunted. She hoped Jessie got a good one in, although, Rhys was basically harmless.

"Stop it," Elsie's voice joined the fray. "Jessie, settle down. We will let you see her. We are simply worried about your control, or lack thereof. I trust you to tell me if you start craving her blood. We have no idea if you will be driven by the same bloodlust that drives skirm. Breslin, Rhys, and I are here, so don't worry, nothing will happen to Cailyn even if you do lose it."

Cailyn perked up at the mention of Breslin. She was glad that the fierce Vampire Princess was there to help Elsie and Rhys. She wanted nothing to go wrong with her friend.

"Thank you. I don't want to hurt her," Jessie said as she entered the room. Tears sprang to Cailyn's eyes the moment she saw her friend. Jessie ran to her side.

"I'm so sorry Jess. This is all my fault," Cai murmured through her tears.

"Stop that. It's not your fault. Oh, Cai you don't look so good. How are you feeling?"

"I'm ok. Just need some more rest and I'll be good to go."

"Don't pull that bullshit with me. You're pale and I can hear how weak your heartbeat is. What did the delicious doctor Jace say?"

Cailyn wanted to put a muzzle on her friend, as it was she looked over at her sister and saw the calculation in Elsie's eyes. She pushed that to the side to deal with later. "Jace said that I have internal bleeding, broken bones, and a concussion, and that he can't heal me because the Fae put a spell on me. He and some of the other warriors went to get me a cure. What I want to know is how you are doing? I can see the physical changes you have gone through already."

Cailyn was unnerved by how sleek and muscular her friend was. Jessie had always been stick-thin, but now she had muscles that people worked years to obtain. Her brown eyes shone in the light, and she moved with an innate grace she had only seen with the other supernaturals she'd met. Jessie's bleached-blonde hair appeared to be even silkier, and had a fullness women envied. Emotions stuck on her throat at the changes to her friend. She loved her either way, but wished she hadn't been put through this ordeal. Cailyn understood that Jessie's life as she'd known it was over.

Jessie began blinking rapidly as her eyes filled with tears. "Cai, I have no idea what is going on and I'm so scared. I woke up in a body I no longer recognize. I look like Lara Croft with the muscles, and I have fangs, for Gods' sake." Cailyn easily identified the lisp as Jessie spoke. Cailyn's heart clenched at hearing her best friend's fear. She knew that there was no way she could return to her life without helping Jessie through this. That's what best friends do for each other. She would never abandon her.

That led to other questions. What would she do about John and her job? She supposed the John issue should be clear-cut given that she had broken off their engagement, but she still loved him. She wasn't entirely certain that she didn't want to marry him. She was still confused, and her emotions were all over the map.

Months ago, her body had taken on a mind of its own and roused an interest in Jace. It was an irrational, all-consuming attraction that had dug its hooks in and refused to let go. The thoughts alone were causing her stomach to tighten, and her feminine places to become warm and hungry. She'd never been torn like this. She cared for Jace and wanted him desperately beyond reason, but she still had feelings for John.

Her three J's drove her crazy. Jessie needed her to be there while she adjusted to an entirely new existence as a supernatural creature. She had planned to marry John in the winter, but then Jace had burst into her life. She wanted things from him she had never envisioned. With Jace it was mad passionate fire. There was nothing mediocre about him and what she needed from him. It was raw and animalistic, yet deeper than anything she'd ever felt. She was a wreck!

"No matter what, I will always be here for you," she promised and stretched her fingers toward her friend. Jessie sat on the bed next to her and picked up her hand with extreme care. The action was a reminder of how very fragile Cailyn was at the moment.

∼

"Where in the name of the Goddess are we?" Gerrick grumbled from the backseat. Jace adjusted the rearview mirror and glanced back to see blue of Gerrick's magic light flitting between his palms. The light sent shadows across Gerrick's scarred face, which was drawn tight, causing him to appear forbidding. He realized that Gerrick was as anxious as he was, which was sobering.

"Middle of the Goddess-damned swamps. Focus and use your sight, I think the weeping willow Tia told us to turn at is up ahead, but I can't see shit through this mist and fog." Jace rolled down his window and pointed out to the left side of the desolate two-lane road.

Finally, Jace spotted tiny, winged faeries flying all around the enchanted willow. The creatures were from the Unseelie court, which was likely where Marie had received much of the information on the potions she sold. The Unseelie were often thought of as the dark and evil side of the Fae, while the Seelie were seen as the light and good. Jace knew differently. All Fae were capricious creatures who thought only of themselves. The Seelie Queen was as prone to mischief and revenge as the Unseelie King.

"Thank fuck," Bhric blurted as he shifted in the seat the sound of his leather pants rubbing across the seat, "I didna think we would ever reach it. And by Lucifer, it smells like the seventh circle of hell out here, eau de nappy twat. Damn, roll the window back up."

Jace shuddered at the thought, but had to agree and rolled up the window. There was a definite decayed-fecal smell that reminded him of a pus demon. Jace took a left at the willow as instructed and began to wind his way down a single-lane dirt road that hadn't been graded in way too long. They drove in silence until they stopped at an old abandoned dock that was barely afloat in the murky swamp. The mist and fog was thicker near the waters' edge. Jace parked the car, heat and humidity slapping him in the face the moment he opened the door.

Zander crossed in front of the car's headlights to stand next to Jace. "Any ideas of what we will face?" Zander asked as he sheathed his claymore in its holster and checked his *sgian dubhs.*

"Not definitively, no. Evzen said there have been various rumors that Marie protects her swamps with anything from a wraith to Wendigos to trolls to Bakulu himself." Jace glanced around, his unease building. He sheathed his own claymore and secured his medicine bag with the stones and salt.

"I suspect we are being watched even now. We must proceed with extreme caution no matter how badly we want to storm through to her front door," Jace said as he considered how dangerous their journey was about to become. One scratch or bite from a Wendigo and they could become flesh-eating zombies, too. As hard as it would be to avoid any contact with the Wendigo, wraiths posed an even bigger threat. They could not be destroyed, and could devour their whole group with ease.

The bayou had a sound all its own. Crickets chirped and

frogs croaked as crocodiles rippled through the water. The moss and lichen waged a battle against the trees, water and mud in the swamps. The trees' lichen-covered limbs gleamed in the moonlight.

Making their way through the knee-high grasses, Jace removed the quartz talisman Tia had reluctantly given them. The mambo hadn't wanted to give them any information, but traded the talisman for all the information Zander could supply about the shifters in Seattle. Being a mambo to the powerful Voodoo Queen didn't immunize her against wanting her Fated Mate.

Jace closed his eyes and called his staff to him. The familiar weight of the Alder wood warmed his shaking fingers. He and Gerrick chanted the words of the reveal spell. The sound of water slapping against a hull sounded long before the small fishing boat came into view.

"We're gonna need a bigger boat, Captain," Bhric chuckled as he jumped, none too gently, into the rickety boat while keeping his eyes on the crocs. "I really hate anything with bigger fangs than me."

"Dumbass," Gerrick muttered as he entered with more caution.

"I canna believe this boat floats. I'm more worried right now aboot sinking than what we might face. Hopefully this thing moves," Zander observed once they were all seated.

"It will. I can feel the power in the crystal," Jace said before he put the white quartz to the bow of the boat. It started forward immediately, the wooden hull slicing a path through the moss covering the water's surface.

Movement on the banks caught Jace's attention. "Liege, we have company. Wendigo, shit. Remember to be careful, and don't get bit or scratched," Jace remarked.

The sound of swords unsheathing joined the cacophony

of the night. The boat slowed its pace before it stopped, and suddenly the banks were filled with creatures. Jace counted at least twenty. That was going to be a problem if they were to avoid the enormous fangs in their gaping maws. Silver glinted in the misty moonlight as they all brandished their weapons.

The gleam of the night highlighted the zombie-like creatures' glowing, yellow-brown eyes. Jace squinted at the closest monster, noticing its fangs were dripping green slime. The grass and water sizzled and popped where the slime hit. A shudder racked Jace's body at how grotesque they were.

Clothing hung in tatters on their bodies. Through tears in their shirts, scales of a vibrant-orange were visible and green pustules oozed from large sores that seemed to cover their bodies. The smell of decaying flesh nearly knocked him out cold. He knew their sluggish movements were deceiving, and that they were supernaturally fast. Their lumbering gait was designed to lull victims into false complacency. Long brown claws flared, and one growled a warning to them. It was the sound of old heavy door hinges groaning in the wind.

"Brace yourselves," Zander instructed.

"Damn, these are some ugly mother-fuckers. Talk about having a bad hair day. I'm renaming them Patches cause shit, that's ugly," Bhric's attempt at humor didn't defuse the situation. They were in deep shit.

Gerrick widened his stance holding his sword at the ready. "Don't leave the boat. We stand a better chance sticking close together."

"Aye, fight back to back. Doona leave yourself exposed," Zander ordered.

For the second time in his life, Jace was truly scared of

what would befall him. He had something he was fighting for, and it felt as if he had something to lose. He called up an image of Cailyn to give him strength.

Their enemies moved swiftly, sending the crocs, toads and other swamp critters scurrying for safety. Water sloshed into the boat as claws gored the sides. Zander's battle cry was deafening as he swung his sword, decapitating the first to reach them with ease. That didn't deter the others. The next used the carcass as a step stool to get its tall, lanky body closer to where they stood in the boat.

Jace rushed to the back of the boat where two were climbing into the craft, unbalancing the boat and threatening to overturn them. Jace muttered a freeze spell and was able to be-head one before the other regained movement. Grunting out a curse, he used the momentum from his first swing to bring the sword around and take out the second. He swiveled around to see Bhric freezing several Wendigo. In that moment he felt like they could do this. When three of the five broke through Bhric's ice as if it was paper, he amended that statement. At least it bought a few needed seconds for Bhric to take down one and send the others flying.

"Jace, your back," yelled Gerrick. He pivoted around with his sword at the ready to cut a monster in half before its claws ripped through his leather jacket. He needed to stay focused. He backed up slowly towards Gerrick and Zander and Bhric.

Jace ducked as Gerrick swung his weapon around, sending orange, pus-filled arms flying. The limb flopped wildly around the boat, grappling for traction.

"Fuck," he yelled out and kicked the appendage into the water before rising from his crouch. "Unattached limbs still attack and carry their poison, so watch it," he yelled.

The demon that created these flesh-eating beings was brilliant, Jace thought. Detached limbs carried the instructions to infest and create more within its DNA. Nothing else would power such devotion to a mandate. The real question running through his mind was what Marie Laveau had done to gain control of them. They were single-minded creatures not subject to domination. There was no doubt that she was a seriously powerful demi-Goddess.

The boat lurched, sending them stumbling and throwing out their arms and swords for balance. Jace stayed low to avoid friendly strikes. "Shit, they're under the boat—" his words died off as they were all sent toppling into the water. He dropped his sword and frantically swam to the bottom of the murky swamp. He searched as best he could with the limited visibility, feeling around for his weapon. He was completely at their mercy without it. Several agonizing minutes passed, but his search yielded nothing. He cursed fate for his luck.

Fate be damned, he wasn't going to fail Cailyn. He kicked up and gulped in mouthfuls of fresh air when he breached the surface. Zander was perched on a pylon wielding his claymore, while Bhric stood on a fallen log, together facing ten monsters. Gerrick was on the other side of the swamp fighting off four beasts.

At that moment, three of the Wendigo battling Zander and Bhric broke off and headed Jace's way. He called his staff to him and grasped the Alder wood below the leather grip, hefting it to shoulder height.

When the first beast reached him, he shoved the end through his throat and sent a wave of power through the staff. The hole widened and Jace wrenched it from side to side. He felt his magic draining, and was relieved when the head plopped backwards into the water, sending the torso splashing after it. As he swiveled the staff and turned to the last two, a flash caught his eye. Gerrick had taken out two with one sword stroke. That warrior was a beast.

Refocusing on his own combatants, Jace put all of his force behind his next swing and took off a quarter of one Wendigo's head, but the damn thing was still coming after him. Directives were definitely imbedded deep in their DNA. Otherwise, survival instinct would kick in and send this one scrambling. He was able to slow it down by pushing it back into the water.

Zander and Bhric were cutting through their numbers rapidly, and Gerrick was down to one opponent. That small distraction cost Jace as claws dug into his biceps. The zombie was pulling Jace up to his dripping fangs. He managed to grab the small *sgian dubh* he kept sheathed at his ankle and sliced into the creature's carotid, ducking to avoid further contamination.

He was in trouble, he thought, as he felt the excruciatingly painful movement of the acid through his veins. Wrenching his arms free he cried out and sliced his knife through its neck, finishing it off before he staggered and fell face first into the murky water.

He couldn't fail Cailyn. He needed to get to the salt in his medicine bag. His arms felt like lead, but he managed to plant his palms into the soft ground and heft himself over onto his back. Stars glinted in his vision and he heard splashing close by. A thousand-pound weight kept his body immobile.

"Salt," he whispered, hoping one of his fellow warriors heard him. He was unable to do anything but turn his head.

He watched Gerrick jump over downed bodies and race after the Wendigo missing part of its head. The idiot hadn't seen Gerrick, thinking it had an easy target in Jace. Jace noticed Bhric and Zander were not far behind. Bloated bodies floated all around them. Bhric made it to his side while Gerrick attacked the last Wendigo.

"Fucking hell, Jace. You were clawed. What do we do now?" Bhric sputtered.

"Grab the...salt, it's...under...my *wampum*," he breathed.

"Och, where exactly is your *wampum*?" Bhric asked, concern etched into his features.

"Grab the bag under his belt," Gerrick bellowed as he fought.

Zander had already pushed his brother out of the way and Jace could tell from the King's expression that he looked bad. "Bluidy hell, I have the salt. Jace, hang in there. What do I do, Gerrick?"

"Bhric, grab his forearms below the affected areas and cut off the blood flow. Let's get his jacket and shirt off," Gerrick instructed, coming to their side.

Silver glinted from Zander's hand and before he processed what was happening, Jace felt warm night air skate across his burning flesh.

Gerrick grabbed his legs and gave further instructions. "Good, now Zander, rub as much salt as you can into the wounds. This is going to hurt like hell and instinct will have him fighting back. Hold tight, Bhric."

"Get ready, buddy. This will be over before you know it," Zander encouraged as fire exploded in Jace's right arm before he could brace himself.

Jace's back arched and his legs kicked out at the iron bands holding them. The fire spread, and his body began bucking wildly against Bhric and Gerrick's hold. He turned his head, expecting to see the flesh of his arm seared to the bone. Zander was grinding another handful of salt into the affected area. It pulsed white-crystalline light, like a strobe light as it devoured the poison. Zander leaned across his body to reach his other arm. Without the command leaving his brain, Jace was biting into the muscles of Zander's chest. White powder went flying into the misty night air.

"Shite, let go of me," Zander snapped. Without taking the time to break Jace's hold, Zander rummaged through his medicine bag and then the fire renewed in his left arm. Twin blazes collided and felt like they were eating him alive.

"How long will this take?" Jace was unable to focus on Zander's voice or any response that was given. His body writhed in pain for what seemed like an eternity. All the while, he imagined Cailyn's beautiful smile to get through it. Barbs of black magic from the Wendigo venom left his blood one cell at a time, and finally, the fire began to cool.

He blinked open his eyes and assessed his body. Expecting to find bloody stumps instead of arms, he was relieved to find them whole and at full strength. His head was pounding out a fierce beat of pain, but otherwise, he was surprisingly good for nearly becoming one of the flesh-eating Wendigo.

Jace raised himself on one elbow and ran his hands across his bare chest. He gazed around the swamp and noticed the zombies had been piled up and he watched as Gerrick threw a match on the heap. Within seconds, a bonfire was eating up the remains. The warriors hovered close, swords at the ready.

Bhric interrupted the silence. "Are you okay? Do you have a craving for my flesh?"

"I'm okay. I'm not infected." Jace shook his head to clear it.

"Thank the Goddess. I didna want to tell my mate or her sister that we lost you," Zander replied. Jace wondered if Zander was aware of the connection between he and Cailyn.

Leaving that issue for another time, Jace assessed their situation. "Now what? She has to be close..." he trailed off as the air to the south of them shimmered and an old, rustic cabin materialized. It looked as if the big bad wolf could huff and puff and blow the house down with its thatched roof and weathered appearance.

"This woman courts death with the creatures she uses for protection," Bhric surmised, motioning to the enormous, black wraith floating above the sagging porch.

"Shut up, she can hear you," Zander's whisper was barely audible even to their supernatural hearing.

Bhric sheathed his sword and voiced what no one wanted to. "We're fucked."

CHAPTER 9

Kyran stalked the night looking for skirm, trying like hell to forget one hot little human female. The moment he had seen Mackendra, he had wanted to do things to her he had never once fantasized about in his seven hundred forty years. He wanted to carefully take her while looking into her beautiful, whiskey-colored eyes. The thought made him shudder.

For centuries, he'd indulged in his carnal pleasures with dominance and power, not sweetness and caring. He was a twisted bastard, and he liked it that way. So did some of the females at Bite, for that matter. It made him perfectly happy. Change wasn't something he dealt with well, and he had taken off the second his desire had taken this turn.

That wasn't to say he didn't get hard imagining Mackendra secured to his cross, or hanging from his swing. In fact, he was harder than he'd ever been at the thought. He imagined her flesh turning pink as he brought his leather crop down across her breasts and ass. He groaned at the thought of her submitting to him. She was a strong, independent woman who would not break easily, and winning her submission was a temptation that he had to deny, even though he relished the thought of being the one to bring her to that erotic place. His every instinct cried out for him to go to her.

It was going to be a battle to stay away from her, one that he was unsure if he was going to fight. He was not magnanimous enough to stay away from her for her own good. He would claim her before he suffered...suffering was for his women.

Thoughts of women being tortured always brought him to the reason for his perversions...his mother's rape and murder. He had been but mere days beyond his stripling years when the demons and their skirm attacked their castle in the Scottish Highlands. His mother had placed him in a hidden room that was concealed in a wall of his parent's suite while his father had taken the twins to hide them in a different location.

When his father returned to the bedroom, he had been overtaken. Skirm beat his father then held him down while more skirm tied his mother to their bed. The thuds of the Behemoth archdemon's boots had echoed loudly in Kyran's young ears. It was a sound that tormented him to this day.

The demon stormed into the room and began fileting his mother as if she were a piece of meat. He cut the flesh from her rib cage, making sure to slowly remove her breasts. As his mother screamed, Kyran had slammed his eyes shut, unable to shut out her whispered gurgling plea, "please don't hurt me." His eyes then opened to the sight of her lying there with her throat being torn out, and the demon shoving body parts where they should never go. He was unable to look away as his mother was violated, then murdered.

Witnessing something like that changed a male.

Witnessing it as a child twisted his desires, and fucked things all to hell. He had accepted what he was long ago.

Leaving the past behind him, Kyran looked around and realized that he was deep in a residential neighborhood, and he sensed that there was a skirm nearby. There was no mistaking the pins and needles that accompanied their presence. Perfect, he had steam to work off and no time to go to Bite.

Sgian dubh in hand, he stalked around the shrubs and evergreens to find a skirm stalking a young human. He sifted behind a detached garage and yanked the idiot behind the building as he passed. They were so focused on the orders of their masters when they were on a hunt that they were easy to pick off. He muffled the skirm's cries and waited to hear the female resume her trek down the street.

"You picked the wrong street, arsehole," Kyran breathed into the skirm's ear as he plunged the blade through his heart and watched the creature turn to ash and blow away in the wind. He glanced down, cursing at the residue on his favorite silk shirt. That had been too easy, and didn't give him the relief he needed.

He glanced at the lightening sky. Thanks to modern technology and his internet stalking, he knew that Mackendra's house was on his way home. He needed to see her before returning to Zeum. He had left his brother's treasured mate vulnerable, and he would never forgive himself if anything happened to Elsie, but he had a burning desire to see Mackendra before he retired for the day.

∼

"Please tell me that one of you knows how to deal with

these creatures because I doona have a clue," Zander said as he looked from Jace to Gerrick to the top of the house. The skeletal creature was clad in a black mist that cloaked all but its face and hands. Jace knew the eye sockets peering out at you from under its hood may appear empty upon first glance, but you saw your destruction in their depths, moments before it sucked your soul from your body and left you a dried up husk.

Jace tried to focus enough to respond to Zander, but his pounding head took all his attention. He did a quick scan and noted that his throat was dry as a desert and his arms burned with pain. He felt as if a cement truck had parked across his chest, and it took all his strength to sit up. Luckily, he had mastered the art of appearing perfectly fine many centuries ago, despite being in utter agony.

"Evzen gave me a way to handle these creatures. We are going to need the boat again, unless we want to swim up to the dock, but I wouldn't advise that. I can only buy us enough time to get from the dock into the house before the wraith rains hell on us," Jace relayed as he conjured himself a shirt and considered the best approach to the house on stilts.

"He couldn't have given us more time?" Bhric grumbled.

"We will be lucky to get those few seconds. You can't kill wraiths, and it's near impossible to stun them," Jace replied.

Gerrick turned an eye on the boat. "Get your ass over here and help me, Bhric."

"I canna believe I have to go back into that water. I already smell like swamp-ass," Bhric complained as he headed towards the boat.

"You and me both," Gerrick agreed as they righted the boat and they all climbed back in.

Once settled in the boat and closer to Bhric, he noted the warrior did smell foul, they all did, in fact. He may not know women, but he knew that they couldn't enter the Voodoo Queen's house smelling like this and expect help. He dried and cleaned his leathers and shit-kickers with a quick spell. Gerrick cleaned his own clothes as Jace muttered another quick spell to clean the king and his brother as well.

"That's much better," Bhric said, plucking at his shirt. "You sorcerers come in handy. I could shrink you and carry you around in my pocket. Or, we could start hiring you both out. You'd make good maids," the warrior joked.

Jace bit his lip to hold back his laugh as Gerrick muttered a reversal spell and added a noxious bit of pus.

"What the fuck?" Bhric roared. "Why'd you do that?"

"*Brathair,* I believe they are telling you they didna appreciate being degraded to mortal cleaning elements. Thank you both for the help cleaning. Now what, Jace?" Bhric shrugged at Zander's comment and smiled.

"Gerrick and I need to cast a confounding spell to blind the wraith, and once it can't track my movements, I will immobilize it with these agates," Jace retrieved the banded black and white agates from his bag. "It will only be paralyzed momentarily, so be ready to act fast and get through the door. Gerrick?"

Gerrick's nod was interrupted by Bhric. "Wait, are you going to clean me again?"

"No, I'm not," Gerrick muttered before turning to Jace. Zander grabbed the ruff of Bhric's thick neck in a hold only the powerful vampire king could get away with before Bhric caused more problems. Gerrick held the crystal quartz to the prow of the boat and it resumed its trek to the cabin.

For the third time that night, Jace had his staff in hand, ready to chant the words to a spell. He loved using his sorcery so freely, but regretted that he was going into a dangerous situation with his energy depleted. It couldn't be helped, and hopefully didn't put them at a disadvantage.

Belatedly, he realized he had been so focused on what they would encounter on the journey to her door, that he never asked how best to negotiate with her. The lack of knowledge didn't sit well with him.

There was nothing he could do about that now, so he made sure Gerrick was focused and began chanting the spell. Gerrick quickly joined in, and the sudden shriek told Jace that the wraith had been blinded by their spell just as the boat bumped into the dock. There was no mistaking the creature's anger.

Jace said a silent prayer to the Goddess that the stones found their mark before they left his hand. Less than a second later, an eerie silence descended over the bayou. Not even the ever-present crickets and bull-frogs made a noise. "Move it, now. We only have seconds," Jace yelled, shoving Gerrick out of the boat.

Moving at supernatural speed, Zander was knocking on the door within a millisecond. Jace had planned on barging in, but Zander's way was probably better for their chances. She had better open the door quickly because there was no telling how long the wraith would be frozen. A couple seconds passed and he silently screamed in his head at the delay.

Forcing a breath through his nostrils, Jace caught a whiff of how putrid Bhric smelled. He was about to take pity on him and clean the poor bastard when the door slowly creaked open. There was no one in the dark doorway greeting them. Four pairs of wary eyes met each other, conveying the apprehension that none would ever admit to out loud. They had to enter before the wraith attacked, so Jace shrugged and quickly walked into the darkness before anyone else, thinking it was the lesser of two evils.

If they stayed out with the creature, even now re-gaining movement, they would be killed. And not only killed, their souls would be devoured. He'd be damned if he allowed anything to harm his Fated Mate's soul. It was his duty to keep it safe.

The door slammed shut once they had all crossed the threshold. Hundreds of black candles flared to life in the next breath. They stood in a large entryway. From the outside, you would never expect to be in such a large space. Clearly, there was a dimensional spell at work here. The room was one massive open area, and if possible, this space was even more cluttered than the shop on Bourbon Street.

Countless shrunken heads and dolls surrounded them while a cloying sweet smell of incense permeated the air. Jace turned his head and gaped at the jars of chicken feet, eyeballs, and unknown skulls. On the set of shelves next to that, he saw what looked like the embryos of various species. He didn't want to know how she used those, given that an embryo was only used in black magic.

Everywhere he looked there were antique bookshelves and sideboards with miniature skeletons, masks, jars of ash and dirt, and random figurines. Jace was amazed at the amount and variety of magical paraphernalia that surrounded them.

There was only one thing missing. Where was Marie Laveau? There were no stairs, no doors, and no hallways. The only place to sit was a velvet-covered armchair set before a blazing fireplace. He looked to Zander and the others.

A soft feminine throat clearing brought all their attention around to the maroon chair before the fireplace, which was clicking shut as the regal female took a seat. She wore a tignon of vibrant gold. The elaborate headdress was adorned with numerous rubies, sapphires, emeralds, and diamonds. She kept her hair under a wrap, but Jace saw that it was black. As she situated herself, she adjusted the luxurious gold and red shawl more firmly around her shoulders.

"I thought you'd have headless chickens hanging from the rafters," Bhric blurted into the quiet. Jace turned incredulous eyes to Bhric. Did he have a death wish?

"A headless vampire runnin' 'round be bettah," she purred in a heavy Cajun accent. Her creamy café-au-lait skin glowed, and Bhric's eyes widened as the pulse of her power nearly knocked him off his feet, and had him gritting his teeth in pain. "Dem chickens is in da soup pot over der," she chuckled and the oppressive power dissipated.

The message was clear, they were in her territory and she tolerated their presence to an extent, but would take them out if need be. They needed to tread carefully.

Zander bowed deeply and addressed the queen. "Your majesty. We come to you in peace and ask for help. We have encountered Fae troubles, and need your expertise. I would bargain for an antidote." Zander reached his massive height once more, and met the female's gaze firmly.

"Me tink you too readily make bargains, young king."

"With respect, my mate is worried that her sister will be lost to us. Cailyn is her only remaining family. And there is nothing I won't do to ensure my mate's happiness," Zander vowed.

"Ta have such love and devotion," Marie shook her head.

"Da body fails because Cailyn's soul has been taken ta da place not of death, but of imprisonment. Da fate in such a place can stretch on foreva. Tell me, what would you bargain ta me?"

Zander was silent while he pondered his response. Jace had no idea what to offer and was completely out of his element here. He was a healer, not a politician.

"I have wealth and jewels to offer but I suspect that will no' do. What I offer is a formal alliance with your voodoo nation."

"I tink I would hear what young Jace has ta offer."

Jace was taken off guard. Why was she asking him this? Did she want something specific from him? He struggled to read the female, but didn't see anything nefarious. In fact, he wasn't able to read her at all. In the end there was only one response. "I will give you anything as long as Cailyn's soul is free and she is healthy." He had nothing to lose, why not sacrifice himself for another, especially someone with as much promise as Cailyn. It would be an honor to give his life for hers.

Marie scrutinized him for what seemed forever. He feared she would reject his offer and not help them. Before he went to his knees to begin begging, she looked to Zander and responded. "Me tinks dat I will be akseptin' dis offer of alliance, Zander. Wit conditions o'course. I spect my kin ta be on dat council. One of my Mambos, Tia, me tinks." Marie gave Zander a knowing smile. It seemed Zander's premonition wasn't wrong after all. "I spect there are bad things to come, and we bes' join forces." She turned those intense eyes back to Jace and he shuddered at the power emanating from them.

"You, Jace need ta be careful of wha' you offer. Your Fated Mate needs you ta be der for her. And, before you go forsakin' fate and make da biggest mistake of your life, stop and tink. I know Morrigan well, and dat old bat never does anytin' wit'out considerin' ev'ry angle. When you find your mate, remember, you are wha' she needs, especially wit' dat sorcery."

The tension clearly left Zander's shoulders and he let out a breath he had been holding. "'Tis an honor to have you and yours join us. We are facing an archdemon unlike any we have ever experienced. The expertise and knowledge that you and your Mambos bring will be invaluable. Tia will be welcomed into the position. Thank you for helping."

Still reeling from Marie's words, Jace barely heard Zander's response. He should have expected that this powerful demi-Goddess knew the Goddess, but he was still stunned. He had a Fated Mate out there somewhere, when he never believed he would be blessed with one. The idea both frightened and elated him. He knew how much he needed his Fated Mate, but he couldn't believe that she needed him. He believed whoever she was, that she was best off without him. He dipped his head to Marie in acknowledgement, and stumbled forward when she hit him upside his head. His gaze shot back to her in confusion.

Her bracelets clanked together as she lowered her arm back to her side. "Stop dat negative tinkin'. Dat sentiment goes bot' ways, you idgit. Der are many trials still before you," she said as she crossed to the kitchen. She may have only been five and a half feet tall but her power was evident in her every pore. Everyone was staring at him in shock over her words.

It was disturbing that she had apparently read his mind. There was no time to ponder that as she gestured for them to follow her. Not missing a beat, Bhric walked up to the stove and peaked into the pot while Marie approached the shelves and began selecting various ingredients.

"Och, you really do have headless chickens in there. I thought you were joking," Bhric chuckled and picked up a wooden spoon to poke the contents of the pot.

Marie turned around and set the bottles down on the counter then smacked Bhric on the shoulder. She re-adjusted her gold shawl around her shoulders in a way that showcased her ample bosom even more. Apparently, she could read vampire minds too, and had Bhric's number. "Leave dem alone. Dey are zombie chickens who eat vampire flesh," she laughed and went back to grab the mortar and pestle.

Bhric laughed with Marie as if they were long lost friends. How did the male do that? Jace had never made friends so easily. He didn't open up with anyone, not even the warriors he had lived with for centuries. There were too many skeletons he wanted to remain hidden, too much shame. He didn't want to look weak and pathetic if they learned he was powerless to stop his own torture for over a century.

"It smells good. What is it?" Bhric asked, obviously dismissing her position that they were vampire-eating chickens.

Marie moved gracefully and worked quickly to concoct the antidote. She emptied small amounts from the bottles into the mortar, eyeing it as she went. Occasionally she muttered a foreign word, binding the ingredients. "Dat will be a Cajun chicken and rice soup when I'm done," she glanced at the warrior with a twinkle in her eye. She grabbed a small glass vial that she had set on the counter and poured the iridescent liquid into the container then replaced the cork stopper.

She handed Jace the ampoule and he was shocked at how warm the liquid was in his palm. "Put dat in her IV and it will release the magic. Now, be gone wit' you all." She shooed them toward the door and opened the portal with a wave of her hand.

Zander took her hand and held it for a moment. "Thank you for your help. I look forward to hearing from Tia."

Gerrick cleared his throat. "What about that wraith of yours? How do we get past it? We have no more agates."

Marie's eyes took on a glow as she met Gerrick's gaze. "Fate, Gerrick Haele, is not done wit' you." Marie waved him off when he opened his mouth to respond. "I won't answer dos questions simmerin' in dat brain. Now, I will control da wraith so you can clear da dock with ease, and I won't replace my Wendigos until you leave da swamp. But dat only gives you thirty seconds ta get da boat moving. Leave, your time is running out." With that, a force pushed them across the threshold and the door slammed shut.

It took the blink of an eye to get everyone, except Gerrick, moving the short distance to the boat. Jace glanced back and realized the warrior was standing there staring at the closed door. He raced back and grabbed his arm. "Come on. No time to think now, we have to go. Get that crystal out, and be ready," he urged.

Within seconds, they joined Bhric and Zander in the small boat and were crossing the swamp. Bhric broke the silence. "I don't know aboot you guys, but I kinda liked her. I'd go back there and see her, but I doona care if I ever see another croc or Wendigo again in my life. Och, now I'm hungry. Whatever she was making smelled good."

Jace tuned out Zander's reply and the rest of the banter as he considered the advice she had given him. She had said he and his Fated Mate needed each other, and that he shouldn't deny fate. He wanted her to be right about that, but six centuries of believing you didn't deserve something wasn't easy to override. Part of him wanted his mate to be Cailyn, and more than anything, he wanted to be the male she needed.

CHAPTER 10

Cailyn listened to Elsie and Jessie talk about the Tehrex Realm. Cailyn listened raptly as Elsie gave a crash course in the realm's mystical inhabitants, going over creature like the Harpies, nymphs, Valkyries, shifters, sirens, and demons, and how things worked in the realm.

She scarcely believed what she was hearing. She was familiar with the myths about harpies being Satan's offspring, but was shocked to hear they were actually beautiful, had wings, and that they partially shape shift.

"Harpies exist, too," Jessie murmured shaking her head. "I can't imagine being half bird, half woman," Jessie voiced, her disbelief evident in her tone. This was a lot to take in and Cailyn prayed that her friend came around and embraced the new world she was now a part of.

Elsie laughed and squeezed Cailyn's hand. "Yeah, they aren't very attractive when they shift, but they are beautiful in their human form and beneficial to have as your ally. Zander has been searching for centuries for a way to get them on his side." As her sister spoke, Cailyn heard several people bounding up the stairs. She didn't have to wonder who it was, as Elsie stood up in anticipation before Zander bellowed loudly through the house.

"*A ghra*, I'm home. The journey was successful," Zander announced as he burst into the room, grabbing Elsie into his arms. Her sister's squeal made Cailyn smile.

"Thank God," Elsie declared as she pressed her lips to Zander's.

Cailyn turned away when Zander deepened the kiss, and met Jace's glowing purple eyes. Relief flooded her that he was alive, and she tingled from the intensity in his gaze. They stared at each other for several seconds. She wanted the extraordinary kind of love she saw between her sister and Zander. She knew too many people where the passion and fire had faded, and they were in a place of comfortable complacency. That wasn't enough for her, she wanted more. Life was full of too much mediocrity, and love should never be subpar.

"How are you feeling?" Jace asked, breaking the silence. The sound of his voice sent shivers down her spine. The sexy sorcerer did things to her she had never experienced. She undoubtedly wanted Jace, and was eager to explore what they could have, but she couldn't discount her feelings for John either. Her conflict begged the question whether or not an all-consuming love was possible for her.

He crossed the room to her side and picked up her hand. Electricity raced from her hand, igniting her body as her heart began to race and her stomach clenched with need. To keep from fantasizing further about Jace, she forced herself to focus his question.

"I'm still here," she whispered as she smiled up at him. His glower made her smile widen. He did feel something for her, and wasn't able to hide it completely. It was a warming thought.

"I told you that I wouldn't allow you to die. You will be healed in no time. I have the cure right here," Jace murmured as he held up a small vial. Cailyn watched as he injected the iridescent liquid into her IV.

A bitter taste, like rubbing alcohol, built at the back of her throat and she wanted to gag when she felt something thick, cold, and painful run through her arm. She jerked her hand away from him involuntarily and her muscles tensed. Jace reclaimed her hand and sat down next to her. "It's okay, Cailyn that's the antidote. I'm sorry you have to go through this," Jace cooed in her ear, comforting her amongst the raging storm. Convulsions shook her body, and she felt a blazing trail of heat across her brow and down her neck to her shoulders. Jace ran his fingers over her skin, and it felt as if he was branding her as his. It elicited a fire that spread from her stomach to her core.

Time stood still as Jace sat there soothing her shaking limbs and provoking arousal at a time she shouldn't be feeling anything but pain. It was unnerving, yet she was unable to escape his soul-deep care and concern for her in his every caress.

"I'm going to try and heal your injuries now," he murmured. His anxiety was evident, and she understood that he feared he'd trigger another spell. There was no choice but to try, and she nodded her head, giving him a small smile of encouragement. He held her gaze as she felt heat spread from his hands to her injured leg and throughout her body. It was like stepping into a hot bath after being out in a snow storm. Within moments, she began feeling better.

A smile crept across his lips, transforming his face and

relaying his relief. She'd never seen a more majestic sight. "There's that sparkle. It's good to see you with your golden glow back, *Shijéí*."

She knew the room was full of people, her worried sister included, but she was unable to avert her gaze and smiled back, curious about his comment. "What does *she-jay* mean?"

~

OVERCOME WITH RELIEF, Jace gathered Cailyn up in his arms and the knot that had tied his gut up from the moment he awoke to Elsie's panic unraveled when she slid her arms around his neck. The pounding of her heart against his chest calmed his anxiety while it inflamed his ardor. "It means my heart in Navajo, my mother's native tongue."

She pulled back, and he was trapped by her stunning hazel eyes. He loved the pink that tinged her cheeks, how it told him she liked the endearment, as well as the fact that she was once again healthy. He saw her need matched his, and for the first time he wasn't afraid of his desire.

Elsie jumped onto the other side of the bed, jarring him and interrupting the moment before Cailyn was able to respond. Jace nearly snarled at the vampire queen for pulling Cailyn from his arms. "Cai, oh my God. How are you feeling? I told you they'd come back with a cure."

Jessie climbed onto the bed behind Elsie and stuck her head between Jace and Elsie's, trying to get Cailyn's attention. With the clamoring and activity in the room, he expected Cailyn's attention to be elsewhere, but she stayed focused on him. That didn't deter Jessie from jumping right in. "Girl, you had me scared shitless. I could hear your heart struggling to beat. I don't know what I would have done if we'd lost you. Likely gone on that killing rampage everyone's been worried about, only I'd have Fae and demons on the menu."

Cailyn responded, but her eyes never left his. "Don't do anything to put yourself at risk. I'm okay now. Glad to be out of pain, that's for sure," Cailyn told her friend, shifting her eyes in Jessie's direction.

Jace felt the loss of her regard keenly. She smiled at her friend and sister then scanned the room. He followed her gaze to Zander, Bhric and Gerrick. "Thank you guys for what you risked to help me, but you can't ever put yourself in such danger again, Zander. My sister needs you."

Zander laughed and gripped Elsie's shoulders. "You of all people know what you risk for family. I would do it again, *puithar*."

Jace saw tears mist Cailyn's eyes. Clearly, she was moved by Zander considering her a sister. Instinctively, he wrapped his arms around her waist and pulled her close. She crawled to him eagerly, surprising him as she sat across his lap. The long t-shirt she wore did nothing to mask the heat emanating from her sex.

He held back a groan, well aware of their audience, as his shaft filled with blood and hardened beneath her. She had an effect on him that both terrified and exhilarated him. He had long lost hope that he could react to a female like a normal male.

Her eyes became saucers and her mouth fell open. As her eyes became glassy with her desire, the world around them melted away. Something inside his chest reached out to her. Without a thought, he traced her lower lip, pausing at the mole on the right side of her mouth. Her tongue darted out, and the tip touched his thumb as she wiggled on his lap, teasing his erection. He couldn't hold back the groan that escaped then.

"Okaaay," Elsie said, shock clear in her voice. "Cai?"

Zander cleared his throat. "I think they want some privacy. Come on, *a ghra*." He pulled Elsie off the bed. Jace hated that Cailyn's attention was snagged by the movement, and he tightened his fingers on her hips. Cailyn looked to her sister and nodded before she met Jace's gaze again.

"I'll check in later Cai," Elsie called as Zander pulled her out of the room and the others followed suit, but if Cailyn heard she gave no sign. Her breathing increased and her face flushed with desire.

"This is your chance, Cai. Treat her right or I will kick your ass, Jace. I can do it now, too," Jessie threatened. Jace would have smiled at the threat, and reassured her that he wasn't going to do anything with Cailyn, but he couldn't, because he hoped to do things to this female he hadn't dared let himself want in too many years.

"Goodbye, Jess," she sassed as she smirked at her friend.

As the others filed out of the room he heard Bhric's fading voice. "Hey El, can you make me some shrimp creole? These arseholes wouldn't let me have any booze or beignets."

When he heard the door click closed, he panicked. He had made out with countless females over the centuries, but it had never gone beyond kissing, and even that hadn't gone well. He wasn't technically a virgin given the unspeakable acts Lady Angelica had magically forced him to do, but he'd never had sexual intercourse with a female of his own accord.

Her pupils dilated as he traced her cheekbone, erasing some of his anxiety. She had flawless skin and her round face and hazel eyes were bright with color. "How are you feeling? Any trouble breathing? Chest pain?" It was easier for him to play the doctor since this was uncharted territory for him. He had no idea how to seduce a female, and he wanted Cailyn fiercely. For once in his life, he wasn't going to allow anything to stand in his way, not even his body's reaction.

"I ache, but it's not from the spell," she murmured as she leaned her cheek against his palm. She turned her head and kissed his palm, leaving no doubt what she was talking about. "I have wanted you since the moment I saw you months ago," she confessed.

He had felt the same level of attraction to her. "You are the most beautiful female ever created," he breathed as he leaned closer to her lips. He paused, giving her enough time to stop things.

She leaned into him and he gave in with a groan. He cupped her cheeks and closed the gap. Electricity sparked between their lips the moment they met. He pressed his lips to hers and slid them across her mouth gently. He pulled back and licked his lips. She tasted divine and he wanted more. His nausea started, but he shoved it down to his toes, refusing to allow it to ruin this moment. He was determined to have this female, right here, right now.

He brought his mouth back to hers and pressed their lips together again. A soft gasp left her and he took full advantage, sliding his tongue inside. Tentatively, he moved his tongue against hers. A kiss had never rocked him to his toes like this. Queasiness was there, but it paled in comparison to the way his body ignited, and his desire exploded. The kiss quickly turned urgent and they tangled. Each tasting, teasing, exploring.

He grazed his hands down her neck and the sides of her breasts to rest at her back. She began grinding herself against his groin and he lost control. He thrust his tongue into her mouth hungrily as he grabbed her ass and pulled her against his erection.

He broke the kiss and realized they were both panting. Her lips were red and swollen from his attention, and he loved it. He prayed for strength to hold back the bile because he didn't want to stop what was quickly escalating between them.

He took her mouth once again, sliding his lips against hers and exploring her depths, mimicking what he wanted to do to her intimate flesh. He licked, nibbled, and suckled her tongue. "I want to taste you Cai. I need to," he whispered. He closed his eyes, hiding his vulnerability. This felt good, and right. This was what sexual relations were meant to be, and he didn't want her to see any hint of his shame.

"Oh God, Jace. I need you too. I hurt for you," she mumbled against his lips. He grabbed her and gently laid her back, careful of her IV and monitors. He didn't have the patience to stop and remove them from her body. His need was too great. He'd be lucky to get their clothes off, never mind the medical apparatus. She clawed at his back as his hand snuck under her shirt and teased her belly. She made pleading sounds driving her hips up, seeking relief.

He found her breast and erect nipple. He pinched the bud between his fingers and pulled, elongating the sensual tip. Apparently, she wasn't one to have her needs ignored he thought, as her hands slid into the back of his pants and grasped his ass, tugging him flush to her. He liked how aggressive she was. It gave him a guide he desperately needed, since he had no idea what he was doing.

He couldn't wait anymore and sat back dislodging her hands, causing her to cry out. He gripped her shirt and ripped it in two, revealing her bra and panties. The sheer black material barely hid her rosy nipples. He plucked the middle and the bra fell open, showing him her ample breasts and flushed nipples.

She was writhing and fumbling with his zipper. He pulled off his shirt, tossing it to the side. She had managed to unzip his jeans and traced the tip of his cock while he ripped the underwear from her body. Pleasure like he had never known raced through his veins, and for the first time in his life, pre-cum slicked the head of his shaft. There was a heavy ache in his balls. But fear slithered in to combine with his desire. He knew his seed would only appear for his Fated Mate. Was this perfect female his?

Rational thought scattered as she spread her legs and he gazed at heaven, her flesh glistening with her desire. He inhaled deeply, taking in the earthy cinnamon scent. Bile rose and he ruthlessly swallowed it back down. This may be all he ever got of this female, and he was damn well going to enjoy it. He stood and was undressed in record time.

"Mmmm, Jace...please," Cailyn moaned. He saw how she had gripped the sheets and couldn't deny her eager, open invitation.

"Cai, you are amazing. Your body is perfect. Let me love you." He needed her permission to continue, needed to know she was with him.

"Yes, yes, yes," she exclaimed reaching for him. The heart monitor's beeping increased as she spoke, telling him how much she liked the idea.

He lowered himself to her and kissed her passionately. He kissed and licked his way down to her breasts, taking one into his mouth and sucked hard while he fondled the other. Her wriggling brought her core into contact with his erection. He rubbed up and down her slit, coating his cock in her juices, but stopped before he lost control.

"No, don't stop. I may have to kill you if you do," she exclaimed.

He chuckled, amazed that this magnificent creature could elicit laughter while stoking his arousal. "Nothing will stop me, but I have to taste you," he informed her as he settled between her legs.

He didn't give her time to respond before he swiped his tongue across her throbbing bud, relishing her cries. Allowing some primal drive to guide him, he licked, nibbled, and suckled her clit like he had her mouth. She was sweet and succulent. He slid one finger, then two into her core, and that was all it took. He lifted his eyes and watched her throw her head back and shout her release. The monitor went crazy with her racing heart.

Needing to be inside her, he rose up and hovered over her. Before he took the next step, a thought niggled. Could she be his Fated Mate? Something warmed in his chest as if trying to provide him the answer.

"Please. I need you inside me," she begged, making his decision for him.

"You never have to beg, baby. Anything you want," he murmured as he surged into Cailyn for the first time.

His intrusion was so fast and brutal it sent her into another orgasm. He held himself still with his cock buried to the hilt in her pussy while her muscles milked him. He held back his own orgasm as well as the bile that threatened to make it past his control. He bit his cheek to stop his body from exploding while she came down from her climax. He pulled out and thrust back in roughly, his balls slapping against her ass. That broke his control and he began a punishing rhythm.

"Oh, God. Give it to me hard and fast. I need to cum

again." She was as lost to the pleasure as he was, ensuring him she liked what he was doing.

"*Shijéí,* you are simply astonishing. I have never felt pleasure before. Are you ready for more?"

She nodded as she whimpered and flexed her muscles around his shaft. All the urging he needed. He slowed and pulled back, then thrust back in. She cried out and tightened around him. Two more deep thrusts and she climaxed again.

He silently cursed when he nearly had to withdraw and rush to the bathroom. He pumped into her slowly as he fought it back. A deep breath brought her sultry scent to his nostrils and settled his resolve. He began moving once again, and her desire heightened along with his own. "I want you to cum again," he whispered against her ear.

She turned her head and claimed his lips in a searing kiss. His pace increased and he felt an unfamiliar pressure. His seed built in his shaft and he was ready to explode. It felt damn good and almost robbed him of control. The full, heavy feeling was something he never thought he would experience in his life. This female was his Fated Mate. He didn't have to wait for the mark to appear to tell him that. So many emotions bombarded him over the knowledge, but they were overridden by the pleasure of the moment. He couldn't stop now if he wanted to.

His hands settled on her hips and he tilted her pelvis to allow him to penetrate her deeper. He lifted one hand to her breast and pinched her nipple while he kissed her fiercely. She detonated again. She was sobbing his name as she came back down. She was the most beautiful thing ever.

"Again," he murmured against her lips.

"I can't," she cried. The heartrate monitor was going

crazy, but he noted that she was in no physical danger. Good, he wanted more.

"Yes, you can. Cum with me," he ordered and pushed his hand between their bodies.

He was close and wanted her to go with him. He pinched her nipple and his other fingers trailed over her mons to find her clit. He worked his cock in and out, hard and fast, while he teased her nipple and pinched her clit.

"I'm close. Don't close your eyes this time. I want you to look at me." He lost himself in her half-lidded gaze and found his home. Within moments, his spine tingled as his balls drew up tight. His eyes went wide in shock at the extreme pleasure he felt when his seed began pumping into her womb. "Goddess, Cailyn," he cried out as he gave her everything he had.

Pain mixed with the pleasure as his mate mark was branded into his skin. His right butt cheek burned from the mark of the Goddess' blessing, but nothing diminished this moment with his mate. The moment their orgasms waned, he had no time to enjoy the immense pleasure because the bile refused to be held back anymore.

He surged from her body and raced into the bathroom, humiliation riding him hard.

CHAPTER 11

Cailyn had just had the best sex of her life, and was dumbfounded as she watched Jace disappear behind a closed bathroom door. She wondered why he had jumped up and raced away like he was on fire. Insecurities swamped her. Perhaps he hadn't wanted her. She put her face in her hands as she recalled how she practically threw herself at him.

She sighed as she remembered the sight of him running away. The man had the hottest ass on the planet, but she wondered about the red, swollen brand on his right buttcheek. It was an incredibly detailed Native-American mask, and she surmised that it held meaning in his culture. It looked painful, and she wondered when and why he'd had it done. It seemed like an odd choice for a doctor, but it fit him as a warrior. Whatever the reason, it made her mouth water to think about tracing it with her tongue.

She stretched her body, expecting to be sore after what they'd done, but instead, she was ready for another round. Sex with Jace was as burn-the-house-down good as it could get. She'd always known it would be. She'd also known that their coming together was inevitable, which was why she broke her engagement to John.

Her heart constricted as it raced wildly in her chest. She had been torn about these two men for months, and despite having the most absolutely mind-blowing sex she had ever had, she was even more confused now than she ever had been.

Sex had never been like this for her, and she wondered if she could give this up if she chose John. John knew her almost as well as Jessie, yet something in her cried out for Jace. It literally felt like something was trying to claw its way to him. She hated being so uncertain.

She felt wetness on her hand and noticed they had ripped out her IV at some point during their interlude. Not wanting to ruin the sheets or blankets, she leaned over and grabbed her shirt, holding it against the wound. She recalled how he had ripped and shredded her clothes in his frenzy to have her. No man had ever come at her with such fervency before.

She heard the toilet flush and water running. What was he doing? She tapped into his thoughts and was met with a jumbled mess of pain and remorse. As she was trying to decipher what was running through his head, he opened the door and walked out. His naked body was distracting, and every thought flew out the window. Her gaze lifted to his face and she saw that his expression was shuttered and completely cut off.

Feeling exposed, she grabbed a blanket and covered herself. "Everything ok? You, um, left kinda fast. Did I do something wrong?" She hoped she hadn't declared her love during one of those moments he propelled her out of her body.

He quickly crossed to her and sat next to her on the

bed, tugging on his jeans and shirt. "No. Cailyn you did nothing wrong. In fact, you did everything right." His beautiful, copper skin deepened with his blush. "Your sister put some of your things in the front room. I have to head out and do my patrols, and we can talk when I get back."

Something was definitely off, and she almost called him back to her as he turned and headed for the door. Her gut clenched at the thought that perhaps he didn't want anything more to do with her. Despite the fact that she was in a quandary over him and John, the idea hurt.

Cailyn brushed off her disappointment and took a shower. Once she was dressed, she headed downstairs, following the aroma of garlic to the kitchen where she found her sister and friend.

"There she is," boomed Jessie. "We wondered how long you'd be going at it. I told your sister it might be days with how long you have lusted after the sexy doctor." Her friend slid a knowing look her way, and as expected, went right for the jugular. "I take it John is out and Jace is in."

Cailyn grimaced. She was further from that decision now than she had been before. "Honestly, I have no idea. I know I shouldn't have had sex with him before figuring that out, but something overcame me and I couldn't stop. I want Jace...more now than ever. Ugh, I'm so tangled up and have no idea what I am going to do."

Her sister looked up from where she was chopping celery and sweet peppers. "I still can't believe you broke off your engagement and didn't tell me. Like I said before, it sounds like what I experienced with Zander. Did he have a brand anywhere on his body after you had sex with him?"

Cailyn gaped at her sister. That mark on his ass...holy shit. "He had a brand on his butt. No," she shook her head, "it can't be," she denied. There was no way they were mates. Surely, he would know if they were.

Elsie beamed as if this were good news. Clearly, this was not a happy moment, or Jace would have told her. "Your attraction makes sense. It's called a mating compulsion, and it will never go away where Jace is concerned. Just so you know it's impossible to fight. Believe me, I tried for months. He didn't say anything to you?"

"No, he didn't. He ran to the bathroom. If what you say is true, I don't think he's very happy about this mating thing." The rejection stung. Cailyn had never felt more inadequate or unwanted in her life. Elsie had to be wrong, she couldn't be Jace's mate.

"Turn your head to the right," Elsie told her. Cailyn obliged, and heard both of them gasp.

"What?" she asked.

"It's true, you're his Fated Mate," Elsie declared. "You carry a mark below your left ear." At her confused look, her sister explained. "Fated Mate marks don't appear until after sexual intercourse. For supernaturals, that mark is a brand that everyone can see, but for humans, it is a mystical mark that is only visible to us. There is no doubt that you are his."

"She's right. I can see the tiny mask on your neck," Jessie added. "It glows iridescent."

Cailyn had no words to describe the chaos in her head at hearing those words. If she thought she was confused before, this news complicated everything even more. Knowing she was Jace's felt right, but didn't erase the fact that she loved John.

She needed to talk to Jace. Did he run off because he had learned that she was his? Was he repulsed by her? More importantly, how did this make him feel?

It was a relief to understand why she had been attracted

to Jace beyond reason. She was still unbearably aroused, while at the same time she was confused, hurt, and scared. How dare he run from her? A little voice in her head told her nothing was as it seemed, and she needed to look deeper.

She wanted to embrace a mating with Jace and all that entailed. She knew she'd have everything she had ever wanted and more with Jace, but she had her own issues to resolve first. It wasn't fair to any of them to be on the fence like she was.

"Is John in Seattle? Did you have a chance to call him?" Cailyn asked.

"Yes, I talked to him earlier. He's in Seattle at a hotel nearby and worried sick. And he's angry that I haven't allowed him to see you. The man is wearing me out. You should call him soon," Elsie suggested as she dumped the diced veggies into the creole she was making.

Her sister was right, but she wasn't ready to call him. Maybe some liquid encouragement would help. "What are you girls drinking? That doesn't look like your Monsterita."

Jessie laughed and slipped off her stool. "Yeah, I'd need some booze before that call too. I, however, am drinking some O positive, but am ready for a Melon Pepper Martini, which is a new creation of your sister's."

Cailyn cringed at the mention of blood. "We have been so focused on me, but how are you doing Jessie?" She welcomed the distraction.

Jessie grabbed two martini glasses from a cupboard then turned around to face her. "You missed my meltdown. I completely lost it when Elsie told me I was no longer human. As you can tell, I am still trying to learn how to talk around the fangs, but I'm holding steady at the moment. I have no idea how I am going to tell my family."

Cailyn took the glasses as Jessie grabbed a pitcher from the fridge. "I can never take away what happened, but I will be by your side every step of the way. And before you say anything, I know being here with Elsie and the Dark Warriors is the best place for you, so that's where I'll be, too. I'm sure I can get a job at a firm here in town. Now that I've missed out on the biggest opportunity of my career, it no longer matters if I stay in San Francisco." Perhaps relocating would be the answer to her dilemma. Somehow she knew it wasn't going to be that easy for her.

Jessie stood gaping at her, making Cailyn squirm. To break the tension in the room, she grabbed the pitcher and filled the two glasses, handing one to her stunned friend. "I can't let you give up your entire life for me. There are still so many unknowns, and Jace and the scientists are doing a ton of research looking for answers. Your sister has already told me I can stay here as long as needed, and I plan to do exactly that. I will be just fine."

She opened her mouth to object but Elsie cut her off. "Nothing needs to be decided right now. Let's focus on the positive," Elsie chimed in and held up her glass. "To Voodoo Queens, magic, and new beginnings, for you both."

That sounded sublime to Cailyn. Everything could wait while she got blotto. They clinked glasses and she took a big gulp. "Mmmm, this is yummy, El. Sweet and spicy, great combo," Cailyn shared as she finished the drink, mustering the nerve to call John.

∽

Jace turned and slashed at the skirm stalking him from behind. He shook off the ash and scanned the street for more enemies. He had joined Orlando and Santiago after hightailing it out of the room before he had to face the truth of the situation. He had left Cailyn hurt and confused over his reaction.

He wanted to deny what had happened, but he was a new male after making love to his Fated Mate. Not only had the pleasure been exquisite when the barrier broke and his seed left his body for the first time, but he had not experienced the same revulsion that usually accompanied sex. Yes, he had thrown up, but his mind and body were ready to explore her again.

The shame of his inability to hold back the queasiness altogether still burned. He had used all his strength to hold back the bile, but it wasn't enough in the end. It was never going to go away. Cailyn was more than he could ask for, and he desperately wanted to be able to have a life of love and passion with her. Unfortunately, he was a damaged male, not fit to be anyone's mate.

He was still in shock that the Goddess had blessed him with a female of his own. Marie's words came back to him. She may believe the Goddess had planned everything out and that he was exactly what Cailyn needed, but he had his doubts. Cailyn's soul stirred in his chest, offering acceptance and comfort. He hated that her soul had been exposed to his worst moments, even if it was the only way he had gotten through the endless days of torture with Lady Angelica.

In his pre-occupation, he missed a skirm approach and was hit in the back. He stumbled then turned and ducked a roundhouse, shooting his leg out, knocking the young male over. Jace was up and on the balls of his feet, his blade slashing out before his next breath. He heard Orlando and Santiago fighting several others who had joined the fight at some point. He stabbed the one he faced through the heart, letting the titanium go to work on the corpse, and turned away from the flash of fire that rendered the skirm to ash.

A quick count told him they now faced eight skirm. He jumped into the fray, deflecting their attention. Two came at him with blades drawn. Tossing his own blade from hand to hand, he sprang at the two. He nicked one on the shoulder and pushed the other into Santiago's weapon.

"You will pay for that," one of them promised before lashing out at Jace.

"They have no brains, do they," Santiago observed, and threw one of his blades at the skirm's back.

Jace watched the blade find its home and turn the guy to ash. This was exactly the distraction he needed from thoughts of Cailyn. He wasn't ready to deal with having a Fated Mate.

One of the skirm began taunting them, drawing his attention. "We have your precious females, you know. We watch those bitches become ravenous killers. It makes it more fun when we have our way with them."

Jace met Orlando's gaze and knew he was thinking the same thing. Who were the females? And, what were they doing to them?

"We are aware that you guys have been kidnapping females. Are you that desperate for company?" Orlando asked then looked at Jace. "We should take him in for questioning."

Jace nodded his agreement and centered himself to caste an immobility spell. Before he knew what was happening, the skirm that had been doing the taunting grabbed Jace's knife from his hand and shoved it through his own chest, piercing his heart. He cursed as he watched the flash of fire and the resulting cloud of ash. His *sgian dubh* clattered to the ground. He scooped it up and turned to capture one of the others, only to find the clearing empty.

He was stupefied at the fact that one of them had actually committed suicide. Orlando and Santiago wore the same expressions of shock.

"What the hell was that? Apparently, they're better controlled than we thought. We need to get back to Zeum and let Zander know what happened," Orlando advised.

"Yeah," Santiago echoed as they headed to Orlando's mustang. "I don't get why they would target females. Jessie surely hasn't shown any signs of being a mindless killer, so what are they doing to these others that cause them to be that way? And why was that kid so terrified of being taken in?"

Jace somehow didn't think that was it. "I don't think he was afraid of us taking him. More like, he didn't want to face Kadir," he observed. "They are taking huge risks targeting females like that."

"Do you think they are trying to breed with them?" Orlando asked.

Jace shook his head as he considered Orlando's question. The thought was extremely disturbing. "Anything is possible. From what we have been able to gather in studying skirm over the years, the males aren't able to reproduce. And even if they were, human females wouldn't be able to carry the offspring. We haven't studied Jessie yet to determine if her conversion left her sterile. The demons are another story altogether, because they are definitely able to reproduce. Let's head back to Zeum."

They were a somber group as they climbed into the car and made their way home. As they drove, they discussed the missing humans and females that had gone missing in the realm. He thanked the Goddess that the San Francisco Dark

Warriors had been able to get to his mate before the demons took her. Anger boiled hot and fast through his veins at the thought of what could have happened if they had taken Cailyn.

Thinking of Cailyn had him wondering if any of the kidnapped females were Fated Mates. He hoped not, because any male whose mate suffered at the hands of such evil was in for hell. He knew better than most that no person should experience pain like that. It irreparably changed one, and had far-reaching effects. Six centuries later, he was still tormented by what he went through. His heart clenched for the females, and Jace felt a sense of urgency to rescue those held captive before any more damage was done.

The opening of the steel gates to the compound broke Jace from his musings. He was close to Cailyn, his Fated Mate. Fear, excitement, inadequacy, and wonder bombarded him, knowing he was going to see her again. She had no idea what she was to him, and he had yet to resolve how he was going to tell her.

After the way he had acted, he wouldn't blame her if she had jumped on a plane and went back to her fiancé. Thinking of the other male had jealousy coursing through his veins. Cailyn carried Jace's soul, and had been made for him. His chest constricted painfully at the idea that she was going to marry another. His instinct was to deny her relationship and fully claim her for his own, regardless of what she wanted. To do that was certain to earn her wrath and hatred, not that it mattered, because he had no plans to claim her. He wondered what his life would be like without Cailyn. If Gerrick was anything to go by, his life was going to be miserable.

The moment they pulled up to the front doors, Jace resolved that it was best not to say anything to her about being his. It was best for her if he lets her go, and lets her return to her fiancé, no matter how painful it was for him. He could only give her a life of dysfunction, and he would never do that to anyone.

As Orlando parked the car, his heart began racing and his palms were sweating. His mouth went dry at the knowledge that his female was just beyond those doors. On cue, his body reacted and hardened. Desire hot and wicked ran like lava. The Goddess was a royal bitch for making the mating compulsion impossible to deny. He hadn't even seen Cailyn and he was ready to ravish her. Excitement joined his trepidation and he jumped out of the car, rushing into the house. He followed the sound of voices to the kitchen with Santi and Orlando following close behind.

He stopped in his tracks, caught by the beauty of Cailyn. Her head was thrown back and she was laughing at something. Her eyes sparkled and her cheeks were full of color. She was breathtaking, full of life and he wanted her more than anything.

"Stop gawking and move it, buddy. I'm hungry and I smell Elsie's creole. Thank the Goddess, there's good food tonight," Orlando remarked as he pushed past Jace.

Jace moved to the side, intending to head to his room but his feet took him to Cailyn's side. Her eyes still glittered with mirth as she turned to him. Unable to stop, he leaned down and claimed her mouth in a soul-searing kiss. The feel of her soft, moist lips sliding against his fueled an arousal so intense it hurt more than the mate mark on his ass. The pain of the incomplete mating was indescribable, but not enough to deter from the moment.

He brought his hands up, hoping she didn't notice how they shook as he cupped her face and deepened the kiss. Instantly, the connection he shared with her soothed the scars left by centuries of torture. In that moment, none of it mattered anymore.

She groaned into his mouth as he coaxed his way in. The slip and slide of their tongues tested his control. He wanted to strip her bare, place her on the bar and devour her before he fucked her senseless. Now, he understood the PDA between Zander and Elsie. A simple thought of his mate roused his beast, the good and the bad. Reluctantly, he pulled back and ran his hands down her back.

Her lips shone with their combined wetness and were red and swollen. She was lost to her lust and eager to welcome him. That he did that to her, and his pride in that warmed him. Another first for him. "Hi to you, too," she croaked out.

"Goddess be damned you two, go to one of your bluidy rooms. As I have told Zander and Elsie countless times, we prepare and eat food in this room. Och, where's the whiskey," Bhric grumbled, entering the kitchen.

"Havena you had enough, *brathair*?" Zander asked from his position behind Elsie.

"Fuck you, *brathair*," Bhric spat as he reached for the bottle.

Tension mounted in the room as Bhric ignored the glasses and turned the bottle up, leaving Zander to glare at him. Jace hoped the two didn't start throwing punches. He didn't want his mate in the middle of a fight.

"I wonder when Killian will have Confetti Too opened," Elsie intoned, breaking the silence and changing the subject. She reached back and pulled Zander's arms around her waist. As if the mention of Confetti conjured him, Killian entered the kitchen. How many of the warriors were in the compound?

"Did I hear my name?" Kill asked as he scoped the room,

casually leaning against the counter as he spoke. "The doors will open in a couple months. My people are hard at work as we speak. I have hired a new security staff, and the Rowan sisters have added a layer of protection so it will be safe to bring your mate back to the club."

"Hayden told me he was assisting with security." Jace was relieved to hear that the shifter Omega was helping with security. Cailyn would be at the club with her sister, and he needed to know she was protected. "And after what we heard earlier tonight, it's going to be needed," Orlando finished as he proceeded to relay what the skirm had told them earlier that evening about captured females.

A tic had set up in Zander's jaw and once again, the tension in the room escalated. "*A ghra*, you are no' to leave the compound without me, period," Zander declared.

Jace saw the familiar ire rise in Elsie's eyes as she fisted her hands on her hips. "Look here, Mr. Bossy Pants. You don't order me around. Have we forgotten how to ask nicely? What I do at Elsie's Hope is important and I am needed there. And, before you go all caveman—"

Zander's growl cut her off as he bent forward and tossed her over his shoulder. Jace expected cursing and yelling, but Elsie began laughing and her cheeks heated as Zander stomped out of the kitchen with his queen in tow.

Zander's vehemence made Jace think. Cailyn was mortal, and easily killed with no way to defend against an attack. His gut turned over at how close she had already come to being kidnapped by the demons. "Cailyn, you can't leave the compound either. You face far more danger than your sister, because you have no defenses. You will stay here where it's safe."

"I appreciate your concern, but I will be leaving. John is in town and I need to see him," Cailyn retorted.

He saw red at her words, and jealousy seared him. She was *his*, not some mundane mortal's. "I don't care if the President of the United States wants to see you. Females are being kidnapped and tortured in brutal ways that is causing them to become killers. I will not allow them to succeed in taking you, too. You are my Fated Mate, *mine* to protect." He relished the flare to her eyes, and possessive glint that entered at his declaration. Hell no would he allow her to put herself in danger.

CHAPTER 12

Cailyn was speechless. He had gone from walking out on her without an explanation to claiming her in front of the other warriors. Apparently, he did know. Anger hit hard and fast. She'd had to find out from her sister and Jessie that she was his mate, not the way a woman wanted to find out she was fated to a man. There had been no loving words or revelation. There had been nothing but his backside as he escaped.

She raked her gaze up and down his body, her anger dying a quick death as she took him in. She hated what the dynamics of this mating did to her. She wanted to hold onto her anger, not become aroused by this. If she were honest, she'd admit how much his authoritative behavior now turned her on right now. No one had ever taken control and told her what to do, and some dark part of her enjoyed it, wanted more. Not that she planned on obeying him. She wasn't the obedient type.

"I had wondered if you knew. Elsie told me that I was yours. Not exactly ideal," she told him crisply, ignoring the current sizzling through her body as he grabbed her hand

and pulled her out of the kitchen. "Look, Jace, I know this whole Fated Mate thing is new to you, and it causes you guys to lose your heads, but you can't order me around. And, you can't walk out on me and then stroll back in like nothing happened," she said wanting to withdraw her hand from his grasp, but his grip was too tight. They entered the media room and she sat on the back of the couch, folding her arms across her chest after he released her.

Jace stepped close to her and insinuated himself between her legs. She refused to acknowledge the way her stomach clenched with need. She tilted her head back and saw he was both frustrated and amused.

"*Shijéí*, I don't think you understand the danger you are under. Kadir is targeting females, and you have already been a target of his. Now you carry my mark," he whispered, running his finger across the left side of her throat, making her moan, "making you more vulnerable. You are mortal, and easily wounded. These skirm boasted of torturing females." He lowered his head and his fingers trailed down her shoulder, gripping her flesh.

He took several deep breaths before he met her gaze. "I don't want you hurt. And you are right about one thing, the compulsion drives us in many ways. I become murderous at the thought of you being in danger. I won't let that happen," he informed her and leaned down until scant millimeters separated their lips.

He was going to kiss her again. Her heart raced at the thought and her palms started sweating. All the reasons for her anger and frustration with him vanished. Breathless with anticipation, she lifted her head to close the distance as one corner of his mouth lifted and he straightened his stance. He was enjoying getting her all worked up and leaving her hanging. He knew the affect he had on her, and was playing her like a well-tuned instrument. It frustrated her even further, but damn, if she didn't find that erotic.

She was attracted to him, and wanted him like no other. If life was simple and straight forward, she'd jump in with both feet, but life wasn't. It was best that he didn't kiss her again; she lost her head when he did. She still cared for John, and felt guilty about being undecided. She needed to make a decision and go forward with it.

"I'm sorry about earlier," Jace said, bringing her head up. "I shouldn't have taken advantage of you after just coming out from under the influence of Fae magic. And more importantly, I shouldn't have left like I did."

"What happened was beyond magical for me, and I didn't do anything I didn't want." She relaxed, hooking her fingers through his belt loop. "Why did you leave?"

He closed his eyes and took a deep breath. After several silent moments, he opened them and looked at her hand where it rested. She blushed as she realized her hand was inches from his groin, but didn't move.

"I left for many reasons. To make a long story short, I am not mate material, and when I realized what had happened I panicked and ran. I wasn't able to handle it and still don't know what to think or do about it. I'm really not meant to be anyone's mate. And yet, I find myself unable to stay away."

"Why would you say you aren't fit? Up until you ran to the bathroom, you were wonderful." She struggled to understand what made this sorcerer feel as if he was unfit to be a mate. She hadn't seen anything to make her agree. Everyone had baggage. It was a matter of finding that one person to help you unpack and find a proper home for that baggage. Question was, did she want to explore more with him?

His gentle caress brought her head down. "Your skin is

torn from the IV. I was too rough and injured you. Are you hurt anywhere else?" he asked trying to turn her as he searched for additional injuries.

"I'm not hurt. It's nothing," she denied. He shook his head then laid his hand over hers, sandwiching it. Warmth spread through her. When he lifted his hand from hers, she saw that he had healed her injury completely. He may believe he wasn't mate material, but in her mind he was one of the most thoughtful, caring men she'd ever known.

"Is healing part of your sorcery?" she asked as she turned her hand.

"I'm not sure what you know about the Tehrex Realm or sorcerers, but no, it's not part of my sorcery. There are no spells or magic that can heal injuries. Most of the Dark Warriors have been blessed by the Goddess with extra powers, and mine is the ability to heal almost any wound. The exception being skirm bites, injuries from silver and mortal wounds," he responded automatically, clearly lost in thought. He was still standing between her legs and she noticed he had begun rubbing a wide silver cuff around his wrist. She wondered about the significance of the cuff.

"I have an ability to read minds, although, I'm having a hard time reading yours, or any of the supernaturals, for that matter." Jessie and Elsie were the only two people she had ever told about her ability. Not having to hide her ability was one benefit of being in a compound full of supernatural creatures. She didn't stand out there. It was freeing to share this with him. She hadn't realized the burden she carried everyday keeping that information secret. She wondered how these supernaturals kept their secrets so well, and for so long.

"I had no idea you were telepathic. Elsie never mentioned it," Jace replied, maintaining eye contact. The way he looked at her made her squirm. He saw straight through to her soul and sought a connection with her. She met his gaze, trying to figure out exactly what he was asking her for. She was out of her league here.

She loved John, and believed they were close, but what she saw in Jace's depths and felt from his soul told her what they could have was far beyond anything she had experienced. There were forces at work here that she didn't understand, and she didn't think Jace was aware of what was driving him either. She was torn, and reminded herself not to accept the invitation in his eyes, or get in any deeper with Jace than she already was.

"She wouldn't have. We made a pact as children. I remember when she was five years old she came home from school in tears after she told her best friend her prediction of her friend's cat dying, and that girl told all their class mates Elsie was a freak. I had to walk her to classroom for a month after that and threaten anyone who made fun of her. I made Elsie promise never to tell anyone about what she or I could do, especially not our parents." She lowered her head, needing to break the building tension between them and noticed he was rubbing the cuff again. She had never told anyone that story. Despite her efforts to remain distanced, Jace was pulling her in.

"Tell me about your cuff. It's exquisite. I love the Celtic symbols," she observed, taking the conversation to less intimate topics. She refused to acknowledge that she was falling for a guy she knew so little about.

He released the cuff and grasped her hand. That familiar zing zipped through her at the contact and she suppressed her shudder. He ran his thumb over her pulse point. It was more sensual than kissing, and went straight to her core. She tried to fight what he incited in her, but it was impossible.

"The cuff was a gift from my father. It is a *Cuff de Draiocht*, and it helps me channel and focus my magic. My da was Scottish and my mother was from the Onyota'aka tribe. Fate brought them together before your human explorers discovered this land."

"How is that possible? How old are you?" She couldn't wrap her brain around what he was saying.

"I was born seven hundred forty-five years ago, and I know to you that must seem impossible, but supernaturals are immortal. We don't age beyond twenty-five, and before the Great War, there were countless of my kind that were several millennia old. As for how they traveled back then, there are many powers in the Tehrex Realm. Its inhabitants have always had the ability to travel to foreign lands through portals. There was a time that we could travel to other realms, but that information is in our Mystik Grimoire. My da was the Guild Master and was especially proficient at portals."

Cailyn was shocked. There were depths to this fierce warrior and caring doctor that she hadn't expected. Despite his age, there was something vulnerable about him that one often saw in adolescence. At the same time, he was confident, had immense pride, and a brutal strength that was frightening to see in action. The combination excited and intrigued her. "Your dad must have taught you well because you're pretty good at portals yourself."

Pain and grief ravaged his beautiful features. She expanded her telepathy and tried again to capture his thoughts. It was muddled, but she sensed that he harbored guilt about events that she suspected were out of his control.

She had this overwhelming urge to reach out and ease his burden. She was definitely falling for this guy.

"All sorcerers are good at portals within this realm. It's the ones to other realms that we can't access without the Grimoire. In fact, I don't think there is anyone alive who has done one since my da."

"By what you are saying I assume these other realms don't exist on earth like you guys," she shook her head at the complexity of this world. "I didn't realize there were other realms out there. There is so much to learn, but what I really want to know is how you feel about me being your Fated Mate. I know you have all the instincts and you said you aren't mate material, but I want to know how you feel about it."

She watched a million emotions wash over his features as he pondered her question. "Honestly, I have mixed feelings about it. The Goddess made a mistake. I'm not someone who should have been blessed with a mate. You deserve far better than me. It is for the best that you are going to marry another."

She wanted to punch him in his gorgeous face for being such an idiot. How could he say that? She must have been a disappointment in bed. He didn't know her enough to reject her for any other reason. "Maybe you're right. John wants me and he loves me," she pushed him away, annoyed with herself for hoping he reciprocated her feelings. She needed to remember that sex for men didn't involve an emotional attachment. Irritated, she huffed and tried to stand. He grabbed her arm and pulled her into the hard line of his body.

"Get one thing straight. I want you more than I want to take my next breath, but there are things about me that you don't know. I wish I were fit to be your mate but the reality is that I'm not. You are perfect, Cailyn. Beautiful, intelligent, caring, and sexy as hell. I couldn't ask for more, but we can't happen." She lost time staring into those amethyst gems while a million thoughts and feelings ran through her.

Part of her wanted to smile and throw her arms around his neck. He did care about her, and he thought she was perfect. No one had ever called her perfect. She wanted to erase the pain and anguish she saw. It was heart wrenching to think that he truly didn't feel good enough for her. A loud ruckus in the nearby kitchen shattered the intimacy of the moment.

"This conversation isn't over," he told her and held her gaze until she nodded an acknowledgement, then turned and tugged on her hand for her to follow him. They walked into the kitchen to find Kyran had returned home bloody, covered in ash, looking like death-warmed-over. The tension in the room was tangible.

Orlando dropped his spoon into his bowl and surged to his feet, knocking his stool over. "Where the fuck have you been?" he bellowed at the disheveled warrior.

"Oot killing skirm. What the fuck does it look like?" Kyran replied as he crossed the room and retrieved a bottle of scotch from the pantry. He twisted the top off and tipped it back.

While he drank deeply, Orlando continued his tirade. "You decide to flip the fuck out and left the Queen, your brother's beloved, without your protection. What if the demons had arrived and overwhelmed us? Zander should put us all out of our misery and take care of you."

The bottle lowered and Kyran disappeared only to reappear right in front of Orlando. He fisted Orlando's shirt and spat in his face. "Fuck you, arsehole. I doona have to listen to this shite," Kyran snapped and strode from the room, bottle in hand.

Orlando leaned his muscular frame against the counter and clasped his hands in front of his stomach. "That went well, I think. So, Jace, Cailyn is your Fated Mate?" Orlando arched an eyebrow in question.

Jace's fingers squeezed hers before he leaned back against the kitchen counter. "Yes, she is. The situation is complicated. Cailyn is engaged to another, and there will be no mating." Cailyn's heart twisted painfully in her chest and Jace's soul protested his words.

"You didn't tell him?" Elsie asked. Cailyn looked at her sister, pleading her to keep her mouth shut.

"Grab me a drink to go, Jess. Elsie said there was chocolate in my room, and I need some girl-talk," Cailyn said, wanting to get out of the room before Elsie spilled the beans.

"I wonder if matings in the past were all this complicated. The Goddess must be rusty. I pray she takes her time getting to mine. I want simple," Orlando said as he placed his empty bowl in the sink.

"You guys solve the problems of your realm. We are going to solve my female problems. Come on," Cailyn intervened, letting go of Jace's hand. Knowing it would throw him off her sister's comment, she brought her face close to his. "You're right, this isn't over, Miakoda," she whispered against his lips then turned and grabbed Jessie and her sister on her way out. She put more sway in her hips and was rewarded with a heavy groan from Jace. *Yeah, I get to him, too.*

CHAPTER 13

Kyran opened the door to Bite and entered the familiar waiting room. A sexy little nymph sat at the desk talking with another customer. His patience was a thin thread ready to snap. He had been entranced by a feisty human female who made him want to perform acts that were completely foreign to him. He didn't do tender, normal sex. His entire world was being turned upside down. His desires had followed a certain path from the day he'd witnessed his parents' murder, and it was a choice he was comfortable with, a preference that excited the predator within. He had embraced his deviancies because they helped him gain power over the memories. He refused to acknowledge Mackendra, or drag her into his hell.

"Hey honey, your usual?" the nymph drawled, catching his attention.

He turned around slowly, careful to keep the nightmare at bay. He was close to breaking and needed to release his demons. "Aye, my usual." He hoped that neither the room nor his regular sub, were currently occupied.

"Head back and I'll send Charlotte your way."

Thank fuck, Kyran thought as he turned on his heel without another word and headed back to the room. He had worked with the owner, Madame Madeline, to outfit the room with every device he needed during one of his sessions. He turned down the left corridor and reached the burgundy door. He twisted the nob and took a deep breath when he entered the small room. The scent of leather, plastic, and metal reached him, loosening the tight knot.

He sauntered over to the large wooden cross, noting the smell of bleach and lemon polish. Soon that smell would be replaced by that of blood, sweat, and fear, his favorite combination.

He contemplated using the cross today, it would provide a sturdy base for his play. The large bed in the corner was too soft for his mood. He selected a paddle, whip and cane. A nipple clamp, vibrator, and butt plug followed. He didn't know what would strike him in the moment and didn't want to have to stop mid-session. He gazed at the kneeling bench, steel stockade, and wooden rack. This was what had kept him sane, not his mate's soul. Nobody had a fucking clue what his world was about.

Charlotte walked in in the middle of his brooding, and like a good little sub knelt at his feet, waiting for instruction. She wore a leather corset and had her collar with nipple clamps already on. He tossed the ones he'd grabbed in the corner. "Grab a ball gag and go to the cross," he ordered.

"Yes, sir," she replied. She stood up and selected a ball gag then dutifully walked over to the cross. She fastened one of her wrists onto the wood as he stalked to her and fastened her other wrist. Her whimpering told him he had been rough, but that she liked it.

He walked around her, each step bringing an image of

Mackendra into his mind. Her silky, short, black hair and her full bust were exquisite. She had smelled of orange and vanilla. His cock hardened at the picture and he fantasized about her being on his cross. But she wasn't the type of female who would submit, and would never be on his cross. In fact, she'd likely be disgusted by his predilections. Hell, the female would stab him in the heart without hesitation if she ever learned what he was. She hated vampires, hunting and killing what she believed were vampires nightly. His anger spiked out of control.

He reached down and grabbed the paddle then ran it across the sub's breasts. A harsh tug on the nipple clamps drew blood. He bent and licked the drops of blood from each breast, his hunger rising to the fore, the taste only wetting his appetite. Needing more, he tilted her head, exposing her jugular and sank his fangs into her slim neck. He bit down hard and drank several mouthfuls of her sweet blood. "You want more?"

The pretty red-haired shifter moaned loudly. "Yes, please sir."

His reached down and tugged the silk thong from her body and discovered how wet she was. He stroked her intimate flesh and was for the first time in his life revolted by a female. Disconcerted, he grabbed the anal plug and lubricated it in her juices, not as effective for what he was planning, but then she liked pain. He inserted the plug roughly into her tight opening and she cried out. He felt her body tense beside him.

"Doona cum or you know I will punish you," he growled.

She trembled, trying to hold back. Ruthless bastard that he was, he pinched her clit and drove her over the edge. "Ah, you should no' have done that." Leaving the plug in place, he dropped the paddle and grabbed the whip. Several lashes to her breasts had her panting and close again to climax. His strokes came down on her core this time. "Hold it back," he ordered and like a well-trained dog she obeyed. He breathed deeply of her arousal.

He ripped open his pants and palmed his erection, but even with her blood on his tongue and scent in his nose he found no real pleasure in his touch. Unbidden, Mackendra's smirk entered his mind and he recalled her fresh scent and his balls drew up tight. His body had never responded to anything so strongly, and it made him angry.

He brought stepping stools under her feet and had the sub step up, spreading her legs. He ran a finger through her moisture and crouched, licking her core. She held still like he had trained her, only letting out whimpers. He toyed with the plug while he tasted her. Normally, he would be rock hard, but the moment he shoved Mack out of his mind, he softened. He stood abruptly and retrieved the cane, returning to his position in front of the sub. He penetrated her with the tip of the cane and she sobbed. "Please, sir…"

"Doona cum, dammit." If he found no pleasure, neither would she. She cried out and her body shuddered, he ripped the plug from her body and brought the cane across her legs. He lashed out and struck her breasts, abdomen, and thighs repeatedly. Her sobbing took on a pained tone. He thought of Mackendra, and what she'd think of him if she saw him at that moment. She would be disgusted with him, and it pissed him off that he cared. The sub's cries reminded him of his mother's rape and murder. Instantly, he was back in that room over seven hundred years earlier.

Thud,
Thud,
Thud.

A menacing laugh was followed by a wet, tearing sound, thick and obscene, something out of a nightmare. A creature unlike any he had ever seen entered his parent's bed chambers. It was well over seven feet tall and had huge black horns on its head.

"Hold her," the demon ordered his minions. His mother fought back and screamed obscenities at the demon. The demon's lips pulled back to reveal huge fangs and before Kyran could blink they were in her throat. Kyran shoved his fist into his mouth to keep from crying out. He wanted to run out from his hiding spot and help his mother, but he was no match for the huge creature.

He closed his eyes. "Please don't hurt me," a whispered gurgling plea from his mother. He glanced up to find his mother's throat torn out. The demon smiled and ran his hand down her cheek. "Shh, bitch. This will only hurt, a lot." His laughter was filled with evil intent. Then he shredded the green, velvet gown from her body.

Unable to look away, Kyran watched as the demon grabbed his mother's breasts sinking his claws in deep and ripping one from her body. He sucked the nipple of the other breast and spread her thighs while she cried. When the demon surged his large, grotesque cock into her body, she turned her head away and met Kyran's eyes where he was hidden in the wall. As he prepared to surge from the closet to her aide, she shook her head, not wanting him to help her. The demon ripped his mother to pieces as he ruthlessly raped her. Kyran swallowed back his bile and was grateful that the demon took pity and beheaded his mother after he had his fill. No female should live with that memory.

Back in the present, Kyran realized he had lived with the pain of that memory every day for over seven hundred years, and needed to escape it. Taking two steps back, he surveyed the female. She was bleeding and bruised in several places. He released her from the cross and smoothed his hands over her back as he walked her to the kneeling bench.

He kissed her neck and brushed her hair away from her face. He grabbed the ball gag and shoved it in her mouth securing the strap. He pushed her forward so she draped limply face first across the bench. He thrust his pants to his knees and gripped his semi-erect shaft. Nothing moved it until he let the sultry orange-vanilla scent enter his mind. When he added Mackendra's whiskey eyes, pre-cum slicked his head and his spine tingled.

He maneuvered his body behind the sub and rubbed the head of his cock in her wet slit. They both moaned and he saw whiskey eyes glaze over with passion. He refused to make love to a fantasy of his female and erased those thoughts. The sub's muffled cries and scent reached him. He went to thrust into her pussy but his cock had deflated. He tried again.

Nothing, no toy, no play, not a thing aroused him. He may be able to feed, but he couldn't fuck. He'd rather starve to death. Enraged, he grabbed the cane and brought it down across her ass.

Crazed, he swung the implement until blood ran in rivulets, and the cane broke over her back. The paddle was in his hand before he knew what he was doing, but that wasn't enough.

Hadn't the Goddess taken enough from him when she took his parents? He was forced to relive the brutal murder and rape of his mother. Now, he couldn't have sex like he wanted without obsessing about a ridiculous human female. He screamed his rage, and reached for his *sgian dubh* tucked into a sheath in his boot.

The sub had gone still at some point, but he was beyond

seeing anything. He pulled the female's limp form to his chest and sliced the blade across her throat, nearly decapitating her. When her head lolled and her sightless eyes gazed at him accusingly, he came back to himself. What the fuck had he just done?

He snatched his cell phone from his back pocket and called Zander. "*Brathair*, I need your help. I'm in trouble," he uttered brokenly.

"Shite, Kyran, is that you? Where are you?"

"Aye, 'tis me. I'm at Bite, hurry and bring Jace." He dropped Charlotte's body and was unable to look at what he had done. He pulled up and fastened his pants then walked as far away from the bench as he could before sinking down on the cold tile floor.

~

JACE AND ZANDER walked into a blood bath. Jace rushed to the broken female across the room, slipping in blood as he skidded to a stop at her side. He immediately laid his hands on her throat and sent his healing magic into the wound. Some throat injuries he could repair, but he feared this injury was beyond his ability.

He looked over at Zander where he crouched in front of an unrecognizable Kyran. He was covered in blood and gore, but the scariest part was the bleak look in his eyes. He realized he was not the only one with skeletons in his closet, and wondered what terrible thing had happened to Kyran to cause him to brutalize an innocent female. Jace was too ashamed to share his own torturous past with his fellow warriors, and imagined Kyran's must be even worse.

"She is close to death, Liege. I will try my best, but I don't think I can save her."

Zander threw blazing eyes at Jace. "Do whatever it takes. She didna deserve this." Zander turned to Kyran and placed a hand on his shoulder. Jace noted the slight tremor as the two connected.

Jace turned back to the female and kept trying to heal her wounds to no avail. She was gone and nothing was bringing her back. He lowered his head in sorrow. How the hell Zander was going to fix this, Jace had no idea.

"Liege," Jace swallowed the lump in his throat, "she is gone. There is nothing I can do to bring her back. What do you want me to do?"

Zander took a deep breath and let it out slowly. Black had swallowed his sapphire blue irises. He was pissed as hell. "Go and gather Madame Madeline. I need to talk to my *brathair*."

Jace nodded his agreement and left the room like Lucifer was hot on his tail. One thing was certain. Kyran's issues ran deeper than his own. He shook his head and made his way down the hall, ignoring the sounds of pleasure mixed with pain as he went. When he reached the reception desk, the pretty nymph's horrified gasp reminded him he was covered in blood.

"We need to speak with Madame Madeline in Kyran's room immediately."

She glanced at his hands nervously. "I will send her right in." He inclined his head and returned to the room. He paused at the door and listened to Zander yell at Kyran. When Madame Madeline, the lithe Rokurokubi demoness, met him in the hall, he opened the door and noted with disgust how she entered the horrid scene without a flicker of emotion. Her gaze skittered over the dead shifter then to Kyran and Zander, yet she remained stoic. She was one cold bitch.

Zander rose from his crouch and drug Kyran with him. "Madame Madeline, as you can see, we have a problem."

"Yes," she said, anger evident in her tone. "I'd say you and your brother have a very big problem. It displeases me to have to clean up this mess and find a replacement for one of my highest grossing females."

Zander clenched his fists and spoke through gritted teeth. "As Kyran's sovereign, it falls upon me to punish him for his transgression, and as part of that, he will be cleaning up his own mess. What I want to know is how much he will need to compensate you for your...losses."

"This will cost him greatly. I never want him to return to my establishment. Bite will be warded against his presence."

Jace couldn't understand what brought Kyran to this point, but he understood suffering, and recognized it when he saw it. Kyran was a very disturbed male. Jace heaved a deep sigh, it was still early but it was going to be a long night, and he couldn't leave Kyran to do this alone. Zander had been there for Jace and he wouldn't let either of these males down. He only hoped he was able to help Kyran come back from this.

CHAPTER 14

"Shhh...quit being so loud," Jessie whispered. Cailyn glared at her friend. She hadn't made any noise.

"I am being quiet," Cailyn hissed from her crouched position behind a cluster of evergreens. The moon shone bright in the late summer evening, like a spotlight pointing her out. She felt like an escaping prisoner who needed to be on the lookout for the tower guards. Paranoid much?

"You sound like a heard of buffalo traipsing behind me. If I can hear you, I am sure Elsie and the others can, so try to make less noise when you walk," Jessie breathed into her ear. Cailyn hadn't heard her footsteps. It was still odd for Cailyn to think about her friend being a skirm-hybrid with preternatural abilities.

Cailyn stuck her head around the trunk of a tree and scanned the back of the house. No one was following them, so they had to keep moving. Jace and Zander were out on patrol, but there were still way too many warriors in the mansion that could stop her. She tiptoed as fast as she could through the property toward the private boathouse and dock, hoping they didn't get caught. Breslin was going to be mad when she returned from her trip and learned that Cailyn had borrowed her boat to go see John.

But there was no other option for Cailyn. She needed to see John, and it was impossible for her and Jessie to leave the compound any other way than on the water. The front gate was protected by the best electronic security system in the world, as well as the strongest magical wards. The wards extend around the property, but there was no electronic system along the water, making it their best bet.

She had stolen the boat keys and codes for the boathouse. She felt like a teenager sneaking out of her parents' house to go joyriding in the car. Hopefully, this ended better. When they were teenagers, her and Elsie snuck out and ended up in an accident, totaling the car.

She breathed a sigh of relief when they made it to the boathouse undiscovered. Excitement over what she'd done with Jace warred with anxiety and anticipation of seeing John. She understood the danger she was in, and wasn't going unprotected, but this was too important to discuss over the phone with him. Jessie was super-powerful now, and able to defend them. Besides, Cailyn refused to allow anyone to tell her what to do or not to do, even if a part of her liked Jace's dominance.

She fumbled with the key and prayed she wasn't being too loud. She glanced at her friend and noted her gaze was fixed on the house in the distance. Once the door was open, she rushed to the alarm panel and entered the code to disable it. When she was about to start the motor for the automatic wench, Jessie stopped her.

"No, I'll get it down by hand. I'm not sure how loud it is, but I'd rather not take any chances," Jessie voiced as she got to work turning the hand-crank. While Jessie worked,

Cailyn pulled out her phone and looked over the map she had Googled.

When the boat hit the water, Jessie turned and opened the door so they could get the boat onto the lake. "Let's go," her friend said as she ushered her into the sleek speedboat. It was intimidating, and made her re-think her plan of driving this boat down the lake to get to John's hotel. She had no idea how to drive a boat, and neither did Jessie. This was doomed to fail, but that didn't stop her from jumping into the craft.

She stood at the wheel and watched Jessie join her. "I don't know about this. It's pitch-black and neither of us knows exactly where we are going. What was I thinking with this hair-brained scheme?"

Her friend pushed her aside muttering, "I can see just fine and this will work. It's the only way, and you have been dying to see him since you talked to him. I, for one, don't want to hear you bitch and moan about it anymore." Jessie snatched the boat key that was dangling from her finger and started the boat.

She yelped as she fell back into the seat when Jessie gunned the boat. They bumped into the dock and a loud screech told her she was going to owe Breslin a paint job. "Jesus, maniac. You don't know what you are doing any more than I do." Cailyn cursed as her friend hit the edge of the building before she cleared it, and they finally hit open water. Add a new door to the list, too.

"Which way is south?" Jessie yelled over the engine. Yeah, they were in deep shit.

"I think it's to the right. Doesn't this thing have a compass?" Cailyn asked as she stood up and checked the controls. "It's right there, see?" Cailyn pointed to the control panel. "Turn to the right and then we look for the public dock for BluWater Bistro."

Cailyn took in the sights as they made their way down the lake. There were countless houses, most of which had private docks. After a few minutes, she began to worry that they'd gone too far. "Slow down. Unlike you, I can't see at night and don't want to miss it."

The boat slowed and a couple minutes later Cailyn spotted the neon sign on a building. "Stop, that's it," she called out and pointed to the docks near the restaurant. Jessie whipped the boat around and made her way into one of the slips. They had no idea how to tie the boat off and looked at how the other boats were secured. Cailyn threw big rubber tubes over the side and tied the ropes to some metal hooks on the dock, hoping the boat didn't float away.

Once they were out of the boat, Cailyn hailed a cab and directed the driver to the Sheraton near downtown Seattle. She was glad she had raided her sister's wallet before leaving, ensuring she had plenty of cash to pay the fare.

As they stood on the sidewalk at the bottom of the stairs, she was suddenly nervous to see John again. She grabbed Jessie's hand for support and they walked into the hotel.

"What room?" Jessie asked.

"He said five-twenty-six," she replied as she pressed the elevator call button. An older couple joined them as they entered the car. The gentleman pushed the number nine button and turned to them. "What floor?"

"Five, please." As they rode in silence, Cailyn's heart raced and her palms began to sweat. She had slept with another man. She felt no guilt, because sex with Jace had been right, necessary even, but John would never understand that.

She smiled at the couple as she exited the elevator then

followed the signs to his room. Jessie placed her hand on her shoulder, offering comfort. "I'll be downstairs in the bar. Come get me when you're done."

"Thank you. Here, take some money." She watched Jessie round the corner then knocked, holding her breath until John opened the door.

"Cailyn! Oh my God. I have been so worried about you," John exclaimed and grabbed her up into a bear hug, causing her feet to leave the ground. He held her tight and carried her into the room.

He set her down and placed his hands on her face. "I'm sorry you worried, but I'm ok now. I missed you." She placed her hands on his chest, pushing lightly to create space. In the back of her mind she registered that Jace's chest was more muscled. Comparing the two wasn't fair because there truly was no comparison. Both men were so different from one another.

John refused the space and closed all distance between them, claiming her lips in a kiss. He mistook her hesitation for permission and deepened the kiss. He held her close when she tried to pull away. She was sad that his effect on her was mild compared to the uncontrollable lust that Jace induced in her.

As she ended the kiss and looked into John's warm, brown eyes she saw unconditional love and caring. This was the hardest thing she had ever faced. "We need to talk."

John slid his hands down to her arms and squeezed. "Whenever a woman says that, it never ends well. I love you, no matter what. You know that, right?"

Tears misted her eyes. "I know and I love you, too. It's not necessarily bad, but complicated. Let's sit down."

He interlaced their fingers and he tugged her to the only place to sit, the bed. She kept her eyes downcast and played with his fingers as she gathered her thoughts. "As Elsie told you, I was in an accident. Jessie and I were both injured in that accident. I am not one hundred percent better, and Jessie has a long road ahead of her. Jessie won't be returning to San Francisco. She has to stay here where there are experts to help her. Elsie's new husband has the connections and money to help her. She is my best friend, and the accident was my fault...what I'm trying to say...is that I'm going to stay here with her, at least for a little bit."

John's shock was evident as he gaped at her. "But what about your job? You can't quit. And your condo? What about us?"

She grabbed his other hand. "I have to quit. I can get a job here if I need it. I'll be staying with my sister as long as I need to."

"Are you saying you want me to move here with you?"

"No, I'm not. You can't leave your job, and I need some space and time. These last few days have been difficult for me."

She saw the heartbreak on his face, but she wouldn't lie to him and tell him everything was going to be alright. "I love you," she said simply.

"I love you more than you know, and I will be there for you anytime you need me. Can I come visit you at least?"

She choked back a sob and nodded her head. A loud knock sounded as he was leaning his head to kiss her again. He cursed and rose to answer the door. A panicked, pale Jessie was on the other side. "Hey John, I hate to interrupt but," she looked over at Cailyn, "we have to go. I need to see Jace right away, something is wrong."

"What's wrong?" she asked as she met them at the door.

"There is this feeling under my skin that I can't describe but it's not normal," Jessie said through clenched teeth. She noticed that her friend was hiding her fangs and was in obvious discomfort.

"What's going on?" John demanded.

Cailyn turned to John and hugged him close. "I'm sorry but I have to go with her. I'll call you soon and will try to see you before you head back to San Francisco," she murmured before kissing his cheek.

"Call me later and tell me what's going on."

Cailyn couldn't answer him so she turned and headed down the hall. She felt John's gaze on her back, but she refused to look back.

∼

JACE PULLED up to the hangar-like garage around the back of the main residence, relieved to be done with the ugly task of cleaning up Kyran's mess. He climbed out of the car and glanced at Zander and Kyran. They had cleaned the room and ridden home in silence. The tension was draining. It was going to be a rough road for the warrior, and Jace worried that Zander wasn't going to be there for his brother. A noise drew their attention to the house.

"What's going on?" Zander asked as he looked toward the back of the house.

"Don't know but something is up. Everyone is racing to the water. We may be under attack," Jace called as he conjured his staff and raced across the lawn.

They caught up to their majordomo, Angus, a dragon shifter, and Elsie. "What's wrong, *a ghra*?"

"Cailyn and Jessie are gone, looks like they took Breslin's boat. I'm sure she went to see John, but she doesn't have a cell phone and John's not answering his," Elsie said worriedly.

Jace cursed and dashed toward the water as a ball formed in his gut. He uttered the words to a reveal spell and saw the traces of Cailyn's aura along with that of Jessie's. "She left with Jessie," he observed when they entered the boathouse. He looked around the scene and noticed the blue paint along the dock and door. Had they met foul play?

"We have to go after her," Elsie insisted.

"We will," Jace promised, wondering where to start looking.

"I hear a boat," Elsie cried out. "Is that them?"

Jace cocked his ear and heard the faint sounds of a boat. A breeze off the water carried Cailyn's cinnamon scent to him. "Yes, it's her."

The boat came into view a few seconds later and Elsie began cursing at her sister. Jace saw that Jessie was driving the boat and Cailyn was in the passenger seat. The female maneuvered the craft into the garage and banged into the dock. "Shit," Jessie cursed, "stupid boat."

Jace ignored her and charged over to his mate. He jumped into the boat before it stopped completely and he crouched down to meet Cailyn's gaze. He was certain his eyes were black with his anger. "What the fuck were you thinking?" he growled. As the tight knot of fear unraveled and Cailyn's soul soothed his tension, he realized he couldn't lose his Fated Mate. He couldn't live without her, but wasn't sure he could live with her, either.

Spunk sparked in Cailyn's eyes. She squared her shoulders and stood up. "I was thinking I wanted to see John, but that's not important right now. Something is wrong with Jessie."

CHAPTER 15

Cailyn gasped as Jace got into her face, distress, fear, and annoyance marring his beautiful features. "I don't give a fuck about her right now. I do, however, care about you and the danger you knowingly placed yourself in."

Her jaw went slack and her eyes widened. How could he say he didn't care about her friend? Obviously, the Hippocratic Oath meant nothing to him. "Yeah, well fuck you too, Jace. I do care about her. She is my best friend and the only one, aside from my sister that I can count on. If you aren't going to help her, I'll find someone who will."

Cailyn turned on her heel and hurried to the house. How had they gone from making love earlier to this? They hadn't made love though, had they? They didn't know each other, and despite being Fated for one another, that didn't necessarily mean it meant anything to him. She should consider it nothing more than good sex. Unfortunately, it was the best sex of her life. He may be able to forget her, but she would never forget this sorcerer and the moments they shared.

Suddenly, she realized she had no idea who to call within the realm that may be able to help her. She turned to ask her sister for suggestions and noticed that Elsie's panic lingered in her eyes.

Cailyn should have known how worried her sister would have been, especially after what she'd suffered. Her sister was one of the strongest women she knew, and it cut Cailyn to the bone to see the worry in Elsie's eyes. She hadn't really thought the situation through, and had only done what she'd wanted to. In hindsight, talking to John in person wasn't necessary and hadn't even given her the clarity she hoped for.

"El, I'm sorry. I didn't intend to worry you," she canted her head and begrudgingly included Jace. She was still mad at him. "Or anyone else. Can you help me find someone who can help Jessie?"

"Please, there's electricity or something pulsing under my arm, close to my heart," Jessie interjected, grabbing her arm. "It was much worse when we were at the hotel, but it seems better now."

"I will help her," Jace offered, glaring at Cailyn. What did he have to be angry about? "Let's get to the clinic downstairs," he barked and headed to the house.

Elsie wrapped her arm around Cailyn's shoulders as they followed. "One thing you will learn is that these warriors have a hard time with being overbearing, especially where their Fated Mate is concerned. Cut him some slack. None of them know how to deal with everything when it hits them all at once."

Zander stepped up to her sister's other side while Jessie walked on Cailyn's other side. "She is right, *puithar*. I have a difficult time with being what Elsie calls a Neanderthal."

Jace stopped as they reached the back of the house. "I

am sorry, Cai. This is all new to me, but trust that I will do my best for Jessie. Although, I'd like Evzen here just in case."

He grabbed her hand and tugged. She met his blazing amethyst eyes and saw his vulnerability for a split second before he shuttered his emotions. She heaved a sigh. Overwhelmed could summarize exactly how she felt. In fact, she wanted to crawl into a big, soft bed and get lost in a good romance novel, anything for a break from everything plaguing her. Between her four J's: Jace, John, Jessie, and her job, she was close to breaking. His reaction was to be expected, and she needed to remember that.

His tension was obvious as they entered the house, but, as Jace intertwined their fingers and sidled closer to her, some of that tension eased. She normally hated reading people's thoughts, but for the second time since the accident, she entered his mind. As with all the supernaturals, it was difficult to gather clear impressions, let alone coherent thoughts.

This time the only thing she heard was a name, Lady Angelica. Jealousy speared her heart at hearing another woman's name in his thoughts. Numerous scenarios played through her head, from him being in love with this woman and her rejecting him, to her being his long-time lover. The sudden urge to rip this woman's head from her shoulders had Cailyn gritting her teeth.

"We have a lot to work through, but right now I am glad to have you on my side." She squeezed his fingers to emphasize her words.

He opened the basement door and held it open for her. "Never doubt that I will always be on your side," Jace replied as he watched Jessie descend the stairs behind them.

"What happened right before this began, Jessie?" Jace asked, changing the subject.

"Nothing. I was riding down the elevator and dismissed it at first, but when it didn't stop and worsened a few minutes later, I panicked. Given all the changes I have been through, I was worried that it was a sign I was losing control. The last thing I wanted to do was start attacking everyone in the hotel."

Cailyn's heart broke and she felt terrible for what her friend was going through. It only served to set her resolve to be there for Jessie as she forged a new life. No way was she leaving her to deal with this alone.

"So, did you have any cravings? How was your bloodlust when you encountered humans?" Jace asked, clearly in doctor mode, and it was hot as hell. Everything about the man was irresistible and sexy.

"It wasn't any worse than it has been since I woke up. I'm not sure why, but I want Cailyn's blood more than any of yours. Is that normal?"

"I'm not certain what's normal for a female injected with archdemon venom. What I can tell you is that male skirm crave only human blood, it's all they can consume. They can't eat food any longer, so on that, you are more similar to vampires given that you still ate Elsie's creole earlier. Vampires can ingest blood from almost any being and it doesn't have to be humans, unlike the myths say. I have only given you human blood, but I wonder how you would handle realm blood."

Cailyn listened to them talk and thought she could listen to him talk all day. She loved the deep timbre of his voice. She watched his lips move and found she was thinking of sucking that bottom lip into her mouth while she explored his body. She hadn't spent enough time on his delectable body before. Remembering how well-proportioned he was all over, her mouth watered.

Mental head shake to halt the erotic fantasy. Her body was out of control, demonstrating once again, how right Elsie was when she said that the mating compulsion hampered your ability to think of anything but carnal pleasures with your mate.

Jace inhaled and his head snapped in her direction. She was on fire, as arousal coursed hot and fast, and from the way his eyes glowed, he was more than aware of what her body wanted. His pupils dilated and he brought her hand to his lips.

Jessie cleared her throat loudly and smirked in Cailyn's direction. Cailyn felt her cheeks heat with embarrassment that her friend was aware of what she'd been thinking. "I'm up for trying realm blood anytime. By the way, the sensation has now stopped altogether."

Zander and Jace shared a look that Cailyn couldn't decipher. "You are within the boundaries of the protection spell. Would you say there was a hum to it?" Zander queried.

"I hadn't really paid attention, I just panicked, but now that you mention it, yes," Jessie answered.

They entered a well-supplied medical room and Jace gestured for Jessie to get onto one of the tables. "Let's take a look. Can you remove your clothes please? I'm afraid we don't have gowns here. The Dark Warriors aren't concerned about their modesty when they come here for treatment. Just leave on your underwear," Jace instructed. The idea of Jace seeing her friend topless made Cailyn see red, and she had difficulty remembering that he was a doctor and this was necessary.

"That's fine, but I want all these guys to leave the room. I do mind *them* seeing me half-naked," Jessie retorted.

"Everyone except Elsie and Cailyn, oot now," Zander ordered. Cailyn appreciated him taking control and not simply dismissing Jessie's feelings. "Let me know when we can come back in. I want to know what is going on."

"Yes, Liege. Now, let's have a look," Jace said as the others filed out of the room. Cailyn grabbed Elsie's hand and said a prayer that everything was okay while Jessie quickly shed her clothes. They had enough unknowns and concerns where Jessie was concerned, they didn't need to add more.

∼

It was a struggle for Jace to remain focused on his patient with Cailyn so close. The smell of her arousal clouded his mind. He continued to be caught off guard by the mating compulsion's effect on him. His thoughts continuously turned in a lascivious direction, and it was extremely distracting. He had never been one to obsess on anything sexual, given his reactions to simple kisses. It wasn't until he'd met Cailyn that his desires were reawakened.

"What exactly are you looking for?" Jessie asked as she lay back on the table, claiming his attention.

"To be honest, I'm not sure. I have a suspicion that they may have placed a bug of some sort in you. It would explain the symptoms, and the wards we have around the property would render any such device inert," he explained as he took her vital signs. He noted there was nothing there to cause alarm and went over possibilities of what could have caused her symptoms.

The most logical was that it was a bug, so he began there. He figured the demon had minimal time to install it, so it would had to have been somewhere easy for them to reach.

He threaded his fingers into her hair and gently probed her scalp. "Any tenderness?"

"No, I don't feel anything."

He moved his hands down the sides of her neck and noted how Cailyn stiffened and stepped closer to him. His head tilted her way and he smiled. His mate was jealous, and that thought made his heart soar, and almost forget about the steaming jealousy he felt when she mentioned her fiancé and being alone in a room with him.

He refocused on Jessie. "Do you remember if there were any areas that were particularly sore after the accident?"

Jessie pondered the question. "Everything seemed to hurt. I ached everywhere. Sorry."

"Well, we will have to do this the hard way. Let me know if I hit a tender spot." He felt around her collar bones and down the front of her chest, stopping short of her breasts.

From the corner of his eye, he saw his mate clench her fists at her sides. He moved to examining Jessie's arms, considering Cailyn's feelings and how out of sorts she was at the moment. They hadn't completed their mating, and her instinct would be to claim what was hers. He was beginning to understand exactly how unpredictable emotions were during a mating, and Cailyn would never forgive herself if she hurt her friend.

He lifted Jessie's left arm, but found nothing. When he lifted her right arm, he saw nothing on a visual inspection, but when he probed her ribcage, he felt a hard object the size of an almond. "Does this hurt? Do you feel anything here?"

"Nope, nothing. Is something there?" Jessie asked as she twisted her head trying to catch a glimpse.

"It may be nothing, but I am going to do an x-ray to make sure. Would you grab the portable machine out of the storage closet?" he asked Elsie who nodded and headed to the door at the back of the room.

"Wow," Cailyn exclaimed, "you guys have everything here. Do you have an MRI somewhere too?"

Jace stopped his exam and turned to face his mate. Big mistake, as his shaft hardened, yet again. He wanted to forget the matter at hand and explore her body. He began to imagine what he wanted to do before he stopped short with a mental head shake, now was not the time for that...later.

"No MRI. Supernaturals don't have a need for that in-depth of an exam with their superior healing abilities. We aren't prone to human diseases either. Any injury not caused by skirm venom or silver heals quickly. And, when you have warriors who are often shot, an x-ray machine comes in handy for bullet extraction. I have added more medical supplies since your accident given that we have no idea how Jessie will heal. As well as to meet your unique human needs."

Elsie returned with the machine. Jace plugged it in and set the necessary settings, then booted up the laptop. "Put your hand above your head," he instructed. Jessie complied and Jace positioned the machine and took a couple pictures.

Returning to the laptop, he uploaded the digital images. He zoomed in on a tiny device in the fatty tissue around her ribcage. "You definitely have something right here," he pointed at the computer screen showing those in the room. "It will be easy to remove. I'll numb the area then make a small incision and retrieve the object using small tweezers. Looks like we will find out how you heal."

"I hate needles," Jessie complained, making Jace laugh. That was a familiar complaint at the hospital, and had him wondering how quickly she'd get over that.

He set about quickly setting up a tray for the procedure,

but his mate's scent was driving him to distraction. It took him longer than normal as his mind kept conjuring her naked while he plunged into her heat. Sweat beaded his forehead and his heart raced as he fought against his arousal.

Gaining a modicum of control over his libido, he turned and numbed Jessie's side. Cailyn had stepped to the other side of the table and while he wanted her back by his side, he was touched at how she grabbed her friends hand and offered her support. He loved how she anticipated what others around her needed, and provided it without ever being asked.

Once he was assured the area was sufficiently numb, he picked up the scalpel. "I'm going to get started now. You might feel some pressure in your side followed by tugging as I remove the object, but you shouldn't feel any pain. If you do, let me know right away."

"Okay," she replied, her shaky voice displaying her nervousness.

"You are going to be fine, Jess. This is going to be over before you know it. Remember that time I crashed my bike when we were six and my arm was bent at a funny angle and you rode with me to the hospital?" Cailyn continued to detail the story, distracting Jessie while he worked.

"Yeah," Jessie laughed. "You screamed like a little girl."

"I was a little girl, I was six."

"I remember when you looked in the mirror and asked the nurse if she'd seen your face. You didn't even care that your arm was broken. You were more concerned with the bloody scabs."

With quick work, he had pulled a small black piece of plastic out from under her skin. He held it up and noticed Zander looking in the window of the door. Without gaining permission, the Vampire King was pushing his way into the room. He heard Cailyn gasp and saw her pull a sheet over Jessie's body.

"Excuse me, Zander. You couldn't wait until she's dressed?" Cailyn snapped.

"Nay, I couldna wait. This is aboot the safety of everyone in this house, not one female's modesty," Zander told her before he stepped up beside Jace to examine the object.

"It's okay, Cai. He's right. This is important," Jessie added. Cailyn didn't look appeased, but Jace saw that she understood.

The object was the size of an almond and had a tiny red light on it, clearly electronic in nature. The fucking demon had bugged her, trying to find their location. No wonder they hadn't simply disappeared with the females before the Dark Warriors got to the car. He had wondered why, and had figured they believed they had control over Jessie. Not to mention the little bomb they had planted in Cailyn. That spell was designed to make the Queen suffer when Cailyn wasn't able to be healed. Shaking his head, he dropped the bug into a jar and handed it over to Zander.

"I'll have Kill see what he can learn aboot it. Surely with his expertise, he can turn this on them, so we can locate their lair," Zander pondered as he held the jar up to the light.

Jace picked up some swabs and turned back to his patient. His mouth fell open. "Shit, that's amazing. And, we have our answer. Your healing abilities far excel any skirm we have ever seen. In fact, it matches our speed of healing. You don't even have a scar."

"What? Really?" Jessie sat up and twisted, trying to see.

He grabbed her shoulders stilling her movements.

"Wait, let me clean the blood," he whispered, lost in thought about everything unique to Jessie.

Before he could wipe the area clean, Cailyn had shoved a shirt over Jessie's head. "You're fine. You can get dressed now," she snapped.

He walked around to his mate, needing to soothe her ruffled feathers. He pulled her into his arms as soon as he reached her and sighed in relief. Unfortunately, at the same time, his nausea reared its head. He wished for one moment that he could enjoy the feel of his mate against him without all the other bullshit. He wanted to rail at the Goddess for cursing him. Warmth spread from his chest out, easing the nausea and settling his anger. They really were Fated Mates, he marveled, as Cailyn's soul attempted to make it better.

He leaned back and tilted her face up with his finger on her chin. "You have nothing to be jealous of, *Shijéí*. I feel it, too." Her anguished expression was killing him. He ran his thumb across her plump lower lip, groaning as her tongue followed in its wake.

"I don't know what has overcome me. I wanted to rip my best friend's face off when you touched her. That's not like me," she shook her head ruefully. "I can't think of anything but how much I ache, and feel like I will die without you right now."

He laid his forehead against hers, aware of everyone leaving the room. She tilted her head back and helplessly, he lowered his lips to hers. The kiss seared his soul. She settled her hands on his hips, pulling him closer. She took advantage of his gasp, slipping her tongue into his mouth.

He danced his tongue tentatively against hers, not wanting things to get out of hand lest he get sick. Her mewls drove him on, and his hand went to the back of her head and tangled in her hair. She angled her head and deepened the kiss, hands roaming up and down his back.

She was his heaven and his hell. He had never felt as at home as he had with her, but he wasn't good enough for her. As her hips began moving against his front, his objections dissolved. The feel of her soft stomach against his erection had him so hard, his balls were drawn up tight and he was ready to explode.

He would deny himself, but saw no need to deny her as she grabbed at him and kissed him frantically. He prayed to the Goddess, asking for a way he could be with his mate, and be the male she needed and deserved, as he slid his thigh between her legs. He rubbed it against her core and he could feel her heat through their clothes.

She climbed up his body, her arms thrown around his neck and her legs around his waist. He held her close as she writhed, ignoring the searing pain in his mate mark. He pulled back from the kiss to see the desire blazing in her hazel depths. "Fuck, yeah, baby. Take what you need," he growled and licked and nipped his way down her neck.

"Oh God, Jace. I need you inside me, now." She arched her back, pressing her breasts against his chest. His cock pulsed, pre-cum oozing at the slit. The sensation was still so new, and the pleasure momentarily stole his breath and his reason. He had never wanted anything more than he wanted Cailyn while at the same time he wanted to run as far and as fast as he could.

Her panting increased and he sucked on her neck, grasping her hips, helping her movements. He may deny himself pleasure to avoid embarrassing himself but he would never deny his mate's needs.

"That's it, come for me. You are so beautiful," he murmured.

"I'm close," she cried. He claimed her lips and slid his grip to her ass and increased the speed and pressure. He burned with pleasure and had never wanted an end to his centuries long torment more than he did at that moment. He loved the sounds she made when caught in the throes of passion.

Cailyn tensed in his arms and cried out his name as she climaxed. He helped her ride out her orgasm and gentled his kiss even though he ached to be inside her. When she went boneless he was both satisfied and in agony. It had never felt better or hurt more to provide his mate pleasure.

"Oh God, baby. That was incredible. Now it's my turn to take care of you," she uttered then looked into his eyes. A female had never called him baby, and he liked it, especially when his mate said it. Panic set in at the thought of her taking him into her mouth. His shaft pulsed, on board with the idea, but his stomach churned. He was doomed to never experience that pleasure, and couldn't allow this to go any further no matter how much instinct was telling him to complete the mating.

"You are a treasure. Come on, let's go find out if they've learned anything about that device from Jessie's side." He needed to get out of the room drenched in the scent of her desire before his resolve dissolved. His balls were ten shades of blue already, he couldn't take anymore.

As he set her down and took her hand, leading her to the door, she stopped and protested. "What about you? Let me take care of you."

He shut his eyes and groaned at an image of her on her knees with his cock buried in her hot little mouth. A sudden, magical blast sent him staggering back and obliterated his erotic fantasy. His eyes snapped open and he caught the bright flash of green light that preceded the appearance of an object he hadn't seen since he was a stripling. It couldn't be.

Cailyn looked around in confusion, gaping when it arrived out of nowhere. It was easy for him to forget that such occurrences were completely foreign to her. He had to admit that this particular time he was as shocked as she was. "What is that?"

"That, Cailyn, is the Mystik Grimoire," he uttered numbly.

CHAPTER 16

Cailyn stared at the huge tome that had appeared out of thin air. Jace's touch was reverent and his expression awed. What had they said about the book? She recalled it documented magic spells and there was something about prophesies, too. It was bigger than an atlas, and ten times as thick. The aged-brown leather was exquisitely decorated on the front with numerous colored crystals.

She peered at the writing on the cover, but wasn't able to read the words. The script was in a foreign language and there were symbols she thought were runes. She watched his fingers linger on the large metal locking clasp on the side.

"So this is the magical book of the realm. Why do you think it appeared now? Do you know what you are supposed to do with it now?" A million questions were running through her mind, but it was clear that he had his own questions and was overwhelmed with some strong emotion.

"The last time I saw this book, my da was using it to

banish a lesser demon back to the Hell realm. It was the last time I saw my parents alive...I was taken prisoner later that night." The lost, agonized look on his face took her breath away, and had her heart aching for her sorcerer.

Wait, *her* sorcerer? At some point in the past few days she had come to think of Jace as her sorcerer. Yes, she acknowledged, she had some difficult decisions to make. And she was no closer to that decision, even if she was claiming Jace as hers. It killed her that regardless of what she decided, one great guy would have his heart crushed, and neither deserved it. What he'd said registered fully, and her eyes widened in shock.

"You were taken prisoner? When? And for how long? Why? What happened?" The questions tumbled out before she could stop them. This humble, giving man was no hardened criminal, and she had a bad feeling about what type of imprisonment he may have suffered.

"As I mentioned before, the grimoire is tied to my family line, and can only be accessed by one of my blood. It is said to be fickle, appearing and disappearing seemingly at random. My da believed it did so in times of great need, either for the realm, or our family. I don't know if it came to me for my sake or because the realm's greatest asset is under attack, threatening the future. I have no idea what I am supposed to do with it right now," he said, ignoring her questions about his imprisonment.

It was obvious he didn't want to discuss the topic, so she let it go for the time being and focused on what he had said. Only those of his blood could access it? Idly she wondered if, as his Fated Mate, she would be able to open the thing. That led to a zillion other thoughts she certainly didn't want to deal with right now.

"This sounds ominous. Sounds like we need to figure

out why this book reappeared, but I want to talk about your time in prison, soon." She grabbed his hand and laced their fingers together, needing to offer him acceptance. She recognized that the ache in her chest emanated from him. The portion of his soul that she carried connected them deeper than she'd realized. Whatever had happened to him, the scars ran deep, and she would have to peel away the layers before either one of them could be whole.

He finally met her gaze. His eyes flared before he settled his composure. She wondered what her soul was communicating to him. "I'm sorry, Cai. I didn't mean to upset you. I can understand your curiosity, and I promise I'll do my best to tell you about it, but right now I need to find Zander and call Evzen. This," he hefted the tome and waved it, "returning is huge for the realm, even if I don't fully understand why, yet."

She nodded and followed him out the door. "I appreciate that. Is there anything I can do to help? I can feel your tension rising again," she smiled sidelong at him, unable to stop the memory of what had caused his tension before the book appeared.

"You have a way of doing that to me." He blushed lightly, and his smile was uncertain and tentative. She was startled to see that he was shy. Surely, this man who was over seven hundred years old knew the effect he had on the ladies, and worked it to his advantage. In his time, he had probably been with thousands of women, so why so shy? The idea of him having been with so many had her jealousy rearing its ugly head. If she were honest, she hated to think of him being with even one other woman, which wasn't fair at all. She was struggling to choose between two men, and yet she hated the thought of him having had a history with someone else. She'd never been a particularly jealous person, and figured it had to be the influence of the mating compulsion Elsie had talked about.

"It's your fault, you know. I can't think straight when I'm around you. I become consumed by my desire to have you, and nothing else matters," she winked at him as they headed up the stairs.

He paused at the landing and tugged her into his arms. "*Shijéí,* you have no idea," he murmured against her lips. He hesitated long enough for her to wonder if he would kiss her before his lips came crashing down on hers.

He swept in and obliterated her ability to think or speak. His lips were silky as they slid across hers, teasing her into a fever pitch. Every thought she had flew out the window as he ravaged her mouth. The touch of his tongue against hers was electric. He wound his hands into her hair and held her close, leaving her breathless. She didn't care if she breathed again as long as he never stopped.

All too soon he broke the kiss. He was panting and sweating, and his lips were wet with their combined moisture. He was gorgeous, and she didn't think she'd ever get enough of him. Abruptly, he turned around and began bellowing into the spacious entry.

"Warriors, get your asses to the war room, now," he yelled with his head thrown back. Cailyn couldn't help but wonder why Jace was always putting space between them every time they became intimate. For her, the mating compulsion was impossible to deny, and his actions made her wonder how he was able to pull away from her. She wouldn't have been able to stop to save her life, but he stopped with seemingly no ill effects.

Jace interrupted her musings as he retrieved his cell phone to call Evzen. Cailyn recalled meeting the man at her sister's mating ceremony. His silver hair was at odds with his youthful appearance. There was no time to think about this further, because they needed to focus on the more important matter at hand.

As soon as Jace hung up, Zander came barreling down one side of the sweeping stairs. "What is it now?" Zander snarled as he buttoned his jeans.

Jace held up the object he had been toting. "It's important, Liege."

"Holy shite! It canna be. When did it return? What preceded its arrival?" Zander uttered as he rushed down the main stair case and took the tome from Jace.

Elsie rounded the top of the stairs pulling on her shirt. "What's going on? Is everything ok?" She reached Zander's side and stood on tip toe trying to see what he had. Cailyn noticed the glow in her sister's eyes. She had never seen her sister happier, better loved, or more content than she had since mating Zander. It was everything she had ever wanted for her baby sister. "What's that?" Elsie asked.

"'Tis the Mystik Grimoire," Zander explained as he resumed walking to the war room.

"Oh, that's the book that's been missing forever, right? I assume having this back is good for us."

"Aye, *a ghra*, this is a verra good thing. Have you called Evzen? I doona want him chewing my ass for not informing him of this right away," Zander asked as he turned his attention from Elsie to Jace.

"Yes, he will be here—" The doorbell interrupted Jace. "In fact, that's probably him now."

Cailyn heard Angus, their majordomo, answer the door right before Zander crossed to the intercom on the wall, pressing the button and hollering, "Every one of you arseholes, get doon here right now."

There was a ruckus as numerous heavy feet tread their

way down the hall and/or stairs. One by one the Dark Warriors come from various parts of the mansion. Cailyn noticed that Orlando wasn't among the group

The missing warrior's voice echoed through the intercom. "I'm going to need a few minutes and a bucket of ice please, Angus. Elsie's creole has created a fire down below," Orlando complained.

Zander jabbed the button, but couldn't hide his amusement. "Get your arse down here, now, you pussy. 'Tis important," he laughed.

"Fuck off," Orlando retorted.

Cailyn and her sister broke into laughter while Evzen and Killian came into the room and were still laughing when Orlando waddled into the room a minute later.

Evzen and Killian's reaction to the book was overshadowed by Orlando's complaints when he entered. The big bad warrior continued complaining as Angus brought him an ice pack to sit on.

"You are a baby if you can't handle a little spice, O," Elsie teased.

"I'm not a baby. You all wait until you take a shit and see who's crying then. And, what the hell kind of peppers were those? Ghost?"

"No, they were jalapenos, you big baby."

"I know Elsie's pepper of choice is critical, but can we focus on the issue at hand?" Gerrick rolled his eyes.

Evzen wasn't able to hide his excitement. With awe, he picked up the tome and touched the lock like Jace had done. "This is incredible. I can't believe it appeared to you after all this time. Do you recall the spell to open the lock?" Evzen asked Jace.

"I can't figure out why it reappeared now, but yeah, I remember the spell," Jace replied quickly. Cailyn wondered if he was thinking of his parents and his imprisonment again. The torment she'd seen before spread across on his face.

"Then by all means, open it. It did, after all, appear to you," Evzen retorted as he set the book back on the table.

Jace placed his palm directly over the lock and chanted words under his breath. She was unfamiliar with the language he spoke, but it worked its magic as a soft snick could be heard before the lock sprung open. Jace took two deep breaths and then cracked the book.

Cailyn gaped at the old parchment that held elegant script on its pages. The ink glowed and the pages were all hand-written, as well as embossed with Celtic symbols and runes similar to the cover.

Cailyn walked up and stood next to Jace who traced the letters reverently. She wondered if his father had written the passage on the page. "What language is that written in?" she asked.

Jace looked up and she noticed the sentiment in his amethyst eyes. "It's old Gaelic." This book meant a lot to him. She suspected it was having this connection to his father back in his possession.

She should have guessed it was Gaelic, given that the realm began in Scotland. "Can you read it?"

Jace chuckled and traced her cheek. She leaned into his touch and his palm cradled the side of her face. He inflamed her and made her feel alive. How could she give this up? On the other hand, how could she break John's heart? This was not the time to think about the decision before her, but she knew she needed to make one soon. It wasn't fair to any of them for her to be in limbo like she was, but she would address that later.

"Yes, I can read it. My da taught me when I was very

young, and there are some things one never forgets," Jace said.

"Why did it come to you, Jace? What were you doing before it appeared?" Evzen changed the subject of their conversation.

Cailyn turned beat-red, recalling what they had been doing. "I was leaving the medical room after we had discovered the tracking device in Jessie," Jace replied.

"Did it return to help us find Kadir's lair? 'Tis aboot time we win this war against the demons and their skirm," Zander commented.

"I have no idea if there is a spell that can locate the lair. But, I believe we can use this to bring down Kadir. The last time I saw it, my da was using it to banish lesser demons. It has been lost for so long that no one knows everything in it. Until we review the entire document we can't know for sure," Jace answered as he flipped pages and read. "This will take some time."

Zander ran a hand through his hair and turned to the majordomo who had been standing in the doorway. "Angus, would you bring us some coffee and lunch? And, bring my mate one of her energy drinks," Zander leaned down to kiss Elsie. The kiss heated, and had Cailyn looking with longing at Jace. She'd love for him to kiss her and claim her in front of his friends.

Finally, Zander broke away from her sister and turned to the group. "Och, we'd better get started."

"Do you think I can start a catalog of sorts to document what's in it?" Killian asked as he leaned against the table.

Jace tilted his head in a way Cailyn was fast coming to recognize he did when he seriously contemplated something. "My guess is it won't work since this is a creation of the Goddess, but it's worth a try."

Evzen read to Killian from a random page and as he went to save it, the document went blank. "Jace is correct. We can read from it, but we can't copy it. We will have to rely on memory as to what it contains," Evzen observed.

Angus and several other staff returned with trays laden with assorted sandwiches, pasta salads, fruit, and chips, as well as a variety of drinks. Cailyn's stomach growled when she saw the food, reminding her she'd worked up an appetite from Jace giving her the most intense pleasure she had ever known.

She grabbed a sandwich to divert her attention. Being in a room full of people with supernatural senses wasn't the place to linger on erotic memories. "Can you put the information in there about the cure to the spell placed on me?"

Jace pulled her back to his front and squeezed her in his arms. She felt his need to have her close, a reassurance that she was healthy and whole. He wrapped one arm around her waist and picked up one half of her sandwich and began eating it. Even the simple act of sharing a sandwich was sensual. "The Grimoire contains a vast amount of information from my forefathers. Any hex, enchantment, potion recipe, or prophecy up till it disappeared has been documented in these pages. If I had gotten the recipe for the potion from Marie Laveau, either Evzen or I could have written it down. I will record the Fae spell, as well as the fact that Marie has the antidote."

"It wouldn't hurt to include her location in the swamps and her network of Mambos," Evzen interjected. His thoughtful tone of voice had her turning to the Guild Master. A quick flex of her ability didn't provide her any clear information. She still wasn't able to pick up clear thoughts from the supernaturals.

"While you're looking, find that banishing spell, Evzen.

It wouldna be remiss of us to have it memorized. Just because we havena faced lesser demons in over a century, doesna mean we willna face them again. It could provide the turning point in a battle," Zander intoned as he sat in a chair and tugged Elsie into his lap.

Her sister was on her second energy drink. As Cailyn understood it, Elsie still struggled to remain awake during daylight hours, like all young vampires. Apparently vampires, as with all supernatural creatures, came into their powers when they sexually matured at twenty-five. That was also the time they passed their stripling years. For vampires, the transition to adulthood was a time when they were forced to sleep during daylight hours. Only the mature could remain awake easily during the day.

"Zander, you need to see this," Evzen exclaimed, waving him over. Zander stood with Elsie and walked around the table as Evzen continued talking, too eager to wait. "According to Jace's great-great-grandfather, Áedán, the Triskele Amulet can kill a demon. And, by that, I mean it actually destroys the demon's soul, ending its existence."

Zander placed his hands on the table and glanced at the open pages. "This is the break we need. Och, now we have to find that lair. To be able to destroy Lucifer's second in command would be a great victory indeed."

"'Tis a game-changer, let's take that to the next battle," Bhric bellowed, fist-pumping the air.

"Nay, it willna be at the next battle. From the premonition, we will be facing new enemies and I need more information before I take such risks, but I will relish the moment I can use the amulet to end Kadir's sorry existence forever." The determination in Zander's voice made Cailyn shiver. She'd hate to be their enemy.

CHAPTER 17

The fervor in the room heightened as ideas and suggestions were thrown out. It seemed as if everyone was talking at once, and Jace was struggling to concentrate on the matter at hand. They had discovered the most important information of the past seven centuries, and he wasn't able to think about any of it.

After the interlude with Cailyn in the medical room, he had been hard and aching, and was left wanting. It had only worsened and was consuming his every thought. The Goddess had certainly made it impossible to walk away from your Fated Mate. He could complete the mating and relieve the searing pain in his mate mark or suffer for eternity. All of that was overshadowed by the insistent compulsion for her body and soul. He had to get out of that room.

"I need a bit of time, Liege. Call if you need me," he told Zander, as he gripped Cailyn's hand and led her out of the room. He knew Zander would understand the turmoil he was experiencing from the mating compulsion, and wouldn't fault him.

"But," his mate sputtered as they reached the stairs.

When they stopped on the landing between the flights, he whirled her to face him. A startled noise escaped her, and her hands landed on his chest, her nails instinctively dug into his muscles.

He cut her off, "I couldn't concentrate on anything in there besides you. If I don't have you right now, I'll go out of my fucking mind."

The groan slipped past his lips when her hands began moving. He didn't think she was aware of what she was doing. She stepped into him and he felt her heat through her clothing. His hands bracketed her hips and he pulled her flush.

"I couldn't concentrate either. It's like I have lost control. I have never wanted or craved anyone like I do you." She stood on tiptoe and kissed him. Her lips brushed over his, teasing before her tongue coaxed his mouth open. She deepened the kiss, making her desire clear, and he was unable to stop this time.

His arms slid around her waist and he picked her up. She wrapped her legs around his waist and he carried her quickly up the stairs to his room, kissing her the entire time. Her lips coaxed, and commanded his to respond. She awakened more than his nausea. He had only ever experienced discomfort with females, and yet Cailyn breathed new life into him.

As he entered his rooms and kicked the door closed, he released her. She slid down his body rubbing against his thickening male flesh. He set her away from him. If they continued to touch they were going to have sex. He wanted that more than anything, and at the same time he never wanted to touch her again.

Already the nausea was building and he pushed back against it. He wanted his mate, and wanted nothing to mar the experience. He needed to gain more control before they continued. He saw the uncertainty race through her pretty hazel eyes when he pushed her away. He never wanted to see that look in his mate's eyes. Pulling her back into his arms, he kissed her deeply, not wanting her to doubt his desire.

She grabbed the bottom of his shirt, trying to pull it over his head. He stopped her progress. She looked up into his eyes. "I know we didn't talk before but you can't get me pregnant, I'm on birth control and I don't have any STDs. It's ok. We can do this. I want to do this," she murmured, shocking him, and succeeded in getting his shirt off. His chest muscles flexed under her scrutiny, causing him to harden further.

As she trailed kisses across his pectorals, he grasped for reason. He should tell her that her birth control wouldn't be effective for them. His mind reeled from the pleasure. He wanted this, but didn't want it to end like the last time. "We shouldn't do this. What about your fiancé?" He groaned as her tongue ran over his nipple, causing it to bead. His hands went to her hair and tangled in its length.

She paused and looked up at him. "I honestly don't know what I am going to do, but what I know is that if I don't have you right now, I will die. I need you, Jace."

At hearing her words, Jace's objections crumbled. He wanted her, too, and he wanted to relish in her and take it slow, unlike the first time. This could be the last time they were intimate. He was going to make this memorable for them both. Being given a Fated Mate was a blessing, and he intended to make her feel so much pleasure she'd never forget him.

Her shirt was gone in moments, and joined his on the floor. She had a sheer white bra on this time, and it made her skin even creamier. He leaned down and licked her nipple through the fabric. The pink bud flushed red and distended under his attention. He blew his hot breath against the wet fabric, causing her to shudder. He turned his attention to her other nipple as he reached back and unclasped the back. When he pulled back, she allowed the bra to slide off her arms to the floor.

"More," she murmured, pulling his head back to her nipples. Her breasts were large, overflowing in his hands. He squeezed the plump globes and plied her with his teeth, tongue and mouth. When he met her gaze, her pupils were dilated and she was panting. If he wasn't mistaken, his mate was close to orgasm. He loved that she was so responsive to his touch. With her, he didn't feel like a damaged male with no experience. He felt like a god of pleasure.

"I love your breasts. The Goddess blessed me with a perfect mate," he whispered. Emotion hit as the truth of his words sunk in, she was perfect, and he was blessed. Her soul flared in his chest, adding to the poignancy of the moment.

"I need you naked, now," she mumbled and pulled his head down for her kiss. As her lips worked him further under her spell, she fumbled at the button on his jeans. She gasped and pulled back.

Her fingers had grazed the head of his cock that had risen above the waist of his pants. She unfastened the button and lowered the zipper. Her hands paused and she met his gaze. He nodded to let her know he was with her. She pushed the fabric to his knees and looked her fill.

"You are killing me, Cai."

"Mmmm," she smiled sensually. The female had no idea the affect she had on him. His cock pulsed, and more precum beaded the slit. It was like a mini-orgasm, and he loved the new sensation. "Paybacks are a bitch, Jace." Her little finger ran along his boxer shorts and then, they too, were at his knees. He watched her as she continued to stare at him.

"Your eyes are like a hot brand," he groaned.

"I knew you were bigger than any other man I had been with, but you are long and thick and gorgeous," she murmured, finally gripping the shaft. "If we hadn't already been together, I'd be afraid you wouldn't fit. As it is, I know the pleasure to be found with you, and can't wait."

He forcibly removed her hand from his cock. If she continued, there would be no slow exploration. "I prepared you for me last time and need to do that again. This time, I plan on taking my time, savoring every inch of your skin."

He kicked off his pants and boxers and set about divesting her of the rest of her clothing. As he skimmed his hands down her legs, his lips followed, tasting as he went. He picked her up and carried her to his bed, claiming her lips as they went.

He paused by the side of the bed and tilted her head to deepen the kiss. She wiggled out of his arms and his hands went to her hips. He tightened his hold and pulled her against his body. His erection fit perfectly against her soft abdomen. He laid her back on the bed, never releasing her lips.

He kissed his way across her cheek and down her neck. He paid special attention to her pulse point and trailed his tongue down to her full breasts. His hands left her hips and rose to stroke and tweak her peaks. His mouth enveloped one nipple while his finger plied the other, all the while, he fought back the nausea. He loved the feel of her skin beneath his hands and mouth, yet something dark rose and fought to steal his attention from his mate. He refused to allow that to happen. Broken male or not, he was giving this experience all he had.

"That feels amazing. I could come from that alone. My breasts have never been so sensitive." Her hands slid down his back. He felt her fingers working his braid free. He never left it free, but loved the feel of her hands in his hair.

"I have wanted to run my hands through your hair from the moment I saw you. It's so silky and long. Oh...god yes, don't stop...I'm so close."

He looked up into her half-lidded gaze and knew his eyes were glowing from his lust. Her hips left the bed and began thrusting against him, seeking release. "Easy, I'm only getting started, *Shijéí.*"

∼

WAS THE MAN CRAZY? She was an inferno, ready to beg him to fuck her but he seemed intent on torturing her. He began to lick and kiss his way down her ribs and abdomen. She shivered at the knowledge that he was going to go down on her again. She had never been fond of oral sex, and it wasn't until Jace that she realized it was because any man who had performed it on her was terrible at it. And, she had to admit, that included John. Her thoughts scrambled as his lips trailed over her moist feminine flesh.

She wanted to curse as his hot little lips passed over her labia but didn't touch on her needy bundle of nerves. His long fingers reached up and tweaked her nipples while he blazed a trail down one leg and up the other. She was close to climax and he kept pulling back, heightening her pleasure, so much so, that she wanted to scream.

"Your scent is driving me crazy. I have to taste you. I'm going to lap up your cream as you cum on my face," he growled. The vibration of his voice had arousal flooding her folds and seeping down her thighs. This man set her on fire.

She was beyond words, only able to whine when his talented fingers left her breasts. She stopped breathing when they parted her intimate flesh, revealing her pulsing clit. Hot breath fanned over the bundle and she almost climaxed. His glowing purple gaze narrowed and held hers for several frantic heartbeats. It was the hottest moment she had ever experienced, and her pussy wept even more.

Holding her eyes, his tongue licked from her vagina to her clit in one long stroke, and her orgasm struck so powerfully she nearly passed out from pleasure. She cried out his name and pulsed as he thrust his tongue into her opening. She couldn't think as Jace feasted on her.

When his soul brushed against her skin, it sent her into the heavens again. Her eyes rolled back in her head and she saw stars. Moments later, she floated back to her body and gripped his hair. He refused to stop licking her clit. She didn't think she could take anymore, but his fingers entered her tight depths and her back bowed.

That quick, he had her passions flared. He played her body like a well-tuned instrument. It was as if he knew exactly what she needed and what would give her the most pleasure. Which was not surprising, since she was made for him, and him for her. She needed him inside her and pulled his hair until he finally lifted his head. His lips were swollen, making them fuller and more kissable. They gleamed with her arousal, turning her on even more.

She pulled him up her body and kissed him fiercely. She tasted herself on his lips and it heightened her excitement. She reached down and grabbed his rampant cock. She ran it through her folds, eliciting moans from them both. His shaft jerked in her hand. "We both need your cock inside me, now," she murmured against his lips.

JACE GAZED into hot hazel depths and knew he was falling in love with his mate. He could still hear the echoes of her screams of pleasure. His muscles vibrated with the tension to claim his mate fully and initiate the mating bond. He had never enjoyed anything more than making Cailyn climax. He reared up to kneel on the bed between her spread thighs. Her glistening feminine flesh called to him.

He waged a battle between desire and revulsion. There was an entity in his head that was fighting the intimacy. He refused to allow it to ruin his time with this female. This may be all he ever had of her, and he planned to enjoy every minute.

He had never felt this ache, and at the moment, he needed to bury himself in this female and hold her pinned to his bed more than he needed to live. Divergent energies flared and clashed, light versus dark, and he swallowed back the bile, gripping his cock. Nothing was stopping this.

He leaned forward, covering her luscious body, resting on his elbows. He pressed his lips against hers and relished the waves of electricity that raced through his body as he let his cock push against her lower flesh. Eager to join their bodies, his erection pulsed and a mini-orgasm hit him, leaving his pre-cum on her clit.

He leaned to one elbow and ran his palm down her side, glorying in her curves. He wanted to stoke her passions higher. He wanted her panting, begging for his possession. His thumb stopped at her nipple and he paid homage while he kept the moist warm pressure of their joined mouths. A back and forth motion started in his hips that rubbed his long cock through her feminine tenderness.

"Do you like that Cailyn?"

"You know I do. Stop teasing me, I need you Jace," she pleaded.

Jace licked his way to her ear and bit her delicate lobe before kissing her mate mark. Insatiable lust almost robbed him of his seed when his tongue touched his mark on her. "What do you want, baby? Tell me."

Her body jolted as if hit by electricity and she groaned. "I want you, now."

"You're gonna need to be more specific than that. Do you want me to lick you?" He continued the back and forth motion of his hips and let more of his weight rest there, creating more friction between their bodies.

"Not...fair. Fuck me, now." She tilted her hips trying to align her core with his shaft.

"Your wish, my command, *Shijéí.*"

He reared up and looked down their sweat-slicked torsos. The sight of his soft sensitive crown running through her glistening flesh and over her clit had the pressure in his shaft building. He was addicted to the new sensation of filling with seed. Her head was thrashing on her pillow as she begged him to take her. He loved her erotic agony. He shifted back and felt as the tip of his cock was hugged in her tightness.

"Fuck, you are so tight and wet. Goddess, baby I don't know if I can stay in control. I don't want to hurt you." He focused on the pleasure and not his churning gut.

Cailyn cupped his cheek and forced him to meet her gaze. He felt her love and care all the way to his toes. "You would never hurt me. I trust you. Besides, I'm tougher than you think, and I hurt so badly right now."

"I lo..." he inhaled and clenched his jaw. He had almost told her he loved her. He didn't love her, did he? "I love the way you feel. I had never ejaculated before we made love yesterday and I can't wait to do that again." He thrust into her, ignoring the sharp pain in his mate mark.

"What? You can't have been a virgin for so long," she exclaimed with a lust-glazed expression. He altered his angle, eliciting a moan.

"No, I wasn't a virgin per-se, but sorcerers do not ejaculate before having sex with our Fated Mates for the first time," he explained, loving the way she struggled to follow as he tortured her with the head of his cock.

"What?" she gasped.

"We can orgasm, but there is no ejaculation until we meet our Fated Mates. And, I have never felt pleasure so intense or wonderful until I met you. It is truly amazing. Let me show you."

He closed his eyes and worked more of his shaft into her core, stopping their conversation. She wiggled, trying to help ease his way. Despite the fact that he had taken her before, he worried about hurting her. He pinched and tweaked her nipple and her arousal gushed around his shaft. His hips moved slowly in and out, taking more of him deeper each time. He laved her breasts, making her so wet that he slid to the hilt within a smooth dream of movement.

Nausea rose, and he kept his movements slow while he once again tamped the beast down. He didn't understand the power this had over him. Being connected like this to Cailyn felt right, perfect. He was where he was always meant to be.

Slowly, his pace increased and he reveled in the tight slide into and out of her sheath. "Goddess, you are heaven."

"Harder, Jace. Faster," she begged.

At that moment, his control snapped and he began a hard quick speed that no human male was capable of. He would burn all thoughts of her fiancé from her mind. He thrust into her and tunneled his fingers past her beautifully trimmed curls and found her clit. He pinched the bundle of nerves and she came, screaming his name out loud.

Her pussy squeezed him so tightly that he was helpless but to join her, despite his intentions to make her come several more times first. He thrust balls deep and stilled as his seed burst into her womb. He shouted as he was taken to the stars while his mate's body milked every last drop from him.

Unfortunately, the beast refused to allow him to bask in the afterglow as the nausea broke past his control. Bile surged into his mouth as his cock spurted the last of his seed. He was pulling out of his mate and off the bed faster than she could blink. As he ran into the bathroom, he heard the hurt and confusion in her voice as she called out to him.

"Jace? What's wrong? What did I do?" He shut the door before the last word left her lips.

CHAPTER 18

Cailyn's head was spinning. For the second time in as many days, she'd had mind-blowing sex that had ended abruptly. She'd had the biggest orgasm of her life after Jace worshipped her body lovingly, only to run off as if she disgusted him.

A sound that echoed from the bathroom had her blood running cold. She craned her neck and heard gagging. Was he vomiting? The thought that he wasn't experiencing the same level of ecstasy as her brought all her insecurities and doubts to the forefront. Sure, she was disappointed in herself for having sex with Jace before she had made her decisions about him or John, but that didn't mean she hadn't enjoyed every second of being with him. She just wished her willpower was stronger where Jace was concerned.

It was becoming clear to her that this sorcerer was her kryptonite, and this situation wasn't going to remedy itself easily. Her love for John was still present, but her love for Jace was growing every day. He fascinated her with his quick mind and compassionate heart. He handled her as if she were a china doll that might break, yet made love to her with a fierce passion.

It didn't hurt that he was the sexiest man she'd ever known, with his amethyst eyes, bronze skin, and long, black hair. He had eight-pack abs, but then every inch of his body was sleek and muscular, elucidating his warrior status. Nothing could measure up to Jace's six-foot-something-hard-body. Yeah, Jace was in a league all his own.

It wasn't all superficial, however. Everything she learned about him from his heritage to his passion for medicine was appealing. She longed to learn more about both his Native American background, as well as his Celtic roots. A violent coughing and hacking brought her attention back to the bathroom door. Insecurities be damned, concern had her feet moving to the bathroom.

Cailyn raised her fist to the closed door and paused. This was the second time she had been with him, and he was in the bathroom getting sick. As she stood outside the door, it was clear that he was indeed in that bathroom losing the contents of his stomach. That rejection hurt more than she would have imagined. Clearly, he was repulsed by what he had done with her, and no doubt regretted it.

It would crush her if she saw the revulsion in his eyes, so she dropped her hand and scrambled into the living room of his suite where her clothes lay in a heap. The sight was a dismal reminder that the man who had given her the most satisfying moments of her life couldn't stomach what he had done with her.

Tears welled in her eyes and she wanted to crumple in a heap on the floor. Her heart was torn in two. She had never felt closer to another being than she had with Jace while they were making love. She had to amend her thinking on that. For her they had made love, but obviously for Jace, it was nothing more than sex.

Hating how naïve she'd been, she ran into the kitchen and grabbed a towel. She was furiously scrubbing away the evidence of her shame when a warm hand settled on her shoulder. Her head dropped to her chest and she wanted to rip his soul from her chest as pain constricted and his soul surged towards him. How could things be so wrong when they were Fated Mates? Maybe he was right. Maybe their Goddess had this one wrong.

"Cailyn? What's wrong?" His voice made her shiver. How did he still have so much power over her? She scolded her traitorous body for wanting him again.

"Cailyn, honey, look at me." Jace placed one strong finger under her chin and tried to coax her head up as he turned her body to face him. She refused to look at him, not wanting him to see her pain.

She added persistent to his list of characteristics when he wouldn't be denied and she closed her eyes as he forced her face up. "Open your eyes and look at me now, *Shijéí*." Like a puppet, her eyes obeyed. He gasped and his eyes widened in shock and dismay. That was not the reaction she expected.

"Oh Goddess, did I hurt you? Was I too rough? What is it? Tell me, please." Numerous emotions flickered through his amethyst depths but concern for her rang strongest.

She took a deep breath and gathered her courage, letting her anger take over. She wasn't going to allow him to take the coward's way out and run. He lived with her sister, and she would have on-going contact with him, so she'd better set him straight now.

"Why did you fuck me again if I disgust you? I don't want a pity fuck from you. And, I sure as hell didn't mean to beg you so pathetically for your oh-so-magnificent dick! Surely, a man as sexy and intelligent as you can get a woman who doesn't make him throw up," she spat.

His eyes widened further, if possible. This time she couldn't decipher what he was feeling. "Is that what you think? Goddess, I've fucked this all up. You couldn't be more wrong. You are perfect in every way."

She snorted with derision. "You are good, I'll give you that. You had me going there for a while. I believed you found me attractive and actually wanted me. I should've known better, given that you acted the same with that skank I saw you with at Confetti. I'm glad I didn't claw her eyes out like I wanted. I am such an idiot!"

Jace reached out and stopped her as she tried to brush past him. "Let me go," she demanded.

"No, not until you listen to me," he retorted as he pulled her flush against him. She refused to shudder in pleasure at feeling his flesh against her own. It had felt like she had found home when they joined. How wrong she was. She couldn't trust her body or her instincts where this man was concerned. A sob escaped, but she choked back her tears, not wanting to give him any more power over her.

"Shh, let me explain." He was the one pleading now. The vulnerable, frightened look in his eyes had her pausing to listen to what he had to say, against her better judgment. Suddenly, she felt more naked than ever. He rubbed her back in soothing circles for long moments, and of course, her traitorous body responded. A hard length prodded her stomach, telling her he wasn't entirely revolted by her. It was the reminder she needed. The mating compulsion really did affect them both equally. She reached up and touched the mate mark on her neck, missing the way it sizzled with heat when Jace touched it.

"As much as I want to take you back to my bed and pay proper homage to your body, we need to talk." She allowed him to grasp her hand and lead her to the leather sofa in the living room.

She sat on the buttery soft cushions and wrapped her arms around her waist. Jace grabbed a blanket and draped it around her shoulders and sat next to her. He ignored her recoil and pulled her into his arms anyways. She was glad to be covered, minimizing any contact of their skin. She couldn't control herself when they touched.

"I am so sorry for hurting you. Please stop shaking, it's killing me," he whispered into her hair.

She hadn't realized she was shaking. She took several deep breaths, willing herself to calm. "I don't want your apology," she croaked past the tears.

He pulled away and captured her gaze for several moments before turning away. She gave him time to gather his thoughts. She was about to give up and leave when he broke the silence.

"I had hoped to keep this hidden from you." He lifted his head and the pain and shame she saw floored her. That was not what she expected to see. This warrior carried deep wounds. "I was kidnapped and held prisoner over seven hundred years ago." He sat forward and balanced his arms on his knees.

She hated to pry, but now that he had opened that door, she had to know. "What happened?"

His head dropped forward and he stared blankly at the floor, lost in his painful past. "An older sorceress, named Lady Angelica wanted the power my family wielded, and meant to garner control over it when she took me. She was beautiful, and I was an inexperienced youth. One moment, she was seducing me in a realm tavern, and the stupid, randy lad that I was didn't see her for what she truly was until I woke up chained to a stone slab."

She ignored the jealous flare she felt when he mentioned this Angelica, whom she had heard in his thoughts, was beautiful. Her gut churned at what he must have experienced. "What did she want? What did she do to you?"

He heaved a heavy sigh that carried the weight of the world. "She wanted the power of the Mystik Grimoire. As you know, it holds many spells and incantations and a person of evil intent could use them to garner power over others. Only those of incorruptible blood, as my father used to say, are allowed to access and utilize the book. That was why she needed me. As for what she did to me, she..." he trailed off, gulping and she saw sweat bead on his brow. His skin lost some of its radiant glow, as well.

She ran her hand over his back and twined the fingers of her other hand through his. He squeezed, as if needing her support. "At first she used physical punishments to try and gain my compliance. When that didn't work, she resorted to using other methods. I had never experienced the pleasure of a woman's body, and she thought it would be easy to use sexual means to influence me, but my body refused to respond to her. She resorted to spells and creams and incense to incite a reaction that I didn't feel. My body may have hardened but I never orgasmed with her, or any other female for that matter." He stopped and a shudder rolled through his body.

He broke her heart with his confession, and it made her fall for him that much more. She was losing her heart to this sexy sorcerer, and once that happened, there would be no turning back.

"After several decades of the torture, I started praying to

the Goddess for the book. I wanted her abuse to end, and knew it never would stop because I couldn't give her what she wanted. I was helpless to the magically reinforced chains...I hated what she did to me," he whispered.

Through her bond to him, she sensed his self-loathing and perceived weakness. That this warrior felt like he should have been able to do something to break free was astonishing. He was barely more than a child, and his powers had been stripped.

That he had trusted her with his pain and suffering humbled her. She had seen that he held a piece of himself back from those around him, and now knew what it was. She understood the shame he felt, even if he was mistaken.

"Oh, Jace, you are the bravest man I have ever met," she crooned. Tears were streaming down her face as she suffered for him. "I wish I could have stopped her. And I understand why you reacted the way you did. You must relive what she did to you every time."

Startled eyes met hers. "That's not it at all. I love sex with you. In fact, I'd venture to say I'm addicted to you. The only way I can explain what happens is that I feel like I am battling a dark beast who always wins, and if I become aroused, I become violently ill. I have never been able to move beyond a kiss with a female. You are the only female to ever bring me such pleasure." He gently brushed her tears away.

Cailyn was shocked that this passionate guy had never been able to experience real pleasure. It sickened her to think that his only experience with sex was of being helpless and violated by someone with evil intentions. She was convinced there was more at work. "So, you're under a spell then?"

"No, it's not a spell. I would have felt if someone hexed me, and the foreign magic would stand out to me."

She gazed into his watery eyes, amazed that such a courageous man existed. Suspicion nagged at her. If she were some crazed lunatic, she wouldn't allow her source to simply walk away. She'd want a way to hopefully gain power over him at some later date. "Even if you were being tortured and didn't fully understand your own powers?"

Jace stood suddenly and crossed to the piles of clothes. "No, that's not possible. I would know," he insisted, agitation clear in his movements. He yanked on his clothing and paced the room restlessly. She wanted to reach out to him but sensed he wouldn't welcome her touch. "I need some space. I'll be back. Please don't leave the compound again."

Mouth hanging open, she watched for the third time as this man walked away from her. She worried about the flash of devastation she saw before he disappeared around the corner.

∽

JACE PACED the deserted beach on the Puget Sound, Cailyn's words replaying in his mind. Pure, beautiful, kind, caring Cailyn. For the past hour, he had been searching his soul for a magical taint. The problem was, that Cailyn's words rang true, he wasn't sure if he would recognize if Lady Angelica had done something.

He was amazed at how intelligent his mate was. She was beyond anything he ever expected. It was entirely possible that Angelica, being a sorceress of immense power, could have unknowingly placed a spell on him. It burned his ass to think of it, but he had been so young and inexperienced.

She had crushed him to the lowest he'd ever been, and

he was ashamed to admit that if he hadn't been chained, he'd have killed himself long before Zander had rescued him. He hadn't thought of anything beyond escaping his torment. Reliving the torture, searching for something he may have missed, made his skin crawl all over.

The Goddess had blessed him with his Fated Mate, and he wanted to win her affections and claim her as his. He wanted desperately to get past the years of his shame and what had happened, rather than feeling dirty and used. He wanted more than anything to be the male she needed, but didn't know how to get past his unworthiness.

A sparkle caught his vision and he turned to see none other than his captor, in the flesh. Fear and dread consumed him. He wanted to run and disappear, but was cemented to the sand. This female had captured and tortured him, and the sight of her made him feel vulnerable all over again. He reminded himself that this time he wasn't without powers of his own.

"Jace, my love. How have you been?" She purred as she sauntered to his side, flanked by her goonies. Bile rose for an altogether different and valid reason.

For a brief moment he was transported back in time, and he was once again that helpless lad. He felt a pull to this vile creature, but had to fight it. Thoughts of Cailyn grounded him and gave him confidence. "You are brave to approach me. I'm not that weak, pliable youth anymore," he ground out through gritted teeth, refusing let her see him as weak.

She ran red fingernails across his chest, making him shudder. Cailyn's soul began clamoring and clawing to fight against Lady Angelica. "You are mine, Jace. Don't fight it. Open up, allow me in," she tried to coax.

He felt a foreign vibration that he would have missed if

not for his mate's suspicion. The problem was, he didn't understand what it was, or how to fight it. "I'm not yours. I belong to my mate, and she, thankfully, is nothing like you."

Surprise and anger flared and she dug her fingernails into his flesh. He missed her muttered words but felt her power enter his being. She tried to distract him as it fought for purchase. "Nonsense, you are mine. Your heart knows it is so."

"No, I'm not. What do you want?" Sweat beaded his brow as he fought with all his strength and called his staff to him. He was going to be prepared for whatever this female may try. He allowed her to feel a fraction of his power.

A smile spread across her face and her nails eased. "I know the Grimoire is back. I felt its magic return. All of sorcerer kind did. This time, the power will be ours to share, and you are going to call it for me. Let's go, I have a boat waiting to take us to my home, where you will do as I ask."

Panic threatened, but that was not going to happen. She began walking away and his feet took a few tentative steps. He chanted spells to immobilize his feet to no avail. As he uttered a spell of protection around himself, Cailyn's soul surged and added strength to his incantation, allowing it to fall into place. "Not this time, Angelica."

Shocked, she whirled and glared at him. She threw several spells at him, which he was able to deflect. "I will win this, Jace. I made you who you are. Your body refuses to accept any but me."

"My mate has changed me and I will find a way to beat you." The truth of his words added strength. Cailyn gave him strength and courage to fight this. He was made for her, and she was made for him. He would find a way for them to be together.

"Watch out for your little mate. She is mortal, after all," Angelica cackled.

Jace shouted his rage and withdrew one of his *sgian dubhs* from his boot. No one threatened his mate. As he readied to throw it into her black heart, she vanished in a puff of black smoke.

CHAPTER 19

Cailyn laid her head back on the lime-green float as her sister and Jessie talked with Breslin. After Jace left, she had been more confused than ever. She felt as if she had lost control. Not once, but twice she was caught up in an erotic storm that wouldn't be denied.

She'd had sex with Jace, despite her continuing turmoil. If she were being completely honest with herself, she was closer to that decision than she let on. There was a driving force to Jace that she was helpless to deny, and it had ridden her constantly from the moment she had first seen him. Every second she spent with Jace, she fell a little more in love with him, with their connection deepening.

The heaviness in her heart gave her one of the answers she needed. She had to let John go, regardless of the outcome with Jace. It wasn't fair to John to give him false hope, especially since she knew things could never be the same between them after she'd had a taste of Jace. She wanted to grab Jessie and go tell John, but she remembered the folly in her previous impetuous actions.

She wasn't a stupid woman, and wouldn't take such risk

again. It was clear that without the direct protection of the Dark Warriors, the archdemons and their minions had the power to reach her. The fact that the skirm were being instructed to kidnap women was frightening enough on its own.

She resolved to try and communicate by phone, but had been unsuccessful in reaching John either at his hotel or on his cell. He hadn't checked out of the hotel, so she knew he was still in town. Apparently he was angry with her, not that she blamed him. He was a kind, caring man who deserved better. She sighed. She did love him, but this was for the best.

There was no denying her connection to Jace. When they were making love for the first time, she felt something click into place, and that bond had only strengthened the second time. The piece of his soul she carried had become more active every moment they were together.

Recalling the look on his face when he told her about what he suffered broke her heart. He had experienced unbearable torture and sexual abuse that would have killed anyone else. She saw that he had come out of it with a beauty and strength that he couldn't see. He was loyal to his friends and gave of himself tirelessly. He approached challenges with confidence and determination, despite the defeat he carried in his heart. But he saw none of it.

She wanted to help him work through his pain, and discover what was causing his reaction to arousal. Of one thing she was certain, there was something prohibiting him from being intimate with any woman, and it wasn't because he had been abused.

The picture of tiny yellow flip-flops waving in her face brought her out of her brooding. Elsie drug her to the pool for some fun after she had left Jace's room and was holding out a cup decorated with flip-flops.

"Here, this will take your mind off things. You are looking far too serious on that float, Cai."

She laughed at her sister's teasing attempt to lighten the mood and grabbed the drink. "What is it?"

Elsie propped her hand on her hip and cocked her head to the side. "A Monsterita, of course. There is nothing better."

Jessie swam to their side and joined the conversation. "The one thing I miss the most, aside from being able to talk and not cut my lip, is not being able to get shit-faced. I barely manage a buzz now. Lord knows, I have many reasons to want to escape reality, but am I allowed to? No."

Cailyn had been so caught up in her own drama that she had forgotten about her best friend, even though she had vowed to help adjust to her new life. She was turning out to be a crappy friend. She rolled off the float and gathered Jessie into her arms. "I'm sorry, Jess. I have been so caught up in my own issues that I've forgotten about you. I'd give anything to get drunk with you right now, if it's any consolation."

"Thank you. So what has you drinking?" Jessie asked, pulling away.

"I don't want to talk about that. What have the scientists said?" Cailyn asked as she watched her friend drain the huge cup in record time.

Jessie smiled at her. "After donating gallons of blood for testing and doing every scan ever invented, and then some, they've determined that the changes to my blood, specifically my DNA, are slowing and near completion. Oh, and it looks like I will be able to continue to eat food. I can't say how happy I am to still enjoy my burgers and fries rather than living off of blood alone."

Cailyn was curious how her friend liked blood. Personally, the thought made her sick to her stomach. "But, you do have to drink blood, right? How is it? Do you like the taste? Elsie insists it's wonderful, but she's only sucked on Zander's neck, so her opinion doesn't count." She laughed as Elsie shoved her. As she flew across the pool and went under, she got a first-hand demonstration of how strong her sister had become. It was a reminder that she was surrounded by super-fast, super-strong beings. She came up sputtering and laughter filled the cavernous room.

"Sorry, sis. I forget my own strength," Elsie apologized sheepishly.

"I bet it's easy to forget when you were a human not too long ago," Jessie observed. "Blood is like drinking milk. I enjoy the taste and am relieved that I'm not driven by a bloodlust that causes me to kill people. I couldn't live like that. I do have to have human blood, though. Supernatural blood makes me queasy."

"I remember seeing the bloodlust when that skirm attacked me. I saw my death in his eyes. That would be awful to try and live with," Elsie shared.

"Yeah, I'll just be happy when my head stops spinning and things settle down. I've had the world's worst migraine for days now," Jessie replied, swimming to the side of the pool.

"Have the scientists been able to do anything about it?" Cailyn asked, getting back on the float.

Jessie put her empty cup down. "Orlando, I need another drink," Jessie called out before she turned back to Cailyn. "No, I'm not immune to everything, only human diseases. I have been feeling this immense pressure in my head that at first I thought was because of the changes in my vision. Apparently, it is the demon trying to gain control over my mind. As if," her friend snorted and handed her cup over to Orlando for refill. "Anyway, he's not able to control or influence me. They aren't sure why, but have theories about my female hormones or something."

Breslin rose from her lounge chair and joined them. "It has nothing to do with hormones. Females are stronger and smarter than males, no matter the species." Orlando returned, followed by Angus carrying a tray with four cups. "My point is proven," Breslin said as she pointed to Orlando and they all burst into laughter.

"Now I understand why you keep rebuffing me. Your eyes aren't working properly. We need to fix that, sweet cakes," Rhys said as he swam up behind Jessie and wrapped his arms around her exposed middle. Jessie wiggled out of his grasp and suddenly grabbed her top, gasping.

"Fucking Rhys," Jessie shrieked. Cailyn noticed one end of the string in Rhys' hand and realized he had to have used his telekinetic power to untie Jessie's suit. She couldn't help but laugh.

"Don't be shy, gorgeous. I only want to play a little," Rhys wheedled.

"Not in a million years, playboy," Jessie mumbled and rolled her eyes, but accepted his attentions with good humor. Cailyn was relieved to see that the most notorious man-whore of the compound didn't offend Jessie. Her friend didn't take promiscuity lightly, and Rhys didn't know the meaning of monogamy, which wasn't surprising given that he was a human-sex-demon-hybrid who needed constant sex to keep his beast at bay.

"You'll come to me eventually, sweet. Until then..." Rhys swam away on his back, giving a view of his large erection.

Cailyn was convinced the guy walked around with a constant hard-on.

Elsie ignored the byplay completely and brought the conversation back around. "What's wrong with your eyesight?"

"Ever since I woke up I have been seeing things in infrared, like I'm looking through heat vision goggles or something. The Dark Warriors are brighter than everyone else. No one can explain it, but it's not the cause of the pressure. As I learned to turn off the infrared, the pressure didn't dissipate, and that's when I noticed compulsions. Thankfully, they have always been elusive and easily ignored, and are reducing in number and strength every day."

"I hate that your life is like this now. I feel like I ruined your life," Cailyn voiced to her friend.

"You didn't ruin my life, it was the damned demon. All that matters is that I'm alive and have a future ahead of me. It will be a very long future, but a future, nonetheless. We both could have died that night. The one thing I am grateful for is that the scientists have reassured me that I am still fertile, unlike my male counterparts. So, our babies can still grow up together like we always talked about."

Cailyn laughed, recalling the many conversations they'd had as teenagers about that topic. They'd had many theories about whom they'd end up with, and who the father of their babies would be. She'd always wanted a guy with jet black hair and dark, smoldering eyes, which was funny because she'd never dated anyone with those features. All of her boyfriends had some shade of blonde hair and blue eyes. Knowing that she was Jace's Fated Mate made her wonder how much their Goddess had influenced her throughout her life. It seemed too much of a coincidence.

She considered what her life would be like. Her sister

and best friend were immortal, and could potentially live centuries, while she would grow old and die if she stayed with John. The thought didn't sit well with her. She didn't know if she would be able to keep Jessie and Elsie in her life under those circumstances. On the other hand, if she mated Jace, she could be immortal too, and have magical babies with the man she loved, and have her sister and best friend for eternity. A frightening thought occurred to her. "What will your babies be, I wonder?" she asked Jessie.

"Unfortunately, no one knows. But, I fervently hope they aren't born with fangs, cause I won't be breast feeding otherwise," Jessie observed. The sober expression told her that her friend was worried about the genes she would be passing on to any children she may have.

"Yikes, I hadn't thought of that. Are vampire babies born with fangs, Bre? If so, I may need to rethink nursing, too. I love my mate's fangs in me but..." Elsie trailed off as she met Zander's heated gaze where he sat talking to Santiago and Gerrick on the lounge chairs.

"Nay, *bairns* are no' born with fangs. Like all striplings, they get their fangs when they get their teeth. Their parents provide the small amount of blood they will need until the come into their powers when they reach maturity," Breslin answered. Cailyn remembered what her sister had told her about all supernatural children being called striplings until they reached maturity at roughly the age of twenty-five. Breslin had been the one exception they knew of in the realm when she came into her power at the age of three.

"Are you guys already trying to have a baby?" Cailyn asked her sister not sure why the idea shocked her.

"Not intentionally, no. With supernaturals, the conception rate is naturally low, and there is no contraception that works on us. So it's all left up to the Goddess. And, you should know birth control doesn't work for you with Jace."

"What? How in the hell is that possible?" Cailyn managed after several shocked moments. She hadn't used protection with Jace, but then, if her sister was right, there would have been no point anyway. Elsie said conception was rare, there was no way she was pregnant, and no reason to panic.

"Divine intervention," Jace answered as he slowly stepped out of the shadows.

Her head swiveled and she was locked with glowing amethyst orbs. She knew what that meant, that he wanted her. The mere thought that this perfect male specimen wanted her made her blood boil, and had heat building between her thighs. An epiphany struck her. Jace had been made for her and carried part of her soul. How could she deny what was so clearly between them? But, how could she be with him when another man held space in her heart?

∽

"What do you mean? How can your Goddess make the pill I take useless?"

Jace couldn't help but smile at his mate's confusion. The sight of her made him yearn to complete the mating. Everything about her was alluring; in fact, his heart had yet to settle into a normal rhythm. When he had entered the house looking for her, he feared that she had left the house again. The sound of laughter and voices had taken him to the pool.

The sight of her in a skimpy black bikini had him rock hard in an instant. Her plush globes were overflowing out of the top, and if she shifted just right she would expose herself. She was the sexiest female ever born, and he wanted to take her to his room and pull the triangles away from her flesh so he could feast on her breasts again. His instinct was clamoring for him to claim her and finally complete the mating. She was an addiction he would never overcome, and didn't want to.

His encounter with Angelica had reinforced the fact that he wanted Cailyn, and he was resolved to try and find a way to be the mate she deserved. Cailyn had been right. There must be a spell forcing him to reject all intimacy, and he was determined to discover what had happened to him, and reverse it. Once that happened, he had every intention of claiming her fully. Cailyn was his mate, and he refused to live without her. He may not be an ideal mate right now, but he had centuries to become the male she needed and deserved.

A smile curved his lips. The first real smile he had felt to his soul since he was a stripling living at home with the love of his parents. "The Goddess' power has no limits. Never forget, she created most creatures of the Tehrex Realm, and has ways of ensuring we continue." He kicked off his shoes and stripped off his shirt.

He enjoyed the way her eyes flared and pupils dilated as his chest was revealed. His mate wanted him as desperately as he wanted her.

"Who is this Goddess? What is her role in your world? Am I supposed to worship her too?" Jessie piped in before his mate could gather her wits.

Zander answered Jessie while Jace shed his pants and jumped into the pool in his black boxer briefs. He made his way to Cailyn's side and wrapped his arms around her.

"The Goddess Morrigan is our creator," Zander explained, "meaning, she created most of the creatures that make up the Tehrex Realm. Her role is complicated, but the most important aspects are that she acts through her subjects to protect weaker beings from evil, and blesses those she deems worthy with their Fated Mate. And, no, you do not have to worship her, but I think you will find that she had a hand in your creation. I believe it is why you are so different from your male counterpart."

"Where have you been for the past three hours? And, who have you been with?" Cailyn asked Jace, ignoring Zander. He smiled at how possessive his mate was of him already. It had clearly been impossible for her to hold her curiosity in any longer.

Jace turned her in his embrace so she was facing him fully. The spark of hurt coupled with anger in her eyes both cut and excited him. "I went to one of the beaches on the Sound to think. I ran into an old acquaintance while I was there," Jace turned and glanced at Zander, "Angelica is here, and she is hunting for the Mystik Grimoire."

Cailyn gasped, "Are you okay?" Cailyn asked at the same moment Zander asked, "What did she say?"

"She approached me on the beach with several of her lackeys and tried to exert control over me. She was confident of her power, and ordered me to produce the Grimoire, saying we were going to rule the world together."

"What the hell is she thinking?" Zander asked.

Jace gathered his thoughts. "She knows the Grimoire has returned, and will do anything to get it. She was surprised to find that she wasn't able to control me. Cailyn had suggested that she may have cast a spell over me when she held me captive, and now I know Cailyn was right. I felt a foreign force when I fought her, but was able to thwart her with the help of Cailyn's soul." He ignored the gasps from in the others in the room. No one but Zander and Cailyn had been aware that he had ever been held prisoner.

Cailyn reached up and cupped his face in her hands. The empathy and compassion in her eyes touched a vulnerable part of his soul. "I am so sorry you had to face that on your own. I can't imagine what that was like for you." She stood on tiptoe and placed a chaste kiss on his lips, a kiss of comfort. Goddess, he loved this female.

He knew he had been falling for Cailyn, but when he had begun to love her he didn't know. The warmth that spread from his soul to encompass hers was the most amazing feeling. He found his home. This was what he was made for, to love this female. He squeezed her tighter and closed his eyes, allowing the feelings to wash over him.

CHAPTER 20

Zander's voice brought Jace out of his reverie. "How did you get away from her?"

"When she realized she had no power over me, and saw that I was about to kill her, she vanished. She hides it well, but was furious and lost control. It was good to see she feared me too." He didn't mention her parting threat to Cailyn. Jace would protect her and make sure she was okay. He'd willingly lie on that stone slab for the rest of his life, or die to ensure his mate's safety.

"How did she find you in the first place?" Cailyn asked accusations in her eyes as she looked up at him.

"I didn't call her if that's what you are asking. I don't know how to get in contact with her, and wouldn't even if I did. Given what she did to me, I never wanted to see her again," he reassured his mate.

"I wish you knew how to find her because I want to rip her to shreds and set the remains on fire for what she did to you." Her lips turned down in a pretty frown, and he couldn't help trace her bottom lip with his thumb. She was a dangerous distraction. Right in that moment, he wanted to kiss her passionately.

"She's a blood-thirsty one," Breslin remarked making Cailyn laugh. Jace matched her smile and lightly pressed his lips against hers. "I like your *puithar*, Elsie. I'm verra glad she's a part of this family, and so is Jace, I'd wager." Cailyn laughed harder and pulled away from him, looking over her shoulder.

"I like your candor, Bre, although you may be jumping the gun a bit," Elsie commented.

"I doona believe I'm jumping the gun. The Goddess has plans for us all, as you well know," Breslin countered with confidence.

"Och, we need to focus on the important issues. Cailyn had a valid question. How do you suppose she found you? Do you think she placed a magical tracker on you all those years ago?" Zander voiced his concern.

"I'm not certain, but I wouldn't put it past her to place a tracker on me somehow. It makes no sense otherwise. I don't hang out at that beach. In fact, I'd never been there before." Jace settled Cailyn into his side and kept her close.

Zander ran his hands through his hair as he contemplated the situation. "'Tis concerning if she has amassed that much power. What do you think her next move is?"

"Whatever it is, I don't think she intends to leave me be. Her disappearance was a regrouping. We need to be wary of her," Jace advised, shuddering when he thought of the look on her face before she vanished.

"I guess it would be asking too much for a way to overcome her," Zander sighed heavily.

"How can we find out what she did? Will Evzen know?" Cailyn asked.

"If I don't know, then Evzen won't either," Jace informed his mate.

"What about the Rowan sisters?" Gerrick queried from his lounge.

"Rowan sisters? Count me in," Rhys chimed in, excitedly.

"No, you're not going," Gerrick replied curtly.

Cailyn tilted her head to the side. "Why not?"

"Because last time I was there, I didn't leave for a month. Best month of my life. I didn't even mind Zander locking me in the dungeons for missing patrols. I'd happily do it again," Rhys answered, flashing his panty-dropping smile.

"Okay, no Rhys. Who are the Rowan sisters?" Cailyn asked.

"They are witches. The only triplets born to the realm, and they are notorious for their love spells. It's all about sex, drugs, and rock and roll for them. They could bespell you to love me," Jace joked, winking at his mate. He loved the sight of her flushing cheeks. "Gerrick, you have the right idea, we should visit them. If anyone can discover malignant magic, it's the Rowan sisters."

~

Prowling the streets of Queen Anne, Kyran searched relentlessly for an outlet for his rage. He needed a vicious bloody battle, but hadn't come across many skirm. Inevitably, his thoughts went to Bite and how he had been banned. He hung his head, remembering the reason. It had only been a few days, and still the image of the battered bruised body he'd left lying lifeless haunted him. That poor female didn't deserve to die, and he was responsible. Self-hatred seethed beneath the surface. He never lost control. From an early age he had been deviant, but had never done anything like that.

To complicate matters, Kyran was fighting the compulsion to seek out Mackendra. He didn't understand his draw to her, and frankly didn't like it. She had come to consume his every thought. He liked the stubborn tilt to her chin, which in itself was astonishing given that he preferred his females submissive. Her ample bosom and her vanilla citrus scent were intoxicating. He chained those thoughts in the dungeon of his mind. No one had free reign with him.

Now, he not only needed an outlet for his rage, but a release for his lusts even more. He hadn't tried another female since the incident. Too many demons had been haunting him, and he feared the changes that had begun. He needed pain and dominance during his sexual encounters, and now those fantasies included a particular female chained to his wall.

A million tiny pins and needles assaulted his flesh, breaking his reverie. A feral smile broke over his face, exactly what he needed. He followed the trace of skirm to a clearing near Magnolia and stopped dead in his tracks. Mackendra was engaged in a battle with three skirm. She was a thing of beauty in motion. He inhaled deeply, and caught her citrus-vanilla scent.

The skintight leather pants and tight black t-shirt made his mouth water. He held back his chuckle when he read 'Make My Day Punk' on her tee. The vixen had attitude. She swung a large blade and pivoted gracefully on her black boots. The soles were bigger that his shit kickers, and it surprised him how fluid she was. Her spiky black hair gleamed in the moon. He drank in her whiskey eyes, getting drunk on the sight of them. She was a fine female specimen, dare he say, the finest he had ever seen. And he had seen many over his long life.

When her blade sunk into one of the skirm's chests and he flashed, Kyran knew her blade was titanium, and he wondered how much she knew about his world. Clearly, she was aware of what type of weapon to use against this enemy.

As she spun and executed a perfect roundhouse kick, he noticed the human male that was fighting with her. He wondered who he was to Mackendra, and why he even cared. It mattered naught to him if this male was sleeping with her. If only that were true, he thought, as he clenched his fists.

He watched as she bounced on the balls of her feet and was caught by the sight of her ample breasts bouncing with the movement. He was distracted by his overwhelming desire to taste those breasts. He wanted to hear her moan and cry out, and imagined her secured to a cross. His cock hardened, and he cut off the erotic images before he pulled a Zander and threw her over his shoulder and carried her off to make the fantasy a reality.

A flash of fire brought his attention back to the battle. The big-burly-muscle-head she was with had dusted his opponent and turned to incapacitate the once facing off with Mackendra. It was obvious that they had worked with each other for some time. There was no communication, but the goateed-bonehead slid up behind the skirm and grabbed his arms and without missing a beat, Mack plunged her blade home. Kyran snuck behind a large evergreen to avoid being seen. He peered around the trunk just in time to see the guy with a death-wish embrace Mackendra and swing her around.

"You were amazing, as usual," muscle-head breathed.

"So were you. I could have handled that last one without

you, but thanks for the help," Mackendra replied easily. Her confidence was sexy as hell.

The goateed-bonehead set her down and cupped her cheek and Kyran heard how the guy's breathing became erratic. Kyran nearly jumped out from behind the tree and freed the guy's head from his shoulders until Mackendra rebuffed him.

"That's not going to happen. You know that, Stitch. Let's finish our patrol. We need to tell the others what we heard." Kyran watched the sway of her fine ass as she walked away, using all of his considerable strength to remain in place. Only after she disappeared did he realize what she had said and wondered what they had heard. If he wasn't so fucking keyed-up, he would have followed and listened in, but that wasn't safe at the moment. He had a sudden craving for a Creamsicle.

∼

Cailyn looked out the window as they made their way through Seattle to the Rowan sister's house. Jace had explained to her that the sisters were triplets who were witches. She was surprised to learn witches were different from sorcerers. Sorcerers were creatures of instinct, magic, and the power of the moon, whereas, witches were creatures of potions, circles and the four elements. The two types of magic were different, yet both stemmed from the Goddess.

These young, impetuous girls had recently hit adulthood and come into their power. The Dark Warriors believed a prophecy claiming that triplets born on a rare blue moon would become the most powerful witches ever known. Apparently, the Rowan sisters were the only set of witch triplets to have been born on a blue moon.

They drove across 520 Bridge and the sight of the lake was amazing to her even in the moonlight. One side of the water was calm and still, while the other was turbulent and choppy. The dichotomy was stunning during the day, but rather eerie at night. Cailyn understood the bridge itself caused the difference, but couldn't help but feel magic was at play.

Water gave way to land and the suburbs, and soon they were exiting the freeway, heading into an affluent neighborhood in Belleview. The opulent houses were stunning. "Are there any poor immortals? I thought you said these witches were twenty-seven or something."

"Yes, there are many poor realm members," Gerrick replied tersely.

"So, there's like a realm ghetto then. That's hard to believe. Your version of a ghetto is probably what I'd call a normal sized home," Cailyn teased the growly warrior.

"No, they don't live in homes at all. Where some live would scare the living hell out of you. Pray you never see it," he said as he looked at her square in the eyes over his shoulder from the passenger seat. This guy was intense and scary, and she shuddered at the lack of emotion in his ice-blue eyes.

Jace grabbed her hand and twined their fingers together, offering comfort. "Gerrick, stop. You're scaring her," he chided. "But, he is right, Cai. There are poor realm members, and it is an area that is best to avoid."

"Don't sweat it, Cai. It's in an area that is generally unsafe in Seattle, and you wouldn't wander there alone. I'm developing a kind of social services for the realm to help our poor, but its slow going. Those with money don't want to part with it to help others," Elsie shared. Cailyn smiled at her sister, thinking how well that role fit her personality.

"I see that the rich aren't any different just because they are supernatural," Cailyn remarked.

"Aye, there are selfish beings in all races, and politics abound in the realm," Zander remarked as trees and houses flew by.

Before she knew it, the car was slowing as Bhric pulled into a long drive. It was too dark for her to make out much, except for several weeping birches scattered amongst evergreens and various shrubs on the spacious property. They approached the house and soft lighting greeted them at the top of the U-shaped drive.

Cailyn glanced back at the lawn and saw that a small patch was illuminated by antique gas lamps. She was surprised to note the lawn wasn't perfectly manicured like you would expect to see in such an affluent neighborhood. She wondered if the young witches received angry letters from their HOA.

She had her door open and was stepping out before Jace made it around to her side. His scowl made her pause and glance up at him. His amethyst eyes had darkened with displeasure. "What," she whispered, placing her hands on his chest.

He placed his warm hands over the top of hers and took a step closer to her. Her body responded to his nearness, making it difficult to focus on the issue at hand. "I wanted to make sure it was safe before I opened your door," he murmured.

"Surely, with you here, I'm safe," she replied.

"Have you heard nothing about the dangers that lurk the night, you stubborn woman?" he breathed and brought his lips down on hers. The world around them vanished, and there was only them. She lost herself in the passion of his kiss until the slamming of car doors and a masculine laugh broke the moment.

Their surroundings returned in a rush, and she blushed to her roots over her public display of affection as Bhric chuckled and approached the ornate red door of the house. An elaborate pentacle surrounded by tiny stars was painted in black on the front panel. She figured the R in the center stood for their last name.

"Come on, let's do this," Jace uttered as he tugged her behind him.

Bhric knocked on the wood and she heard a woman's voice calling out from inside the house. She thought she heard her say this had better be good or she was turning whoever was interrupting into a toad. Cailyn was suddenly frightened of what they may face.

Wanting to be prepared, she accessed her own power and tried to read the minds of the witches. When she opened her mind numerous words and images flooded in. She wasn't able to make sense or identify who was thinking what. They lived in close proximity to numerous humans, and she was bombarded by so many thoughts that she was forced to shut it down.

Before she could regroup, the door swung open to reveal a tall, exotic woman with black hair that hung down to her hips. The young lady was drop-dead gorgeous, and her brown eyes glittered with amusement when she saw Bhric standing on the stoop. "Hello Bhric," she purred and draped her body against the door jamb.

A black smoke rose from a ring on her finger. The smoke had a sweet smell, but surprisingly didn't choke her out. Cailyn shrieked when a black bat fluttered from her finger and settled on the witch's shoulder. "Not you, sweetie. My other Bhric," the witch cooed, petting the animal.

"Hello Suvi. 'Tis good to see you again, lass," Bhric replied as he picked up her hand and kissed the back.

"Mmmm. Always a pleasure," Suvi responded. It was obvious the two of them had a history.

Another woman with bright red hair poked her head around the door and greeted the warriors. When she rested her arm above her head in the door frame her silver bangles jingled as they shifted. The bracelets coupled with the colorful skirt reminded Cailyn of a gypsy. "It's good to see you all. Now, before Suvi gets too distracted by Bhric, what brings the Vampire King to our door step?"

"Ah, Isis, 'tis been too many months. How are you and your sisters settling into your powers?" Zander greeted the red-haired witch.

Isis waved her hand dismissively. "We're settling. The house is still standing, and that's something, I suppose. You know how it is. Please come in," Isis said as she turned, calling out to Pema. Cailyn assumed that was the third sister. She wanted to laugh as Suvi grabbed Bhric's hand and pulled him along. Jace shrugged his shoulders and they all entered the house.

"Have you been training with Cele?" Zander asked as they entered the home. Cailyn glanced down and noticed what she thought was a line of salt along the threshold of the front door. She craned her neck, taking in the entryway. The walls in the small area were black and the floor was a dark brown oak. Cailyn thought it was an odd color choice. The overhead light fixture was turned off in favor of white candles on sofa tables flanking the door.

Isis' red hair was swaying in in the candlelight as she shook her head and continued walking. "Cele isn't exactly easy to work with. She wants control of our power for her own selfish purposes. I know she believes the prophesy about the power of three, but that doesn't mean it's about us. Besides, we chafe under her tutelage. We are doing a fair job of honing and controlling our craft. We have each other."

The sisters stopped at the end of the hall and slid a wood door open. Cailyn was surprised to see that there were no electrical lights on in the house. Every room they passed was lit with candles, and there were wall sconces down the hall. She couldn't see a whole lot, but each room they passed seemed to be painted a different color.

Suvi muttered foreign words and the bat vanished to become a silver ring on her right index finger before she got down to business. "Surely, you didn't come here to talk to us about our training. What can we do for you?"

CHAPTER 21

Jace kept hold of Cailyn's hand as they stepped into a large, open room. "We are here for me. You see, I have reason to suspect I have been under a sorceress' spell for about seven centuries, and I need your help."

He would have laughed at how the Rowan sister's eyes bulged at that, but it was too serious. It was Suvi who found her voice first. "How do you not know if you are under such a spell? That's a long time to be under someone's influence. You should have felt when the enchantment was cast."

Jace lowered his head in shame. She was right, of course. Only a weak sorcerer would not have recognized the casting of an enchantment. He suddenly wished Cailyn wasn't there to witness his weakness, yet he needed her there supporting him. There was no way he would get through this without her to keep him grounded. "It's a long story. Suffice it to say, this would have happened shortly after I passed my stripling years when I was under great duress."

"That only explains why you didn't counter act a spell. Even a sorcerer coming into his power is able to detect magic, especially if there is malignant intent. Please have a seat, this may take a while," Pema said as she glided gracefully into the room. Cailyn jumped when Pema spoke and Jace pulled her closer, realizing she likely hadn't heard her approach.

He glanced around the room for the first time. The walls were painted blue and white and the hardwood floors continued throughout. The furniture displayed the sisters' youth with its modern designs. He saw that the kitchen was surprisingly similar to Marie Laveau's. There were jars with herbs and flowers, as well as crystals and incense. He guided Cailyn to a nearby sofa and took a seat.

"We need to hear everything you can tell us about the person and circumstance surrounding the spell," Pema instructed.

"I will try, but this isn't going to be easy." Jace took a deep breath and briefly explained what he experienced at the hands of Lady Angelica, leaving out the details about how she sexually tortured him. Zander and Cailyn had known what he suffered, but the others couldn't hide their shock over the news.

"Goddess," breathed Bhric, scrubbing his hand through his hair. "I always wondered where you had disappeared to, and why Evzen took power when you were next in line. I had no idea."

"We are going to have to start calling her the Royal Bitch. I can't believe you have left her alive all these centuries. If that had happened to one of my sisters, I'd kill her with my bare hands," Isis remarked as she brought her waist-length, red hair forward, braiding the ends.

Jace noticed Isis' agitated movements and how she became angrier by the moment. It was a sharp contrast to Pema's composure. The calmer Pema was, the more Isis settled down. Suvi grabbed Isis' hand and she was once again under control. Jace was amazed at the impact they had on each other.

Cailyn squeezed his hand. "I couldn't agree with you more, Isis," she said.

"That certainly would explain why you didn't feel a spell casting, but why, after all this time, do you now believe that you are still under an enchantment?" asked Pema, smoothing her purple shirt as she sat on the edge of a chair.

Bile rose in his throat. He didn't want to divulge his problem. He would look like an idiot if there was no spell, and he became ill during intimate moments because he couldn't handle the abuse he suffered. He had no desire for anyone to hear about this, and suddenly wanted to run from the home and never look back. This had been a mistake. He couldn't lose the respect he had worked so hard to earn over the centuries. It was bad enough to have his mate aware of his shame.

He was about to get up when Cailyn broke the silence. Sweat broke on his brow as he prayed to the Goddess that his mate didn't betray his issues. "I am the one who suggested there was something going on. Do you really need all of the details to get the answer to our question? I don't know anything about magic, but it seems like you want to know out of curiosity." He wanted to kiss this female. If he thought he loved her before, that was nothing compared to how he felt now. His heart swelled with the emotion.

"I like you, you're feisty. I see that you are his Fated Mate," Pema observed, pointing to the mate mark behind Cailyn's left ear. "No need to get bristly. We aren't a threat to you or him. We would never do anything to harm him, because our society would fall to pieces without the Dark Warriors. They are the only thing standing between us and the skirm. That being said, we need some information. You see, magic must have a focus and we need to know where to concentrate our energy. It is not mere curiosity. Although, now I must admit to more than a passing desire to know details."

Cailyn smiled with saccharine-sweetness and tilted her head to the side. Jace had come to know that look well over the past days. He debated stopping what he knew was coming. His instinct was to jump in and protect her from these witches who could crush her with a thought. But, he trusted in the goodness of the Rowan sisters. They would understand her protectiveness as his mate. "You might want to be careful. I'd hate to see curiosity kill the cat. Suffice it to say, you need to focus your energy on anything that may sabotage our intimacy."

Pema stared intently at Cailyn, but she didn't back down an inch, and he saw a grudging respect light the witch's sea-green eyes. Finally, Pema nodded to Cailyn and turned her attention back to him. He suddenly wasn't sure he was ready for this. What if they did discover a spell? Worse yet, what if they couldn't remove it?

All of a sudden, he choked on the dread that he would be asked to leave the Dark Warriors. A weak warrior was a liability, and danger to others. He didn't feel fit to protect Cailyn, and wouldn't be able to do that without the warriors at his side. She would be better off without him.

Pema's voice broke his mental bashing and he had to shake out of the gloom. "Fair enough. We will take this on, but this won't be cheap, and it will take us all working together. Are you willing to give us Rhys for another month?" she spun and asked Zander directly.

Bhric blurted, "What am I, chopped liver?" at the same time Zander replied, "Nay, we canna allow that. We need every warrior on duty, which brings up another issue. You need to beware when you leave your home. The danger has increased exponentially, and the skirm are kidnapping females of all races."

"I will gladly stay home with Bhric," Suvi purred, sliding the warrior a hot glance.

Isis smacked her shoulder. "Focus sister, we have work to do."

Jace took a deep breath. It was now or never. He girded his resolve, and faced the sisters. "What do I need to do?"

∽

JACE HAD BEEN PACING the Spell Room for the past ten minutes while the witches made their preparations. The earth tone walls and hardwood floors were closing in on him despite the twenty foot ceiling and large circular skylight. He had wondered how they were able to perform magic in an interior room. Witches needed the four elements to cast their spells, and the moon aided in their ritual.

Isis pushed a button and vents along the side of the window opened, allowing fresh air in. Jace admired the Celtic design in the leaded glass of the dome. The inner circle of the design was done with clear glass to allow maximum exposure, with vines and flowers interwoven around the edges in blue, purple, and green glass.

His gaze returned to the sisters. They had swept the room with a besom and placed their cherry wood altar directly under the skylight, yet weren't performing the ritual. How long was this preparation going to take? Jace's sorcery was vastly different, in that he channeled his magic through his staff and very little preparation was required.

Jace anxiously rubbed his wide, silver cuff as he watched them set a trio of white rune-carved candles, and a ceremonial athame in precise positions on the altar. A scrying bowl filled with water was surrounded by numerous colored crystals. Finally, each of the sisters lit one of the candles, and then Pema grabbed the bowl of salt and dried lavender from Suvi.

Snakes writhed in Jace's gut, they were ready to cast the circle and begin. He suddenly wasn't so sure about this. He wanted to run away and forget everything, including Cailyn, but there was no backing out now. He forced his fears and trepidation into a vault, because any negative energy would taint the space and could alter the spell. He closed his eyes and called forth an image of Cailyn and found his calm amidst the storm. As scared as he was of the outcome, his Fated Mate had become his everything.

Jace came to attention when they moved him into the south position of the altar. "Okay, Jace. We are going to cast our circle now and get this show on the road," Pema informed him with a reassuring smile. She turned to her sisters, "Ready?"

"I was born ready, ask Bhric," teased Suvi as she fell into step behind Isis. Jace was amused at their energy and youthful zest. Their excitement was infectious, and gave him hope.

Isis rolled her eyes at Suvi while Pema removed her green silk robe. She neatly folded the cloth and placed it out of the way under the wood table. Jace tried not to gape; she was naked as the day she was born. He didn't know why he was so shocked, because he knew witches performed magic best when sky-clad, to better draw energy from the moon. He gulped as he remembered that they also performed strong magic when sexual elements were involved.

He found himself praying that the sisters didn't include those sexual elements in this ritual. The thought made him uncomfortable, and for once it had nothing to do with the nausea it induced. He'd never had a problem with the carnal aspect of the craft, but he had been blessed with his Fated Mate, and he held that sacred. There would never be another female for him, no matter how things turned out between them. Cailyn was it for him.

Once all the sisters had shed and stored their respective robes, Jace watched as Pema then began casting the circle. She took the salt mixture and walked deosil in a perfect circle. After she had completed her first circuit, Jace saw white light projecting from the salt.

On her second turn, she began chanting, "I cast this circle to keep us free of all energies that are not of The Light," she glanced back and gave him a meaningful look. Apparently, he wasn't doing a great job with his energy. He recalled Cailyn's image and held it in the fore.

Pema continued, "I allow within this circle only the energies that are of The Light. So Mote It Be." On her third circuit, Jace listened as she consecrated the space and marveled once again at how different witchcraft was from his sorcery. He had been told how earth-based the craft was, but it was amazing to see and feel the power. His magic was much more mystical, derived from the heavens. He would say his came from Morrigan directly, but he felt the Goddess in the magic they were calling forth.

Isis picked up a white piece of chalk and knelt to call the quarters. As she scribed the pentacle, she invoked the element in each direction as she went. "Hear me, Sentinels of the East, I summon the powers of Air! Hear me, Sentinels of the South, I summon the powers of Fire! Hear me, Sentinels of the West, I summon the powers of Water!

Hear me, Sentinels of the North, I summon the powers of Earth! As above, so below. As within, so without. Four stars in this place be, combined to call the fifth to me! So mote it be."

Jace was so accustomed to seeing magic in terms of color, and while the white light did brighten, it paled in comparison to the sudden influx of power he felt within the circle.

The circle having been cast and the elements called, Suvi began chanting. "Live and learn, learn and live. I endeavor to receive what life can give. Bring to me the lessons true. And knowledge of what to do. Amid the mess and chaos fierce. Shine a light to darkness pierce. Show the way to knowledge deep. Which to let go and which to keep. Clear the way so I might heed. The lessons that I truly need. Show me what I need to learn. As life's pages I do turn. So mote it be," Suvi called out. The sisters closed their eyes and threw their heads back. Jace expected to feel or see something, but nothing happened.

He should have known better than to hope. There was nothing magical wrong with him. He was a broken male, not fit for his mate.

The sisters looked to one another and then into the scrying bowl. At Pema's nod, Suvi repeated her spell two more times before they looked into the water once again. Jace began to sweat. It sucked receiving confirmation that he was as screwed up as he had believed for centuries, and that meant he had to give Cailyn up. His chest ached and his heart fractured at the thought. He would rather die, but he refused to force his mate to accept a broken, unworthy mate.

"Jace, you need to find your calm again. We are going to try another spell, combining our powers, and we can't afford your negative energy interfering in our circle. I don't want to have to throw you out and recast everything. It will be far more effective with you in the room," Pema directed to him.

Jace gave her a curt nod. She was right, and it was reassuring to know they weren't giving up. There was hope.

The witches flanked the altar across from him and joined hands. They chanted in unison this time, the power building with each verse. Light glowed between their clasped hands where he had seen those odd stones.

"We are Earth, grounded and strong.

We are the receptacle through which Her true will is delivered.

We are Air, forceful and fierce.

We are Fire, searing and complex.

We are Water, instinctual, and enchanted.

The ripples of our inner consciousness are peaceful and pure.

We are Spirit. We are all that is.

We are poise and harmony.

We are that from which Her true will comes. By the power of three, so mote it be!"

White light pulsed, and the air crackled with electrical energy. Jace felt it as a vibration within, like a hive of bees had been agitated. There was a distinct signature to the sensation. He followed the sisters' gazes to the water in the scrying bowl.

A mist had developed above the liquid and silver light shone from within. Pema chanted a reveal spell in Latin and pursed her lips then blew her breath across the bowl. The mist cleared and Jace saw himself shackled to Lady Angelica's stone slab. The sight of his bloody, broken body caused him to shudder. Angelica was straddling his hips, taking what he never wanted to give her.

The horror of what he had suffered was overshadowed

as the Great Bitch came into view. For the first time, Jace heard the words of her enchantment, the words that had given her power over him. Holy shit, Cailyn had been right. Angelica had been controlling him for over seven centuries.

Horror and relief washed over him. The female was sick and twisted to want to subjugate another in such a manner. She had stolen everything from him, including his ability to experience physical pleasure. His free will had been taken, and he had been her prisoner far longer than he knew. She had robbed him of his pride when she had repeatedly raped him.

If not for his imprisonment, he may have been able to save his parents. He hadn't even been able to say goodbye to them. He failed them, and his kind, because she'd rendered him too weak to fight back. She'd neutralized his magic, depriving him of everything that had ever identified him. His faith in himself was so shaken that he refused to even entertain the idea of being Guild Master after his release. Anger surged through his veins at everything she had taken from him. He wanted to hunt her down and tear her to pieces.

Pema met his gaze and he saw pity reflected in her sea-green depths. He didn't want her pity, and hated that she would see him as weak now. "I understand why you didn't want to say anything before. I can't imagine the strength it has taken you to live freely while still under her influence. The fact that you haven't spent the last several hundred years serving her speaks volumes." She released her sister's hand and bent down to retrieve the robes.

Suvi spoke as they slipped the fabric on their backs, covering their nudity. "Jace Miakoda, you are a fearless warrior, never doubt that. Your mate is a lucky mortal, indeed."

"What that creature did to you is unspeakable, and she needs to pay for what she has done. I know you sorcerers don't ascribe to the same code that we do in the craft, but it can't be so different that harming another is acceptable. I'd love to help you hunt her down," Isis declared, her outrage clear by the fire that flashed in her grey eyes. He was touched that she would experience such outrage on his behalf.

He was overwhelmed at the moment, still shocked to his core that he had been living and battling against nefarious powers within himself his entire life. The big question now was how to rid himself of the enchantment. "I...thank you. I can't express how much I appreciate what you've done for me. I have one more request. Do you know how to annul such a spell?"

They shared a look amongst themselves, then Pema grabbed the athame up while Isis and Suvi snuffed the candles. "We cannot counteract it for you. Only you can cancel out the magic," she said as she crossed to the side of the circle. She looked over her shoulder at him. "Magic is all about the intent, Jace. Consider what her intent was, and you will have your answer. My best suggestion is that you counter her nefarious control with love, pure and simple. You will gain more power if you follow your name sake and utilize the power of the full moon." With that she turned, thanked the Goddess and cut a path in the circle with the athame, dispersing the energy safely.

"Thank you, again," he said, nodding his head in agreement. He followed them from the room while he probed his mind. He now sensed the ugly signature, and was amazed at how deeply it was buried. The fact that these three young witches were able to reveal the enchantment at all was a testament to how powerful they were going to be. When they finally settled down, and focused on something other than selling lust potions and tarot readings, their power would know no limits.

A spark ignited as the hope he'd been harboring consumed him. There was a way for him to be with his mate. Perhaps Marie Laveau was right, after all.

CHAPTER 22

"It's about time you guys got back," Jessie called out the moment they entered the house. Jace saw Cailyn's friend peek her head around the corner from the media room, her anxiety telegraphed clearly. It was obvious to Jace how much the female loved his mate, and surprisingly, she seemed to be rooting for him rather than Cailyn's fiancé. Just thinking of the male set Jace's jealousy raging. It was near impossible to ignore the corrosive emotion.

"How'd it go? We are dying for details here," Jessie blurted out as their group entered the room.

"You know, Jessie, it's been a long night for all of us. Jace will tell us when he's ready," Cailyn replied, coming to his defense.

Cailyn continued to surprise Jace. He hadn't earned her patience and support, but was soaking it up. His mate had no problem speaking out in his defense, and had done so several times that night. He expected to be offended that this female felt that he, a proven warrior, needed protecting, but he wasn't. In fact, he cherished it, and wanted her all the more.

"Thank you, Cailyn. I needed to gather my thoughts, and I was waiting until we returned home. I knew Evzen and Killian would be here and I have no desire to repeat this information more than once," Jace murmured, making eye contact with his Guild Master, nodding his acknowledgement before he made his way to the bar and poured two fingers of scotch.

"In that case, we are no' all here yet. Where's Bhric, *brathair?*" Breslin asked Zander as she muted the television.

"Where do you think? He stayed at the witches' house for a few days," Zander replied with a smirk, as he pulled Elsie into his side and held her close. Jace wanted that same easy closeness with Cailyn. He glanced at Cailyn and caught the longing in her gaze as she watched her sister. Without intending to, Jace crossed to her side and wrapped his arm around her shoulders, drawing her close. When she melted into his side, he felt like a king.

Her closeness was a double-edged sword. His mate mark burned a path across his hip, reminding him he hadn't completed the mating. His body was constantly on fire for Cailyn, and the pain kept increasing as more time went by. Knowing now that there was magic interfering with his ability to be intimate with a female, Jace was ready to move forward with this mating if Cailyn would have him.

Rhys jumped up, knocking the recliner over in his haste. "What the hell? You didn't let me go because you said we couldn't afford to be down any warriors," Rhys yelled, faking an attempt at outrage.

"Nice try, Rhys. Bhric will only be there a few days at most, whereas we'd have to send an entire extraction team for you a month later," Elsie teased and winked as Rhys set his chair to rights and resumed his seat.

"Do you need more time, Jace? If so, I can tell everyone what I found in the Grimoire," Evzen said, bringing them back on track, instantly sobering the mood.

Jace threw back his drink. "I'll go first. I have to get this off my chest." He tightened his arm around Cailyn, needing her close for the next part. He looked down into his mate's hazel eyes and saw tears gather there as if she hurt as much as he did. Suddenly, Jace realized that through their bond, Cailyn was aware of exactly how he felt. Goddess, he loved her.

"Not all of you are aware of this but...shortly before my parents were killed I was taken prisoner by Lady Angelica. She tortured me for over a century before Zander rescued me. Recently, Cailyn brought to my attention that she could have cast a spell on me during my captivity. We visited the Rowan sisters and discovered that my mate was right."

He ignored the gasps and focused on the single tear that slipped down Cailyn's cheek. No one had ever cried for him, and it gave him hope to win her heart and complete the mating.

"That fucking bitch," Killian spat, clearly pissed off. He sat forward in his seat, resting his folded arms on his knees. "I can't believe she would pull that shit. How could she break the oath? What kind of spell, maybe we can help?" Jace had stopped wondering how Angelica could do anything. All sorcerers took an oath never to manipulate another's power and sealed it in blood, making it impossible to break. Jace knew without doubt that even if Angelica had said the words, she had never bound her oath with her blood.

"She used dark magic, but I'm not certain what spell she

used. The Rowan sister's suggested countering the spell with love." He squeezed Cailyn's waist and met her gaze once again. "Under the full moon," he husked, enjoying the way his mate's eyes darkened with her desire.

"Dark magic is dangerous and unpredictable," Evzen shook his head, "that female plays with fire. She knows it's forbidden, and when she is brought in, you will be given the opportunity to kill her. My guess is that she has already disappeared, but our search will not stop until she is found." Jace relished the thought of beheading the sorceress.

"Dark magic is tricky," Killian began, offering his advice. "Your intent must surpass hers. The full moon is upon us. Let us know if we can help."

"I plan to take advantage of it, thanks. I don't want my mate to be at risk of her wrath," he glanced at his mate and smiled at the shock in her eyes. He let his intent show in his gaze. He was going to claim Cailyn and complete their mating.

Her eyes widened even more as he bent over to place a reassuring kiss on her lips. His joy of the moment was shadowed by the knowledge that Lady Angelica was furious with him for overcoming her control, and would only be angrier when he shattered her hold over him.

"I hope you will be able to put this behind you at last, my friend. You deserve happiness," Zander declared before turning to Evzen. Zander had been the one to save Jace from Angelica's dungeon, and knew better than anyone what he'd been through. It wouldn't be an easy path, but Jace had a chance to travel down the road to find true happiness. "Now, what news do you have, Evzen?"

"We need to schedule a formal council meeting, but this is too important to wait for the others to gather. As you all know, the Mystik Grimoire contains the realm's magic, as well as prophecies. Well, amongst the text, I discovered a prophecy that sounds ominous. I think it could be pertinent right now, Zander," Evzen shared with the group as he sat down on one of the leather couches and placed the Grimoire on the table in front of him.

Jace sensed his discomfort sharing realm secrets. Jessie was an undetermined threat, seeing as she was created by demons, which made it understandable that Evzen would approach such sensitive issues with caution. "It's okay to speak freely. Jessie isn't controlled by the archdemon, and she isn't going to betray us. Are you, Jess?"

Jessie's eyes widened in shock. It wasn't a surprise to her that she wasn't trusted, but he could tell that it hurt her deeply. "Oh my God. I'd never do or say anything to put any of you in danger. I'm nothing like those weak males controlled by their creator. That piece of shit has nothing on me. In fact, I want to be called a dhampir. I might have been created by a demon, but I'm closer to vampire than skirm."

Breslin chuckled and stood up to join Jessie. "I havena heard that term in decades. I find it amusing that humans have the myth that a human and vampire mating would produce a dhampir. Our offspring will always be full vampire, given our dominant genes. 'Tis official, Jessie is the first dhampir." Breslin exclaimed.

Jace wondered if there were more like Jessie out there. He had wondered that from the moment he learned females were being kidnapped. Jace filed the thought away, and focused on the issue at hand.

Zander shook his head as if exacerbated with Breslin, but Jace knew the Vampire King indulged his sister. She had been the apple of his eye, until he found Elsie. "Now that we have that oot of the way, Evzen, please share what you discovered," Zander instructed.

Evzen placed his hand on the book and nodded to Zander. "I have shared this information with Hayden and Dante already, but have yet to inform Nikko," he said as he flipped through several pages. Jace noted the change in ink and writing style as the pages passed. His ancestors wrote those words, documenting magic and prophecies for the realm. Bitterness hit at the thought that there had been no one to keep track of things for the past seven centuries. That duty fell to his family, and he had done nothing to further realm knowledge.

Evzen stopped about halfway through and began reading. His voice echoed through the now silent room. "The return of the sacred sign heralds a melee between the forces of Lightness and Dark in the woods where the great beasts are imprisoned. By the blade of a mortal, evil is vanquished under the red moon." Jace shivered at the omen in the words.

"I believe the sacred sign refers to Elsie and the blessing of Fated Mates once again. The passage may refer to a full red moon, and if that's the case, than this melee is right around the corner. I took the liberty of checking the lunar calendar, there is a full red moon coming up in August," Evzen finished.

"Fuck," Zander cursed. His tension was evident in the lines around his mouth and eyes. "I had hoped to annihilate this archdemon's soul once and for all, and then finally have a time of peace. It canna be that easy. Let's break it doon. It mentions that this battle will take place in the woods where animals are captive. Fucking oracles, that could be anywhere in this world or several others."

Jace crossed to the couch and joined Evzen, reading over the words of the prophecy, hoping to gain some clarity.

"Lightness and Dark is clearly us versus the demons and

their minions," Gerrick said, joining the conversation and running a hand over the scar on the left side of his face. "If the red moon is the full moon next week, then that leaves where have great beasts been imprisoned, and who is the mortal that vanquishes evil?"

"What great beasts are they referring to though? They couldna be referring to the Kraken since he was imprisoned in the depths of the ocean," Zander reasoned.

"Do you think this is talking about the Unseelie that were banished to the Fae realm?" Santiago asked.

"That wouldn't make sense because mortals aren't allowed in the Fae realm, and neither are the demons for that matter. None of the players could travel to that realm to have a battle. I highly doubt they are referring to the Frost demons, who have been confined to their realm," Orlando added as he leaned against the back of one of the couches.

"Could they be talking simpler than you guys are thinking?" Cailyn asked as she looked at him across the room. His blood heated as their eyes met. It still shocked him that this exquisite creature was made for him. His mate mark pulsed with pain, reminding him that he hadn't completed the mating yet. He was determined to have this female.

Jace had to take a couple deep breaths and clench his fists to keep from reaching out to her and giving into his desires. "What are you thinking, *Shijéí*?"

"Well," she said, licking her lips nervously, making him hold back his groan. He wanted to forget this conversation and lose himself in her kiss. "There is the Woodland Park Zoo. I mean, they don't have great beasts of myth, but they do have wild animals. And, they are in captivity," she explained, pointing to the television where a story about the zoo was on the nightly news.

"Of course. You're brilliant, Cai!" Elsie exclaimed and

looked over her shoulder at Zander. "Do you think it could be that easy? It makes sense to me. You guys do tend to overlook the mundane."

Zander smiled at Elsie with what could only be described as utter devotion. "You're right, I doona consider things that are strictly related to humans. If the realm isna connected in some way, then in my mind it doesna exist. This is an oversight on my part. Okay, so until a better opinion is brought forth, we operate under assumption this prophecy is referring to the zoo, and a battle next week. That still leaves the mortal who vanquishes evil."

"Do you think that could mean there will be mortals present? It is a popular public zoo and park. I hate the idea of people being in danger like that. Is there any way we can clear the area at dusk, Orlando?" Elsie asked.

"We need to make sure Mackendra isna at the park that night." Everyone turned around abruptly at the harshly growled words emanating from Kyran's throat. At some point the disturbed warrior had returned, and now stood in the doorway to the media room with an armful of...Creamsicles? What the hell?

"Aboot fucking time, *brathair*. Next time you decide to disappear, you will tell me." Zander and Kyran shared a meaningful look full of reprobation. Jace knew where it came from, thankful that no one else was aware of the death of the young shifter at Kyran's hands. Zander was right with his concern. The knowledge would only drive a wedge between the warriors. "Obviously, you've heard some of what Evzen discovered. Your opinion would be appreciated. What exactly are you eating, anyway?"

"Ice cream."

"Awesome. I love these things. Can I have one?" Orlando asked and attempted to take one of the boxes from Kyran.

"Touch them and I'll break your fucking hand," Kyran barked. The male was losing his ever-loving mind. First he killed a female, and now he was acting like a possessive lunatic over some silly ice cream treats. Jace made a mental note to talk to Zander about this situation.

Elsie approached Kyran. The female was the only being brave enough in the room to approach the feral warrior at the moment. "It's okay, Ky. These have to be melting, why don't you let Angus put them in the freezer?"

Kyran looked down at Elsie and some of the savage heat left his eyes. "The one in my room."

"Alright," Elsie motioned to Angus, who had come when he heard Elsie say his name.

"I'll just put them in the freezer in your room. Would you like me to add them to the shopping list?" Angus was quick to reassure the agitated warrior. The majordomo had a sixth sense when any of them were on edge. It was likely a benefit of his dragon genetics. It still amazed Jace that such a strong creature served as Zander's majordomo. Of course, he did more than act as majordomo. Having a dragon on hand for protection was far better than a pack of wolves.

After several long, tense moments Kyran handed over his bounty, keeping one box. "Aye, thank you, Angus. So, tell me more aboot this prophecy," he said as he unwrapped an ice cream bar and ate it in three bites.

Zander gave Kyran the condensed version about the prophecy and what they had already determined and the conversation came back to concern for mortals. "My biggest concern is for Mack and her group. I can see her patrolling the area and getting involved in such a battle. She is a warrior and would never turn her back." Jace questioned the protectiveness he heard in Kyran's voice. "We need a way to make sure she is nowhere near the park that night."

"Keeping any humans away from the park that night will be impossible," Orlando said responding to both Elsie and Kyran's concerns. "But, Mackendra will be another issue altogether. She is a force unto herself and doesn't strike me as the type that if asked nicely will stay away from the park. In fact, I think approaching her with anything will ensure she will be there that night."

"I agree with, O. Best option will be to set up a distraction so she patrols another area that night," Santiago added from the side of the room where he stood with one booted foot against the wall.

"Speaking of patrols, you four head oot now," Zander said, pointing to Orlando, Santiago, Rhys and Gerrick. "We've left the city unprotected long enough. We will continue to discuss these issues here."

"We will have to pick this up later. I have a spell to obliterate," Jace informed the room and grabbed Cailyn's hand, dragging her to the back door, ignoring the good luck wishes sent Cailyn's way and the knowing chuckles of the males.

He knew how to break Angelica's hold over him.

CHAPTER 23

"What the fuck is that?" Orlando whispered, gazing at what had to be a demon. The thing stood on two legs, and had mottled skin the color of smoke. It looked up from the neck of its victim as the moonlight reflected off its eyes, causing them to glow brightly. The creature had huge fangs that dripped blood onto the pale skin of the female in its arms.

"I'm going out on a limb here, but I think that is the enemy spoken of in the prophecy," Gerrick commented. "I don't think he is an archdemon, but I sense low levels of power."

"Let's ponder that crap later. We need to stop them from killing any other innocents," Rhys remarked as he headed across the street. Orlando hated that one innocent was already lost, and kicked it into gear.

"Any ideas about how best to kill them?" Orlando asked Gerrick as the rest of them followed suit.

"No idea—" Gerrick was cut off by Santiago's urgent warning. "There are half a dozen more coming out of the park!"

Orlando whipped out his blades and rushed the newcomers. He had never seen these types of demons, but they smelled to high heaven. Why was it that demons and their minions always smelled? Didn't they have showers in Hell?

He heard Rhys taunting the one he had engaged. "Damn, you're an ugly motherfucker, aren't you? Bet you've never been laid." Orlando would have laughed at the warrior's taunting but he was too busy fighting. Orlando swung his *sgian dubh* out and connected with the demon's stomach.

"Ugh," Orlando groaned, keeping his feet, and dinner, in place as the smell of burnt flesh intensified. "You are a rank bastard," he yelled as the creature slumped to the ground, groping for his intestines.

Orlando had enough time to kick it in the head before Santiago called out a warning. "Watch your back, O." Orlando swung around, his blade up and ready. Metal clanged loudly as Orlando met every blow delivered by the newcomer. He took in the scene while he fought.

Rhys had injured his first demon, and was facing another while Gerrick and Santiago each battled their own. When Gerrick lost his weapons, Rhys threw his to Gerrick and had new ones in his hands before Orlando blinked. Lucky bastard. Orlando loved Rhys' telekinetic ability, thinking it sure came in handy during battles.

The two injured demons crawled after the warriors, drawing Orlando's attention. "These fuckers don't stay down," he warned.

"Chop their heads off, idiot. That'll stop them, it stops everyone," Gerrick chided as he swung and sliced cleanly through the demon he battled. Orlando laughed at the satisfying sight of both the head and demon toppling over.

Orlando renewed his efforts against the demon standing before him. These demons were tough as shit to kill, and they were going to need to regroup and refocus their strategy before the big battle.

The thought of Elsie facing these new enemies sent fear racing through him. He had no doubt that she could hold her own against skirm and ash them easily, but these were another story. These demons were stronger, faster, and far harder to kill. He worried about her no matter how much he told himself she wasn't his to worry about. He was very aware that she belonged to Zander, but that didn't mean his feelings for her had changed. It was a knife to the chest every time he saw them together. No matter how hard he tried, he wasn't able to erase her from his mind.

While preoccupied, a blade nicked his bicep. He'd chastise himself later for his distraction, and swung out at the offender. He missed anything vital, and ducked to pick up a second blade from the sidewalk. He crossed his arms and brought them back together, cutting through half the demon's neck. Before it could regain its balance, Orlando twisted his body, coming up behind and finishing his opponent. Head and body met pavement as Orlando looked around to scope the scene. The others were finishing off the rest of the demons. Orlando was out of breath and his heart was racing by the time all was said and done.

"I know I wished for tougher opponents, but I take it back. It makes me shudder knowing these creatures are out there. They are posing far more danger to any unclaimed mates than we previously assumed," Gerrick groused.

"What the hell were those?" Santiago asked as he kicked a headless corpse.

"Lesser demons of some kind. Gerrick was spot on with

his power assessment, thank the Goddess. Had they been more powerful..." Rhys trailed off and shuddered.

"Let's call for clean-up and head back to Zeum. The council needs to be updated on this new threat. I've never smelled so bad in my life. Why the hell couldn't they ash like skirm?" Orlando observed as he stabbed his titanium blade into its heart for good measure.

～

CAILYN STUMBLED BEHIND A DETERMINED JACE, blinking away the raindrops. "Slow down. I can't see as well as you and I'm tripping over every branch and rock out here."

"Sorry. I forget you don't have super-senses," he replied as he looked back at her over his shoulder. He finally stopped and bent next to her. She yelped when he placed one arm behind her knees and the other behind her back and hefted her off her feet.

"I wasn't asking for you to carry me. I am perfectly capable of walking on my own, at a normal *human* pace," she pointed out as she twined her arms around his neck. She loved his strength, and marveled at how easily he carried her across the property. She had never felt dainty like her sister, but this man made her feel like a tiny fairy. She had never felt more feminine, or safe.

"I like carrying you. Besides, I need you close, especially right now." He clasped her closer and buried his nose in her hair. She shivered at the heat of his body, and loved that he openly acknowledged needing her so much. She sensed how she calmed and inflamed him at the same time. She'd never felt more powerful than she did seeing how she affected him.

His breath stirred in her hair as he moved gracefully and

surely through the woods. She rested her head on his shoulder and breathed him in. He smelled of sage and masculine musk, and it went straight to her core. She kissed his neck and felt his pulse race against her lips.

Feeling bold, she swiped her tongue across his pulse point. He groaned and stumbled. She reveled in the power she had over this male. Not that she wanted to control him, but she liked knowing that she could cause him to lose control.

She kept up her exploration of his neck and twisted her hand around his long, black braid. She brought her other hand down the front of his chest. When they reached a small clearing in the trees he stopped and gazed down at her. His eyes glowed purple, which just happened to be her new favorite color. "You are playing with fire, mate," he growled.

"Maybe I want to be burned," she murmured, wondering where her courage had come from. Every time she came together with this man, she lost her senses. All her good intentions to square her life away flew out the window, and she was swept up in the passion.

He let go of her legs and let her slide down his hard, muscled body. Their eyes remained locked together and she rested her hands on his shoulders while he ran his hands down her back to cup her hips. She had to kiss him and stood on tiptoe, lifting her hands to tug his head down.

His pupils dilated as he realized her intent. She saw the moment he gave in to temptation, meshing his lips over hers. Like a match to tinder, he set her body on fire. She clutched his braid and pulled him closer. He met her urgency, deepening his kiss and teasing the seam of her lips. She imagined him teasing other far more sensitive flesh.

He licked at her mouth and she opened, inviting him in.

She loved the way he dominated her and elicited sensations she had never experienced before him. Their tongues slid sensuously together and tangled passionately. His hands began an urgent exploration. This would be another fast, hard coupling, and she couldn't wait.

When his hands cupped her ass and squeezed, her abdomen clenched with need. His mixture of masculine beauty and brawn struck her; it was a heady combination, impossible to ignore.

"I need you, Jace," she begged as she wrapped one leg around his hip and began rubbing up against his hard shaft. She knew how that enormous piece of male flesh made her feel and she wanted it more than was good for her. One thing was certain; he had ruined her for anyone else sexually. She had never had a lover like him, and if she chose not to be with him, she never would again. She questioned if she could let this go. Then all coherent thought left as he met her thrust for thrust, causing more friction between them.

"I want you more than I can say, but I need to get rid of this spell first. I will not have our lovemaking sullied by that filth any longer." How could she have forgotten the reason he pulled her out here? He made her lose her mind the moment he looked at her, that's how.

∼

"No, I need you right here with me. Your closeness makes this easier. I don't want to lose this." Jace pulled her leg back to his hip, and when that wasn't enough, he picked her up and coaxed her legs around his hips. He rocked gently against her core and reveled in the way she gasped, clutching his shoulders.

"Isn't this distracting you?" she groaned as he thrust and reached up with a free hand to cup her breast.

He lowered his head and bit her nipple through her fabric. "Not at all. I need this, trust me." It was vital that she trust him, and he found he was holding his breath for her response.

"I do trust you, Jace, with my heart and soul." He felt victorious and his heart swelled. He was going to beat this, and win her over. He continued to tease her until he felt the familiar nausea rise. He examined the sensation and located Lady Angelica's signature.

He lifted his face and meshed his lips to Cailyn's and focused internally. Several blissful and tormented minutes later, he was finally able to identify the weave of the spell. He mentally tugged at a strand, trying to pull it apart. Nothing happened. He recited a release spell in his mind while maintaining a mental hold on the strand, but nothing. He continued to kiss and caress his mate, allowing his love for her to envelope him.

His arousal hit a fever pitch and Cailyn was lost to her need, reaching for the hem of his shirt, trying to divest him of it. He allowed her to pull the fabric over his head while he increased his efforts to tug and pull on the threads of the spell. It began to unravel.

He could do this. The key was his love for Cailyn. "I love you, *Shijéí*. I have from the moment I met you, and am not afraid to ask that you give me a chance. Broken male that I am and all."

"Oh, Jace," Cailyn whispered, kissing him with renewed vigor. He refused to give the spell the power he had for seven hundred years. He was going to love his mate and win her heart.

He gathered his magic once more and grabbed the

remaining elements of the spell, casting it away. A ten-ton weight lifted off his shoulders as the enchantment disintegrated, and he imagined Angelica screaming in defeat. He was finally free!

He pulled back and met Cailyn's stormy hazel eyes. "Ah, Goddess. I'm free. I'm finally free," he expressed and kissed his mate brutally, feeling nothing but bliss. His body surged into his love play with Cailyn. He cupped her breasts and teased her nipples. Her heat seared him through their fabric. His cock was hard as a rock, yet there was no nausea.

"You did it. I knew you would." Cailyn wiped at his eyes as he broke the kiss for them to catch a breath. He realized he had tears in his eyes, but didn't care. He was no longer bound, and knew what it was like to feel true pleasure.

"You're in for it now, baby," he warned as his need became feral.

"Jace," she yelped when he set her down and ripped her shirt from her body. Her nipples pearled under the black satin, making his mouth water.

"Let me love you, Cailyn." He reached back to unclasp her bra and stole her reply with his mouth. He didn't want to hear a denial. Her tongue met his, and he knew there would be no denial. He let her bra fall to the forest floor along with his past. The rain had lightened to a mist and it mingled with the sweat on her skin, making her glisten.

"Mmmm, yesss." She arched her back and rubbed her breasts against his chest. His mate mark chose that moment to burn hotly, demanding that he finish the mating. It was harder than he imagined to stop from taking those final steps.

He set her on her feet and knelt in front of her. He grasped the waist of her pants, took a breath and looked up into passion-filled eyes. "I have to taste you, *Shijéí.*" He needed this with a desperation that was painful. He had to have her coating his tongue. He loved that she widened her stance at the same time she blushed and turned her head as if shy. Not that he had experience in pleasuring a female, but her combination of carnal abandon and shyness drove him crazy. Ignoring clasp and zipper, he ripped her jeans apart in one swift move.

"Holy shit, Jace," Cailyn gasped. "I liked those pants, but you can rip anything off my body anytime you want." A twist of his fingers and her silk panties fluttered to the ground as well. He glanced away from her flushed face to her exposed core. It was glistening with her arousal. He lifted a finger to trace her moisture and his eyes traveled up to her face, stopping to admire the way her exposed breasts rose and fell rapidly with her breaths.

His hand ran up her leg, luxuriating in her satin-soft skin. His fingers sank into her silky, slick flesh. "You are mine, Cailyn. My mate, my soul and I will win your heart." He swooped in and licked up her channel. Her response was lost as she mewled and panted her pleasure. One taste wetted his appetite and he savored her like a starving man. Going on instinct, he licked, nipped and sucked on her aroused flesh.

"Oh God, Jace. Please, whatever you do, don't stop." Her head dropped forward and he wrapped his arms around her waist as she wavered on her feet.

"You taste like heaven, love. I wouldn't dream of stopping," he murmured against her intimate flesh. He inserted one finger into her quivering flesh while he sucked her clit into his mouth. Her core clenched, and he added another finger, stretching her, preparing her for him. She writhed in his arms, rubbing against his mouth with abandon. He loved that she was so responsive to his touch.

He bit down on her bundle of nerves, making her squeal. He smiled and renewed his efforts, plunging his fingers in and out. As she convulsed and cried out his name in climax, joy swept through him that all he felt was an unbearable desire to join her in ecstasy. He refused to let up, despite her pleas. He was a male possessed by his Fated Mate.

As he continued his assault on her body, he marveled at the intense feeling of the pre-cum building in his cock. The pleasure was even greater this time without the nausea hampering it. She cried out as she came against his mouth a second time.

Driven by an urgent demand, he stood and headed for a nearby evergreen. "I can't wait. I'm sorry, love, but this is going to be hard and fast. The mating compulsion has me firmly in its grip," he leaned in to whisper in her ear, "I'm going to fuck you so hard that you have no doubt who you belong to."

"Oh," she cried as he impaled her on his cock in one smooth stroke. She was wet and more than ready for him. He did that to her. His chest puffed with pride that he could arouse his female. He began a slow rhythm trying to be gentle as he walked forward to the tree.

"How does it feel to have me deep inside you?" he demanded, and thrust hard, pushing her into the bark. He needed her to acknowledge that he was the only male for her. "So deep, I can't tell where you end and I begin," he groaned. He pulled his cock out of her pussy and saw her cream glowing along his length under the moonlight. He nearly lost his seed at the sight.

"Oh God, you feel so good. Fuck me, Jace," she managed, thrashing her head back and forth, using the tree to meet him stroke for stroke. He wanted to take more care with her, but he was an animal possessed right now.

Every sound she uttered made his cock harder. At the moment he was hard as steel and could pound nails. Instead, he speared into her tight little sheath while her walls squeezed him deliciously. He had never experienced the sensations bombarding his body, and he wanted more. He was greedy for it.

He realized he needed to complete the bond with this female, who not only carried a precious part of his soul, but had made her way into his heart. He needed her to accept his claim, and mate with him.

"You will accept me as your Fated Mate. We will spend the rest of eternity together. This I promise you, *Shijéí*." She yanked on his braid in response, making him buck and pound harder. He tried to remind himself that she was human and fragile, but was unable to stop the building orgasm that drove him deeper into the mire of insane arousal.

He reached down with one hand to play with her clit, stroking it harshly, demandingly. She tensed, signaling her orgasm was but a breath away. His was even closer, and he felt the pressure of his seed building, ready to explode. It threatened to melt him to ashes in the best way.

His spine tingled and his balls drew up tight. Her spasms began milking him as she cried out his name and her body shuddered violently with her release. She quaked over him and he roared out his victory as he joined her. He had won much this night, freedom, but a pleasure so great that it destroyed and remade him.

He felt the brush of their souls at the moment of climax, and it sent them both spiraling into another, deeper orgasm. He trembled as he held her against the tree, both their breaths coming in pants. He would never be the same after this night, and prayed to the Goddess that she felt the same way.

CHAPTER 24

Cailyn was still shaking as she followed Jace back to the house, and her mind was reeling. She'd had the best sex of her life, and he hadn't run away to throw up this time. Truth be told, she had felt the moment the spell was lifted. She was honored to have played a part in such a momentous moment for this formidable, yet vulnerable male.

It would not be easy to walk away from Jace, and yet she hated to break John's heart. He was a good man. Life wasn't clear or easy when you loved more than one person, because no matter what, you have to let one of them go, despite the pain it would cause. Sometimes you had to do that which you wanted least, in order to gain that which you wanted most. It was impossible to deny that she was made for Jace, and Jace alone. His every touch made her come alive.

Still, she struggled with how to walk away from John when he was familiar and comfortable. She knew what life would be like with him. She'd keep her job, marry him, eventually have a family then move to the suburbs. It would all be average, happy and…safe. She was okay with an average, safe life. It was what she had been raised to know, and didn't need a life of unending excitement and intrigue to be happy. But, with John, there wouldn't be the passion and thrill.

With Jace, it was as if she'd finally found home. His world might be filled with danger and violence, but she was protected by him and the warriors. Her life had been threatened too many times to count, her sister had been changed into a vampire and her best friend was a dhampir. Excitement, peril and intrigue were the mainstay of life at Zeum, but with Jace she had never felt more alive in her entire life.

"I need to talk to John before we can go any further. I know you want me to declare my love for you, and I know you don't want me to see him, but this is something I must do," she blurted, hating to ruin the afterglow. Despite the trudge back to the house, they were both still humming from the intense encounter. But sure enough, at the mention of John, he tensed, and the easy-going feeling vanished.

He squeezed the hand he was holding and stopped abruptly. She looked into angry, amethyst eyes. A firm tug brought her chest bumping into his. It was difficult for her to ignore the feel of his hot, hard flesh pressed against her naked breasts.

"I know that you have things to work out, but know this. You are my mate. You belong to me, and I will not stop until I have all of you. That human will never have you," he growled at her then kissed her. It was a hard kiss, full of dominance and ownership. She couldn't deny that he had a command over her. His free hand tangled in her hair, holding her close.

After several long moments he tugged at her hair,

pulling her head up. His lips were red and swollen and gleamed in the moonlight. His expression was fierce and possessive, and she was thrilled at how deeply this strong warrior wanted her. Still, she bristled at his dictation. "No one tells me what to do. I would've thought you had learned that by now. I am my own person and make my own decisions."

"I don't deserve to have you, but I will not stop until I have won your heart and soul. I fought what you represented to me, because you deserved better than what I was, and I refused to force you to be with a mate who was wrecked and unable to be what you needed. *You* changed all that. I walked the earth for centuries filled with bitterness and anger, and I never truly lived. And then you came into my life, bringing hope with you."

He untangled his hand from her hair and wrapped his arms around her waist, pulling her into an embrace. "I meant what I said in the clearing. I love you, Cailyn, so much it hurts."

She was stunned, but she felt the truth in his words through their connection. She had no words, and wasn't ready to explore her own deep feelings. "This is not what you want to hear, but I need a little more time." She stood up and placed a tender kiss on his lips.

"Come on. Let's get back to the house. We have time to figure things out, and I have waited seven hundred years for you. I think I can wait a bit more." He twined their fingers again and began walking before she could respond.

The big house came into view and the lights flooded into the yard. Suddenly very aware of their nudity, she ducked behind Jace.

"Jace, we can't go in there without clothes," she hissed. Laughter and talking emanated from the kitchen.

"We can grab something in the pool room. Don't worry, I don't plan to let anyone else see what's mine," he replied with laughter dancing in his eyes. She had never seen him so light and carefree before, and it elicited a smile from her.

They approached the enclosed patio and as she crossed the threshold, she recalled her sister's mating ceremony that was held in that room days ago. The intricate design inlaid in the center of the floor was vital to the realm. It was a representation of the Triskele Amulet, which was a magical talisman that allowed communication with their Goddess. The downside of the amulet, and the reason for the war with the demons, was that it could free Lucifer from his frozen prison in hell. She shuddered to think if he indeed got free and wreaked havoc across the earth.

They hurried to the pool room and quickly donned robes before heading to the others. As they walked back through the patio, Cailyn found herself wondering if all mating ceremonies were held in that room.

The idea of her and Jace standing before the realm and Goddess surrounded by the twinkling lights and magic was more appealing than she was ready to admit, just like Jace's insistence that she belonged to him. It would be easy to accept Jace and all that he offered. She may have grown up expecting an average life, but she was more than ready to begin a life living on the edge. Putting that thought out of her mind, she entered the kitchen to find nearly every resident of the house gathered while her sister cooked.

She smiled at the sight her sister had always wanted. She could remember Elsie playing restaurant with her and their friends. Elsie was happiest when she was whipping up a meal with those she loved around her, and now she had a large family of hungry warriors. Cailyn wanted to be part of this world with her sister, Jessie, and most of all Jace.

"There you guys are. I was about to turn the sprinklers on if you didn't stop soon. We have big news and can't afford for all of us to get caught up in your mating frenzy," Elsie joked. Cailyn blushed to her roots knowing they were all aware of what they had been doing. She could kill her sister for bringing even more attention to it.

"Mmmm, that smells delicious. What are you making?" Cailyn asked, changing the subject.

"One of your favorites, enchiladas and taquitos. Want to help?" Elsie motioned to the roast in front of her. Yum, suddenly Cailyn was ravenous, and realized she hadn't eaten since early that morning.

"Sure. What's your big news?" Cailyn walked past Kyran to reach Elsie's side and noticed he was eating creamsicles again. In fact, the warrior was double fisting them, and had a box in his arm. She wanted to laugh at the sight of one of the most intimidating warriors in the bunch obsessed with ice cream treats.

"Before we get into that," Zander said, turning to Jace as he picked up some meat her sister was cooking and popped it into his mouth. "From the shock wave that reverberated through the grounds, I take it the spell is lifted."

"Yes, it is. I couldn't have done it without my mate." Jace came up behind her and placed his hands on her hips, staking his claim verbally as well as non-verbally. She ignored the meaningful looks Elsie and Jessie threw her way. The questions were in their eyes, but they held back for the moment. She knew the second they had her alone, they would let loose. She would have to avoid them until she had spoken with John.

"Many are hunting Lady Angelica as we speak, we will find her. You will have your chance for vengeance. Now, back to the matter at hand. Orlando, please share what you told me earlier," Zander ordered, picking at the food again.

"Well, it seems Kadir has upped the ante once again, and somehow brought lesser demons into our realm. On patrol tonight, we faced half a dozen unknown creatures. They were bent on destruction and difficult to kill," Orlando shared as he walked over to grab some roast.

Elsie smacked Orlando's hand with her hot tongs. "Between the two of you, I won't have enough to finish these taquitos." He stuck his tongue out at her and they started laughing.

"Whatever they were, they seemed to feed off of our anger. And the cleanup sucks. They don't turn to ash like skirm," Gerrick steered the conversation back on track.

Rhys reached around Elsie and grabbed a bit of meat and retreated before Elsie retaliated. His movements were faster than Cailyn could follow. It was comical that the big bad warriors were afraid of her sister. Or, maybe it was Zander they were afraid of, Cailyn amended. "Kill," Rhys mumbled with a full mouth, "can you check the database? Maybe it'll tell us what type of demons they were. I think it's safe to assume that we will be facing these lesser demons, as well as skirm, at this prophesized battle."

"It's worth a try. I need to grab my laptop, I'll be right back," Killian answered as he left the room.

Cailyn watched the guy disappear, and thought about the last battle that occurred outside his club. She recalled those terrifying moments, and didn't want any of these people she had come to care for, especially her sister or Jace, facing that type of danger again. The thought had her stomach knotting, but this was part of life at the compound. A poignant reminder of what to expect, should she mate with Jace. She looked over her shoulder at her sorcerer, and something told her it would be worth every risky second.

"I had no idea that demons were so fucking hard to kill. We had to behead the bastards with our *sgian dubhs* and it was a bitch. Skirm are so much easier to battle. We will need to carry our claymores to this battle next week. And it wouldn't hurt to bring in more warriors either," Santiago said as he leaned against the granite counter.

"I vaguely recall the lesser demons my da banished. They were ferocious and there were too many of them for us to overcome without risking others," Jace explained. "What did these demons look like? The spell he used in the Grimoire may be effective against them, too."

Killian breezed back into the kitchen. "Hold those thoughts. Let me get the database up and running so I can compare while you talk." Killian flipped the computer open and before long he was typing away, giving the all clear to proceed.

"The ugly fuckers had mottled, smoke-colored skin," Orlando shared, running his hand through his short white-blond hair, causing it to stick up more. "They had the typical horns, fangs and claws of a demon. Only they had four red horns and sharp black fangs. They weren't overly tall, about six feet."

"And, they had glowing yellow eyes. And Goddess, they stunk like shit, or rather dead animals," Gerrick added.

Elsie stuffed and rolled the various tortillas she had been lightly frying while Cailyn stuck toothpicks through them, skewering the yummy tubular concoctions. They had done this many times before, and it helped Cailyn calm her nerves as she listened to the talk of demons. She marveled at how fearless her sister had become as she jumped right in the conversation without a break in her cooking. "Who were they targeting? Are there any victims we need to worry about?"

"The only victim we saw was a young human female. She will be found in the park where we encountered them. An anonymous call was placed to the SPD, so she won't be found by innocents. Don't worry, it will be attributed to an animal attack and the realm won't be exposed. Also, I personally notified her family and offered the assistance of Elsie's Hope," Orlando assured her sister. Cailyn had seen Orlando's attraction to her sister many times, but this was the first where she saw his respect for her as the Queen.

Elsie acknowledged with a nod. "Thank you for that. The families are often the forgotten victims in these cases."

Killian cleared his throat and interrupted, "From what I see here, we are facing fury demons. Now, keep in mind that most of this information is based on lore that has been passed down from generation to generation. The information indicates anger and fury only makes them stronger. If this is what we are facing, we could be screwed. There is no way to block rage while fighting."

Elsie dropped the taquitos into the deep fryer and the room was filled with the sound of crackling and popping. Soon the aroma of chili sauce, enchiladas and fried food filled the room. More than one stomach rumbled in response. Angus bustled about the kitchen and Cailyn had the feeling he wanted to join the conversation, and it was difficult for him to hold back.

Zander came up behind Elsie and placed his hand on her shoulders. "We need to increase patrols. Killian, send oot a bulletin from the council, informing citizens to keep an eye out for the new threat. I will notify Hayden, and have Nikko bring in Dark Warriors from Vancouver, Portland and

San Francisco. We will plan more about the battle in the days to come, but for now, let's eat."

Cailyn was starving, but with the talk about demons, death and war, she didn't know if she could eat. "Rhys, do you have any of that *hey juice*?" she asked, needing a strong drink.

∽

CAILYN STOOD in the grand entry way of Zeum having a stare down with Jace. It had been a crazy week of Dark Warriors coming to help with the battle. The house was full to bursting.

The visiting warriors stayed in the quarters that were located in the basement. Thane and Jax came from San Francisco, while Kellen and Mikael came from Portland and Caleb and Phineas flew in from Vancouver. The new warriors fit in seamlessly, and the house was focused on getting ready for the battle.

She was surrounded by gorgeous men with hard muscled bodies, so she wasn't complaining. Testosterone was abundant around the compound, and Jessie was in heaven. Cailyn was certain her best friend had hooked up with at least one of the new Dark Warriors. The warriors helped Jessie learn control of her new abilities, and it was good to see her settling into her new life.

Cailyn had been busy making changes to her life as well. She wasn't going back to San Francisco anytime soon, so she called her boss and tendered her resignation before calling her insurance company and handling the car accident. Putting her home up for sale was a difficult decision, but she knew it was for the best. The decision had come down to one of necessity. She wasn't able to pay her mortgage without her job. She refused to allow her sister to pay her bills. It had always been Cailyn's job to take care of Elsie, not the other way around.

She had tried to call John numerous times with no luck. He had checked out of the hotel and wasn't answering his cell. Countless text messages went unanswered, and most disturbing was that he hadn't been to work since leaving for Seattle. She recalled the hurt in his eyes when she called off the wedding, but she didn't think he would ignore her so completely.

And then there was Jace. She had been walking on eggshells with him. They hadn't been intimate again since the night they broke his spell. She suspected that he was waiting until she came to him, ready to accept his claim.

Jace had been busy preparing for the battle to come, but that didn't stop him from seeking her out every chance he had. They talked all hours of the day and night, and she realized they had more in common than she would have guessed. She was coming to love everything about him. Their connection deepened daily, and she was choked by fear for him every time he left for his patrols.

Tonight wasn't just any night when he went to the hospital or was on patrol. Tonight was the night of the Red Moon, and they were all headed to Woodland Park to face demons. She didn't want him to go. Hell, she didn't want any of them to go. They had all come to mean too much to her, even the new guys. At the same time, she understood that they were all that stood between evil and humans.

"I don't want you to go," she whispered to him, her lips trembling with her emotions.

Jace cupped her cheeks with his warm hands and looked deeply into her eyes, letting his love for her show. "I have to go, but I will come back to you. I have too much to live for now. We have a mating ceremony to plan, *Shijéí.*" He smiled that smile of his that melted her heart before kissing her deeply. When their lips finally parted, she saw her sister and Zander in a similar embrace. Before she could respond, Jace had walked out the front doors.

Trembling with fear she turned to her sister and grabbed hold. For as long as she could remember they had been a team. She couldn't have faced this night without Elsie. "How can we just let them go?" she asked her, as an overwhelming feeling that she needed to be at this battle refused to leave her.

Her sister smiled a mischievous half smile. "We aren't, I had one of my premonitions. We all need to be there. I have no idea what we will face, or if we will all come back. I don't understand all of the changes to my ability, and this time I didn't get as many details, but it was clear that the three of us have to be there. Angus!" Elsie called.

The elegant and handsome majordomo of the house came in and bowed. "Your Highness."

"Are you ready to take us to the park?" her sister asked the servant, shocking her. What the hell?

CHAPTER 25

"Yes, your Highness. But first, follow me, lasses. We must get you into battle leathers and ootfitted with weapons," Angus replied before he turned on his heel and headed down the stairs to the basement.

"There aren't going to be leathers that fit us, Angus. We are all short compared to the warriors, even Breslin. Somehow I don't think it will work to roll them up. Jeans will be the sturdiest we can manage," Elsie replied as she and Jessie easily kept pace behind Angus. Cailyn was practically running to stay close to the trio. She might not be a marathon runner, but she thought herself fit. It was a poignant reminder that the two people she loved most in the world were no longer human.

For a second, Cailyn envied their supernatural status. She wanted to have super speed, be able to see a tick on a horse's ass from a mile away, and be strong enough to take on Lady Angelica. The fact of the matter was that she was only a human, with human strength and speed, and she would be killed if she attempted to go after Angelica.

Angus' voice shook Cailyn out of herself. "I have taken care of what you will need, your Highness," he turned and his smile was full of mischief and affection. "I knew from the second you walked in the front doors of Zeum that they'd be needed. You are no' one to sit idly by."

Elsie's laughter was sharp and quick. "You are right about that, Angus. I cannot sit here in safety while my mate is in danger."

Elsie's mention of the danger had Cailyn's palms sweating. She'd be a liability during the battle. She didn't have the fighting skills her sister had, or Jessie's newfound strength. "I don't think I should go with you guys, no matter how much I want to. I'll just be in the way. You will be distracted by worrying about me and Jace will too if he sees me." The thought of everyone she loved being at risk had her anxiety skyrocketing. But she wanted desperately to be there so she could protect them, as crazy as the idea was.

"You are going, Cai. Yes we will worry about you, but you have to be there. You were part of my premonition. The four of us were there. Besides, Angus is going to remain glued to your side, no matter what, so you will be protected," Elsie looked straight at the dragon-shifting majordomo while she said the last. Her sister's insistence that she be there both frightened and reassured Cailyn.

She refused to think about the last battle she had been in the middle of, otherwise, she would be frozen by fear. "Okay," she responded weakly then tried again, "okay, I trust you guys."

Jessie grabbed her hand as they entered a room Cailyn had never been in. The room was filled with shelves upon shelves of weapons of every kind. The smell of oil and gunpowder assaulted her nose. She wasn't surprised to see so many medieval weapons as much as she was to see so many automatic rifles. Somehow, the rudimentary arsenal fit more with the Dark Warriors.

"Oh my God, you guys could outfit an entire army," Jessie blurted as she picked up a large sword from the wall.

"That is exactly what we do," Angus responded matter-of-factly. "His Highness leads the realm's forces. At any given time we have Dark Warriors from all over the globe visiting, in addition to a great many weapons being lost in battle." Angus walked into a small closet and came back loaded with black leather garments. He laid them out on a table and the three of them approached.

The smell of new leather was potent and she inhaled deeply. She loved the smell of leather. She reached out and was shocked at how soft it was. This wasn't the cheap stuff that held a degree of stiffness. This was like butter, and she couldn't wait to feel it against her skin.

"You guys don't skimp on anything, do you?" Jessie asked.

"I wouldna buy anything but the best for our weapons and armor. This is all that stands between you and the enemy. You are no' familiar with our world yet, but there are demons whose saliva is like acid. These will protect you from that, as well as minor blows from blades. Now, I'll leave you to get dressed."

The moment Angus was out the door, Cailyn had her shirt over her head and was slipping into one of the shirts. By the time Cailyn was slipping on her pants, Jessie and Elsie were already changed and putting on their boots. "This feels amazing on, and is surprisingly easy to move in," Elsie commented as she stepped back and tried some maneuvers. "Let's grab some weapons."

Unease shot through Cailyn. "I have never used a gun

and don't have the first idea about what I will need. Maybe I shouldn't go."

"We aren't going over that again, Cai. You are going. Here, you will need some of the titanium *sgian dubhs*. They are small and the titanium will turn any skirm you face to ash. Angus will try and protect you from everything, but I don't want you unarmed," Elsie said, placing several small blades in various places on Cailyn's body.

"Thank God one of us knows what they are doing," Jessie remarked.

"I wouldn't go that far," Elsie replied. "I may have fought skirm, but this is only my second big battle." Those words had Cailyn's heart racing as her anxiety flew out of control. She hoped she didn't have a panic attack.

∽

JACE WALKED across the large grassy field next to Rhys, wondering if they had the wrong location. The night was quiet and the mist changed to light rain as the Dark Warriors and council stood looking around.

"Do you suppose we are wrong about the prophecy?" Rhys asked.

Zander spun around and pinned him with a glare. "Nay, we were no'. The battle will occur tonight. Question is, when?"

Jace went rigid. "You feel that?" he asked Evzen before black and red lights flashed in the middle of the clearing. All heads turned in that direction and they watched as fury demons and hellhounds poured out of the portal like black lava oozing down the side of a volcano. There were already too many to count and they were still coming.

"How the hell are they doing a portal without going

through the Cave of Cruachan? I thought that was the only place where the veil between earth and hell was thin enough to allow passage between the realms." Gerrick inquired as he withdrew his claymore from the sheath on his back.

Every warrior followed suit and silver glinted in the night off the dozens of weapons. "I don't give a shit about how. We need to block this portal or earth will be lost," Evzen yelled back.

Jace called his staff to his free hand and looked over, seeing that Gerrick, Killian and Evzen were at the ready. As one, they began chanting in the old language, using the red moon to power their spell. Jace held his love for his mate close, using its power as well. Between that and the red moon, the surge of energy almost knocked Jace off his feet. It was as if billions of tiny bubbles fizzed through his veins. With a loud blast, the portal snapped closed on a dozen demons. Torsos and heads fell to the ground, emitting a foul odor of brimstone.

No time to wonder if their spell would hold, the demons were upon them and the others were already engaged. Jace released his staff and began swinging his sword.

"Watch out, Jace," Rhys called out before he threw his *sgian dubh*. Jace ducked and spun around to see a hellhound choking. Knowing that wouldn't kill the beast, Jace delivered the final blow, lopping its head off in one slice.

Jace rushed to Zander's side when he noticed the focus of the battle was on him. "Fight back to back," Zander ordered. They fell into a familiar fighting stance, managing to keep those around them at bay.

Kyran flashed to their side and joined them. The Vampire Prince was merciless in his attack. Movement in the corner of his eye caught Jace's attention. Kadir and Azazel appeared at the edge of the clearing, and they held at least twenty skirm between them.

"Skirm," Jace called out, pointing to where the archdemons were. He began racing that way, eyes blazing with the need for vengeance. The bastards would pay for what they'd done to his mate.

Jace didn't make it ten feet before he was once again surrounded. His arms never slowed as he swung his sword. He couldn't let these creatures win this battle or his mate would become one of their victims, not to mention the countless humans they would kill.

Jace glanced around quickly, noticing that each of the warriors were in a similar predicament of being outnumbered. He sent up a prayer to the Goddess for help. They would need a miracle to turn the tides of this battle. He fought harder, refusing to give up. He had yet to win his mate's heart, and he wasn't dying before that happened.

~

THE RAIN FELL LIGHTLY as Cailyn stood on the back lawn gaping at Angus. He stripped revealing an exquisite body. She knew the guy was gorgeous and no cream puff, but having always seen him in suits belied that he was so large and muscular. As Angus stood there with his short black hair blowing in the wind, naked as a jay bird, Cailyn marveled how unselfconscious supernaturals were. For good reason, they were all perfect tens.

He flexed his muscles and seemed to tense, then relax, and suddenly his entire body shimmered, and colored light enveloped him. Cailyn shielded her eyes and when she blinked to clear her vision, she was looking at an enormous dragon. He took up the entire lawn in their backyard, and had to be the size of an airplane. His scales were as black as his hair, and had an iridescent quality. His pale-green eyes were set wide apart in the long, reptilian face, and were bigger than basketballs. She marveled at the magnificent creature before her.

Jessie stood next to her, clearly in as much shock. They had told Jessie about shifters, but she had not seen the transformation, so this was new to her. Cailyn had seen Orlando and Santiago both shift during the battle outside Confetti, and that had been surreal, but that experience was nothing compared to watching the enigmatic Angus become a dragon - the largest, most magnificent creature of myth, in Cailyn's opinion. Orlando as his snow leopard and Santi as his wolf were both larger than normal, but they were still animals she was familiar with, animals she could visit in a zoo. But this dragon simply took her breath away.

"Incredible, isn't he?" her sister voiced as she approached the black dragon.

"What, can you read minds now too?" Cailyn joked with Elsie, shivering in the cool night air. "Yes, he is exceptional. Have you thought about how mad Zander is going to be?"

Elsie stroked the dragon's snout as he lay on the lawn resting his head on his huge paws and looked back over her shoulder. The dragon's head was a good two feet taller than her sister. It was simply enormous.

"Yes, I have, but you should know better than anyone that I cannot stand the thought of my mate facing danger. It's a good thing Angus here," she patted the beast, eliciting a snort and a puff of smoke on his exhale, "feels the same way about his Liege. He has been with Zander for centuries and refuses to stand by and not use his strength and fire to help fight the demons. I know my mate thought it best to leave him here to protect us...he will soon realize he didn't mate a wilting flower."

Cailyn couldn't help but smile at her sister's vehemence, and knew the on-going battle she'd had with Zander's overbearing, caveman attitude, and how he wanted to shelter her from the world. That vampire had no idea what he had bit off.

"I'm surprised Angus is willing to take you. I mean, he could leave without us and help the guys," Jessie pointed out.

"Angus and I have become close since I joined the household, and he has come to trust my premonitions as much as I do. He knows the Goddess has a hand in them and that they shouldn't be ignored. Besides, I bribed him with his favorite meal," Elsie added and the dragon seemed to smile, baring the largest incisors she'd ever seen.

Jessie eyed Angus dubiously. "So, are we riding or rather flying on him? Cause I have to say, that idea doesn't appeal to me. I was granted immortality and don't plan to die one week into it," she stammered, as his huge, leathery wings extended. Both she and Jessie jumped when lighting flashed the moment his wings arched into the air, and thunder boomed.

Elsie laughed and leaned against the dragon's side, showing her comfort. Cailyn loved her sister even more for trying to put her best friend at ease. "Yes, we are flying on Angus to the park, and no, we can't take a car and meet him there. He's our best chance at safety while still being close to the fight until we are needed. I don't plan to take any unnecessary risks with myself or you guys."

A curious excitement raced through Cailyn's system at the thought of flying on a dragon through the night sky. She considered herself a pretty adventurous person, and was totally on board with it. She eagerly awaited the adrenaline rush that would soon follow. She recalled the zip-line she had traveled at Mount Herman in the Santa Cruz Mountains and how thrilling it was. But, then she had been securely fastened to the steel cable with little chance of falling to her death. "I am totally on-board with that idea. Is there a saddle or some way to tie us to his hide? I'm not a fan of free-falling without a parachute," Cailyn said, eager to get into the air.

A smoky chuckle echoed in her head. *"No, little one, I have no saddle. Doona fash, I willna let any of you fall. My reflexes are good, and if I need to maneuver during battle, I will set you some place safe."*

Cailyn gaped at the harsh, dragon voice that spoke in her head. This was the first time she was able to hear a supernaturals thoughts so clearly. She loved being a part of this realm, there was always something new and exciting, no matter the danger. "Thanks for the reassurance. I trust you. Come on, Jess," she replied as she climbed onto his bent knee and hoisted herself to his back. "Have a little faith. This is going to be fun."

Jessie grumbled as she followed suit and reached for Cailyn's hand. "Easy for you to say, you love all this adventure crap. Don't forget, I'm afraid of heights."

Elsie chuckled as she squatted down then sprang up and did an elegant somersault into the air and landed smoothly behind Jessie. The move was shocking. When Elsie was human, she had been a mediocre athlete, at best. Cailyn attributed her grace to her new vampire genes.

Cailyn would never have vampire genes, but that didn't stop her from wondering what she would be like if she mated Jace, becoming immortal. How much would she change? Would she have super hearing and vision? What about her strength and speed? The idea wasn't as upsetting as she might have thought.

"Okay, Angus," Elsie's voice broke in. "We are seated and ready." The dragon inclined its head and the huge wings began to beat, stirring up leaves and debris. Cailyn hunkered down and grabbed hold between the shoulders and wings at the base of his long neck. A subtle tingle built in intensity as they left the ground. The lift off was surprisingly quiet and as she looked over to the lights of the house. It became obvious what the tingle was when Cailyn noticed the air around his wing was shimmering like it did off the cement on a hot day. "What is that?" she called over her shoulder as she pointed.

"That lass, is my magic. An invisible shield. It wouldna do to have a giant black dragon seen flying over the city, now would it?"

Her words were swallowed by the air currents, and in moments they were flying over the city. Angus seemed to be flying toward the lightning. Cailyn enjoyed the heat coming off Angus as her skin chilled further. The rain pelted her face with the speed of their flight. The houses and building were a blur beneath them and before she knew it they were approaching the park.

Even from a distance she heard the clang of metal. "Can you see anything?" she called out to Elsie and Jessie.

"I can see the battle, but I can't see Jace or Zander," Elsie responded. At that moment they passed over and she looked down at the bloody battle. Angus angled up before she could make any sense of the scene before her and the moon caught her eye.

The large, red-orange globe was haunting in its fullness and presage. It echoed the brief glimpse she had gotten of the battlefield. Angus swooped back around and she felt his sides swell as he took in a breath. They passed over the outer banks of the park and he bellowed fire upon the demons and skirm skirting the edges. She felt the heat from his flames waft up into her face as the vile creatures ignited and fell to the ground writhing. The putrid smell of burnt flesh reached her before he flew them away. Her stomach roiled and her heart began to pound in her chest. She hadn't seen Jace yet, and needed to find him. She searched the ground as Angus continued flying.

It seemed there were countless demons. Some looked like the ones Orlando had described, and others looked like big black dogs. And, then there were the skirm she recalled all too clearly. Even though they brought in more Dark Warriors, they were outnumbered. She sent a prayer to their Goddess asking for their victory.

She saw Santiago standing on the ground with his arm extended toward the sky. Lightning struck at that moment and she watched in amazement as Santiago directed the bolt to the nearest demon. The creature exploded in a spray of black blood and guts. Santiago didn't bother to clean the debris from his face before his arm was back in the air once again. He repeated the action time and time again eliminating several skirm and demons. Unfortunately, more took their place.

Her anxiety eased when she saw Hayden run from the trees followed by a large pack of shifters. Wolves and a variety of large feline breeds roared as they ripped into the demons. She hoped this gave them the edge they needed to win.

She scanned everywhere, but still couldn't find Jace anywhere. She hoped he was okay. He had to be alright, she couldn't lose him. She needed him, and hadn't had a chance to tell him how she felt about him. His soul surged in her chest, reaching out to her. It was such a comforting feeling in the midst of this chaos. She realized that during her most trying moments throughout her life, his presence had always been with her. She just hadn't known it was Jace's soul.

She saw Zander heft the longest silver sword she had ever seen, and lob head after head off demons and skirm alike. He was an awe-inspiring sight, and she could see why he was the vampire king.

White fur streaked toward the dragon, cutting a path while yowling furiously. Orlando, she realized, and he had seen them. Angus stopped belching fire and began chomping the enemy with every pass. The sound of bone crunching caused bile to rise in her throat as he devoured the enemy.

Something cold rushed past the left side of her face as her sister called out a warning to Orlando. Startled, Cailyn realized Elsie had hurled a ball of ice at a skirm who had been coming at Orlando from behind. The ice slowed the skirm enough that Orlando was able to claw its heart out. Black blood sprayed and stained the snow leopard's white fur.

"Take that, motherfuckers! Get 'em Angus," Jessie called out. Cailyn glanced over her shoulder at her friend and noted the excitement in her eyes while she watched the battle. This was not the same girl she had grown up with. Before, Jessie would have balked at such violence, not relish in it.

Silver flashed out of the corner of her eye as a small blade flew into the chest of a skirm that was trying to jump onto Angus as he flew low. She looked back and saw Rhys call the knife back to his hand as the skirm flashed on fire and turned to ash. She broke out in a cold sweat at the close call. She was feeling very human and wanted to be anywhere but where she was. She told herself to suck it up because she wasn't leaving everyone she loved in this alone. She may not be able to do much, but she could try.

She refocused on the ground and noticed black blood and bodies were strewn about the field and amongst the trees. She saw Kyran swing his sword through necks only to disappear before the severed heads hit the ground. She thought that ability would keep him from harm until he was caught by one of those demon dogs when he reappeared. She and Elsie screamed out at the same time when the dog bit into Kyran's leg, shaking its big head from side to side.

Elsie jumped off the dragon's back when they got close. "Zander, help Kyran," she called out and had two blades in her hands the second she touched the ground. Zander was running in their direction while Elsie stabbed the dog repeatedly. Cailyn's heart sank when skirm seemed to sense Elsie's appearance and broke off to head her way. No one had seen the danger approaching her sister.

"Angus," she yelled, "we have to do something. Can you get those guys running to Elsie and Kyran?" She felt rather than saw his nod, and faster than she could blink he had several of them in his jaws. There were still too many of them, she could not lose her sister like this. Scanning about she searched for something, anything. Recalling her own weapons, she withdrew one from the waistband of her pants.

Warriors were crying out in anguish all around her. She saw Thane go down and he didn't get up. She screamed out her denial. She hated to see any of these powerful men hurt, and refused to believe he was dead. She sat upright and searched for Jace but didn't see him. She did see Rhys. "Rhys," she called out, "help Thane!" He drew his hand back and let lose one of the small knives. Silver glinted in the red moonlight before the blade sunk into skirm flesh.

"He has to get up," Jessie breathed against her ear. "Come on, Thane." Cailyn reached back and briefly squeezed her thigh.

Scanning for Jace again, she finally saw his distinct braid. He was a beautiful and ferocious sight. Her chest swelled with pride as she watched him. She lost sight of him as Angus increased his height to avoid the trees.

When they came back around, she noted that they were making a dent in the demons. Angus had continued his low swoops to either breathe fire on or eat the combatants. She was relieved to see that Zander had reached Elsie and Kyran's side. Kyran was limping, but still fighting. In fact, the three of them had formed a triangle and stood shoulder to shoulder. Elsie was a better fighter than Cailyn had thought, and had taken out her share of enemies. The sword her sister wielded looked far too big for her petite body, but she swung it with ease.

For the first time, she thought they could win this until a loud shriek pierced her ears.

CHAPTER 26

The world pitched end over end for several terrifying moments and suddenly, Cailyn was momentarily transported back in time to the car accident when she heard Jessie scream. Strong hands grabbed her and pulled her into a warm body before she found herself flying through the air. She remembered the Fae, and how he had yanked her from the wreckage. Thank God this time it was Jessie that had grabbed her, catapulting them off the dragon. They landed roughly in a tangle of limbs, snapping her out of the memory. Even though Jessie had shielded her from the worst of the fall, Cailyn hurt all over.

Cailyn looked up and saw Angus hit the ground, taking out several skirm and plowing a furrow several yards long. Dirt flew and rained over them as they hurried to his side. Her left side hurt the most, but she didn't think anything was broken. She had lost her weapon in the shuffle and scooped up a random blade she saw as she approached the downed dragon. "Are you ok?" she asked the dragon.

The large creature blinked his eyes open and spoke in

her mind. *"I will live, unlike the two demons who dared claw my wings. Get doon, lass."* She ducked as his paw pulled her safely under his belly, along with Jessie, before a searing heat left his throat. The flames engulfed the skirm approaching them.

"You ok, Jess?"

"Yeah. You?"

"Yeah. Did you see Jace before we went down?"

"No. You stay here, I can help them take out the rest of these guys and I'll look for him."

Before Cailyn could respond Jessie had taken off and was scooping up a new weapon. Cailyn stood up, more sore than before. Adrenaline had her heart racing and her body ready for battle. She took breaths to calm herself, and looked around for her sister and Jace. Coughing, she placed her hand over her mouth when the stench of rotten meat suffocated her. These demons didn't turn to ash when they died, and smelled far worse than a sewer.

"Stay under my flank, lass. I will protect you with my life."

"I knew I should have stayed home. You should be helping the others not protecting..." she trailed off when Kadir and Azazel appeared at the edge of the clearing. She would never forget the large, ugly demon. While Azazel looked like a beautiful male model, Kadir was a seven foot monster. He had gray skin and horns on his head. His eyes and hair were red as blood, and his black fangs were the size of small swords.

She realized that they were holding someone between them and her heart stopped when the young man turned around. She knew him, it was John! She couldn't believe what she was seeing, and she screamed a denial when she saw his glowing eyes and fangs. They had turned him into a skirm. Her world collapsed around her as she saw the wild need in his eyes to kill and consume. The confident, loyal, independent man she had known was gone and she wondered if he recognized her.

Her heart ached for the man she had loved. It didn't matter that she didn't want to spend the rest of her life with him, he deserved better than the fate he now faced. Maybe there was a way to save him. Could they come up with a cure for John with the new information the realm scientists had gathered from studying Jessie's envenomation? She was determined to keep him alive so they had the chance to find out.

As she looked around she had no idea where her best friend was. Jessie had disappeared in the midst of the battle and all she could hear was yelling and cursing and the clashing of metal. Her sister was fighting back to back with Zander and they were surrounded. Jace was MIA and she was close to losing her shit. If anything happened to those she loved, she would be left with nothing. There had to be something she could do.

∼

JACE HEARD Angus go down and began running toward the bloom of dust. Panic had him cutting through everything in his path. He had heard Zander curse when the dragon first flew overhead and had looked up to see his mate riding on the back of the dragon. Jace's heart had stopped when he knew she had gone down along with Angus and she was so close to danger. He tried with all his might to send a message to Angus that the bastard had better keep his mate safe.

A large hellhound stepped in front of him, stopping him in his tracks. Jace slashed out and stepped into the demon, but it repeatedly sidestepped out of the way. After several minutes of dodging blows, Jace roared his rage and rushed the hellhound, taking it to the ground. The dog got in a couple swipes and flayed Jace's side. His worry and anger blocked the pain and Jace put all of his effort behind his swing, finally removing the demon's head.

Panting, he jumped to his feet and searched for Angus and Cailyn, trusting the dragon would keep her close. At the edge of the clearing, he caught sight of Kadir and Azazel with several skirm, surrounding Breslin. The feisty Vampire Princess looked tired and wasn't producing any of her fire. He had to help her and rushed toward her, still searching for his mate.

He saw Cailyn safe by Angus' side and continued to Breslin. He hoped she stayed by Angus, Breslin needed him. He swiped up a fallen claymore as he ran.

"Breslin," Jace called out as he got close, "here! Take this!" He tossed the sword to her and she reached out, catching it without stopping her attack. Jace liberated three skirm of their heads with one swing of his sword.

"Thanks, Jace. These arseholes have been bragging aboot setting this up and getting us to leave Zeum unattended," Breslin gritted out as she blocked blows. "Och, and they claim that skirm is going to take down Elsie's sister, and thus, Elsie."

Jace's head swung to the skirm Breslin had pointed to and noticed he had started to walk away from their group. Jace ignored the taunts Breslin and the archdemons were exchanging and really looked at the guy. There was no way Jace would allow this guy within inches of Cailyn, but what made the archdemons put so much faith in this particular skirm evaded him. He wasn't anything special, and certainly wasn't stronger than the Dark Warriors.

The male picked up his pace, and the closer he got the Cailyn and Angus, the more panicked Jace became. He didn't want to leave Breslin alone with the archdemons, but he had to get to Cailyn. He glanced back and was happy to see that Zander and Elsie had fought their way to Breslin's side, and between the three, they had the archdemons and their skirm in hand.

Jace turned around and leapt forward, grabbing the skirm's shoulder before he made it two more feet. He tackled him to the ground and scrambled to find the claymore he had dropped in his efforts. The male flipped over and snarled in Jace's face. "Let me go, sorcerer. That's right, I know who you are. I was told about the sorcerer with the braid who stole my girl from me."

Shocked, Jace crab-crawled backwards and took in the male. This had to be Cailyn's fiancé, John. Several things hit Jace at once. Cailyn was going to be heartbroken over John's envenomation. This was going to devastate her, and she was undoubtedly going to blame herself for his turning. She felt it was her responsibility to take care of those she loved and would see this as her failure. He also knew without doubt that she would want to seek a way to save him. The way she had fought for Jessie had made him proud of her, but now he cursed how vehemently she fought for what she believed in. There was no saving male skirm. The centuries of study by realm scientists hadn't even garnered enough information to develop a treatment for their venom.

John lunged at Jace with knives in both his hands. Jace knocked him back and jumped to his feet, snatching one of the blades. He dodged John's next blow, reluctant to cause the male any harm. "You will never have her. Kadir has promised to turn her and give her to me," John spat.

Jace was surprised at the amount of reasoning John had

for a skirm. Of course, it was a ploy. If Cailyn saw a piece of John's personality, she would trust him. She would believe there was a way to save him, and wouldn't allow one of the other warriors to kill him either. Jace's gut clenched at the thought of the hopelessness of the situation. John needed to die, there was no saving him, and Jace was the one who stood between him reaching Cailyn.

Jace stabbed out, catching John's arm. The black blood flowed to the grass where it sizzled and popped. They circled one another and John tried to catch Jace. Jace danced back a few steps with John following him. Jace had an opening when John stumbled, but Jace hesitated to deliver the killing blow.

Cailyn would never forgive him if he killed John. Jace had no doubt that the demon had made false promises and would kill Cailyn after he used her to capture Elsie. That could never happen, John needed to die. What stopped Jace was the fact that Cailyn would never be able to look at him without seeing a cold-blooded killer. He wanted to win her heart, not her wrath. How could he kill the male his mate loved?

John slashed Jace's arm and Jace responded by slicing John's cheek. At that moment, he heard Cailyn cry out John's name and he swung his head around, making eye contact with her.

The distraction was all John needed to sink a blade into Jace's back. He felt the titanium nick his heart and cursed before jumping away. Jace fought hard as they scuffled and felt the blood pour down his back. His power waning and John now had the advantage with his strength leaking with every beat of his heart. Jace didn't have the time needed to heal. John swiped up a sword from the ground and Jace's heart sank when he realized he was done for. Normally, beheading an immortal was difficult, but right now it would be easy for John to end Jace's life. He had no more power than a human male while John had the strength of a demon coursing through his veins. He may have lived for over seven hundred years, but wasn't ready to die. His life had just begun.

He looked back to Cailyn and saw the tears flowing from her eyes. "I love you," he whispered.

∼

CAILYN WATCHED in horror as John drove a knife into Jace's chest. As she had watched them fight while she made her way to their side, she noticed how John was more agile than she had ever seen him.

John hadn't hesitated in injuring Jace, but she saw Jace holding back. Jace typically fought with vigor and confidence and she hadn't once seen him pause. Through her connection to Jace, Cailyn felt his debate and knew he didn't want to kill John because of her.

She foolishly had held onto the idea of a man whom was safe and comfortable. She wasn't at risk of losing her heart or anything else if she stayed with John. If she lost him, she would move on and be fine, but if she ever lost Jace, her life would be over. To acknowledge that she loved him would be giving up everything to him. He owned every last cell in her body and would literally change them when they mated. He wanted centuries together. She'd known this the entire time and had been afraid of opening herself up. She had been a fool. Now, she wanted to run into his arms, proclaim her love for him, and accept his mating claim.

Jace whispered that he loved her and she saw the acceptance of his death in his eyes, sparking anger in Cailyn that roared from her mouth. She ran as Jace's knees gave out and he toppled to the ground, his eyes never leaving her.

She looked away from Jace when she saw John's arm rise. The glint of silver from John's sword sent her heart racing with determination to save her mate. Putting all her love for Jace into her legs, she flew across the space, and without hesitation, she plunged the knife she was holding into John's chest. She must have missed his heart because he snarled at her, revealing bloody fangs. She didn't have time to stop and think, he was going to kill her and Jace, so she pulled the blade from his chest and shoved it back in.

She had loved this man, and had wanted to give him a chance at a cure, but she wasn't willing to sacrifice Jace for it. Pouring all her anger at the demons into her force, she shoved the blade deeper. She cried out and snatched her hand back as flames flashed and John turned to ash. He remained an eerie ash statue for a timeless moment, and the look of betrayal would forever be etched in her mind.

"Jace," she cried out as she sank to her knees by his side.

"*Shijéí*," Jace murmured.

She grabbed his hand and brought it to her chest, looking into stunning amethyst eyes that never failed to captivate her. She wrapped her arms around him and buried her face in the crook of his neck, careful of his wounds. His warm, masculine scent soothed her, and the steady beat of his heart reassured her that he was going to live. She clung to him for several long moments as she let the tears flow. He cooed words in her ear and kissed the top of her head. Her heart broke as the enormity of the situation hit home.

She had killed John.

~

MACKENDRA SLUNK through the back alleys and ducked behind a greasy dumpster to hide from the vampire she was following. Last week, she had been on patrol with Stitch, when they heard the vampires talking about kidnapping women. Since then, every SOVA member had been trying to discover more information about vampire activities while they researched missing persons' reports. They had increased nightly patrols, but unfortunately, they revealed nothing. There hadn't been one vampire sighting, and everyone was burnt out.

Stitch had called it an early night, making her promise that she would do the same. She had every intention of going home, she really did. In fact, she was headed that way when she hit pay dirt. A lone vampire was stalking the shadows through her neighborhood east of downtown. Instinct had her reaching for her blade to end this parasitic creature. Her first instinct was always to strike without hesitation, and it took all of her will power not to attack. She said a prayer and followed it, hoping he would lead her to the missing women. Finding these women was more important than vengeance right now.

She peered around the edge of the dumpster and noted the guy had stopped moving to sniff the air. Shit, she hoped the rotting trash hid her presence and she flattened against the wall. That familiar dump of adrenaline preceded her racing heart and rapid breathing. Normally, she used this extra dose of energy to beat the super powered leeches, her legs crouched automatically, ready to pounce. She slicked her sweaty palms down her black fatigues and forced herself to stand straight. Don't move, she repeated over and over as she clamped down on her muscles. Sweat poured down her spine as she stood there for what seemed like an eternity.

She waited while the footsteps carried danger away from her. Gingerly, she made her way from behind the trashcan and down the alley. She was forced to pick up her pace or risk losing him when the vampire disappeared around the corner. It was hard to be quiet when her combats boots were loud as thunder.

She came up short when she noticed that he had stopped and was looking around. He clearly wasn't aware of her as he resumed his sure-footed pace through the buildings. She was curious as to why he was in the midst of downtown.

The streets were relatively empty save for a few stragglers. She wanted to shout to the drunks stumbling from the bars and the people leaving work that a killer walked among them. But they were safer not knowing the danger that lurked nearby.

She kept her hand on her blade beneath her jacket. The vampire all but flashed his fangs as he passed several people. The guy was hungry, and she would slash him before she allowed anyone else to become his victim. They reached the outskirts of Pioneer Square and he ducked into an old warehouse. Curiouser and curiouser.

She looked through dusty windows and when she was satisfied that she wasn't walking into a room full of bloodsuckers, she cautiously followed him into the building. The large room was mostly empty except for stacks of crates and empty aluminum buckets. Cobwebs covered every square inch of the place, and she swore she felt spiders crawling up her legs. She hated spiders almost as much as she hated leeches.

Several sets of footprints in the dirty floor lead her to a door that was barely hanging on its hinges. This was a highly traveled area, and she almost turned back to return with reinforcements during the day. The thought that women were suffering at the hands of these creatures kept her moving forward.

She crouched her five foot nine inch frame and ducked under the door. She refused to ring the dinner bell by moving the thing. On her hands and knees, she found herself at the top of a flight of stairs and stopped, listening for several long moments. She heard several different male voices talking. She slowly stood from her crouch and heard a rip. She looked down and saw the tear on her black t-shirt. She loved the snarky saying, 'Friday, my second favorite F word,' and she made a mental note to order another one.

One stair at a time, she descended into what she realized was Underground Seattle. It was a frightening thought that these parasites were living in close proximity to a popular tourist attraction.

When she reached the bottom stair she paused and noted the majority of the voices were coming from the left so she slipped into the right corridor so as not to be seen. Through dim lighting, the area appeared to open up to a bigger space that was under construction.

Voices approached and she inched backwards slowly, bumping into something. She reached behind her and ran her hands over an object, finding scaffolding. She hid against the leg of the structure and breathed in the stench. She held her breath and waited until the voices retreated.

A faint scream at the end of the passageway caught her attention. She debated turning back or proceeding. There were an unknown number of vampires and she was alone with one weapon. Going forward was definitely a stupid move. Another stronger scream sounded, and made the decision for her. That was a woman's voice, and from the sound, Mack bet that she was in trouble. Mack surmised that she had been living on borrowed time since surviving her own attack years ago, and she'd be damned if she was leaving another to face a worse fate.

Forward it was. Several feet down the hall, purplish-blue light shone through the glass squares, illuminating from up above. She recalled the story behind these skylights, and how they had been installed during the rebuilding after the Great Fire. She had walked over the sidewalks countless times, but would never have guessed at the evil that lurked beneath.

Something scurried over her shoes and she bit down on her fist while shudders wracked her body. Fucking rats, the only thing she hated more than spiders. She took a deep breath through her nose to calm her nerves which was a mistake. The full scope of the smell slammed into her - rotten meat, feces and urine. No wonder there were rodents close by.

She continued on, passing several boarded up and burned out buildings. Sobs and feminine voices sounded from a room ahead. She slowed her steps and tried to listen for any of the vampires.

"Who's there? We can hear you," a woman whispered.

"You aren't one of the demons. You don't smell like them. Whoever you are, please help us," a small female voice pleaded, bringing tears to Mack's eyes. That bloodsucker hadn't been lying.

Without thinking, she rushed into the room and stopped dead in her tracks. Several things hit her at once. A lone bulb illuminated three large metal cages that took up most of the area and there were a dozen women locked inside. The bars were three inches thick and there were no visible locks on the doors.

The women were disheveled and filthy, their clothing

tattered and two of the women were naked, huddled in one cage together. What she could see of their flesh was bruised and riddled with injuries. The moment she walked in, all but the two naked women rushed the bars and gripped them, shoving their faces through the gaps.

"Help us. Please let us out before the demons come back," cried a short blond woman.

Mack was stunned speechless. The woman had fangs that cut into her lip when she spoke, and unbelievably were healing before her eyes. Her gaze flew to the woman's dirty, battered face. She wondered why their other injuries weren't healing. "Who are you? Are you vampires like those guys out there?"

One of the naked women, a lithe redhead stood and approached the bars of her prison. "No," she spat. "We aren't vampires and neither are they. They are skirm and were created by the big ugly demon. How are you here and not being turned by them too?" Skirm, Mack turned the term over in her mind. She had heard it before, from that detective Elsie brought to tell her about Ellen's death. He had told her that she had been fighting skirm, not vampires.

Another female called out from the back of the third cage. "I don't care why. Just get us out of here."

Mack watched them closely and realized they were nothing like the vampires she had encountered. These women weren't slavering to suck her blood and were definitely victims of these creatures. "I'm here to help you. Tell me how to open these cages," she uttered while searching the room for a lever or switch.

"You have to leave, they're coming and will turn you if they find you," warned the redhead. They locked eyes and she gasped at the glowing jade green that stared back at her. Mack hadn't heard anybody approaching, but the fear in her eyes told her to trust what she said. "Please tell the Dark Warriors and the Vampire King where we are. They are the only ones that can help. No one else can defeat these demons. Don't bring your human police back here unless you want them to die. Go, now," the redhead urged.

"I can wait and try to get you out. I don't want to leave you here," Mack argued.

Mack could see the fear and desperation in her eyes. There was no telling what these women had been through or how long they had been down here. It'd been too long, and they'd been through too much for Mack's liking. Her stomach knotted with the possibilities. "I don't want to stay here any longer, but there are too many of them for you to handle alone. I won't be responsible for them getting another victim. Go," the redhead ordered, and pointed back down the hall.

The other women began clamoring and rattling the bars causing a ruckus. Creating a distraction, Mack realized. "I will come back for you. I promise," Mack vowed before she ducked back into the hall and hid out of sight. She watched as an enormous black dog with glowing red eyes loped down the passage alongside a vampire that was arguing with what could only be described as a demon. She hadn't felt fear like this since she was attacked by a vampire herself. There was far more danger lurking in the night than she ever realized.

The moment the coast was clear she inched her way back into the hall and continued to the exit. She tried to ignore the taunting and snarls that came from the direction of the captive women, but the sounds of a whip and screaming almost had her turning back.

She forced her legs to carry her in the opposite direction, and she carefully made her way back onto the street.

As she made her way home, she thought of the redheads parting words. She was supposed to find Dark Warriors and the Vampire King. Her mind reeled with the possibility that what she believed were vampires were actually skirm, created by a demon, and of all things, she needed to trust the vampires. She would never trust vampires, leaving her with a dilemma...how she was going to rescue these women?

~

JACE SAT at the big oak table and listened to the warriors talk while they enjoyed the snacks Angus had brought in to them. It had been a week since the battle, and the buzz in the compound was finally winding down.

Jace still had heart failure when he recalled the sight of his mate flying overhead on the back of a black dragon. A feeling he and Zander shared, and had talked about many times.

"Thank you, Angus," Jace said tersely. He still hadn't forgiven the male for bringing his mate to the battle. Zander had been a breath from ripping the shifter's head from his shoulders when Elsie stopped him. She had given the dragon a direct order that he wasn't able to ignore, especially given that Elsie had had one of her premonitions that they needed to be at the battle.

Angus inclined his head and left the room. The visiting warriors hadn't returned to their compounds because they were still convalescing. Thane looked much better, and was finally able to join them for planning. He had been close to death when Jessie had placed herself between him and danger. The male was lucky to be alive. Kyran's leg had healed but left him missing a chunk of skin and muscle.

Hellhound bites, Kyran learned, were far more painful than skirm bites. Jace was monitoring the injury closely to see if he was able to rejuvenate any of the missing flesh.

They had been outnumbered, but their awareness had given them an advantage. Without the previous encounter with the fury demons, they would not have been prepared. Also, Jace hated to admit it, but they wouldn't have won the battle without the dragon. Angus' flames and teeth took out a large number of demons, and allowed them to gain the upper hand.

The prophecy had come to pass that night when Cailyn killed John. He had been bleeding out on the ground when John came at him, clearly intending to kill him. Cailyn had stabbed John, killing him. Jace knew how hard that had been for her, and he also knew she did it for him. That had warmed his heart more than she could ever know. She had been inconsolable though, but he had been able to comfort her while the others wrapped up the battle. Breslin and Angus cleaned up the grizzly scene with their fire and the humans still had no idea what had really ravaged Woodland Park and nearly destroyed the zoo.

Jace shook off his maudlin thoughts and looked over at Cailyn where she sat next to him. She had been healing ever since that night as well. Her physical injuries were minor and gone with one of his healing touches, but her emotional scars were taking their toll, and he felt helpless. He was the realm's most powerful healer, but he was unable to take her heartache away. He wanted to see her smile and hear her laugh again. He wanted the light to dance in her eyes.

He grabbed her hand where it rested on the table and he laced their fingers together. She gave him a half-smile and went back to staring into space. They'd spent every moment together since that night. They made love, slept and talked endlessly, but the shadows never left her eyes. He needed to do something.

Nerves overwhelmed him as he got down on one knee and turned her chair to face him. He had never felt for anyone the way he felt for her. She gaped at him and swallowed visibly.

He pulled the little black box from his pocket. "*Shijéí*, I love you more than I thought possible. I was broken and unworthy, but you believed in me. You are intelligent and caring and devoted, and I want to spend the rest of eternity with you. Your soul has kept me alive for over seven centuries and I don't want to spend another minute without you. Marry me, and mate with me. I don't want to lose you in mere decades. That isn't enough time with you."

He flipped open the box and presented the antique ring to her. Tears brimmed in his eyes and burned as he held them back. All the emotions that he had never experienced before Cailyn rose to the fore in a jumbled mess. His chest constricted, he loved this female and wanted to be her everything. The room had gone silent and he felt every eye on them.

Cailyn watched him for several silent seconds before she answered. "Oh, Jace. Yes," she cried. "Yes. I will marry you and mate with you. I love you. I love you so much it scares me." She held out her left hand and he slid the ring onto her finger. "I can't believe you got my mother's ring…"

Jace's soul erupted in flames and filled his chest as she launched herself out of her chair and onto his lap. The friction tantalized his shaft and had him close to losing control. He grabbed her waist stilling her movements. The pain in his mating mark flared. It had become unbearable unless they were making love. "You are going to have to stop that," he whispered in her ear.

She gasped and pulled back to look in his eyes at the same time her body melted further into his. "Is that for me?" she whispered with a seductive smile. He stood abruptly and carried her from the room, ignoring the hoots and hollers.

"Only you," he kissed her mouth brutally as he walked. "It's yours and yours alone, *Shijéí*. I am going to love you so thoroughly that you forget there was ever another," he growled against her neck as he took the stairs two at a time to their room.

"Hmmm, that may take some time," she taunted and licked his throat.

"We don't have to leave the room until the next full moon in three weeks, love."

"Sounds like heaven, but what's in three weeks?"

"Our mating ceremony," he announced then tossed her on the bed, eager to show her how much he loved her.

CHAPTER 27

Cailyn marveled at how her life had changed so drastically over the past couple months. Jace expertly twirled her through Zeum's ballroom as she beamed up at him. They were mated and married, and she couldn't be happier.

The mating ceremony had happened moments ago, and every description Elsie had shared about the experience paled in comparison to the reality. The magic of the moment was mystical and life changing. She lifted her fist off Jace's shoulder and opened her hand with the exquisite amethyst stone.

She was still shocked that the river rock Jace had held between their hands had been transformed into the one she now held. The surge of magic that flowed through the seemingly ordinary stone as Zander blessed their mating was near orgasmic. The mating ceremony wasn't anything like a human marriage. Every word wove a spell that bound her and Jace together. She felt the chains form between them, and knew that nothing could ever come between them again.

Her love for Jace was her weakness and her strength. She could study every language spoken for millennia and still be unable to find the words to describe what he meant to her. He completed her in every way, and they had yet to do the infamous blood exchange, the final step to their mating.

Her stomach clenched with need to take this last step. From the moment she entered the patio for the mating she had wanted to ravage Jace as he stood there in his traditional Native American garb. He was shirtless, and his mouthwatering bronzed skin was displayed to perfection by the bone and Buffalo horn breastplate. The tight leather pants were handmade and likely centuries old, molding to him perfectly.

She trailed her hand from his shoulder to his waist, tempted to untie the drawstrings and explore his hard flesh. Instead, she ran her hand up his chest and through his hair, careful of the eagle feathers that had been woven into the long tresses. She saw how his nipples beaded under the breastplate and her fingers lightly grazed his nipples, making him shudder.

"Careful, love. You're playing with fire," Jace whispered into her ear before he sucked her lobe into his talented mouth and bit down.

She stepped in closer to him, reveling in the hardening shaft that brushed her soft belly. "I like fire. I want to be burned, and can hardly hold myself back. I ache to have you fill me, Jace."

"It's the mating compulsion. It's driving us both harder than ever to complete the final stage of the mating."

"I'm all for that. We can skip out and leave the rest of them to enjoy the party." She glanced around the room and found Elsie and Zander in a similar embrace. Her sister gave her a sheepish smile and she winked back at her.

"Okay, let's go but we have to be back for the bonfire. I probably won't want to leave the room, but we have to be there for our mating bonfire. My mother told me stories of my parents' mating fire and I want to experience one of my own."

"What is a mating fire?" Cailyn asked her mate. Her mate, she would never tire of saying that. And surprisingly she loved the term mate far more than husband. It held so much more meaning and depth that the traditional human connotation, and it certainly bound her more securely to Jace.

"It's something only sorcerers experience," he murmured as he kissed her neck.

"You can tell me later, blood exchange now," she demanded as she followed him out through the double doors. She struggled to keep up with him as he raced up the stairs, anticipation bubbling in her veins.

~

JACE KICKED the door shut behind Cailyn and walked her into the bedroom. She was a vision, and had taunted him from the moment he had seen her earlier that night. Her full breasts were all but spilling out the top of the low-cut wedding gown. The white silk garment gloved her luscious curves and revealed her perfect bosom.

"Stay like that. I plan to take my time peeling every layer of that dress from your body," he husked to her.

He noticed the goose bumps on her arms, and knew he was driving her mad with arousal. He turned her around and started on the hundred buttons that ran the length of her spine. He bent and kissed her bare shoulders, the sweet taste of her skin exploding on his tongue.

Suddenly impatient, he ripped the dress down the back not bothering with the buttons any longer. The fabric pooled at her feet as she turned around to face him. The white satin cups of her bra barely covered her nipples. He licked his lips wanting to taste the berry tipped peaks that tightened under his scrutiny.

He finished his perusal of her body, expecting to find white silky panties to match the bra but was met by a neat thatch of dark curls. His blood sizzled, the inferno within fueled to scorching.

"Elsie warned me about the rampant lust and I had hoped you'd fuck me in the pantry, so didn't bother with them," she demurred, clearly using her ability to read his thoughts.

"I like the way you think. I hope the bed is okay. This moment is too important for the pantry." He reached behind her and undid the clasp of her bra. Her breasts bounced when set free, calling to him.

The white silk fell from his numbed fingers as he leaned down and sucked one pert nipple into his mouth. Her hips began moving and his free hand slid between her damp folds.

"Yes, Jace. Jesus that feels good."

"I thank the Goddess for you every day, Cailyn." In truth, she was more than perfection. "You are my goddess...my salvation. And, I am going to devour you, love." He propped her up on the high bed and spread her legs, displaying her lush petals. He knelt in front of her, prepared to worship her. He would worship her for eternity.

He dipped his head and his tongue snaked out and licked her lips. He spread her to his view and the scent of her desire, spicy cinnamon, made him hungry for more. He attacked and tongue-fucked her slick channel as she tangled her hands in his hair and held him to her. She was close to orgasm. Her hips undulated against his mouth and took what she needed from him. She came, crying out his name. He was so hard he thought his dick had petrified.

She was so wet her clit glistened with her desire. He sucked the little bud into his mouth, driving her passion higher. "Now, Jace," she panted. "I need you inside me. I'll die if you don't fuck me, now."

"The lady's wish is my command," he smiled down at her and swiped his tongue over his lips, tasting her.

"I'm not a lady right now. Fuck me, Jace."

"Aye, wench. I think I have what you need," he teased, grabbing her ankles, bringing her bottom to the edge of the bed. She reached down and tugged his laces in a frenzy. He left her thigh-high stockings and little white heels on as he removed his breastplate and tossed it away. She had his leathers undone and his aching cock in hand.

He groaned and jumped when she squeezed his shaft. He snatched her hands and held them above her head laying her back on the bed. She wrapped her legs around his waist and her heels dug deliciously into his ass, causing his mating mark to burn and nearly robbed him of control. He wanted to surge into her and fuck her hard and fast, but held back, wanting to make this unforgettable.

He felt the build of his seed, something he had only ever experienced with this female. It was almost his undoing. Hastily, he shoved his pants to his knees not bothering to remove them.

He pointed the leaking head at her dewy mound and entered her slowly, their groans mingling in the heated air between them. He watched his cock disappeared into her hot, tight pussy. He reminded himself that they had a ceremony to complete, before he lost himself completely.

"Ah, God. Faster, Jace."

He pulled out and slammed back home. "Patience. We have a mating to complete, *Shijéí.*" He twisted without separating their bodies and felt her muscles clamp down on him, keeping him deep inside her sheath.

He tore the drawer from the nightstand nearly spilling the contents and grabbed the ceremonial dagger, a small, silver blade engraved with Celtic symbols and his family name. It was one of the few keepsakes that Zander had recovered from the ruins of his parents' home. "Sorcerers don't have fangs so we have a familial dagger for this part of the bonding."

Cailyn's lust-filled eyes widened and he saw her fear when she took in the blade. He refused to allow fear in this moment and reached down and plucked her clit, fully bringing back her arousal. She writhed and moaned and he made shallow thrusts while he played with her engorged nubbin. "Do it, Miakoda," she demanded. He loved when she ordered him around.

He brought her palm to his mouth and licked and sucked the area preparing it. He struck quick and made a shallow incision. "With this exchange," he murmured as he sliced his own palm, "we will be joined for all eternity." He held up his hand offering her everything he was. Speechless, she nodded before she latched on. Lust shot through his cock and balls as she sucked and swallowed. He took her hand to his lips and felt the moment their souls united.

It was a blinding gold light and he began plunging into her pussy like a piston and all too quickly his seed exploded from his cock like a freight train. Their souls rushed from his body as her head tossed from side to side and her fingernails dug into his shoulders. They were both gasping for breath. He felt the spasms of her orgasm continue and strengthen in volume. In a purple haze, he saw their souls entwine and join their intimate dance.

He didn't know how long he fucked her tight little sheath or how many times they came, but in one final hot explosion more intense than the last he poured all he had left into her.

After long moments of him gently rocking his still erect cock into her core, their souls drifted back into their bodies. For the first time in his life, Jace felt whole and complete. Jace probed and prodded his soul. His was joined so tightly to Cailyn's that there was no way to distinguish them, and he didn't want it any other way.

"Oh my God. That was *unfuckingbelievable*. I want to do that again," Cailyn cooed as she lay back and threw her hands above her head in abandon. As she stretched, he noticed her mate mark had inked into her skin. He leaned down and kissed the mark, eliciting moans from his mate.

"I will never tire of making love to you." He continued to pump in and out of her welcoming body. She responded so well to him that her desire was already returning. He was loath to stop but they needed to be at the bonfire. With a regretful sigh, he pulled from her body.

"I'm not ready to stop. I want that magnificent cock fucking me all night long," she objected.

"I will make love to you night and day for the rest of our lives, but right now we have to make an appearance at the bonfire," he replied.

Instantly, her eyes widened and she had her hand to her mouth. Only then did he realize she had not spoken. He had read her thoughts. "You didn't say that out loud. Apparently, we have already shared our powers with one another."

"Does that mean I can heal now?"

He nodded and watched her place her warm little hand to his shoulder where she healed the wounds she had left during their love play. He had risked everything to let Cailyn see his pain. He'd been forced to expose his shame and weakness, and give up his entire way of life, but he would do it again without hesitation to have this female by his side.

～

CAILYN LOOKED through the patio windows as she followed Jace. The moon was full and the weather was perfect. The property was decorated so differently for them. Elsie and Zander had thousands of twinkling lights and candles, but she and Jace had an illuminated path that lead to a raging bonfire at the water's edge. The scene was surreal, and she was able to feel the strength of the magic that surrounded the area. She instinctively understood that this was as important as any other part of their mating ceremony. "It's so beautiful, Jace and I can feel the power envelope me," she commented as he held the door open.

Jace looked at her and smiled that smile that never failed to melt her heart and instantly she wanted him again. He had fucked her to the point where she was shocked she could still walk, and still it wasn't enough. His chuckle told her he read her thoughts. Her cheeks flamed. "This is all for you, *Shijéí*. And don't worry, by morning you won't be walking," he promised and pulled her into an embrace.

She stood on her tiptoes, her lips drawn to his like a magnet. The kiss caught fire and she felt his hot hand sneak up under her skirt. "My naughty little mate. I love that you aren't wearing anything under this skirt. It's going to be impossible to concentrate knowing this."

Before she replied, Kyran brushed past them carrying a box of creamsicles and grumbled. "For fucks sake can you take that shite to your rooms? I canna stand all the sex around here."

"What's wrong with him?" she asked Jace as they followed the warrior out of the house.

"Kyran has issues that he has to work through. I have a surprise for you." He quickened his steps and she found she had no problem keeping up with his pace. Apparently, she was already faster and had better vision she thought as she looked around and saw their way clearly in the darkness of the night. In no time at all, they had reached the ring of stones and the ten-foot flames.

Jessie ran up to her and hugged her tightly. "You smell of sex," her friend said. Cailyn smiled at the blunt comment, appreciating that Jessie was still the same woman she knew despite all her changes. "I see you completed the mating. Your mate mark is a tattoo."

"I know, I love it. But, you should see Jace's. It makes his ass look fine as hell," she sighed, recalling the sight of his muscular globes.

Jessie laughed. "I'll trust you on that one. I don't want you to claw my eyes out for sneaking a peak," her friend teased as she hugged her. "You look happy, happier than I've ever seen you and I am so glad to see it."

"I am happy. Thank you," she released her friend as a delicious chocolate aroma reached her. "Do I smell s'mores?"

Jessie smirked and turned around. "Yeah, we told Angus they were your favorite. They're right over there," Jessie replied, pointing to the side of the fire.

"Have a seat and I'll be right back. I'll cook your marshmallow just right." Jace's voice turned husky and he leaned over to kiss her. Cailyn went to the wicker lounge with her friend trailing behind.

"So how does it feel to be mated?"

Cailyn looked around the bonfire seeing that everyone was there. Her sister and Zander were in an embrace talking with Evzen. All the Dark Warriors were laughing and relaxing, which had been rare of late. There had been so much going on between her car crash, the search for a cure, the Mystik Grimoire appearing, the battle, and the recovery. It hit her that this was now her family.

Finally, she turned to her friend. "I have no words for how this feels, Jess. I only know that this is right for me. That I am whole in a way few ever experience."

"I wonder if I will have a Fated Mate now that I am a dhampir," her friend mused as she picked up a stick to poke the fire.

Thane came up behind Jessie and wrapped his arms around her. "You will have a mate surely enough, Jess. I will just have to enjoy you until that lucky man claims you." Cailyn smiled as her friend bid her adieu and went off into the shadows with the San Francisco Dark Warrior. After everything Jessie had been through, she deserved to find the same happiness Cailyn had. She said a silent prayer to the Goddess to send a mate Jessie's way.

Jace returned with chocolate, marshmallows, and graham crackers on a platter. He handed her the plate and then maneuvered his body behind her. His masculine strength surrounded her and made her want to eat her treat off of his body. "Careful what you think, my love. I may take that as an invitation," he growled in her ear. "Watch the flames," he murmured.

As if on cue, everyone gathered around and focused on the fire. When her eyes made it back to the flames she gasped at the colors rolling through them. Purple and pink dominated the colorful scene and rose into the air. The cloudlike images morphed into her face and formed a slide show of images of her with Jace. In each one she was smiling and laughing. She was beautiful in a way that she didn't see when she looked in a mirror. A flood of emotions raced through her as she watched the most romantic gesture ever created.

The love and devotion Jace had for her was obvious in every flame, and she was awed by its intensity. She vowed to show him how much she loved him every day. Maybe then she would deserve one tenth of what she saw.

"This is how I see you, *Shijéí*. I hadn't lived before you came into my life. I love you isn't enough to tell you how I feel about you." Tears built in her eyes and overflowed as the images continued.

"I love you too, Jace, more than life. You are a part of me, the best part," she murmured and turned in his arms, kissing him passionately.

An abrupt blast of heat broke their lip lock and she glanced over her shoulder to see what caused the fire to flare. She felt Jace's entire body go stalk-still and tense. The flames turned black, making her gasp, before the image of a stunning female appeared in the center of the flames. Jace whispered, "Angelica," through gritted teeth as he wound his arms around her waist and tried to pull her behind him.

So this was the evil creature that had kidnapped and tortured her mate for over a century. She wanted to slowly rip her to shreds, and appreciated that every warrior felt the same and had weapons out, battle-ready.

"How is she able to project onto our property? Can she find us?" Zander barked out at the same time Jace leapt from behind her. Before she could blink, Jace, Gerrick,

Killian, and Evzen were poised at the edge of the fire with their staffs in hand, chanting in a foreign language.

"You will regret casting me out, Jace Miakoda. I will have the Grimoire, and every one of you will submit to my will," Angelica shrieked before she disappeared. Cailyn was shaking as adrenaline rushed through her veins. What had just happened?

"Like I suspected, she has aligned with dark magic. With the addition of the Rowan sisters' power, we will cast spells against blood magic, and this will never happen again. Rest assured, Liege, she will never breech our property," Jace answered. He walked back to Cailyn's side and had her wrapped in his arms, and only then, did her shaking stop.

Evzen interjected, "It was no secret that we were having Jace's mating ceremony tonight and I believe she made a blood offering to dark fire spirits. Her power is greater than I anticipated."

"Shite," Zander cursed. "How much of a threat is she to this compound and the realm as a whole?"

"The compound is secure, Zander. None outside your circle and the council can locate this place, and we will reinforce those protections. The realm as a whole is another issue altogether. At this point, we need to assume that she poses as much a threat as the archdemons," Evzen shared ominously.

Even Jace's warm arm couldn't stop the shiver of fear that racked Cailyn's body. As she looked to the night sky and saw the black flames die out, she vowed that she would never allow Angelica to harm her mate again.

Elsie's curse garnered the attention of the entire group. "I really wanted to have one night of peace," she said as she met Zander's gaze then turned to Jace and Evzen. "Will she be back anytime soon or are we safe to pursue other matters?"

"She won't be back tonight, and I will make sure the Rowan sisters are here before dawn to cast new spells."

"What's on your mind, *a ghra*?" Zander growled before Jace had finished speaking.

"Mack is going to be in a house fire and we need to save her," Elsie replied.

EPILOGUE

Elsie jumped out of the car the second Orlando stopped at the curb in front of Mack's house. Worry for her friend had been eating at Elsie's nerves ever since she'd had the premonition. It hadn't helped that they stood around arguing for a half hour before Zander finally agreed it was safe to leave the compound. She understood he put the safety of the realm and those under his roof above that of her friend, but she had a sense of loyalty to Mack.

The slam of car doors told her that the Dark Warriors were right behind her as she raced up the path to the house. A hard hand grabbed her arm and stopped her. "Stop, *a ghra,* we canna rush in before we know what we are facing."

Elsie knew her mate was right, but it was difficult to stay put when her friend could be dying. She cocked her head, opening her senses and took in the house. She didn't sense skirm in the vicinity, but easily smelled smoke and the fumes of plastic burning within its walls. One side was soot-stained, and flames were shooting out of the broken windows. She looked in the driveway and saw that Mack's car was parked there. She strained her ears and after several minutes she was able to work through the sounds of destruction and detect two heartbeats.

"There's no skirm, but she's in there with somebody. We have to get them out!" she yelled and began running to the front door.

A sudden blast, followed by glass shattering, sent her to the ground cursing. She lifted her head to see that the side of Mack's house had exploded along with a nearby propane tank. She was getting to her feet when she heard a woman screaming. She recognized the irate voice as Mack's.

She looked to the back of the house where the yelling was coming from and gaped when she saw Kyran carrying Mack over his shoulder. Mack was beating Kyran on the back and yelling at him to put her down, but he wasn't listening. As she watched, Mack's protests lost steam and her movements slowed. Her face was pale and covered in ash.

Kyran was striding quickly through the backyard and away from the street, likely wanting to avoid the sirens Elsie could hear in the distance. Elsie started rushing to Mack's side to help when in a flash of white light Kyran disappeared, carrying Mack with him.

EXCERPT FROM PEMA'S STORM, DARK WARRIOR ALLIANCE BOOK 3

A loud crash startled Pema, making her look up from her computer. Cursing echoed from the front of the store, and she cocked her head to the side, catching snippets of the argument raging between her sisters. Apparently, Suvi had dropped a box of fluorite crystals, and Isis was on the verge of going postal. Just a typical day at Black Moon. Shaking her head, Pema ignored them and wound her long blonde hair into a twist at the nape of her neck and went back to the papers she had been reviewing.

She didn't particularly enjoy the bookkeeping portion of their business, but someone had to do it. For two straight years business had boomed, allowing them to pay Cele, their High Priestess, back the money she loaned them. She had given them a loan to start Black Moon Sabbat, and it had taken a mere eighteen months to pay her back. They were proud of that fact, given the economy and Cele's astronomical interest rate.

More quarreling reached her in the back room, and with

a sigh, she stood up. Time to play peacemaker. Pema was beginning to rethink her idea of opening earlier in the morning to service more of their human clients. There were too many nights they stayed up late trying to find the perfect martini. Prosperity came at a price, she thought, as she made her way from the office to see what had happened. But it wasn't like they were going to give up their pursuit of the perfect martini any time soon.

Glancing around the shop, she swelled with pride. They had built Black Moon from the ground up. The store was as unique to the Tehrex Realm as Pema and her sisters were. Neither should exist, yet they did and were thriving. Pema and her sisters believed the ignorance of their youth was partially responsible.

They were the youngest witches in the realm, and were impetuous enough to take the risk to create a business that brought humans into close proximity with the realm. They enjoyed interacting with humans, and thrived off of the unique verve for life they had. However, that didn't mean they were completely senseless. They understood the Goddess' edict to maintain secrecy, and would never do anything to risk exposure. But they liked to toe the line.

The pungent odor of lavender and jasmine claimed Pema's attention and almost knocked her over when she entered the front. She glanced around to see Suvi standing amidst a mess of books and various teas, with the pricing stickers in hand. She noticed the decks of tarot cards had already been labeled and set off to the side.

"What are you two bickering about?" Pema asked.

"We are too damn tired to be up and functioning this early, and butterfingers here, dropped a case of fluorite. The entire box is damaged. Thankfully, I managed to save the potions we made last night. Had she broken those, we would be looking at an even bigger mess," Isis griped. "I mean, seriously, those magics, if mixed, would be lethal. When we stay out 'til two or three, it isn't wise to open at ten." Pema pursed her lips at the familiar argument her sisters made to push back her new hours.

"But, you did save the potions, and this," Pema gestured to the mess around Suvi, "is nothing. We're a team, remember? We couldn't run this place without watching each other's backs. And, lest you forget, Suvi sells more crystals and leather pouches than the two of us put together. I'll bet she can sell the damaged ones, just as easy," Pema told Isis as she crossed the room and pulled Suvi into a hug.

"Ugh, whatever. I won't say I'm sorry to her. She needs to try and pay attention for once. All it will take is one serious mishap with our potions to prove Cele right, that mom and dad should have forced us to stay at Callieach Academy all those years ago, and I'll be damned if I prove that witch right about anything." Isis stomped to the big, wood bookshelves that had been in the Rowan family for centuries, irritation in her every step. Isis was easily upset, but Pema shared her disgust about Cailleach Academy. Pema never wanted to be under Cele's thumb again.

"I don't know why you let that female get under your skin. I don't like her, but I'm not going to spend my time worrying about her unnecessarily. I'd rather talk about Confetti Too opening tomorrow night. I wonder if the Dark Warriors will be there," Suvi sang as she flitted about, placing books here and there haphazardly. Pema smiled as she watched her sister, wishing she was more easy-going like Suvi. Everything seemed to roll off Suvi's back, barely ruffling her feathers.

"I'm sure they'll be there. This is Killian's club, I

doubt they'd miss the grand opening," Isis offered with a sly grin, her temper finally cooling down.

"On that note, I'm going to change the stone on this wrap to a rose quartz. I want some lovin' in my future," Pema said, waggling her eyebrows as she crossed to the RockCandy Leatherworks display, glad to have the mood lightened. It was her favorite jewelry, and she always wore one of the handcrafted pieces.

"That isn't the right choice of stone if sex is what you want, sister. You need the red jasper. It stimulates vitality," Suvi commented as she walked over to help her pick.

Pema shuddered, Suvi was right. No way did she want love. Love brought nothing but heartache and trouble. "Thank the Goddess you are so much better at remembering that stuff than I am," she replied as she looked through the assortment of stones. "That could have backfired on me," Pema admitted as she unscrewed the rose quartz from the leather band and replaced it with the red jasper.

Being a witch and connected to the earth, Pema felt the power in natural objects like these stones. As the effects of the stone began humming through her system, she turned to the less pleasant task of cleaning the store. "Help me grab the ladder, Suvi. I want to dust the candles on the top shelf. Have you heard anything more about the updates to the club? When we added our protections it was all steel beams and brick, but I've heard it has a whole different feel to it, and that Killian hired additional security. That doesn't surprise me given the skirm attack."

Pema was going against her better judgment in asking Suvi to help her, but her sister needed a boost after the fiasco with the fluorite. As they reached the storage room and gazed at the tall wooden ladder, Pema briefly rethought her decision when she saw the shoes her sister had on. Suvi was always dressed to the nines, no matter what they were doing, and today was no different with her six-inch heels. She sent a silent prayer to the Goddess that they managed without further destruction.

"I heard that Killian had the council members send him their strongest males," Suvi shared as they maneuvered through the halls, "Of course, that means there will be new, highly-mackable males."

Pema released the breath she had been holding when they managed to make it into the open area without breaking anything else.

"Yeah, but can they dance? I'm ready to hit the floor and shake my thang," Isis said as she sashayed over to the stereo and changed the music to a club mix. Pema and Suvi started laughing as Isis began to bump and grind to the sound as she spoke.

"Stop shaking your ass and grab some black candles from the back," Pema told Isis as she climbed up the ladder. "I sold the last we had out here to Camelia a couple hours ago."

Isis winced as she headed to the back. "No telling what crazy Camelia is conjuring with them."

"I heard she was trying to bring her son back from the dead," Suvi said, handing Pema the feather duster.

"You can't believe everything you hear. She may be trying to communicate with him, but she's not crazy enough to believe she can bring him back, resurrection isn't possible." Pema figured Cele was spreading the rumor to discredit Camelia, given the bad blood between them. There was nothing worse than sibling rivalry, and Pema thanked the Goddess that she and her sisters were as close as they were. She reached over and the ladder swayed under her feet, so she quickly muttered a stability spell. It would hurt like a bitch if she fell from the very top.

"I know. It's as insane as what they say about us. I mean, we could never be part of a hostile takeover," Suvi replied from below where she was now rearranging necklaces on the glass counter.

Pema nodded her agreement as she ran the duster over the shelf and candles. "That's the problem with prophecies. They are vague, confusing—" She stopped talking when the tinkling of the wind chimes above the front door signaled they had a customer.

A cool breeze blew through the room, chilling the air. She twisted around to see the most stunning male walk through the door. He was easily six feet tall and had thick, brown hair that fell in soft curls around his ruggedly handsome face. He had a strong, square jaw that she immediately imagined running her tongue over. His warm, brown eyes invited her to share her secrets, and suddenly it wasn't so chilly anymore.

Her gaze traveled over him and she noticed that his jeans were tight in all the right places, and she could easily make out his firmly muscled legs. He took her breath away and she desperately wanted him.

Her sex tightened with need, and arousal flooded her panties as she was overcome with an uncontrollable lust for this stranger, and she couldn't focus on anything but getting him into the office for a quick tryst. She became light-headed when a feathering sensation in her chest set her heart racing. She wondered what was wrong with her. She was no blushing virgin, but she had never responded like this when looking at a male.

Reaching up to wipe the sweat from her brow, she lost her hold on the ladder. As she felt air rush past her, she never once thought to utter a spell. She blamed it on the fact that her brain malfunctioned from hormone overload. Rather than landing in an ungainly heap on the floor, she was caught by big, strong arms and an electrical current raced across her skin the moment they touched. She wanted to climb to the top of the ladder to have this male catch her again. Then again, that would mean him putting her down, and she had no desire for that to happen.

"Are you okay?" His voice was gruff, and she loved it. The sound sent liquid heat spreading from her abdomen to her core and had her melting into his body.

As much as she didn't want to, she needed to put space between them or she was going to lose control. She pushed against his broad shoulders for him to let her go. She didn't fight it too hard when he refused to release her. "I'm okay. Nice catch, by the way. I'm not usually caught off-guard like that."

She should tell him to let her go. Her lips parted to say the words, but they were trapped in her throat. She breathed in his earthy, pine scent and a new flood of heat traveled through her. She needed to gather her senses, and added more force to her shove until he finally set her down. Her body slid down the hard length of him and she took a couple steps back before acting on impulse to rub against him like a cat in heat.

"I didn't mean to startle you. Are you one of the Rowan sisters?" he asked, holding out his hand. Did he crave contact with her as much as she did him? It seemed like an eternity to Pema since he had touched her, and she would die if he didn't touch her again. Okaaay, she was losing her mind and she needed to stop this behavior.

Her brain and hormones weren't on speaking terms, and she eagerly grabbed his hand and held it tightly.

"Yes, I'm Pema and this is my sister, Suvi," she nodded her head in the direction of her sister, keeping hold of his hand. "And you are?"

"My name is Ronan Blackwell," the hunk said, keeping intense gaze into her eyes.

"How can we help you, Ronan?" Suvi asked, awakening Pema from her daydreams of ravishing his body. Realizing how odd it must seem to be holding onto his hand, she pulled from his firm grip and immediately felt a loss. She turned around to face the counter, needing to break eye contact with him.

"I'm not exactly sure. I need to win my female back. I believe her mother forced her to end things between us. I have never believed in this hocus-pocus shit, and I think it made her mother dislike me. I'm a shifter, and I believe in what I see in front of me," Ronan said. Two things happened. For a brief second, Pema wanted to rip this female of his to shreds. She quickly dismissed the notion, reminding herself that she was only fantasizing about the male, nothing more. And, who the hell was he to call their magic hocus-pocus shit? She swiveled and took in this alpha male, and his confident stance amped her body's response, making all other thought flee from her mind.

"I'm not sure what we can do for you. We refuse to make or sell true love potions, so we can't force this female to love you, and we certainly can't create a potion to make you believe in our hocus-pocus shit," Pema said, acid dripping from her tone. "Who is this female anyway?"

Ronan was quiet for several long moments while he stared right through her soul before he answered. "Claire Wells. Surely you have something for me. I was told that the Rowan triplets are supposed to be the most powerful witches in the realm. I want to convince Claire to follow her heart. She has loved me for almost two hundred years, and I don't believe that has changed." He moved closer to Pema as he spoke, angling his body toward her. She wasn't going to be a fool to think that he was as affected by her as she was by him. She was a means to an end for him, and she sure as hell wasn't getting in the middle of his relationship problems.

Still, Pema had to bite her tongue. This magnificent male could not belong to this particular female. She wasn't surprised that he was taken, but why did it have to be with Claire? The male was making Pema crazy with lust, and now disgust. Not a great combination.

She shuddered in revulsion. Claire Wells was Cele's beloved daughter, and Pema hated them both. She didn't have a jealous bone in her body, so why she was so upset over this couple was beyond her. Something had taken over her, and Goddess help her, she may embarrass herself yet.

Suvi jumped right into sales mode. "Of course we are, and if anyone can help you, it's us. We have several truth potions. And, if you want to remind her of the passion you shared, we have pink tourmaline to enhance libido," Suvi winked at him.

Pema watched their interaction, bewitched by his perfection and her desire for him. It had to be the red jasper messing with her. Her libido was working overtime with this male two feet from her. She needed to raise the price on these stones, and order more. This was obviously some powerful mojo.

Pema listened to him talk to Suvi and found herself wondering why he was with Claire. Those thoughts brought up the memory of her last interaction with Claire. It was the day Claire had moved back to Seattle, and Pema and her sisters were making their final payment to the High Priestess.

Claire stood in Cele's office with her hands on her hips, her long mousy-brown hair flying around her shoulders in agitation as she snarled at them. "No matter how much money you make at that store of yours, you three are still just the poor kids in rags. You'll never amount to anything."

Isis sneered back. "This coming from the one who relies on mommy for everything. We may have started in rags, but we aren't in them anymore."

A deep rumble brought her out of the memory. "Bag up whatever crystals or potions you recommend." That quickly, his sexy voice conjured images in Pema's mind of him hovering over her while he slowly thrust into her, driving her to climax.

She clenched her teeth together, telling herself that she *had* to stop thinking about sex. She unclasped the magnet of the wrap around her wrist and dropped the bracelet onto the counter. She walked a few feet away, placing more distance between her and the sexy shifter, and pretended to organize the tarot cards.

Ronan inched closer to her then stopped. He ran his hands through his hair, ruffling his curls and shuffling from foot to foot. His gaze returned to Pema's face again and again. Something in Pema stirred at the way he was staring at her. She couldn't decipher the look in his chocolate brown depths, but it was intense.

Suvi bagged several items for Ronan, telling him how to use each one as she took his payment. Pema didn't think Ronan heard a word her sister had said, given that his gaze never once wavered from her face. For someone who was so hot to win his girlfriend back, he sure didn't seem too concerned about it at the moment. That was *not* wishful thinking, Pema assured herself.

"I need to get to work, but thank you for the help. See you around?" Ronan asked, but didn't move to leave.

"If you are ever at Confetti Too then you'll see me plenty," Pema replied, hoping her invitation wasn't too blatant.

"I guess I'll see you often, since I've just been hired as part of the new security. Will you be there tomorrow night?"

"Yes," she nodded. "We wouldn't miss the grand opening."

"Save me a dance?" he husked.

"Dancing with me is certainly not the way to win back another female," she responded.

"You're right," he said. They stood staring at each other for what seemed like forever before he turned and exited the store. He gazed back at her from the street then hopped into a large truck. There was something about a male in a truck, Pema thought.

"That is some heat you two were throwing off. I need a walk-in freezer to cool down," Suvi broke the silence, fanning her face.

"Shut it, Suvi," Pema mumbled, staring out the window, captivated by glowing, brown eyes.

Authors' Note

With new digital download trends, authors rely on readers to spread the word more than ever. Here are some ways to help us.

Leave a review! Every author asks their readers to take five minutes and let others know how much you enjoyed their work. Here's the reason why. Reviews help your favorite authors to become visible. It's simple and easy to do. If you are a Kindle user turn to the last page and leave a review before you close your book. For other retailers, just visit their online site and leave a brief review.

Don't forget to visit our website: www.trimandjulka.com and sign up for our newsletter, which is jam-packed with exciting news and monthly giveaways. Also, be sure to visit and like our Facebook page https://www.facebook.com/TrimAndJulka to see our daily themes, including hot guys, drink recipes and book teasers.

Trust your journey and remember that the future is yours and it's filled with endless possibilities!

DREAM BIG!

XOXO,

Brenda & Tami

OTHER WORKS BY TRIM AND JULKA
The Dark Warrior Alliance
Dream Warrior (Dark Warrior Alliance, Book One)
Mystik Warrior (Dark Warrior Alliance, Book Two)
Pema's Storm (Dark Warrior Alliance, Book Three)
Deviant Warrior (Dark Warrior Alliance, Book Four)
Isis' Betrayal (Dark Warrior Alliance, Book Five)
Suvi's Revenge (Dark Warrior Alliance, Book Six)
Mistletoe & Mayhem (Dark Warrior Alliance, Book 6.5)
Scarred Warrior (Dark Warrior Alliance, Book Seven)
Heat in the Bayou (Dark Warrior Alliance, Novella, Book 7.5)
Hellbound Warrior (Dark Warrior Alliance, Book Eight)
Isobel (Dark Warrior Alliance, Book Nine)
Rogue Warrior (Dark Warrior Alliance, Book Ten)
Tinsel & Temptation (Dark Warrior Alliance, Book 10.5)
Shattered Warrior (Dark Warrior Alliance, Book Eleven)
King of Khoth (Dark Warrior Alliance, Book Twelve)

The Rowan Sisters' Trilogy

The Rowan Sisters' Trilogy Boxset (Books 1-3)

NEWSLETTER SIGN UP

Don't miss out!
Click the button below and you can sign up to receive emails from Trim and Julka about new releases, fantastic giveaways, and their latest hand made jewelry. There's no charge and no obligation.

SUBSCRIBE

Printed in Great Britain
by Amazon